Northern Hunt

Northern Wolf Series
Book Two

Daniel Greene

ISBN 978-1-7333704-0-0

For Brady, Tim, and Mike -
the stalwart guides on a warrior's journey

CHAPTER 1

February 11ᵗʰ, 1864
Union Lines, Near Stevensburg, Virginia

Johannes Wolf's feet froze in his wet boots. Having no remedy to save his feet, he wrapped his heavy woolen sky-blue greatcoat even tighter around his shoulders, trying to squeeze out some warmth. The corporal chevrons on his sleeves poked out beneath the cape of his coat.

His resistance to the cold developed over a decade spent in Michigan had diminished during his year in the War of Secession, his body slowly forgetting the harshness of winter. Any pre-enlistment fat gained from too many steins at Kusterer's brewery in Grand Rapids had melted off with each passing day, leaving a leaner, harder version of his previous self.

He manned an advance picket line along a bucolic country road two miles from the heart of Stevensburg, Virginia, a humble town that had grown exponentially as the winter encampment for the Army of the Potomac's 3ʳᵈ Cavalry Division. They were more scouts or vedettes for the actual pickets, over forty men, about a mile down the road. He raised his hands to his mouth and blew hot air on his gloved fingertips, more interested in staying warm than watching the empty country road.

Directing his attention back to the muddy turnpike surrounded by naked timber, he eyed the trees for movement. He waited for something, anything to come their way. The emptiness lulled him into a sense of security.

On any given picket duty, they may run into a handful of Virginians, maybe a messenger, but boredom was the main enemy in the winter season. And in good form, Wolf always seemed to be tasked with a long picket shift.

He scratched at his beard that was a couple of shades darker than his honey-blond hair, happy to have the extra layer of insulating warmth on his face. Beneath the bristly whiskers, harder lines had been chiseled on his face, and although he hadn't looked in a mirror more than a few times, he knew he'd changed.

Smoky scents drifted from a campfire and his stomach grumbled with hunger. Daydreams of his mother's pork with dumplings, crunchy breaded schnitzel, and the crispy outsides of a hearty pork knuckle washed down with a cool golden pilsner from the brewery danced before him. He sighed and the trees wavered as wind ran through, over, and around them. He tightened his father's black sash around his neck like a scarf beneath his greatcoat.

Wolf's short comrade stepped close to his side, almost as if he were trying to steal whatever warmth he managed to generate. The young man had dark, almost black, hair. It hung near the tops of his eyes, threatening to overtake them any day. Every strand resisted his attempt to corral it beneath his slumping forage cap.

The young man's cheeks were barren of all but a few hairs although a sufficient mustache took over his top lip, making him look far younger than he should. He wiped his nose with the sleeve of his greatcoat, egregiously too big for the short fellow. "All is clear. No rebels in sight. I will say we do a mighty fine job defending the Republic." He sniffled again and swiped his nose with his thumb. "Say, Wolf, how about a nip to keep off the cold?"

He ignored Roberts for a moment, scrutinizing the forest. They'd joined as boys, he was sure of that, and if they survived, no one could deny their manhood as veteran soldiers. After Gettysburg, he knew more about war than he'd ever care to know. "You know if Wells catches us drinking on duty, he'll whip us."

The poor young man from Grand Rapids licked his dry lips. "How's he gonna know?"

"He'll smell it on us when we return to camp." He glanced toward Roberts. "You know how close he gets."

Roberts shook his head. "Prude." He turned toward a tree near the side of the road where two other men sat. "Hey, Dan, when's it your turn over here?"

The bullish Polish soldier glanced over at them and waved. "No. Ten."

Suspicion narrowed in Roberts's eyes. "It was ten like ten minutes ago. Say, Wolf, you gotta pocket watch?"

"No, Uncle Shugart does."

"Old bat keeps jabbering poor Dan's ear off."

Bogdan, who the men called Dan, sat with another corporal from the unit. Zachariah Shugart, the aging Quaker abolitionist, warmed himself with a hand-stitched quilt wrapped around his shoulders. He was very religious, but despite his religion's objections to war, he had joined the effort anyway. A tuft of hair stuck off the top of his skull, and his face was skeletal enough to see every bone and each nook and cranny. A thick gray beard hung from his cheeks like a tangled mass of spider webs.

He spoke to Dan without relenting, preaching the gospel to the man nonstop. Dan stuck a stick in the fire and nodded every now and then. Wolf was sure he didn't understand a lick of anything the abolitionist preached, but the man humored him.

The earth squished beneath Roberts's boots as he shifted. "I can't say which is worse: standing here staring at an empty road in the miserable wet and cold or sitting next to a nice little fire with Uncle Shugart trying to save my soul."

Wolf studied the men staying warm and readjusted his Sharps carbine in the crook of his arm. Dan grinned underneath his beard as Shugart spread his arms wide, gesturing toward the sky. "I think I'd rather take the watch."

"Damned if you do, damned if you don't, literally, as me ma always used to say."

Wolf's brow creased. "I thought you didn't have a ma?"

"Well, everyone's got a ma."

"I thought you didn't know her."

Roberts stretched his neck. "Didn't know her for long, but that's what I remember her sounding like."

Wolf nodded, wiggling his toes as he tried to remind them of their rightful place on his feet. His metal knee brace emitted a tiny squeak. The elements were taking their toll on the contraption that kept his knee from giving out on him. It probably wasn't made for prolonged exposure to the wind, rain, mud, and snow of Virginia.

Traces of wet snow, the kind that made every step heavy and everyone soggy, layered the muddy road they guarded. Even the trees bent in agony from the horrible condensed melting whiteness.

The air was warm enough to send the snow into meltdown but cold enough to kill a man at night, especially if the cool air got in his chest. It was the leading killer of men in the winter season when most of the South's soldiers took leave to go back to their families.

"Just a nip," Roberts said to himself. He took a small bottle and tipped it back quick. He offered it to Wolf. "You sure?"

"Give it over." Wolf upended the bottle, taking a long swig of the whiskey. The alcohol burned all the way into his belly, warming his insides. Everything except his feet. His feet still felt frozen on this wet back country road. He handed the bottle back to Roberts, and it disappeared inside his coat.

Roberts slapped Wolf's chest. "Now ain't that better?"

A smile crept on Wolf's face. "It's better."

The two men chuckled. Wolf readjusted his Sharps carbine in the crook of his elbow and shifted it to the other side. He tried to wiggle his big toe, finding a needly numbness instead.

"They say the war will be over by the end of spring."

Snow crashed onto the ground in weighty clumps, sounding like falling wet sacks of wheat. The men turned wary eyes on the forest. It was natural instinct. The horses tethered to a nearby tree didn't bother with it, their heads bowing near the earth. The men lost interest, their eyes finding the empty road again.

"I doubt it. You know Old Lee. He's always got a trick up his sleeve."

"True." Wolf's eyes lingered over the route. Having stared at the same empty space for so long, his eyes grew unfocused. Even when shapes caught his eye in the distance, he didn't believe his own eyes. The dark shapes transformed into running men. Mud splashed as they slipped and stumbled over the corrupted road. He'd been lulled into a sleepy nothingness despite the defined men. He squinted. "Roberts? You see that?"

Roberts cocked his head to the side. He'd proven himself to have the best eyes in F Company, perhaps even in the entire 13th Michigan Cavalry. "Aye, I see 'em. Two of 'em. Running hard."

One of the men fell, splashing brown water and mud into the air. The other stopped, tugging his arm. He hoisted the man upright and they ran side by side. It was clear that one was black and the other white.

"We got men on foot," Wolf shouted at the other two troopers. Dan and Shugart stood, snatching their carbines and joining them.

Roberts continued to stare intently. "There be horsemen closing fast behind them.

"Horsemen?" Moments later, Wolf could make out four men riding their mounts hard over the road. The men on foot struggled to gain proper footing but would beat the riders to the picket line. "Dan, get about twenty yards on the right. Shugart on the left." The men's greatcoats flapped as they hopped over fallen logs to their positions, hiding behind barren trunks and gray leafless branches.

Roberts and Wolf let the two men close in on their position, concealing themselves in the trees. When the two men ran close enough, he stepped from cover into the road. Their eyes gaped when they registered his presence, and it brought them to an abrupt halt. Wolf raised his carbine gut level. "Where you boys going in such a hurry?"

The two men glanced behind at their pursuers and deemed Wolf the lesser of the two threats despite his broad shoulders and newly grown blond beard. They ran at him.

"Stop!" Roberts shouted from his right. He sighted them in from the other edge of the road with his carbine giving him an offset advantage.

The colored man was lighter than other black men Wolf had seen, his skin a pecan brown. The other man was pale with fiery hair and broad shoulders, his beard colored orange like a citrus fruit and soiled with dirt and mud patches. He wore tattered plain clothes like a beggar. They halted within ten feet of Wolf, hands slowly raising in the air.

Lifting his Sharps carbine to his shoulder, Wolf said, "That's far enough." The horsemen continued to gallop in their direction, horses furiously tossing mud into the air as they galloped.

The white man pressed a hand to his chest, heaving with effort. "I'm a Yank and you're wearing blue, so I suppose you're a Yank."

Wolf peered around him at the men whipping their horses, attempting to catch up. Concern welled inside him. It had been months since he'd seen the enemy.

The filthy man spoke again, "By God, man, don't you tell me I ran all the goddamn way from Richmond to run into a group of lily-livered rebs in disguise."

"We ain't graybacks. We're with the 13th Michigan."

"Well, let us through because those boys behind us are."

"They're drawing guns," Roberts said loud.

The men on horses could have been anyone. They wore common civilian coats and brown or black hats. Pistols in hand meant ill, and in Virginia it was already difficult to tell secessionist from unionist.

"I'm Captain John Yates, 3rd Ohio Infantry."

With each passing second, the horsemen gained on their prey. They whipped their mounts even harder as if they could smell blood on the horizon.

"Who's the contraband?" Roberts asked.

"The colored boy?" Yates said.

"Yeah," Roberts retorted.

Yates looked at his accomplice. "That's Martin. Fine lad. Now let us through or we're going to die." He shook his head fiercely. "I ain't going back to that godforsaken prison, boy." His thick jaw set hard. "So you best shoot me now 'cause I ain't." His bright icy blue eyes made a promise that he spoke the truth.

"Get near the fire." Wolf pointed.

The riders zeroed in for Wolf. Mud covered the men just like those they hunted. He could see the muscles beneath the horses' flesh rippling as they galloped. Snot and foam flew from the horses' mouths. The mean snarls of the rebels formed on their faces. They saw him. They knew he stood in the way of their capture and they charged on, not caring a lick.

With a flick of his wrist, he flipped his sight upright and quickly adjusted the range on the elevating sight. He took aim with his carbine. Not as good as the Sharps rifle for range, but at a hundred yards, he could land a hit. He squinted his left eye, letting his right do all the work.

"Dan!" he yelled. "Shugart! Get ready."

The riders heard his shouts but continued galloping for them. Their battle focus was all on him and their fleeing victims, so they paid no notice to the men in the timber.

Gunfire popped and Dan fired first followed by Shugart. Wolf couldn't tell which one hit the second rider, but he fell from his saddle with a slap into the mud.

The horsemen discharged their pistols at Wolf. Smoke clouded the air behind them. He was their primary enemy now. Pooled water, unsettled by the thundering hooves, rippled in rings. He let the front runner, a fellow with a long brown beard, enter his sights. All he did was keep his weapon steady and wait. With a firm finger, he let the trigger click backward.

Bang! His carbine erupted with fire, fumes, and violence. Bluish-gray smoke puffed from the barrel like a miniature cannon, and the explosion echoed out like a wave toward the enemy, filling the damp forest with his battle call. The lead rider spasmed, his hand leaping to clutch his side. He yanked his reins, rearing his mount on two legs. The other two riders slowed, firing pistols in his direction. They were quick smaller pops. At this range, it was a mere display of force.

Roberts's carbine reported, and seconds later, more gunfire came from the woods. The riders snapped their pistols with successive shots into the trees on either side of them, not knowing which way to shoot. They drew more pistols from their belts instead of reloading. The leader rocked in his saddle, clutching his side. He lifted his head into the air and howled. Their horses spun in circles. One of the horsemen fired harmlessly in Wolf's direction. Another miniature salvo from the trees sent the rebels into retreat.

In a chaotic cluster, the rebels spurred back in the other direction. One of the riders lifted their fallen comrade on his saddle. Wolf tracked the men with his eyes.

"Should we go after them?" Roberts asked. "You know what Wilhelm always says. Where's there's one there's always more."

The healthy rider mounted with apt horsemanship and they galloped double in the other direction.

Wolf swung the lever out, simultaneously opening the breech of his carbine and slipped in a new linen cartridge. He glided the lever back into place, sealing the breech. He placed a new percussion cap from his sardine box on the metal nipple then pulled the hammer back to full cock, watching the riders flee. "No, we have what they want." He scanned for Dan and Shugart. With a flat-palmed hand signal, he motioned for them to stay put while he figured out who this Captain Yates and this Martin were.

Wolf marched over to the fire. The fiery-haired captain leaned near the flames with his hands as close to the blaze as he could without burning his fingers.

"You came from Richmond?" He couldn't keep the sound of wonderment from rolling off his tongue. The rebel capital was always within spitting distance of the Union forces, but Richmond may as well have been a mythical place farther away than the Orient.

Yates stared at the flames, rubbing his hands. "Aye. You know how long it's been since I had a fire in this godforsaken winter? A real fire?"

"No."

"Long time."

Yates's shoulders trembled as he tried to find warmth. Martin hovered near the flames, staring dumbstruck at the Union soldiers.

"We escaped six days ago. Nothing but me and this Negro to keep warm with. Goddamn Home Guard hunting us. We were lucky for the head start." He glanced at Wolf and then Martin. "Not that I don't appreciate the colored boy's help, but I'd rather have a little lass to share my bed with." His eyes dared Wolf to deny his claim.

Martin's eyes watched the fiery captain, but he held his tongue. He quietly extended his hands, warming them.

Wolf went to his horse, his brace squeaking as he went. The brown gelding had a white patch on his nose. He patted Billy as he walked by, digging in his saddlebags. He removed hard tack, a stale dense cracker like bread, and his canteen. He gave it to Yates and Martin.

"Thank you, lad."

The two starving men bit into the steely bread with their molars, eating fast as if afraid Wolf might take it away at any moment.

"Never seen a man eat tooth dullers like that." Roberts said softly. "Must be real hungry."

Captain Yates greedily swallowed the food with a half-grin. "Never thought tack could taste this heavenly."

Martin stared at his but ate it all the same.

"Ain't that right, boy?" Yates nudged his comrade with his fist. "Speak up."

"It's good, sir."

After Yates finished shoving the rest of the sheet cracker in his mouth, he continued. "There were a hundred and nine of us officers that walked out of Libby. Colonel Rose was our leader, stout, first-rate fellow. He never wasn't going to escape that one."

They'd all heard of the infamous Richmond prison, but only in passing. Rumors held that the conditions were appalling, but all he had to base it on was his hometown jail, so he just accepted the idea of don't get captured. "Where are the rest of them?"

Fire lit in Yates's eyes. "Don't know." His mouth formed a thin angry line. "We ran in groups of twos and threes as to not garner suspicion. I was in the first group. A woman sympathetic to the Union, gave us her Negro to guide us. Martin here."

"We should get you back to camp so you can report to the captain."

"Farther away from the front the better."

Wolf turned to Roberts. "I'm going to take them back to camp. We'll take the others' horses then I'll return."

"You putting Shugart in charge? Come on."

A smile settled on Wolf's lips. "He'll have you confessing all your sins by sundown."

CHAPTER 2

February 12th, 1864
Stevensburg, Virginia

A twelve-man brass band played a peppy holiday tune, one that dominated the grand ballroom despite the din of well-watered chatter. Women in all shades of pink, blue, orange, and red hoop skirts were twirled by men leading them in an upbeat waltz. Union officers in their dark blue dress uniforms, their brass buttons and belt buckles shining, ushered the well-dressed ladies along with civilians in black double-breasted frock coats.

Ulric Dahlgren stood with his back against the wall. His torso leaned to the side, his left leg bearing most of his weight. He twisted a jeweled ring on his hand while he scanned the crowd.

Sweat ran down his cheeks and dampened his forehead. He took a white handkerchief from his coat pocket and dotted his brow.

A young debutante with black curly hair and a vibrant blue dress curtsied to him. Her blonde friend nudged her, and he overheard them whispering as they gained whatever courage they needed to be the pursuer rather than the pursued.

The young woman's plump lips curved wide. She was much prettier when she smiled. "Excuse me, sir. Would you care to dance?" Her cheeks reddened with every word as if she knew she overstepped the social norms. Her dark eyes glanced back up at him.

He was tall, by a good estimate well over six feet, so most people looked up to him. God had given him a slender but athletic frame made even thinner by his time in the hospitals. His nose was long and his cheeks gaunt as if he sucked a candy at all times. He gave her a weak smile and wiped his sweat-dotted brow again.

"I'm afraid I would do you injustice, my lady." Each one of his words was proper, projecting his education.

Her eyes drooped as if he'd reached out and slapped her.

"Look here, my lady." He lifted his pant leg from over his boot. He kept pulling it upward.

She gulped when he'd exposed enough, her eyes filling with fear then pity. He'd rather have the fear than the pity any day, but it was always the same. Pity. Nothing drove him madder than to be pitied. It was the same way his mother looked at him, and when his father thought he wasn't looking, his eyes held the same sentiment.

Blinking her eyes in watery sympathy, she curtsied again. "I'm sorry, sir, for your loss. I feel that we would have had a splendid waltz."

He raised his chin, shrouded in a short-cut rounded goatee. "It could have been." *But we will not.*

The two young ladies circled back around the room for more eligible bachelors like crows hunting carrion. The blonde spoke loudly to her dark-haired friend. "He must've been a wonderful waltzer at one point."

"He had a divine look to him."

"He did. Such a sad affair." She lamented and disappeared into the crowd of soldiers, ladies, politicians, and other Union citizens of noteworthy wealth.

The part of his leg that he still had attached ached fiercely even with the very fine prosthetic strapped to his thigh to hold the piece of wood to the bottom of his knee joint. It was the finest, his father had told him. Surgeons made advancements in the technology every day, but it did not feel right to him. The itching, rubbing, and scratching all day was real enough. Nerve pain would shoot along his leg and end abruptly as if the electrical pulses searched for something, but the connection was severed. Then the nerves would circle back and the cycle would repeat over and over. Falling and stumbling around like a drunken fool humiliated him. The smooth piece of wood placed into his shoe like a false lump to give the appearance of normalcy was the exact opposite. Burdensome and fake.

They'd taken his leg below the knee, leaving him with a mound in its place that no amount of alcohol or medicine could bring under control. A knob of pain that hadn't fully healed made the wood of his prosthetic even worse. Outside of Gettysburg in Hagerstown, a Minié ball had passed through his ankle and into his foot, shattering and fragmenting the small bones. It festered, and five days later, a surgeon was sawing off a part of his body so he wouldn't die. The man expected him to be thankful for the mercy, but daily, he thought maybe it wouldn't have been as bad to fade away as a man whole. He licked his lips, scanning the room.

A short officer stood in the center of a group of people. He had a wicked beak for a nose that dominated his small face. His sideburns hung low off his cheeks like Spanish moss leaving his chin bare like a tree trunk. Dahlgren thought he had the stature of a mythical goblin, but you would never know it the way he stood. His stance was that of a nine-foot-tall man, a giant of confidence. Perhaps it was the stars on his shoulders signaling to others he demanded respect, but there was something else that gave him that imposition. *Ambition.* He held a drink in one hand and smiled at a story a man with a bowtie recited.

Gripping the handle of his crutch, he hobbled across the floor. His shoe flopped uselessly, tapping with every step, and he was thankful for the general din to cover the horse-clopping wooden leg. Piteous eyes followed him, fused with a natural curiosity as to his story. Every lost limb came with a story of heroics and bravery, or at least, battle. He struggled past them all like a circus act on display for all to see. He ignored their commiserating eyes but always felt them. He stood behind the group for a moment, waiting for them to notice him near the edges.

Single stars on the small officer's coat confirmed his identity. He noticed Dahlgren with a politician's smile. "What say you, boy? How many years the rebels have left in them?"

"Hopefully only a few months."

The group of the wealthy and officers laughed. The small general took a swig of his drink and grinned. There was nothing handsome about it. "Optimistic, aren't we?" He pointed. "Must be one of Grant's lads." This caused another round of chuckles from his entourage.

"May we speak in private, General Kilpatrick?" he asked.

The undersized general tilted his head to the side. "We can talk in front of my friends. What do you have to say, boy?" He gawked for a moment.

"I would prefer we have this discussion in private."

"I'm sorry. I don't know you, do I?"

A man in a fine suit smiled at him. His goatee hung almost to the knot of his necktie. "I know the lad. This is Admiral Dahlgren's boy. You have his look."

Dahlgren dipped his head. "You do me honor."

"Your father was a great supporter of mine when I ran for Senate in '60. I do not forget my supporters."

"Senator Cowan, it's nice to see you again. My father spoke very highly of you. Where is the lovely Mrs. Cowan?"

"I'm afraid she is feeling ill tonight." A slight tinge in the senator's voice masked something about his wife. *An affair? Irritation? Disdain? Worry?*

"A pity. She makes lovely company."

Cowan's smile faded like a memory of peace during a long war. "She does."

"General, would you speak with me in private? It won't take long."

Kilpatrick nodded with a smile. "Of course, laddie." He bowed his head to the others filling his circle. "Will you excuse me? I am sure Colonel Henderson can keep your drinks filled while I am absent."

"Have any of you fine folk been to Connecticut?" Henderson asked.

"Only on my way to Boston," said Cowan. This brought about another round of laughter.

The din faded as Dahlgren followed the general across the room to a study.

The room was well-kept, and a fire blazed in the fireplace. Kilpatrick walked over to a glass decanter and refilled his drink with the mahogany liquid.

"Your father is a powerful man. Has the ear of the president." He turned around and took a long swig of his liquor. His eyes weighed Dahlgren's, a malevolent interest laced with greed filling them.

"Is that why you're talking to me?"

Kilpatrick shrugged his shoulders. "Could be, but there are other influential men outside." He smiled at Dahlgren, his eyes still holding some delight of knowing what Dahlgren did not.

"Not like my father. President Lincoln travels regularly to the Navy Yard to confer with him. He visited me when my leg was amputated." Those words tasted like gut bile on his tongue, making him want to spit.

"And the man I was speaking with is a prominent Republican, a man that could put me in the right position after the war, and you cut me off and led me away to a study to talk. Say something worthwhile."

"I know what they call you behind your back."

Anger flared in Kilpatrick's eyes, and his mouth formed a sneer. "Do you?"

"I do. Kill-Cavalry. I also know you are in dire need of a victory."

Kilpatrick gave him a slight nod and took a sip of his alcohol. "I think this conversation has reached its end." He turned his back on Dahlgren, refilling his glass again.

"I know this party is to lobby for support for just that kind of raid."

Kilpatrick spun on him. "A daring raid, *boy*. A raid that will mean something. I want to steal our men back. There's over ten thousand of them right beneath our nose, and the high command is sitting on their hands instead of freeing them. Do you know what their conditions are like?

"I do not."

"Libby Prison is a tobacco warehouse not meant for men, and if it was, a couple hundred. Now imagine it with six times that number. No beds. Sawdust for food. Hell, they can't even feed their men in the field let alone a bunch of prisoners. Rats running rampant. Those are the officers. The enlisted they keep across the river in Belle Isle. Might as well call it Hell Isle. They are treated like no more than beasts. Days without food. No shelter. Sleep in ditches. Freeze in ditches. Listen, pup. I don't care what you think of me or what I've done. Those men deserve better from a grateful nation and I want to give it to them."

"I want in, General."

Kilpatrick smirked and pointed with his glass. "You got no leg. Hagerstown, right?"

Dahlgren gave him a stiff nod.

"I bet you ain't even healed up yet." He took a step closer. "Still raw isn't it? Fresh grown skin rubbing on that coarse wood? Every step agonizing, right up the thigh."

A slight heat rose in Dahlgren's cheeks. Sweat began to bead on his forehead like a summer dew. His crutch dug painfully into his armpit, bearing most of his weight. The general was right on every account, and it made him sick to his stomach. He fought the rising nausea, attempting to stay erect.

Kilpatrick continued. "I'm sure your father can secure you a safe position as an aide somewhere near the capital." He slurped his drink and his mouth curved into pity that never touched his eyes. "Play out the war, and be thankful you didn't have to go bottoms up."

"General, you want a raid. Correct?

Kilpatrick lambasted him with a confident grin. "I'll get my raid."

Dahlgren resisted the urge to wipe his beading brow. "Let me lead under your command, and I'll get you your raid. I can assure you of its issuance."

"What would make you think that I want you on my campaign?" Kilpatrick's lips twisted into a sneer.

Dahlgren's chin shifted a fraction of an inch upward. He dared not let his eyes leave Kilpatrick's pale blue ones that reminded him of a cold winter sky. "Not only will I secure your raid, but you will be a legend in the Union. A man who will be talked of in all the right circles. A man who will gain so much political capital he will acquire rank, politics, business ventures, wealth beyond your imaginations. A man who will be connected to all the right people, to those far greater than Senator Cowan outside."

Kilpatrick laughed heartily. "You are but a boy. What would you know about these things?" His smile faded when Dahlgren didn't respond in kind.

"War leaves no boy not a man. I lost my leg rushing to save Meade at Gettysburg. I've killed men. Seen men killed."

"Suppose it doesn't. Makes men harder. Makes men who lead even harder." Kilpatrick poured some of his drink in his mouth and grimaced as it drained into his belly. "I try not to think about all the boys who've died under me. Those thoughts would be enough to drive a man insane. Let me tell you." He lifted a finger off his glass and thrust it toward Dahlgren. "If you're going to survive this war up here, don't even think of them as real. Mere pieces on a chessboard. That's how we win." He stared off for a moment. "Let's say I might be interested in what you have to offer. How will you, over all those men out there, acquire me my raid? How could you make me a legend?"

"I will make us legends."

Kilpatrick removed a short cigar from his pocket. After rolling it in his fingers, he stuck it in his mouth. He twisted it, wetting the tobacco brown wrap. "Would you like a Cuban Por Larrañaga? You can bet you can't find many of these sneaking though the embargo now. We can thank your father for that."

"No sir, I don't smoke." He wiped his brow. The ache in his leg had progressed to a throb, pulsating where his lost limb should have been, his wound enacting wicked revenge on the rest of his body. After the wounding, his father had the missing piece buried in a grave at the Washington Navy Yard's foundry wall with a little plaque to commemorate his loss. Unusual when so many men and their various parts lay in shallow graves around every battle site in the nation. It was a perk of having an influential admiral as a father.

"Too bad, but your loss either way. I have pipe tobacco around here somewhere," said Kilpatrick out the side of his mouth.

"No, thank you."

The general opened a matchbook and struck the red-tipped stick off the coarse edge. The flame sparked bright on the tip and he held it close to the cigar end, puffing to get the blaze going, the orange embers flaring in response. Sweet cigar smoke filled the air like a foggy summer morning. "You got yourself a deal young man. You get me my raid, and I'll get you a command under me."

Dahlgren found himself straightening, a slow cruel smile filling his thin lips. He could taste the victory in the back of his throat. The pain of his missing limb tempered for a moment. The time had come to grab it by the horns.

Kilpatrick inhaled with a nod. "You are a bold lad." He smiled. "We will need a first-class colonel to lead in the raid if we are to free my prisoners." He exhaled. "And burn Richmond."

"With all due respect, General, I don't want to burn Richmond."

Kilpatrick puffed his cigar. Gray tendrils formed a cloud around the short general. "You don't? There must be a misunderstanding in our purpose." A resounding rendition of the "Battle Cry for Freedom" kicked off in the ballroom. Voices of men and women rose in patriotic fervor as they sang at the top of their lungs, "The Union forever!"

The band belted the tune with proud amusement. It was only the third time they'd played the song in the night. Muffled, "hurrah, boys, hurrah," were shouted on high, probably with fists in the air.

Dahlgren locked eyes with the little general before him.

"Well, be out with it."

The people continued to sing in the adjacent room. "Down with the traitors."

"I want to kill Jefferson Davis."

Up with the stars.

CHAPTER 3

February 12th, 1864
3rd Cavalry Division's Encampment, Stevensburg, Virginia

Campfires dotted the winter military camp near Stevensburg, a tiny village surrounded by farmland roughly five miles southeast of Culpepper, Virginia. The Army of the Potomac encompassed almost forty miles around in the Northern Virginia countryside. The I, II, III, V, and VI Corps were growing restless.

The 3rd Cavalry Division's small corner of the massive federal presence was a cluster of homes near the intersection of two roads. On the surface, the inhabitants were friendly enough to the Yankees' faces, but it never felt genuine as if they waited for the rebels to return and stake their rightful claim over the secessionist Virginian soil. Despite the resentment, they tolerated the presence of the Union troops like a dog does fleas.

Roberts, staring at the fire, sipped his coffee that Wolf knew had an ample amount of shine layered in it. "I'm in love, boys."

The fire lapped the faces of eight troopers with shadows in the night. Shugart frowned beneath his gray beard. "Idle hands are the devil's workshop, Mr. Roberts."

"An idle soldier's hands are the devil's playground," Sergeant Wilhelm Berles piped up from the other side. He sharpened his sword with a whetstone.

"Why you sharpening that thing?" Van Horn said.

"You know what's not more than six miles away and on the other side of the Rapidan River?"

"No."

The sergeant didn't look up from his task. "Ewell's Corps in their winter encampment."

Van Horn dismissed him. "Somebody'd sound the alarm."

"If you don't think it's a possibility, then you don't know Lee or Stuart or Clausewitz for that matter."

"Who's Clausewitz? Never heard of him." Van Horn spit to the side.

Sergeant Berles was a former light cavalry soldier with the 1st Baden Uhlans and was in his fifties, almost the oldest on the squad behind Shugart. Gray consumed his temples like dusty vines, the same shade that hounded his mustache. He'd quickly adopted the young men, becoming like a father to them. He ignored the tall Dutchman, focusing on his work. "He's a famous Prussian general." His blade ground over the stone. "He wrote a book, *On War*. You should read it. Think of it as a general's bible."

Wolf recalled his father mentioning him in the past but knew little in the ways of war before joining the Union Army. "What's his book say?"

Van Horn spoke before Wilhelm could explain. "Wolf, don't be stupid. What's some dead Prussian gonna teach us about war in America? Seem to remember the last empire to walk through here thought they were all fancy, and we defeated them."

"Book 3, chapter 9. Surprise is the foundation of all military undertakings," Wilhelm said.

With a downtrodden expression, Roberts took off his forage hat and scratched a lice-ridden head. He held his cap over the fire for a moment, the lice popping like corn. "Excuse me, fellas, I was professing my feelings, and nobody was listening."

"What's his name?" Van Horn said, his face steady, no mirth despite his jest.

Roberts continued ignoring Van Horn's dour jab. "I know it's hard to fathom," he said, shaking his head. "A young bachelor like me'self, a valiant gentleman and hardy soldier through and through. Who wouldn't want to be with that?"

Wilhelm looked on with a sliver of mirth beneath his curled mustache. He didn't say anything to Roberts, only watched him as if he knew the answers already. He'd grown callous and reserved since the death of his son at the hands of General Wade Hampton, who the men simply referred to as "The Brute." It was as if his joy had been smothered inside him. Even though he'd gained a whole squad of sons, his pain was clear to the other men despite the fact he kept it well-hidden.

They sat in the center of four log cabins around the campfire. Erected in the fall, the shelters provided the men with humble yet surprisingly comfortable lodging. It was much better than lying open air under the stars or freezing in a canvas tent.

Each cabin had its own small chimney, but the men of the squad would congregate around a larger fire throughout the day. He'd heard elsewhere men suffered terribly and was thankful to be where he was despite the occasional picket duty.

Trees around the camp disappeared daily as the men cut them farther and farther back, scarring the land with jarring stumps and turning the earth with horse hooves, boots, and waste. The terrain around them reshaped into a barren form save for the soldiers' presence.

In spite of the constant threat of illness, ample amounts of food, rest, and refitting had gone on throughout the winter. Fresh recruits had come to the brigade and men from the 1st Michigan, one of their sister regiments, were even allowed to furlough home for a month if they'd reenlist.

Roberts looked around the campfire at the blue-coated men. "I've finally found her. She's something real special." He shook his head reminiscing about her warm embrace.

Wolf grinned beneath his beard, tossing a stick into the flames. "She part of Hooker's Division?"

"Yes," Bart said. The round-faced brothers spoke softly to one another in Polish, smiling at Roberts, forage caps pushed high atop their heads.

The love-stricken trooper ignored the jibes of his comrades. "She got emerald green eyes and red hair the color of a summer rose," he said, slurping his coffee and shine.

"She also's got something that will make you sick," Adams said with a smirk. His hair was coal black and his complexion swarthy with a sharp nose and an easy smile. Some men called him Turk but never to his face. His uniform was always a wrinkled mess and Wolf wasn't sure he'd started the war like that, but he had whatever his affliction was now all the time. It was even rumored he'd been a lieutenant before an incident demoted him back to private.

A dozen soldiers had been transferred from the 1st Michigan, having been deemed troublemakers, and the reputation that followed them was fierce. In turn, Colonel Moore had transferred the troublemakers to his least favorite company, F Company. With wisdom beyond his age, Captain Peltier had split the dozen men into different units attempting to diffuse any debauchery before it started.

Adams nudged Private Nelson, a willing accomplice in their mockery. He was more grizzly than man, with thick hair running seamlessly from his head to his feet, his hands the size of cannon balls. It was said he singlehandedly tossed a rebel and his mount to the ground at Gettysburg after his had been shot out from beneath him.

Roberts shook his head. "No, she don't. She told me she was clean."

"Cleaner than the dirt," Nelson said. He wore a scowl perpetually beneath his beard. It was hard to discern if he was serious, angry, or making a joke.

"She ain't no whore, nor one of Hooker's gals." Roberts wagged a finger at Nelson.

"Be careful, where you point that, little man," Nelson responded.

"What's her name?" Adams asked, seeing room to torture the smitten man some more.

"Her name is Rosie Staton. And I just feel like a thousand dollars when I'm with her."

"Hope you didn't pay her a thousand dollars," Van Horn chimed in.

The men laughed and laughed, and Roberts peered at them in angry confusion. "She said she was gonna volunteer to be a nurse once the winter's over."

Wolf nudged his friend, trying to help him come to the realization the rest of them had already come to. "Why wait? They always need nurses around an army."

"I. I. Don't know."

An evil grin fell across Adams's face. "Aye, they always need hookers too."

Roberts stood and pointed at the men. "I don't like the way you talking about my lady. We're in love and you can't stop it."

"You like that thing between your legs then be careful where you stick it," Wilhelm said. He scrubbed his sword with a gray cloth, holding his curved saber in the air to observe his work in the firelight.

Nelson growled, "Now I told you once, half-man. Don't point at me." He went to stand, pointing back at Roberts.

"I'll fight for her honor," Roberts said defiantly.

Nelson laughed a deep bass rumble. "Come on over here and get some."

Wolf tugged Roberts back down to a seated position. "Let's not antagonize the bear."

"You want a fight, you'll get one," Nelson said, clenching his fists.

"Careful, Private Nelson. Don't let this fun get the best of you." Wilhelm didn't look at the man, all his attention on his soldierly task. Nelson scowled, his face reddening.

"I don't take no orders from a dirty Dutchman like yourself."

"What you got against the Dutch?" Van Horn said.

Wilhelm continued to ignore the brutish man who'd found a new victim. "I'm not Dutch. I was born near Baden and swore an oath to be an American."

Nelson leaned closer, growling. "I don't like them neither."

"Careful, Nelson, you're surrounded by Germans and Dutch."

"Polska," Bart said. He beat his chest with a heavy fist.

"Polska," Dan repeated what his brother had said.

Veins bulged in Nelson's neck. "Fuck all of 'em, especially you." A hand went to a knife at his belt.

"Don't be stupid, Nelson. I'll split you from navel to chin." Wilhelm flicked his wrist, and in one fluid motion, slit Nelson's belt off his waist. His equipment plopped on the ground, dragged down by the weight. He let his saber follow the length of Nelson's belly to the bottom of his jaw. "Navel to chin."

Nelson leaned backward, stepping out of saber range.

"Dutch or not, you remember who you're talking to. I'm your sergeant, and if I catch a whiff of you doing something to a member of this unit, I'll cut you down."

Nelson picked up his equipment and ruined belt from the ground. He growled and stormed off, kicking piles of firewood and stomping the wet earth. When men yelled at him, he roared and they backed down.

Adams smirked, watching his ally rage away. He crinkled his nose. "Some people just can't take a joke. He'll come back around. He's lucky you didn't cut his sack off."

"He's lucky I missed," Wilhelm said. He inspected the tip of the blade that could have sliced the big man open like a sack of wheat. Or if he really missed, removed an essential manly part.

Wolf whispered to Roberts, trying to spare the little man's pride. "She ain't no lady. You know that, right?"

"She is to me."

"Okay, friend. You just don't get too attached," Wolf said, wrapping an arm around him.

Roberts calmed. "Can't a man just be in love and bugger the rest?"

"Never that easy."

"Red hair?" Adams said. His eyes veered upward as he tried to recall.

A bit of cheer shone through Roberts's voice. "Yeah, like a red rose."

"That's it. I remember her now. Great tits." Adams stood and scratched at his groin area. "Might need to get me some horizontal refreshment tonight."

The men laughed.

"You young heathens, do not succumb to the wants of flesh. Focus on your true purpose. Defeat of the Rebellion," Shugart postulated with fierce conviction.

"But can purpose give me relief?" Adams questioned. "And doesn't God want me to populate the earth? As far as I know, there's only one way to do so. Unless you care to enlighten me, Uncle?"

Shugart exhaled harshly. "Dear God, man, control yourself. We're not animals ruled by desire. We are men of conviction. Act like one."

"And men have needs that need satisfied."

"At least this misguided boy is only tempted by the flesh, not ruled by it."

"Say, Roberts, where's her cabin?" Adams said, standing. He pointed to the left and then the right and shook himself, waiting for directions.

Roberts became defiant. "I'll never tell the likes of you."

"Red-haired whore. Can't be hard to miss." He shrugged his shoulders. "Or I won't. Who knows, maybe I'll get a freebie if she likes me." Adams slogged away after his friend.

"She only takes favorites!" Roberts shouted at his back.

"Sure she does," Adams yelled from afar, waving an arm.

Roberts sat down, shaking his head. He stared at Wolf in desperation. "I love her. I really do."

Wolf laughed and patted his back. "I know you do, buddy. I'm sure she loves you too."

Shugart shook his head at the retreating Adams. "God save us from these men and the Southern wretches."

"Adams got Uncle all worked up," Wolf said.

"I am only guiding my flock, trying to keep you from burning for eternity for your indiscretions," Shugart said with a frown.

Wolf placed his hand on his chest. "I meant no disrespect, Uncle. You may save our souls in peace. But our boy here is in love, and isn't that what the Lord sings praises of?"

Shugart's cheeks reddened. "The heart of the righteous ponders how to answer, but the mouth of the wicked pours out evil things." He stood, puffing out his chest. "You remember the Lord is always watching."

"As is your sergeant," Wilhelm added.

"I bid you goodnight."

A round of "g'night, Uncle" came from the men.

"When do you think we'll march out?" Wolf asked Wilhelm.

Wilhelm worked some light oil into his sword, letting the fire shine off its blade. "Captain says to be ready at a moment's notice to strike south."

They'd all heard this time and time again. "That's all he ever says," Wolf said.

A twinkle of amusement filled Wilhelm's eyes. "Finally you're learning the ways of a soldier's life. What's the motto of the army boys?"

Nodding their acceptance, all the men let out an exasperated, "We hurry and we wait."

"Exactly. You should learn to enjoy it. It's one of the joys of being in the army. Heard you ran into an escaped prisoner."

"We did. Red-haired captain, 3rd Ohio."

Wilhelm raised an eyebrow. "Roberts's lass?"

"Sadly, it wasn't her. But if it was, we wouldn't have any trouble getting him on picket duty."

Roberts stood, his eyes growing dim. "I sure would. Any moment with her is worth an eternity on picket duty." He threw back his drink and left the fire.

"The heart falls easy for the young and is steady for the old." Wilhelm peered at the young man's back.

"Who would have thought our little gutter rat would fall in love?" Wolf continued. "The captain was from Ohio. Had a colored boy with him. Came from Libby prison. You heard of it?"

Adams returned with a bottle of liquor, glancing at Roberts retreating. "Shame the boy left. Came with a peace offering. Did I hear you say Libby?"

"Yeah, an escapee made it to our lines yesterday. Tunneled out, but almost none made it."

"Rat Hell? Don't get captured boys. Only thing worse is Belle Isle," Adams said.

"What's Belle Isle?"

"Roberts, come out here," Adams shouted.

The short man opened the door to his cabin. Adams waved the bottle and tossed it to him.

Roberts caught the bottle and bit the cork off the top. He wafted the aroma into his nose. "This smells like the good stuff."

"It's from Nelson."

He pulled back in suspicion. "Nelson?"

"Consider it a gesture of reconciliation." He gave a half bow. "Some men lack certain social skills."

"Thanks." Roberts gave a quick smile.

"A real Southern Belle Isle that one is. Give you the old crotch rot before you keel over and die, she will."

"I thought it was an island." Wolf said.

"It is, Wolfie. An island filled with sickness, scant food, dirty water. You don't want that Southern belle if you catch my drift." He raised his voice at Roberts. "Even if you love her."

"Suppose it pays to be an officer," Van Horn said.

Adams shrugged. "In more ways than one, but Libby ain't that much better. But it's better."

Wilhelm glanced up from his work, holding the saber out in the firelight. "Lesson number one. Don't get caught." He sheathed his sword and set it to the side.

CHAPTER 4

February 16th, 1864
Kilpatrick's 3rd Division Cavalry Corps Headquarters,
Stevensburg, Virginia

George Armstrong Custer couldn't take his mind off Libbie Bacon, officially now Elizabeth Bacon Custer. The marriage was fresh and so was the love. The kind of love that made him want to spend every waking minute with her and every sleeping minute beside her. He wanted to gaze upon her, watching her sleep. Even the faintest rise and fall of her chest were the most exquisite actions of a goddess. His dream of her faded before the excited voice of his commanding officer. Kilpatrick had droned on and on about his glorious raid, torturing him, who was unable to think about anything except the most wonderful Mrs. Custer.

"This will go down in history. The bastards are ripe for the picking," Kilpatrick said. "Hell, we could end the war."

Custer's eyes glazed over, his thoughts turning back to his love. She was short, shorter than him by almost six inches. He was tall compared to most men, and she was short compared to most women, making the soldier's appearance even more commanding next to his wife.

Her beauty was perfect, and his blood pumped harder in his veins dwelling on her. Even the newspapers acknowledged her allure despite wide-set eyes and a petite face. He didn't care because to him she was perfect. He also didn't care about Kilpatrick's fantastical chatter.

"They are weak. So weak. Did you read this report?" Kilpatrick held a piece of paper in the air. "Here Van Lew is saying the Confederate capital is ripe for the taking. Ripe." His eyes seemed to swell as if they could absorb even more information. "Only invalids and old men guard the deplorable Jeff Davis and his pretender cabinet." A broad smile stretched across the entirety of his face. His tone was searching even if it was for approval from a man he had history with. His supporting lackeys—Henderson, Davies, and Whitaker—had already stroked his ego enough for one day. "General Custer, what's your take?"

Once again Custer was shaken from the lustful daydreams of his wife, her pleasant smile evaporating in his mind. He adjusted himself in his chair. "Sir, I love a good raid as much as the next man, but General Wistar conducted a similar raid not more than a couple weeks past to ill effect. Not to mention that Stoneman failed last year."

Kilpatrick wouldn't be swayed, his own pomp and circumstance guiding him along a rotten path. "Stoneman was ineffectual. I penetrated the outer rings of Richmond with but a few men! With a proper command, I'd run rampant through her, ravaging her at my whim." His eyes grew distant, witnessing his glory in his own mind. It had been a brisk march in the reverse direction for Kilpatrick to survive his daring jaunt near the outer defenses of the Confederate capital. "And Wistar is a fool. He's got a little shrunken member with no balls to back him up. His men ran at the first sign of resistance."

"I believe the opposition was sufficient to not be taken lightly, but don't you think they would be on high alert now?"

Kilpatrick barked a laugh with an evil grin. "You, General Custer, have never been one to shy from an enemy, alerted or not. Growing timid, are we?"

Custer stiffened, his pride prickling while challenged. He'd been called a dandy, a boy, a lad, an upstart, and he was sure many other worse names, but a coward he was not. "I do not shy from the enemy, sir."

"Good. You've only been married a couple of weeks. I wouldn't expect you to be so soft yet."

Custer blew air through his nostrils, hiding his anger but also an ounce of empathy for his commanding officer. Kilpatrick's wife and infant son had passed in late '63, leaving him devastated. It only redoubled his investment in making a name for himself in his military career, which had been in need of a major boost since the thrashing they'd received at Buckland Mills.

The rebels affectionately called the battle the "Buckland Races" for the whipping they'd given the Yanks. Custer remembered that event in earnest because he had been on the receiving end of that gut punch as well. It was easier to grow from failures than victories as long as you could string together enough victories to keep your rank and your men alive.

It was a thorough reminder of the formidability of their opponents. J. E. B. Stuart, Wade Hampton, and Fitzhugh Lee were still on the field. They lurked somewhere between Stevensburg and Richmond like gray ghosts in the shadows waiting for their chance to strike without warning.

Lieutenant Colonel James Henderson, part of Kilpatrick's staff, lifted his chin. He had an average build, but his head was too small for his frame. Jovial eyes twinkled, but not much went on behind them. "Sir, the men believe that if you had led the Wistar raid, we would have captured Richmond in a few days."

A sigh escaped Custer's lips. That was then, this is now, and his thoughts again drifted to his new wife and her tender smile. Hopefully soon she would have a babe at her breast, and she could be a mother to his children as well as the love of his life. Henderson wasn't wrong. Morale was high in the Union camp. The lull in winter actions and relatively comfortable accommodations for the men had everyone in high spirits despite the failed Richmond. Despite the abortion of a raid by General Wistar, his command suffered few casualties, and at the end of the day, not getting killed sat well with the men.

"I believe there is much confidence in this raid's success from the highest levels of command," Henderson said.

"Respectfully, I must disagree, Colonel. Neither General Meade nor Pleasonton would be so apt to attempt another foray, while the rebels have only just repulsed one. You can only kick a wasp's nest so many times before you get stung. Surely they are prepared for us."

A knock echoed out from the door. Kilpatrick's aide-de-camp Captain

Whitaker, a sturdy young man, moved to answer it.

Custer wondered what his precious wife was doing at this very moment as he was forced to entertain the ambitions of his commanding officer. Was she reading by the fire? Her nose crinkling as the plot thickened? Was she meeting with the other wives sipping tea and giggling over the latest gossip? Did she think of him while they talked, desperate for his warm embrace? Of course she did. Love took two willing participants, an ever-rotating back-and-forth of affection.

A tall man entered the room, probably a match for Custer in height. His uniform was neatly pressed without a wrinkle despite the wooden crutch wedged underneath his armpit. His face had a youthful appearance and held more than its fair share of aristocratic features.

Kilpatrick smiled. "Colonel Dahlgren, my boy. I'm pleased to see you again. You look well."

The man's wooden leg thumped the floorboards. "And I you, General Kilpatrick." The two men shook hands with a good deal of vigor as if Kilpatrick were running for political office.

"I believe you may know of my subordinate, General Custer?"

The young man ducked his head in respect. "I have heard extensively of your exploits near Gettysburg."

"And I yours. Forgive me, but how is your leg?"

"Stiff," Dahlgren said, with a short smile. "I come with a dispatch for General Kilpatrick.

Kilpatrick's face lightened with glee. "Do you?"

Dahlgren handed a white envelope to Kilpatrick. He snatched it from his hand and lifted the seal with his thumb, removing the stationery like it contained a precious treasure map. Unfolding the paper, he held it close to his eyes as he read.

Custer continued on with his negative assessment of a potential raid. "I just don't see Pleasonton granting such a raid so soon, sir. He's expressed no stomach for it."

The general didn't respond, engrossed in his letter. His eyes darted across the page, his smile growing beneath his beak of a nose. "I'm not sure

Pleasonton has much of a choice in the matter."

Unable to discern his meaning, Custer narrowed his eyes. He knew their superior well; their relationship helped propel him into the position he was in now. He wouldn't allow another waste of men and horses for something that would gain little. A setback so close to the spring could cripple operations later in the year. "I don't understand, sir."

"You see, General Custer, I don't need his approval." A smiling Kilpatrick handed him the letter. It had been penned in exquisite penmanship.

Custer's eyes consumed the page's contents. He wasn't a fast reader, but the message was succinct enough and even more so was the name at the bottom of the dispatch. *Abraham Lincoln.*

"Sir, this is from the President?"

"You see General Custer. I don't need Meade or Pleasonton's approval. I only need one man to approve of my *foray*. Would you not want to free the prisoners from Libby and burn the enemy capital? Is this not a worthy goal?"

Custer was almost flabbergasted by his commanding officer. The number of connections to get the president to sign off on a raid was a testament for Kilpatrick and a little terrifying.

"That's not what I meant. Just the other day, my men brought in an escaped captain from Libby. Horrible conditions. If it was feasible to free them today, I would in a heartbeat."

"Ah, but it is. We have an order from the president to do such a thing. Our nation demands it." He held the paper in the air. "But much more than that. We have an opportunity to end this war." His eyes glinted with glory, as if he witnessed his star rising in the Union sky.

"The rebels will pay for their impetuous lack of regard for the well-being of our prisoners," Dahlgren said.

"Their folly will be our gain. We will be saviors of our men and the nation. Glory will be ours." Kilpatrick's eyes were alight with the trumpets of victory. He came back into his own. He walked over to a writing table and removed stacks of paper covering a map of Virginia. The officers joined him, gathering around.

"I have already thought long and hard about what this mission would look like, and I never would have proposed something to the president without assured success."

Nothing is assured, Custer wanted to say. He kept his mouth shut and his voice silent. The military was as much politics as it was service.

"Our assault will be a two-pronged attack. I will be leading the main thrust into northern Richmond while Colonel Dahlgren conducts a flanking maneuver sealing the city from the south. I expect significant support from General Butler's forces at Fort Monroe on the peninsula."

Custer sucked his cheeks in surprise. "Sir, I beg your pardon, but what part of the raid am I to conduct?"

A sharp grin settled on Kilpatrick's lips, genuine mirth surrounding his eyes. "You'll be taking second fiddle so to speak."

It took all Custer's restraint to keep his mouth flat and the anger down deep in his gut. Their history went back almost a year and Kilpatrick had been less than thrilled about his subordinate's stellar performance at Gettysburg a few days after being starred. He'd overshadowed his commander, while Kilpatrick's assault upon entrenched positions after the battle was decided had gotten one of Custer's friends, Elon Farnsworth, killed and solidified Kilpatrick's nickname, "Kill-Cavalry." He didn't want to play second fiddle, especially to this man whose ambition outshone his individual glory.

"General, you are to lead a diversionary jaunt threatening Lee's flank near Charlottesville. This will draw reinforcing rebel forces west and away from our real intentions. Stuart will bite. I know he will. This will free up Lee's right, and we can proceed directly south to Richmond."

Custer calculated the jab into the heart of the enemy bringing his command to a swift end. All those Michigan boys would be buried in Virginian soil for Kilpatrick's foolhardy grasp at a name and then a congressional seat. With his rival and nemesis Stuart hounding him the entire way, his command would be whittled away piece by piece. Dashing and daring aside, it was going to be a deadly sprint to survive. "I'd have to cut across the entirety of Lee's rear to reach you again or go southwest and hope to connect with Sherman."

Venom oozed from every word Kilpatrick spoke. "I have full faith in your abilities, *General*. Old Sedgwick will support."

Sedgwick's name gave Custer slight relief. The veteran major general was a mentor to the younger Union commanders, and he was well-liked and regarded by his men. Custer digested that his men would be in for one hell of a ride, but they were his men. They were reliable and like Toledo steel in a firefight. He had a cadre of quality officers that would easily understand the need to push the men hard and fast. "My Wolverines will do our very best, sah," he said loudly.

Kilpatrick's grin became mischievous. "Yes, they will. General, you will be leading men from Merritt and Gregg's Division. I thought since you preferred Gregg's command, you would want to lead his men and an assortment of other companies suitable for your action, of course." He faced Dahlgren. "We will split detachments of the Michigan Brigade between us."

"I will take care of them," Dahlgren said to Custer.

Bowing his head a fraction, Custer clenched his jaw tight so the muscles in the back of his neck strained. "And I'm sure they will take care of you, Colonel, just as they have me." He'd be giving up his boys, letting Kill-Cavalry and his handpicked minion, however brave, lead his men on an ill-fated mission.

"A leader who speaks so highly of his men has nothing to fear," Dahlgren said.

"He has everything to fear, but with brave men at his back, how can he be afraid?"

"Enough. Whitaker, bring in the colored boy and that feisty captain, the prisoner."

Whitaker disappeared. When he returned, he had two men in tow. A red-bearded captain and a black boy no more than eighteen. The bearded captain had a gaunt hollow exterior like he'd been starving and was willing to bite your ear off for a piece of bread.

"I present our guides for this quest. Captain Yates here was held at Libby before escaping. Tell us, man, how was the place?"

"Unfit for a rat. I'd do anything to free my comrades still trapped inside. No man or beast deserves to suffer so."

Kilpatrick nodded gravely. "I agree, Captain."

"As do I," Dahlgren added.

Eyes turned toward Custer. "I'd break them out today given the chance."

"But this boy is the one that knows it best." The captain nudged his black comrade. "Chin up, boy, especially when you speak to a general." Yates addressed them again. "His name be Martin. He's a good lad and true. One of Van Lew's servants."

"What's your last name, lad?"

"Robinson, if it please you, sir."

"Pleases me just fine. One of Van Lew's servants? What's she like? Heard she's got a thing for General Butler?"

"I. I. Don't know 'bout no generals, sir, but she's fair and kind to us, feeds us well," he said with a timid smile. "She said to help these men so we did."

Yates gave a terse nod and a gruff response. He slapped Martin on the back. "We can get you back."

"Most importantly, can you guide Dahlgren's command around Richmond unseen?"

Neither man answered.

Captain's Yates's growled an answer. "Yes, sir. We'll do our best."

"Dahlgren must travel swiftly and undetected."

"Yes, sir."

Kilpatrick grinned in the firelight. "You are to not speak of this mission unless absolutely necessary. There are enemy spies all over this secesh state. You are dismissed."

Custer gave Kilpatrick a short nod. He stepped toward the door along with the other men.

"General, wait."

Standing, Custer waited for the other men to leave. The door closed, leaving the two rivals alone.

"Need I remind you of our last discussion in the tavern last summer?"

Custer held his tongue. He remembered their exchange after Gettysburg like a scarlet letter pinned to his chest. "I remember, sah."

"You will carry out your part of this mission, or I will have you court-martialed." His hand lifted the written orders from the president himself, wielding it like a sword. "You see what kind of backers I have. I'm going to the top. You can ride those coattails or you can get trampled beneath my boot." He stepped closer to him.

Custer wanted to take a step back from this short inept man, but he held his ground.

"You complete this mission, and we will be heroes. Promotions all around. I know you have ambitions like me. Join me and we will rise."

Only a few words dribbled emotionlessly from Custer's his mouth. "I will conduct the orders as was requested by my commanding officer."

Kilpatrick's eyes tried to read him for some sort of overt sign of loyalty. "Very well, then you may take your leave. And hold your wife close tonight because soon, we ride to win this war."

CHAPTER 5

February 28th, 1864
3rd Cavalry Division's Encampment, Stevensburg, Virginia

Horses neighed and whinnied as the 13th Michigan stood in parade formation in the miserable pouring rain. The shower was cold and cheerless, zapping any energy that could be derived from a dash into the field.

The troopers' mounts could feel the men's discomfort on top of their own. Hooves stamped on sloppy ground, and the animals tugged and pulled relentlessly at their reins in an attempt to find some sort of comfort.

F Company's wolf head guidon lay limp on its pole, water drenched and sticking to the shaft. The top half was red, and the lower half was black with a golden emblazoned wolf head sewn on the bottom. It was cut in the fashion of a company guidon, a dovetail splitting the flag into points.

Venerable Sergeant Berles held the company guidon's pole with a meaty hand despite the weather's tireless assault. He'd carried the standard into every engagement since Gettysburg and lived. He'd been tireless in his efforts to keep the rest of them in one piece and had easily gained both the enlisted and officers' trust.

Time dragged along at a pitiful pace. The camp had been a thing of movement for days. Cavalry units from the 1st and 2nd Division arrived daily to augment the upcoming secret raid of which everyone spoke about in earnest. Hearty-looking bearded men from Maine with a pine tree on their flag, the 4th and 16th Pennsylvania regiments, arrived along with the 9th New York.

Despite the camp's stream of movement and swelling of soldiers, the six companies of the 13th Michigan waited under the impatient gaze of Colonel Moore.

The rotund colonel sat perched on his horse, looking more like a heavyset possum than a leader of soldiers. Rain dribbled off his slouch hat, forcing him to keep leaning his head to the side to give the water a clear path off his brim. He shifted every few moments as if being mounted was the last thing he wanted to do, which Wolf knew was most likely the case. The colonel was a political appointee, and while it seemed he liked the idea of leading, he'd done almost nothing to garner respect.

"Psst," Roberts said.

"What?" Billy shuffled beneath him, and Wolf ushered him back into line.

"You hear anything about this fabulous expedition the old colonel has lined up for us?"

"Secret raid."

"Secret raid? Not much of a secret with all of us sitting out here in the open."

"That's all I know."

Removing his cap, Roberts shook his dampened black hair and wiped water from his cheek. "I'd kill for a drink."

"I'd kill for a fire."

Roberts wavered. "Fire and a drink? Count me in. Anything to make this a little less damp." He sighed heavily. "I mean, look over there our snug cabins empty. And there look at those pukes." He gestured with his chin. Union infantry stood in doorways of tents and cabins, curiously watching the troopers. "What you bet all those bastards be in our cabins when we return? I swear to Christ I'll whip 'em on out. I'll fight 'em, swear it."

"Those be scrapping words for sure."

"Aye, they be."

"If we make it back."

Roberts turned toward to Wolf. "Don't put that evil on us. Rosie be saying her prayers for us and promised not to touch another man until I return."

"So after we return, she'll start back in?"

A scowl puckered on Roberts's face. "No, Wolf. I'll be back. Then we'll be together like we supposed to be." His horse stomped and he changed the subject. "I heard we're going to win this war."

"It's all part of the game of war."

"I ain't playing. I like the game where you live a long time before you die."

Wolf shushed him as mud-splattered riders slogged past them. He watched the blue-coated soldiers pass. Black-bearded Captain Peltier walked his black horse before the troopers. He stared at a piece of paper for a moment before shoving it into his coat. "We need ten men to volunteer to join Colonel Dahlgren's command. You will operate independently from the 13th."

F Company was silent in their rows. They only numbered sixty-two men. The Gettysburg campaign, Buckland Mills, and the deadliest assault of all, illness, had ravaged them. Together they'd grown harder over the year, tempered by the flames of war. The whole Michigan Brigade had. New recruits had swelled the ranks of the 5th, 6th, and 7th Michigan regiments while only a few leftovers and troublemakers found their way into the 13th Michigan.

Wolf wouldn't have called them exactly professional, but they were seasoned. They'd been on the receiving end of a whooping and had doled out their own. Through all those times, they'd earned one another's respect. Enough respect to have pride surrounding their company's wolf head guidon hand-stitched by Johannes's sister before the men departed for war.

Peltier scanned his troopers. "I'm going to have Lieutenant Wells make a pick then. I understand the apprehension of reporting to a new commander, and while I don't personally know Colonel Dahlgren, he served with distinction at Gettysburg. I won't lie to you. His part in the raid will be dangerous."

Wolf had heard enough. He knew whom Wells would pick given the opportunity. He wouldn't consider their lieutenant an enemy, but the man wouldn't mind shifting some of his troublemakers to a new command. He patted Billy's neck.

"Don't you do it," Roberts whispered next to him. "I can tell when you're getting all fire in your gut."

"Shouldn't we own our fate?" With a smile, he gave Billy a gentle spur in the side. The seasoned horse didn't need much encouragement. He could feel what his rider was feeling as he was getting ready to do it. The horse's hooves squelched with every step into the muddy ground. He raised a hand in the air. "I'll go."

Peltier's dark eyes judged Wolf for a moment. He wiped water from his coal beard with a gloved hand. "Thank you, Corporal." He searched his men. "Anyone else?"

Sergeant Berles nudged his horse forward, bringing it in line next to Wolf. He still held the company guidon. He spoke from the side of his mouth in anger. "What did I tell you about volunteering?"

"Never do it."

"And here we sit volunteering." He growled. His graying curled mustache quivered. "You trying to get yourself killed?"

"I'm taking control instead of letting Wells deal out our fate."

"Scheisse," Wilhelm said under his breath.

Roberts maneuvered his mare nearby. His brow creased and his eyes took on a quizzical glare. "I thought we weren't volunteering for anything?"

"You don't have to," Wolf said with a smile. Volunteering for a duty no one wanted was always better with your pals, but no one ever asked you to volunteer for a task that was any good.

More horsemen from their small unit joined them. The old religious abolitionist Shugart. The two Polish brothers. Their third brother, Berry, had been sent back to Grand Rapids to recover after his injuries at Gettysburg. The brothers were almost indistinguishable from one another, broad-shouldered, round-faced, and pug-nosed big men. Gratz, a sturdy Austrian with a tireless work ethic, the Dutchman, Van Horn, and swarthy Adams. The last to join the ranks was the grizzly man, Nelson. It made Wolf's hackles stand on end, but he was glad to have the brute on his side as opposed to across from him on the field of battle.

"So these ten men?" Peltier said. Wells sat on a horse next to him, and it wasn't immediately apparent if his smile was happiness to be rid of Wolf's squad or some sort of perverse pride.

"I count ten, Captain," Wells said.

"Very well. Sergeant, the guidon stays with the company."

"Yes, sir," Wilhelm shouted. He walked his horse over to Roger Smith, a former blacksmith with stout shoulders and a round jaw. "Sergeant." He handed the slick shaft to him. "You take care of that, ya hear?"

"We'll watch over her with our lives. I can tell you that for certain."

Wilhelm nodded his acceptance. He trusted the men to come back with her or not at all. The bullet-hole-marked and bloodstained flag was their little shred of pride.

"You men may join your new command. Good luck. We will see you in Richmond." The captain gave a short salute.

Wilhelm and Wolf led them away from their company to a cluster of cavalrymen congregating together near the other side of the camp: companies from 2nd New York, 1st Vermont, 5th New York, a smattering from the 1st Maine.

Groups of a dozen troopers from the various Michigan regiments trickled in. Most of the Michigan troopers coming from the 5th. The 13th had been riding with the 5th for some time, and their men had a stellar reputation. All in all, about fifty men from the 6th, 7th, and 13th Michigan joined the 5th to make up the last part of the command.

A fire-haired captain gathered all the random Michigan units surprising Wolf. He had a large frame but almost no meat on his bones. His beard resembled peeled orange rinds, thick and unkempt despite the captain's bars on a loose cavalry jacket. Next to him was an equally gaunt colonel wearing a kepi and a dark blue officer's greatcoat. He was slender and sat tall on in his saddle inspecting his men.

"Can't be more than twenty and he's wearing birds on his shoulders," Wilhelm said.

"You said the same about Custer when he first came on," Wolf said.

"Aye, I did. I may have been wrong about him so far, but I trust my gut, and what does this boy know that so many other men don't?"

"Say isn't that the captain from the road?"

Squinting, the man did look much cleaner now and his beard even had a trim. "I'd say that it is. Captain Yates."

"Didn't he say he was infantry?"

"He did."

"What have you gotten us into?"

Wolf raised himself in his saddle, pushing off with his feet. He estimated roughly five-hundred troopers. The other regiments were presented in some sort of order to the colonel. The mishmash of troopers from the various Michigan units, on the other hand, were an unorganized mass.

The captain cupped his mouth. "Form it up, you Michigan pukes."

"What you got against Michigan?" shouted Adams.

"From Ohio," the captain said back, a fierce glint in his eye.

"Who decided a Buckeye should be in charge of a bunch of Wolverines?" Shugart spat.

"What do you mean Buckeye?" Wolf said.

Shugart shook his head in disgust at the thought of an Ohioan leading the men. "President Harrison was from Ohio. You know Tippecanoe and Tyler too."

Wolf didn't know a thing about Tippecanoe. He suspected most the young men in the command didn't either. "Nope."

"He was the log cabin president. The buckeye was a symbol they used for his presidency. Buckeye canes, buckeye cabins with buckeye strings decorating them. It's how Ohioans got the name. They shouldn't be leading us after the dispute." Shugart stared at the reddish-haired Captain, shaking his head. "They gave fine Michigan men to a dirty Buckeye. Ain't right. They know we got bad blood."

"Bad blood over what?"

"Youth today." Irritation crossed Shugart's already crinkled brow. "The Toledo dispute. We fought a war over it. My pappy went down with the militia to sort them boys out. They'd been encroaching on our land. Cheated us out of it really. The man who did the survey was an ex-Ohio governor. Took that prime farmland away and gave us that forested frostbitten wilderness in the north filled with nothing but deer, redmen, and some trappers." The older man's voice shook. "They also snagged the trading center of Toledo. We remember the injustice."

"Isn't the general from Ohio?" Wolf said.

Shugart's mouth opened. "I bet not. He's a hearty Michigan boy like us."

"Wolf's right. He was born in New Rumley, Ohio," Van Horn said.

"How'd you know that?" Shugart's mouth twisted in disappointment.

"Ain't no secret, Corporal. Men talk in camps," Van Horn said.

"Probably part of the disputed Toledo lands. He grew up in Michigan, and that's all that counts." Shugart nodded his head furiously.

The fiery captain gestured with a gloved hand. "Enough chatter, you ladies. Form up."

The troopers knew enough to form a semblance of a company, congregating into their own squads of men. Horses allowed themselves to be steered into ranks.

After they formed a veneer of formation, the captain spoke. "Men, I'm Captain John Yates. Special envoy to the south." He gritted his teeth in the semblance of a smile. "I was in Libby until recently."

"I thought we weren't doing exchanges anymore," said a trooper near the front.

"They aren't. I escaped." He stared out over his men. "And I'll be damned if I let any more of our boys spend another night in that godforsaken hell hole in Richmond." The fire and conviction in his voice was pure. He turned, staring at the young colonel, whose horse shifted, revealing the absence of a leg. Straps encircled his thigh ensuring balance in the saddle. "This here Colonel Dahlgren is going to lead us."

The rain continued to fall on the troopers. Richmond was the enemy capital, and surely, the rebels would fight tooth and nail to retain its possession, escalating any danger involved in the mission.

"And you pretty Michigan lads and I are going to burn it all down."

CHAPTER 6

Evening, February 28th, 1864
3rd Cavalry Division's Encampment, Stevensburg, Virginia

Colonel Dahlgren had a short goatee hanging from the front of his chin. His facial hair appeared to be an attempt to appear older than he was. His right leg was strapped to his saddle to accommodate for his missing limb, and Wolf felt a connection with the young man. Although he still had his leg, they both were invalids, pitied by some, laughed at by others, deep chips on their shoulders.

"I heard his father is a important admiral," Van Horn said.

Dahlgren removed a glove and held his hand in the air. "Men, this raid will bring reconciliation to the Union." He stopped speaking, his eyes running over each and every one of his men, a seemingly practiced orator. "As Captain Yates can attest to, the rebels are of low moral character. They hold our men, even our officers in the dankest, darkest, most miserable conditions possible without chance for parole, without an opportunity for decency." His voice rose in anger. "We cannot stand." He extended an index finger. "We will not stand for such war crimes to take place while we live. No, we cannot because we are Union men, men of conscience. But most importantly because those are our brothers who suffer, and who will save them if not us?" He stopped, the only emotion boiling inside him righteous anger. "What say you, Union men? Will you deliver us from evil? Will you save your brothers in arms?"

The men gave a resounding cheer. Hats were tossed in the air. Troopers lifted carbines on high. Dan drew his saber, thrusting it in the air.

"Private," Wilhelm said in a sharp tone.

Dan lowered his head in shame, sheathing his blade.

Wolf found himself sharing a glance with Roberts. This colonel had fire in his belly. It was awkward to hear such strong words after so long under Moore's lackluster leadership.

The troopers raised a trio of calls. "Huzzah! Huzzah! Huzzah!"

"Maybe this wasn't a bad move, Wolf," Wilhelm said. "This man has conviction."

"He's really selling this raid."

Van Horn's face appeared softer than normal. "I know it ain't going to end the war, but it's better than getting chopped to pieces for nothing."

"As long as we don't end up like Wistar's raid, we should be fine," Roberts said jokingly.

A bugler sounded the call for assembly, and the men turned their horses to face the proper direction. They formed ranks of four across. Wolf took his position on the outside of his row with Roberts and Gratz in the middle and Wilhelm on the other flank. The bugle trumpeted high shrill notes again and the column moved to a march.

The ground smushed beneath their horses, the mud greedily absorbing their hooves. Roughly five-hundred Union troopers passed in front of General Kilpatrick.

Captain Yates's command was the last company in the march. Kilpatrick gave a terse salute as they crossed in front. His shaggy sideburns dripped water beneath his slouch hat, his diminutive head appearing even smaller in such a spacious head cover.

"Do this thing clean for me, and then ask anything you like, Captain," he shouted at Yates.

The young colonel removed his kepi with a fierce twirl in the air. "You will find it all right by me, General."

"What's that all about?" Roberts asked.

"Beats me. Must have some sort of pleasantry together," Wolf said.

Men in brown and black overcoats with no military insignia sat nearby the general. Some wore unkempt beards and others were clean-shaven, but all possessed wary eyes.

"Say, who are those gents?" Wolf asked Roberts.

Roberts shifted in his saddle, trying to steal a better vantage point from the center of the column. "Can't be for certain." He strained his neck. "But if I were a betting man, I'd say they look like BMI."

"What are you betting?"

An offended expression settled on Roberts's face. "Say it was only a guess, but I'd wager you a bottle of Madam Scarlet Grey's that I'm right."

Wolf eyed Roberts for a second to see if he was trying to pull one over on him. "Bold bet. You bluffing?"

Shaking his head, Roberts said, "Nope."

"All right, smart alec, what's BMI stand for?"

Roberts stuck his chin out a hair further, pride beaming through the drizzling rain and dreary skies. "Bureau of Military Information."

Wolf eyed the men again in public scrutiny. A handsome gentleman with graceful limbs and smooth cheeks glance at him. "What they do?"

"Spies, Mr. Wolf. Those are our spies," Adams said.

"Spies? Sounds so European." Wolf twisted in his saddle to stare again."

"Oh, come on, Wolfie, you remember them coming through picket. They always had real official papers. How you think the leprechaun Kilpatrick is going to have any luck?" Adams asked. His diminutive reference to the general made a few of the men chuckle.

"Seems like that'd be cheating or something."

"You ain't trying if you ain't cheating, Wolfie," Adams said.

Wilhelm chimed in. "Hopefully Kill-Cavalry has enough sense to not get us butchered like Farnsworth."

Wolf thought it made sense. Secret raid probably had secrets and spies loved secrets. It never occurred to him to consider much about spies and the like. Didn't seem very gentlemanly like for a war. But as he thought longer, killing one another didn't seem very gentlemanly like either.

"Nothing like a glorious cavalry charge. Meeting your foe face-to-face with a clash of steel and the cap of gunfire. Or even like a fist fight. Let me get my hands on a man. Then it's a fight."

"Hogwash," Roberts said. "You feint and jab all the time. You're telling me you don't size up your opponent before you fight? You see the way he holds himself. You study where his power comes from so you can avoid it. You examine his weak spots so you can hammer it home. You use your opponent's information to win at anything."

Wolf chewed on his friend's shrewd words. "You're smarter than you look."

Roberts's eyes shifted toward him. "It's called survival, my dear friend. Survival. You don't grow up on the streets without listening and learning stuff."

The column continued through the camp. The men in civilian clothes trotted toward the front of the column, following Colonel Dahlgren with his entourage of officers.

They passed different commands, some staying in camp while others were to ride with Kilpatrick's contingent. Men from F Company gave their farewell waves. A chilly wind picked up and with it the guidon. It flapped with long swooping whips in the drizzling rain. Eventually the wolf-head standard disappeared from view.

"Little late to be marching out," Wolf said. The mellow winter sun made a rapid descent for the horizon.

Wilhelm eyed the sky. "Not if you want to move under the cover of darkness."

The mounted troopers walked out of the camp and past Rose Hill, a white Greek-revival plantation house that served as Kilpatrick's winter headquarters. Southward they traveled in the direction of the Confederate capital. Spirits were high despite the rain. The men were on a righteous mission of a magnitude that they hadn't even begun to comprehend.

Captain Yates turned around, guiding his horse toward the rear. He made his way along the column with the suspected smooth-cheeked BMI agent.

"We're looking for a squad of men to secure our passage over Ely's Crossing."

The captain stood high in his saddle, staring at the men in expectation. He raised his voice to a little less than a shout. "Come on, you Wolverines. Thought you were a bunch of fierce rodents."

Wolf felt a sharp jab in his ribs meant to get his attention.

"Don't you even think about it," Roberts said. He gave him a warning eye, promising trouble if he volunteered again.

In return, Wolf gave him a mischievous grin. "Would never."

The captain continued to walk his horse alongside his men. "Let's move, boys. Don't let us look bad in front of the colonel. Our reputation's at stake."

A few men whispered to one another, more grumbles than not. In the dying light, it was hard to tell who was speaking to whom.

Captain Yates reached the rear of Dahlgren's detachment and spun his mount in stride with them. "End of the line, boys. You telling me none of you want to volunteer?" He shook his head. "Can't blame you, I suppose." His horse clomped its hooves into the drier edges of the lane. Curses about Wolverines snuck out under his breath.

Wolf raised his carbine from his hip into the air. "I'll go."

Captain Yates's eyes lit up. "Holy shit. A man with spine."

Roberts punched Wolf again. "What are you doing?" he hissed.

Sergeant Berles glared in his direction.

Shaking his head with a murderous glare, Nelson growled.

"All right, boys. Where'd you come from?"

"13th Michigan, sir," Wolf said.

Yates's eyes shone with recognition. "Say, you were the pickets that found me?"

"We are."

"I'll be damned. Great to see you men again." His smile faded. "Sadly, we don't have time to make conversation. Mr. Hogan will guide you to the ford."

A tall and lithe Irishman with brown curly hair sticking out from beneath a brown cap gave a chuckle. His face was smooth and his eyes bright. "Rough looking lot. Perfect."

Roberts nudged Wolf. "He's one of the BMI agents."

"Come on, laddies. Let's create havoc on dem bastards," Hogan chimed in.

Wolf's squad peeled off to the side of the column and trotted their horses past toward the front, splashing mud as they went.

CHAPTER 7

Evening, February 28th, 1864
Southeast of Stevensburg, Virginia

The naked trees danced in the wind, rustling and creaking in the darkness, old men with silent stories to tell. A swollen river rushed before them almost a hundred yards away. It had pushed higher on the banks in its pulsing flow, making what was once an easy crossing now somewhat hazardous, especially in the night.

Hogan dismounted his horse. "I need a volunteer." He stripped off his brown overcoat and rolled it behind his bedroll.

The country road between Stevensburg and Ely's Ford wasn't nearly as horrible as the camp itself. Despite the rain, the horses only sank a fraction of an inch into the mud, meaning there was solid earth there somewhere. The strain on the animals mitigated for the scouting party.

Dahlgren's command scouted the route southeast passing thru W. Maddon, Shepherd Grove, and Richardsville, all tiny villages with no doubt with a sympathetic rebel or two living in around them under the cover of darkness.

Nelson gave Wolf a shove in the back. "You go, volunteer."

Wolf gave him a steely glance, but the men around him stared back defiantly.

"You should go," Roberts said grimly.

"You got us in this mess," Van Horn said.

"Seems fair to me," Adams added.

Throwing his hands up in retreat, Wolf said, "All right." He dismounted from Billy and handed his reins to Roberts. "I'll be back." He approached the tall Irishman, winding a rope in circles about his arm.

With a quick smile, he said, "Don't act like I'm gonna kill ya, but throw these on."

Hogan tossed Wolf the rough rope. He went about straightening his jacket, and in the darkness, its color was a nighttime smoke.

"That's a Rebel coat," Wolf said.

"Aye, it is," Hogan said, matter-of-factly.

"You get caught in that and they'll hang you."

"Wear a blue one, they'll shoot me; wear a gray one, and they'll hang me. Not much different if you ask me. Both ways muster ya out."

"They won't take you prisoner."

Hogan twisted his head. He worked the rope over Wolf's wrists, the rough-hewn hemp scratching at his skin with fibers. "Not trying to die, not trying to be a prisoner neither." He surveyed his work. "But you're going to be my prisoner."

The rope was lightly bound but with enough bulk to give the impression of a wicked unsolvable knot. He held them closer to his face. "I can't fight like this."

Hogan reached to Wolf's side and unbuttoned his revolver holster and removed his Colt .44 caliber Army pistol. He gave him a playful grin. "Won't be needing it anyway." He took his sheathed saber and carbine, securing them on Wolf's saddle.

The thought of being without his arms made him pucker up. If things went bad, he was going to be solely dependent on Hogan to do the dirty work. "I'm not sure about this."

Hogan ignored him, flipping Wolf's coat open. "But I'm hiding it, so you can grab it if need be." Hogan tucked the gun through Wolf's belt behind his back. "There you go." He stood back surveying his work. "Not quite." He eyed his prisoner from side to side, judging to see if his captive passed inspection. "Here." He ripped off Wolf's forage cap and tucked it into a saddlebag. Then ruffled Wolf's hair.

"Trying to get lice, old boy?" Adams snarked.

Smiling broadly, Hogan said, "Not any more than I already have." He directed his attention back at Wolf. "You are a regular old yellowbelly no-good deserter picked up by the brave and handsome rebel captain."

"I ain't no yellowbelly," Wolf said. Being called or threatened to be called a coward was no laughing matter. His men knew better, but once a seed was planted, it was hard to stem the roots from spreading.

Hogan gave a short soft chuckle. "Today you are. Now you gents." He stared at the rest of the unit. "You sit tight until I give the signal. If we don't get this right, this raid will be over before it begins just like Wistar. Secrecy."

"We'll keep mum," Wilhelm said. He gave Wolf a nod and the men disappeared off the road and into the trees, becoming shadows in the night.

"Come on, Billy yellowbelly Yank." Hogan gave him a soft shove in the back.

The clouds had masked the moon and the river was higher than it should have been for a ford. Hogan guided his horse on foot along with Wolf behind on a rope. Water quickly flowed around his boots and soon was tugging and pulling at the men's waists and legs. Every step threatened to send them drifting downstream in the icy waters.

His boots slipped over the rocky bottom, but he kept his feet. They made it to the far bank and Hogan shook himself off.

"Giddy-up, yellabelly."

"I ain't a coward."

They walked through the mud in the dark trying to keep their feet. "Ya are, ya yella and ya caught. Something I don't have to worry about."

Wolf stayed close to the rear of the horse, its hindquarters swishing as they moved farther into territory not held by the Federal government.

An unhurried voice called out from the trees on their right. "Y'all gone far enough."

Hogan drew to a halt, raising a hand in surrender. "Now easy, boys." His accent had changed dramatically, taking on a much slower dialect, drawling each word, not in a charming southern accent like a Virginian, but in a much more country tone with a touch of backcountry gentry money.

Wolf's heart started to thump in his chest as four raggedly clad men emerged from the trees. One foul word and they would be shot to pieces.

"Step closer and we'll put more holes in ya than a honeycomb."

Hogan took a confident step, tugging on Wolf's rope. "No need to get all huffy with me. I'm Captain Hogan, Jeff Davis Legion. I'm on duty to see General Hampton."

"Is that right, Captain?"

"That's correct, good sir. Now you boys hail from Georgia, is it?"

"'Tis so. Cobb's Legion."

"Hearty boys. Strong Southern stock. Crème de la crème as far as I hear." Hogan took a few steps forward, towing Wolf along behind him.

"With all due respect, sir, what you doing coming from the wrong side of the river?" He pointed with his musket at Wolf. "And what you doin' with that dirty Billy Yank?" With cruel shadowed eyes, he glared at Wolf. "I could smell his perfume from here."

Hogan twisted his neck. "Now, boys, you have done a superb job on your picket line tonight." His voice took a much more stern tone. "But I'm gonna to have to pull rank on you."

The rebels raised their guns to shoulders. The man in front spoke. "Answer the question, Captain, or you'll be a dead one, no matter which side you fight on."

Scratching his curls, Hogan took a few steps closer. "You see, there is a lady just north of here that I've taken a liking too. I had a few too many drinks, lost my way, and came across this no-good, dirty, yellowbelly Billy. After a very short scuffle, I took him prisoner, and now I'm headed down to see Hampton and drop this coward off along the way."

Wolf bristled at his sharp tongue but kept quiet, keeping his hands to his right side so when the time was right, he could draw his pistol and fire.

"You risked going north of the Rapidan for a piece of northern tail?"

"You don't know about this Virginian woman. Round hips. Perfect bosom." He nodded at one of the men. "I can hear you panting from over here." He stopped, shaking his head, and sighed. "They just need to be set free from the yoke of the nasty abolitionists."

The Georgians chuckled and lowered their weapons. The front man tucked his musket beneath his arm. "Sorry 'bout the questions, sir. We been on alert since the last time Billy tried to sneak past us." He gave them a black tobacco-mouthed grin. "Sent them back yelping last time."

Hogan led his horse near the rebels until he was only a few feet away. "You are a true Son of the South. Surely we will win this contest by the end of the year with such stout defenders."

The bearded man smiled at the officer's praise. He pointed back toward a cluster of humble buildings. "Captain Young and the reserve are over yonder. You can bunk up with them if you need rest. They'd be happy to have you. Sounds like they been havin' a bang-up time since we been out here." He nudged at Hogan. "The captain loves a good game of poker and a bare-knuckle fight."

A musical laugh came from Hogan. "Ah, a gambling man. I might have to take him up on a game, but I must warn you, I have an excellent poker face." He jabbed his revolver into the unsuspecting gut of the picket and he let out a soft *uff*. "Let's set them weapons on the ground."

The picket didn't register for a few seconds that a gun had been shoved right into his bowels. His eyes grew larger, revealing more white in the corners. "Sir?"

Wolf shook off his ropes and grabbed his pistol and pointed it at the other pickets, all still gawking at the lecherous rebel captain aiming a gun at their leader.

"Nice and quiet if you want to live," Wolf said.

The butternut and gray clad men set down their muskets. "Pistols too. Real slow," Hogan said. He shifted his gun, pointing it at one man and then the next. "Get in a tidy little line for me."

"You'll never take Young without a fight. You're only two men," the leader spat.

"Don't you worry about that." Hogan turned toward Wolf. "Bind these men together."

Wolf took his rope and wrapped it around a brown-toothed old man, weaving the rope around his wrists, lashing each man with the last.

Hogan let out a short, low whistle that inflected to a high pitch at the end. Dark blue shadows emerged from the dusky trees along the other side of the ford. The men urged their horses into the cold sweeping waters, splashing their way across.

"We got a group of rebel pickets in that house there," Wolf said as Wilhelm reached them.

"More than us?"

"Don't know, but we have surprise, my friend," Hogan said.

"Nelson, stay with the prisoners."

The bullnecked trooper growled, "Aye." He edged his horse closer to the four men. "I'll skin ya if you make a sound."

Adams leaned off his saddle toward the rebels. "He means it. Seen it done." The pickets silently watched them pass.

The ten men walked their horses no more than fifty yards to the cabin across a small field. The sounds of drunken men shouting and jeering seeped from the building along with the golden glow of a fire.

Hogan glimpsed back at them. "I'll get them to open. I'm going to go in with my prisoner here. Take stock of what we're dealing with. Then we will rush 'em when they least expect it. No gunfire if we can avoid it. Any one of these houses could ruin our chance at surprise."

Wilhelm nodded, ushering the unit to dismount and take their places near the edge of the house in the murkiness of the night. They crouched, taking knees on the damp earth, holding pistols. No carbines for this close of a fight.

"Give me your pistol," Hogan said to Wolf with a smile.

Wolf hesitated. "Asking a man to give up his gun twice in one night is a lot to ask."

"And you'll have to trust me, or this won't work." Hogan gave him a cheery wink. "I'll keep her warm for you."

Wolf handed him the pistol, and the BMI agent shoved it through his belt and wrapped his wrists with a piece of leather from his saddlebags. "Remember, same as before. You're a coward yellowbelly traitor to the North."

"I don't like the way you keep saying that." This man was beginning to irritate him with his playful quips. Hogan was the kind of man that might swindle you out of your shoes while you wore them, and Wolf didn't trust that kind of man. The man might need a swift beating to quiet his tongue. He reveled for a moment in the image of punching the agent in the face.

Hogan tugged Wolf's bonds and got close, smile curving on his bare face. "Yellabelly. Let's move."

CHAPTER 8

Evening, February 28th, 1864
Ely's Ford, Virginia

Firelight danced from the windows, illuminating a two-story clapboard home. Dragging Wolf behind him, Hogan marched up the steps and knocked on the door. The yelling and rabble-rousing died down only a fraction.

The door swung open and piercing light penetrated the darkness, revealing a long brown-goateed man. Whiskey and tobacco stained his breath and teeth. He wore a rich brown jacket and tan trousers. A pistol was hung on either hip along with a long knife. "Ain't time for shift change." He studied Hogan for a minute trying to decide if someone was playing a joke on him.

"Captain Hogan, Jeff Davis Legion," he said with a slight bow.

"Yeah, whatdaya want?"

"Your pickets were kind enough to direct me this way for lodging for the night."

The drunken yelling continued in the background. Glass broke and a cheer went up, none of which was a concern for the man before them. "You got money?"

"Why sure. Greenbacks or graybacks?"

"Greenbacks'll do."

The man opened the door wider and let them in. He eyeballed Wolf as he followed Hogan inside. "What's this un?"

"Prisoner for General Hampton."

"What's he want with a lowly corporal like himself?"

"This one's a real important prisoner. One might say a spy?"

The man snarled and pulled the long knife from his belt. "Then I say we make him squeal right here and now."

Hogan lifted a hand. "Not until the general has gathered intelligence from him. He can really help our noble efforts. Alive, of course."

The man pointed his knife at Wolf. "You lucky, boy." He licked his cracked lips. "Fine then. Come back our way when you're done, I could use a Yankee scalp for me collection."

"This yellowbelly scum. Nothing would suit him better." He gave Wolf a broad smile.

The man sheathed his knife with a wise eye for Wolf. "You a betting man, Captain?"

"A fervent gambler. I'd wager my mother's bowel movements, but alas, she's no longer with us."

The Georgian thought this was hilarious and let forth with a booming laugh. He wrapped an arm around Hogan. "Then we have a game of poker to play." He led them into a parlor with all the furniture removed.

Rebels stood around its edges, cheering on two combatants in the center. Each man was stripped down to his trousers, their torsos glistening with sweat. They swung, blocked, and parried one another with clenched fists.

One man looked to be the relative of a bear. Hair sprouted from every part of his body, and he brandished fists the size of young Virginia hams. The other man was more nimble. He danced around the behemoth, his jabs and punches thrown with every ounce of weight in his agile athletic frame.

The hulking man threw a lazy swing. In a flash, the smaller man ducked to the right and slammed his fist upward. His fist caught the larger man's chin. He darted away, standing back to observe his towering opponent. The bear man stood for a moment dazed, fists barely raised in front of his body in exhaustion. He blinked and toppled sideways into the men near the wall who couldn't hold up his weight. After a short struggle, they all went crashing to the floor in a heap of limbs and shouts.

The men cheered, some with joy, others with the shame of watching their champion defeated, and their money disappeared from their open palms as their opponents collected.

The smaller man offered his opponent a hand. The big man let himself be hoisted upright. The victorious man slapped his competitor's shoulder, sending beads of sweat into the air.

"Nice punch, Captain." The hairy man shook his head and rubbed his jaw.

They clasped hands again like brothers. "Remind me not to run into you in the dark, McNeal. Your jaw is like a fieldstone." He turned on the newcomers. "We have guests." He spread his hands like a confidence man making a deal. He approached the newcomers with a short swagger.

"Where you boys come in from?" he asked.

"On my way to see Hampton with this prisoner."

The captain smacked himself in the forehead. "I almost forgot. I'm Captain Young, Cobb's Legion, Georgia's finest." He stuck a thumb out at McNeal and stuck out a hand. "Don't catch a lick from that one."

"Captain Hogan." They shook hands.

"And this Billy Yank?"

"Johannes Wolf."

"Unit?"

Wolf was silent for a moment. They hadn't gone over what kind of story he was supposed to give.

"I assure you, boy, it makes no difference to me. You're our prisoner. Nothing changes that." A smile flashed on Young's face. "We'll whip it out of ya sooner or later."

"13th Michigan Cavalry."

"Far from home, trooper. How's the South treating you?" He grabbed a rag and wiped his hands and then his face.

"Could be better."

Young threw the rag down and put a bottle to his lips. "Suppose it could be better on the account of the war." He clapped Wolf's back. "After all this mess is done, you come down and I'll show you a right old time." He leaned closer. "Provided we win, of course. If we lose, well, just wouldn't be the same." He eyed Wolf fiercely as if he were studying an opponent that he didn't know existed until now. He took a long swig of the alcohol, swallowed, and wiped his mouth. "You look like you could scrap. Say, if it please your captor, would you care to go a few rounds in the ring?" He faced Hogan. "Captain, you a betting man?"

Hogan laughed a musical note. "You want me to bet on his yellowbelly?"

The man who answered the door laughed. "The captain loves to bet."

"No one said you had too. How 'bout you, boy? You want to go a few rounds with me? Maybe we'll let you go if you win. Seems fair?" Young said.

Wolf eyed Hogan from the side. Mirth settled into the corners of Hogan's eyes and a smile crawled over his lips. "You know. What the hell? I'll put five dollars on the lad. He's yellow, but maybe he wants a crack at a reb."

"I got ten greenbacks on the captain," McNeal boomed, holding a spread of numbered bills in his hands. The Georgians started pulling out money and a rebel with a red-checked shirt began to collect and stack piles of cash.

Wolf held out his hands to be untied.

Hogan leaned close to his ear. "It'll be a good distraction." He unraveled the leather thong. "Now, no trouble out of you, yellabelly." He drew his pistol and shoved Wolf in the back toward the ring of rebels.

"What are you scared of, Captain?" Young asked, letting out a short chuckle. "You afraid this unarmed bastard is going to escape? He's surrounded by a dozen of Georgia's finest."

Turning the pistol upward, Hogan grinned. "Meant no disrespect. You're absolutely right."

"I'll beat the fight out of him," Young said.

Hogan slipped his pistol back into its holster. "I'll fancy a proper licking will break his spirit."

Shadowboxing a sequence of jabs and strikes, Young moved his body with the confidence of an experienced fighter. "My pa always used to say, a good beatin' will set any man straight. Teach him some manners."

"Own 'em," shouted a rebel with a straw hat.

Wolf removed his jacket and tossed it on the ground. He unbuttoned his cuffs and rolled his sleeves to his elbows.

"You some sort of invalid?" Young asked, staring at his leg. "Ain't no pleasure in beating a cripple."

"I ain't crippled."

"Sure as hell looks like it."

Young peered back at Hogan. "You were scared of this fellow escaping on foot? A little jumpy aren't we, Captain?"

"I'm a careful man. Calculating to be exact."

"Are you?" Young eyed Hogan closer, his eyes judging him.

"That's why Hampton loves me."

Loudly, Wolf said, "I can fight." He could and he'd show both these loudmouth overconfident asses he was no coward.

Young turned back, an impressed look on his face. "Hopefully, you got more fire in your belly for a fistfight than you do a battle. We've been gettin' tired of whipping your boys all over this state."

Hoots went out from the men forming the ring around them. One spit a glob of tobacco toward a spittoon, but it fell short by a foot, splatting on the wooden floorboards and leaving a dark stain.

"You musta not been at Gettysburg," Wolf said, sizing up the captain. He had plenty of weight on the Georgian, probably twenty to thirty pounds and a decent reach on him. Young was definitely quicker and favored a one-two jab-crossover punch. He glanced over at Hogan and the BMI agent gave him a nod.

"I got money on you, boy. Win me money and I'll make sure that Hampton takes care of you. Get you exchanged quick."

A playful smile crossed Young's lips. "I'll do you one better. You knock me out, I'll set you free."

"He's my prisoner. You don't have rights over him."

"Captain, this is my post you're in. I can do damn well as I please."

Eyes went to the rival captain to see who would win the dick-measuring contest. Hogan threw his hands in the air and dipped his chin. "I'll do you one better." Hogan pointed at the Young's gear. "Throw in that pretty bone-hilted Arkansas pigsticker if he wins, and you got yourselves a deal."

Young eyed his fifteen-inch heavy double-sided dagger with his gear. It had a cream animal-bone hilt polished down so that it shone in the firelight. "That's a quality blade."

"And he's a quality prisoner. If I lose him with nothing to show for it, I risk the wrath of Hampton." Hogan shrugged his shoulders. "Nobody wants him angry."

"Not if he don't know better, but you got yourself a deal." Young took a step forward. He held his hands clenched in fists near the center of his chest, his left arm extended farther from his right, which was held close to his chest. He threw a punch at Wolf's face. His arm snapped as he fired his fist into Wolf's nose with his left hand. It wasn't a full-on punch but more like a "hello, nice to meet you" jab to the bullseye of his face. Wolf's head kicked back, and dots erupted like stars on the Union flag. He'd not even had time to think, let alone dodge or block the strike. All he could do was blink and try to gain control over his tattered vision.

"Wake up, boy!" Young shouted.

Grinning and laughing faces surrounded Wolf, shouting incoherent calls of glee.

Young threw an uppercut and Wolf barely shifted out of the way, feeling the wind wash over him from his iron-ball fist. Blood ran from his nostrils and he could taste the coppery liquid as it dribbled into his mouth. He took a step back as Young pursued him, keeping his hands high on his chest.

"He's afraid!" shouted a man from behind.

Young took a stride toward him and swung an over-the-top haymaker. If he landed the punch, it was over. Wolf weaved, asking his bad leg to do more work than it could handle. He stumbled into the ring of men. A rebel shoved him back to the center.

Young wavered, his head shifting from side to side, a moving target. The man was like a slippery eel, always moving. Wolf jabbed with all his might. The captain sidestepped and gave him a quick body jab to the ribs. *Huff!* Air was forced from his belly. The rebels roared with delight.

Wolf remained upright, covering himself, but all he wanted to do was stay bent at the waist. *He's fast. I have to control his movement.* At an angle, Wolf circled, driving his opponent to the side. He continued to do so, presenting a defensive target. Young hit his elbow and then his shoulder as Wolf circled him into the corner of his men.

Young dodged back and forth like a slithering serpent on the offensive. He'd be on Wolf's left and then his right, fists punching like viper strikes. There was no time to blink, only to deflect the blows and back the man down.

The gradual herding of the smaller adversary started to pay off. His strikes came less often the more Wolf corralled him. He waited until the man had little space to dodge and faked a jab, knowing that Young would shift to the left to evade. Wolf wound up on his crossover punch with his right hand and socked Young straight on the tip of his chin. He then unleashed a salvo of rapid body shots. One-two-three-four, the punches fired into his hard belly. On the third hit, he felt the captain's core weaken, and he knew the fourth punch really hurt the man. The captain fell back into his men who shoved him away from Wolf and back to the center.

The captain stretched his neck. "Been hit harder from a bummer."

As a veteran of countless fistfights, Wolf knew this man should be more shaken than he was. Hands shoved Wolf's back, forcing him to the center. *The man must be hurting. I know I hurt him, and he's standing in the center waiting for me.*

Young egged him on. "You ready to hang that fiddle up or earn that freedom?"

"Let's fight."

"Stupid Dutch," Young said, shaking his head.

He'd been called worse, but it was something in the man's tone that made Wolf's hackles rise and the blood pound in his veins. The disdain this man held for him precisely because of his birth. Wolf swung wildly, his fists connecting with air.

Young retaliated with a combination of body shots fluidly transitioning into an uppercut that grazed Wolf's chin but made his teeth clank nonetheless.

The rebels around them shouted "Ooooo," thinking that their captain had done him in. Wolf bit his tongue, shaking his head. His blood was hot. Amused, Hogan watched instead of capturing the enemy soldiers.

Wolf spit blood on the floor and charged his opponent. A swift fist to the gut knocked the wind out of him, but he swung with the ferociousness of a badger. He swiped and hooked punch after punch. Young's eyes grew larger as he tried to evade the strikes then tightened around the edges as he concentrated on not getting knocked out.

Wolf punched everywhere, his only thought to beat this man to death. He missed several and Young blocked a few, but a single hook caught the captain in the cheek. He staggered backward and was clutched by his men. They held him for a moment, his eyes scrambling to different corners. They shoved him back out with a few pats on his back. "Get 'em, Captain. Teach that bastard a lesson."

The door slowly opened and blue-coated men crept inside. "That all you got?" Wolf shouted.

All eyes in the room focused on him, angry and threatening. Their champion was getting bested by a Northern dog, a prisoner no less. "Show that colored-lover we ain't no equals."

Shaking his head multiple times, the captain tried to collect himself. He took a shaky step forward.

Hogan's voice rose over the clamor. "Wolf!" Rebels turned his direction. He tossed a pistol in the air and Wolf caught it, leveling it at Young's face. The scene unfolded and the Georgians gawked. Guns were cocked by the firing squad of blue-coated men standing inside. Hogan pointed his at the man next to him.

Wolf smiled, wiping warm crimson from his nose. "You hit hard, Captain, but I'll accept your surrender now."

Young stopped and lowered his fists, realizing that Hogan and Wolf had bested them, and the tables had been turned on his men. "You really are a yellowbellied bastard. To think I was going to let you go if you won." He shook his head. "Hot damn, son. You pulled one dirty trick on us. Rotten, no-good, Negro-loving, stinking bastards."

Wolf grinned like a wolf. "That we are."

Young waved at him with his fingers. "Put that gun down. Finish the fight like a man."

Wolf didn't bite on his bait. "Not today, Captain. We have a war to win."

CHAPTER 9

Near Midnight, February 28th, 1864
Ely's Ford, Rapidan River, Virginia

It took the body of Dahlgren's command forty minutes to rejoin with their scouts. They crossed the Rapidan, stealthily entering Confederate-controlled territory with no impediments.

The rains began to die in the darkness, and the roads held enough of their soupy composure for the horsemen to march at a quick pace. Dusky clouds dissipated, leaving pinpricks of light that dotted the black blanket of the nighttime sky. A half-moon with a pale-yellow glow cast dark shadows over an ashy land preparing for the rebirth of spring.

Dahlgren directed his men to water and rest the horses before gathering the entirety of his command to continue their southward thrust toward Richmond.

Wolf and his unit were already warm and well-rested by the time the other troopers had finished watering their horses. Hot coffee and bacon warmed the scouts' belly, courtesy of their rebel hosts. Roberts restocked his saddlebags with a clear shine.

Still dressed like a Confederate captain, Hogan approached Wolf. He held Young's dagger in his hands. He unsheathed the blade, wielding it in his hand for a moment. "Fine piece of craftsmanship. Reminds me of a Scottish dirk." He sheathed it quickly. "Don't have much use for it, but I figured you'd earned it." He tossed the knife to Wolf.

Wolf caught the blade. Its weight balanced like it belonged in his hand, the hilt comfortable, seeming to form to his fingers. He unsheathed it. "Well worth a few licks."

Hogan leaned closer. "You still didn't row him up Salt River."

Wolf snorted a laugh. "I'll split it with ya. You want the sheath?"

"No, no. Our story will be that you laid the poor fellow out." Hogan winked.

Wolf secured his new dagger on his hip, and the order to mount up trickled through Dahlgren's command. The men pulled themselves atop their horses while the prisoners were placed under a light guard near the rear of the column.

The colonel's tall wraith-like form walked his horse near the front of the column. He was followed by a group of his officers. Hogan shifted closer to Wolf's scouts.

"That one there is his signal officer, Lieutenant Bartley," Hogan gestured with his chin to a young, lightly bearded man. "That slender major with a drooping mustache is Major Cooke and next to him is Lieutenant Peters from the 1st Vermont. Used to be a schoolteacher that one."

Dahlgren signaled his men closer like he had a secret. "Men, bring it in close. I don't want to yell." Horses complained with smacking lips and whisking tails, but the troopers squeezed even tighter.

Hogan whispered, "And that mean-looking captain back there with the scar on his cheek. That's Captain Mitchell, 2nd New York. Meaner than the devil himself."

The men quieted down, trying to catch the young colonel's words.

"Hogan's scouts did well." Dahlgren tried to see his scouts in the dark to no avail. "We've crossed unopposed onto Confederate soil. Soil that will soon fall permanently back into the Union hands. Its proper place."

A soft cheer rose from the Union troopers. Bringing their rebel brethren back into the fold was one of the reasons they risked their lives. They risked their lives for their nation. Born to the United States or not, they fought to hold it together. Dahlgren held a hand upright for silence. He placed a hand in his breast pocket and removed a piece of paper. He unfolded the letter as his troopers quietly watched.

"You men know this raid is to free your brothers being held captive in the darkest, dankest, most horrible prisons ever known to man." Angry mutterings sounded out from the men. Dahlgren lifted the paper high for all to see. "This raid is more than that."

"Burn Richmond," called out a man.

A fierceness gripped Dahlgren's eyes. "More than that. This raid will win us the war, but I need a full commitment from you men. Here and now. An absolute and utter loyalty to our mission. We will not stop until our task is accomplished."

"We're with you," a trooper said from the back.

Dahlgren nodded gravely. "Our mission, once Kilpatrick attacks Richmond from the north, is to storm the city from the south." He peered down at the letter in his hand almost lovingly. "You are to free prisoners, yes, but your primary objective is to kill the president of the Confederacy, Jefferson Davis, and all members of his cabinet that can be found, severing the head from the snake of the rebellion for good. Signed Abraham Lincoln, President of the United States of America."

Shock washed over the troopers, and every single man stared at their new colonel. The assassination of their enemy's leader was not a formal part of warfare. There was always a rumor of a Southern plot to kill Lincoln, but it never came to fruition. It was only ever gossip, a tactic to threaten and intimidate the Union, but this was a declaration of a different kind of war. Not the war of armies but a shadow war behind the scenes and offstage, one that could change the course of the war and history itself.

"We are to kill Jefferson Davis and end this war." He waved the letter at them, and it kept its firm structure as he gestured with it. "There is no more noble cause and no other action that will end this war faster and reunite us with our lost brothers." He tucked the letter back into his interior breast pocket, letting the men break down into rapid discussion.

Roberts nudged Wolf. "Kill the president?"

"That's what he said."

"By God, we will be the most beloved men of the Union and the most hated men of the South. Notorious. Men who did what was necessary in our nation's darkest hour."

Excitement built in Wolf's chest as he watched Dahlgren. "We could win this war."

"We do this quick, men, and they won't even know we were there until it's over. We must be quick," Dahlgren said over them.

Wilhelm peered over at them, his eyes calculating. "We need more men. They will fight like the devil when they catch wind of us."

"God ordains us. He will grant us swift victory over the slavers," Shugart said. He raised a bony fist at the heavens.

"He should have ordained us with more men," Wilhelm said, eyes steely. "Men fight harder for their own land."

"We still have stealth on our side. We'll be knocking at their front door before they know we've snuck in the back and robbed them blind," Adams said.

"I hope you're right."

"No, Wilhelm. Our cause is just. If we can end this war, we should do everything in our power to do so," Shugart said.

Wilhelm eyed him for a moment, scrutinizing him. "I reckon you're right. No doubt this is a noble endeavor; every man should strive to end a war if he can, but we march to the heart of the Confederacy. No easy task."

"Nothing but young boys and old men guard Richmond," Hogan said. "I've seen the reports."

"A boy or an old man can kill a man like any other. They'll be in every window and every doorway as we ride through their streets. They'll defend their homes out of principle."

"Fuck 'em. Let's kill the bastards and go the fuck home," Nelson said.

Wolf's feelings were mixed. An end to the violence would be cause for celebration. He could go home and see his family. But then what? Where would he find purpose? Who would he be without the army at his back? More so, who would he be without these men around him? Johannes Wolf, the drunken cripple. No job. No money. Nothing again.

He was here because of the men around him, and as long as they fought, he'd stand with them. When he returned home, he would have to figure the rest out. And to be the men that ended the war would be an epic tale to tell down at Kusterer's brewery back home. "I'm in. Let's end this affair."

"Get back to the farm and start preparing to plant," Van Horn added.

"Get Roberts back to his camp follower," Adams threw out. The men chuckled.

"She's waiting for me, yes she is. We'll be together."

Wolf had no doubt in his mind that Roberts was in love with his red-haired prostitute, but to think that the words she whispered in return were anything except a way to squeeze an extra dollar from the poor man was ludicrous. He clapped his friend on the back. "She'll be there."

Dahlgren raised a fist. "Enough." The men quieted down. "This raid will be filled with danger. Expect no mercy. Expect no quarter. Once they know we are coming to free our men, burn their capital, and kill their president, they will fight like a rabid cornered dog." He scanned his men searching for the infirm and weak. Men without the resolution to carry on. "I will not look down on any man that will not partake in such a dangerous mission. No man here will carry any shame if he turns back now; I'll make sure of that." He paused a moment, letting the men know he meant every word he spoke. "I will ferret out any man who speaks ill of those who do not have the stomach for this dirty yet necessary fight." He pushed himself higher on his mount. "The way back to the camp is clear and safe. Any man may walk away now."

The men turned and eyed each other, the tightly encircled troopers drawing strength from the closeness of their comrades and the conviction of their leader. A hoof stomped into the earth. A saddle creaked as a man readjusted himself, yet every single man stayed in place.

"I implore you, if you do not have the stomach, leave now. For where we go, there can be no hesitation in your heart and no doubt in your mind that we go to do God's work and end this feud that has plagued this great nation for far too long."

Not a man moved an inch.

"We are with you," called out a man.

"End the war!"

"Dahlgren and his raiders!"

Dahlgren held up his fist again. "I knew you when I saw you. I knew that you men were mine. Now let's go kill a president."

A heartfelt cheer rose up from the men in the early morning beneath the star-filled heavens. A clear-cut declaration of their intent. After a few moments, the cheers died down.

"Captain Yates, your scouts can lead the way. They deserve the honor for a job well done," Dahlgren said. Despite the coolness of the night, sweat beaded on his brow as if the very act of sitting upon a horse strained him.

Major Cooke placed a hand on the colonel's back. "Sir, should we rest longer?"

The colonel swatted his subordinate's offending hand. "Do not coddle me because of my leg. We move forward with haste."

Long-faced, Cooke gave a stern glare, but his face softened. "I only wanted to ensure your longevity for the raid. We still have many miles to go."

"You would do well not to touch me again, Major." Dahlgren threw a finger at him.

"My apologies, Colonel." Major Cooke stiffened in his saddle. He gestured at Captain Yates. "Get them moving."

Captain Yates pointed at Wilhelm. "Dutchman, go on ahead with Hogan."

Wilhelm's jaw clenched when the Captain referred to him by a derogatory name for Germanic peoples favored by Southerners.

"You heard the captain!" Wilhelm steered his horse around the cluster of soldiers reforming into ranks.

The ten-man unit spurred their horses to the lead position on the road, a position of honor for the marching command but also a place of danger.

The sergeant kicked his mount into a trot, and they followed him without question. Soon the beating of hooves over the wet earth could be heard echoing out from the road. Any farmer rising in the night to relieve himself would hear them, but the horsemen disappeared almost as soon as they could be discovered. Not that any farmer was seeking out a band of roughly five hundred men hurrying past in the night.

Time was still against them. The very land they traveled through was against them, and given the opportunity, the people were against them. It was only a matter of time before word of their efforts reached the right people.

Every single man had been given a way out and denied it. Wolf doubted every man had stayed because of a wholehearted fervor for the Union. A soldier submitted himself to danger for any number of reasons. Trying to save face in front of his comrades. It was known that the newspapers back home printed the names of heroes and deserters alike, and one did not want to carry that public shaming with them forever.

It could have been loyalty to the men around them. Perhaps the glory of being the men who killed Jeff Davis and won the war. Or maybe some men like Nelson excelled at killing like a wicked painter with an endless canvas. For a few, it may have been a religious crusade against the slavers. It could have been that the men didn't want to ride back alone to the camp, didn't want to pass the faces of the brave men who stayed. Some men loved the thrill of adventure, but Wolf was sure that the adventure of war had worn off all the men.

The Gettysburg campaign had brought the realization of the war to Wolf. Horrifying images of what he had seen flashed at him in his dreams and were forever seared in his brain like a brand on a steer. The jagged wound in Franz's neck where General Hampton had cleaved his neck. The silent tears of Sergeant Berles mourning the loss of his son. His comrade Lent had been shot through the cheek, and his teeth and flesh exploded from his face. The vibrations of his saber as it ground against a man's bones having bit through his flesh. The screams of men shredded by canister, writhing over the earth. And the bodies, the dead men, lying unmoving, husks of skin and bone, their souls gone like they'd decided to forever sleep in a field. He supposed the death of one man to end the war was a noble enough endeavor, something he could throw his weight behind. It was better than picket duty.

Regardless of what was in the other men's hearts—hate for the enemy, or love for their brothers—every single trooper stayed. They'd signed their fate over to Colonel Dahlgren and his secret mission. It meant they would be hoisting the black flag, no quarter given and none received. And although all the men from the command came from different regiments, their faces all held the same look of determination. There was no alternative.

Wolf touched the hilt of his saber and wiped the hair out of his face as his unit separated from the column. He felt alive with his brothers around him and took strength in the knowledge that they would fight for each other. Being captured wasn't an option. The only option was to kill Jefferson Davis or die in the process.

CHAPTER 10

Early Morning, February 29ᵗʰ, 1864
South of Chancellorsville, Virginia

The men leading Kilpatrick's raid drifted through woods and over country roads like ghost soldiers of the night. The fast pace they'd set from Ely's Ford had waned and now the men moved at a walk with only the empty road to guide them.

They'd passed through Chancellorsville as the town slept. Not a person stirred, and no candles were lit to see who marched on the main street. A trooper from the 5ᵗʰ New York traded his lame horse for a stabled one.

A few men went about snatching up chickens and smoked meats from the slumbering townspeople. Living off the Southern supporters was a key component of Kilpatrick's plan so he did not have to be burdened by a long sluggish baggage train. The men only brought three days' worth of tack, bacon or salted pork, and coffee. Not a single man was bothered by the expropriation of supplies from the Southern sympathizers. The line in the sand had been drawn, and these people had chosen the wrong side.

Now in the twilight of morning, a few troopers slept in their saddles while others talked quietly. They eyed the woods with intense scrutiny when an owl hooted or the wind cracked a brittle tree branch, expecting rebels among the trees.

Wolf found himself riding next to Private Adams. Nelson lumbered behind them like a shadow of death in a saddle.

"Why did you volunteer with us?"

Adams gave him a mocking hurt expression, pressing a hand over his heart. "What? We aren't a part of the unit?"

"That's not what I meant."

The swarthy man stared ahead. "Listen, we didn't want to be here, but Elmira happened, and we found ourselves reassigned. Now we do what we do here instead of with our mates."

Nelson barked a laugh. "We'll do what we do all right."

"Union army just can't do without us. They should've hanged us." Adams eyed Wolf and held up a finger. "But they didn't. So now we go back to doing their bidding. They want the South destroyed. We're up for the task."

"What happened in Elmira?"

"Burned her down," Nelson grunted. "Fuckers got what they deserved."

"Isn't Elmira in New York?" Shugart added.

"You burned down a Northern city?"

Reproach fixed upon Adams's features. "It wasn't our fault." They rode in silence for a moment. "Equal blame to go around. Just a bit of a spree for us." He swayed with the movement of his gelding as he told his rendition of the story.

"Who's to blame?" Wolf said, intrigued by the man.

"You see, we were coming back from our furlough. Gave us a month at home before our reenlistment."

"Not long enough," Nelson said.

"I agree, but we were itching to get back to the field. Once men like us taste war, it's hard to get that taste from our mouths. It gripped us, never letting go." He exhaled as if it made him lust for bloodshed.

"We took our leave from our train car to find some chow." He stopped for a moment. "That be rations for those who don't know nothing about Chinese folks. Anyway, when we returned an hour later, we found some Pennsylvania boys had commandeered our ride. We asked nicely for them to surrender our car back to its rightful owners." He thought for a moment. "They declined. That's when we started having trouble. Some words were said and a fight broke out."

"They needed the car when we were done," Nelson said.

"They did. We allowed them to take the car and went looking for something to wet our tongues. First stop was Flanagan's. We departed when they ran out of beer. Then there was O'Hara's. Every bottle was drank dry, but the owner didn't like all us men in there and tried to kick us out. We trashed his place and left. Then there was." He stopped, tapping a finger on the side of his cheek. "What was it, Nelson?"

"Was Murphy's tavern."

"Ah yes, the tavern. They met the same fate as poor O'Hara's. You see, we were just having a jolly old time. Blowing off some steam before we hit the front lines again to take it to Johnny Reb, but these folks in Elmira just didn't seem to care. It was as if they have no respect for men fighting on their behalf. Smith called the constables. All they could do is watch us have a grand old time until they got the Home Guard involved. You see, the thing about the Home Guard is, there's a reason they're home. In one way or another, they ain't fit to be in the field, so they stay home and sit around waiting for the fight to come to them. Graybeards, invalids, boys without a sprout of hair on their balls. Well, they showed in force, told us to leave town, but we didn't have the same inclination."

"We were having fun."

"That's right, we were having fun, and you know we weren't about to let a bunch of constables and coffee coolers turn us away while there was still a bottle left in town."

"What'd you do?"

Adams raised an eyebrow. "We fought them in the streets."

"After we started fire to that tavern," Nelson grunted behind them.

"Are you sure? I thought the fire happened after the confrontation?"

"It was before."

"Ahh, it was, wasn't it." Adams shrugged his shoulders. "Anyway, there was a fire. Nobody knows how it started, but it spread quick."

"I started it," Nelson said. Horses' hooves clopped in the mud. The men turned in their saddles to glance at the brute.

Adams narrowed his eyes. "Now don't be lying."

"I don't lie."

"Why'd you do that?" Wolf asked.

"Barkeep said they were out of whiskey."

Wolf glanced back at the thick man. "You burned down a tavern because they ran out of whiskey?"

"The keep was lyin'."

Wolf and Adams shared a glance.

Adams lifted his eyebrows. "Fair enough. So there was a fire that was spreading from building to building, and the Home Guard and company came out to deal with us. We duked it out in the streets for a good bit. Ended pretty ugly for them. Seven dead, if I'm not mistaken, twenty-some wounded. Nelson killed a man with a single punch."

"Killed two. Broke a man's arm and another's jaw."

"As you can see, it didn't go well for the Home Guard. Then the officers got involved, and a few of us ended up in jail."

"How many?" Wolf inquired of the roguish men.

"Ah," Adams said, doing a quick calculation in his mind. "Forty-six, but then, they went pinning all the bad stuff on the likes of us. I mean, we weren't innocent, but that doesn't sound fair, does it?"

Burning down a city, fighting everyone, and drinking a town dry sounded like a sure way to end a military career with a court-martial and jail. The outrageousness of it all made Wolf laugh aloud. "By God, you men are insane."

"Corporal Wolf, I resent that statement. We are but misunderstood veterans. That's all," Adams said.

"My apologies." Wolf couldn't believe that men could behave in such a depraved fashion. There was a part of him that envied the cutthroats who lived by no rules aside from rip-roaring revelry with no cares for society's expectations or responsibilities. He was no stranger to a barroom brawl or a few too many drinks, but murder and arson were a whole new level of roguishness even for him.

"Seems you need some better sergeants," Wilhelm said. He kept his eyes forward.

Shrugging his shoulders, Adams continued, "Sergeant Thom led us around town. He'd been there before. Had a fine lay of the land."

"You men should be ashamed of yourselves. You need the love of Christ in your life," Shugart added.

"Bugger off, old fart," Nelson said. "I look out for meself well enough."

The aged abolitionist shut his mouth, leaning away from the brutish man.

Adams chimed in. "Corporal Shugart, how is this any different than what we are being sent to do right now?"

"We raid Richmond to win this war."

"And what will we do when we arrive in Richmond?"

"Free the prisoners."

"And?"

"Kill Jeff Davis if we can."

"And burn the enemy capital to the ground. We're going to murder, burn, and cause so much mayhem that the rebels will quit this war."

"It's different, Private."

"Is it?"

Nelson grunted. "No different to me."

"We do it to free the slaves and preserve the Union."

"Do we? You might, but I know men here don't feel the same way you do."

"Of course they do."

"Not everyone is as righteous as you are. Other men have more basic needs."

"I need the old woman to shut the fuck up," Nelson said.

"Leave Uncle be," Wolf found himself saying.

The hulking man growled at him. "Crippled boy getting brave."

Heat simmered in Wolf's blood. He was well aware of his leg's limitations.

"Enough," Wilhelm added. "That's an order."

Adams grinned, intelligent eyes weighing every man there. "Truth is, Shugart, there's a reason why they keep men like Nelson and me around."

"What's that?"

"It's because they need us. You see, any man can carry guns, ride horses, and yell real loud, but only a few of us can do what needs to be done when it needs to be done. That's why we ain't in no prison. That's why they put us in F Company. They need men that get things done. They need men who will do the dirty work, like making Jeff Davis stop breathing. Have you even killed a man yet?"

Shugart paled and he ran fingers through his beard. "I fired like everyone else at the enemy. Couldn't tell if I was the one who dealt the killing blow."

"But have you killed one? Have you stuck a man in the belly and watched him die crying for his mother?"

Shugart's voice shook. "I. I. Don't know."

"You don't know." Adams nodded, confirming all his suspicions.

The rest of the unit rode in silence, each remembering the men they were responsible for sending to the next world. Wolf had stabbed and shot men, he wasn't sure what happened to them later, but he knew he'd done it. And he knew by default at least some of those men died, and he was the man responsible.

"Well, I do know. I shot 'em, knifed 'em, sliced 'em up, and beat 'em until they was all dead. I look 'em in the eye when they're dying 'cause I want to know what they're feeling and thinking in their last moments. Some of 'em scream, some of 'em cry, others curse, and others are real quiet like as they go yonder, but in the end, they're all dead. Every single one of 'em. If you look real close, you can see something in their eyes grow dark. Or maybe it's just the darkness that takes 'em. Don't know. Don't care." He spit. "But don't tell me I need God when maybe God needs me to keep the righteous men like you alive."

"I killed my share," Wolf said, cutting through the men's spat.

Adams gave him a queer smile, staring him in the eyes. "I believe you. You got some hot devil blood in you."

"No one needs to talk about killing," Wilhelm said.

"Sounds like a normal conversation piece since we're in the army. Doing killing," Adams said.

"That's an order."

"Yes, sir," Adams said with a wink for Wolf. "Too much like a business for those Prussians. Take no joy in it, so damn serious."

The soldiers rode in silence contemplating the tirade of Adams and what capacity for violence each man held in his soul. Wolf knew it was in his, but he wasn't so cavalier about killing. He knew it was something that needed to be done so his brothers-in-arms could go home in one piece. Although he believed in God, he was by no means righteous. In fact, many a time his father had called him a lazy drunken good-for-nothing. That was part of the reason why he was in the military: to prove that despite his injury, he was a man capable of fighting for a cause greater than himself.

They passed brown dirt fields. Nothing grew in the dreary February Virginian winter. Trees grew aplenty but had yet to produce buds on limbs or leaves on branches. Frankly, everything appeared dead.

The creak of leather saddles was accompanied by the rise of the sun in the east. Its warm rays filtered through the naked trees, touching the men and battling the cold air for supremacy.

A single gunshot exploded in the air, penetrating the softness with violence. Men turned in their saddles. Their carbines went to hips as they searched for the offender. Pistols scraped across leather as they were drawn. Smoke clouded the air.

Private Gratz's eyes were wide with shock. He held his carbine in one hand as if it had offended him.

"What the hell are you doing?" Wilhelm yelled at him.

Gratz shook his head. "I. I. It slipped in my hand."

"Who told you to slip, Private? By God, man, we are on a covert raid. Blödhammel!" He swung at Gratz's head with a free hand, cuffing him like a child. "You idiot, boy."

They could hear the thunder of hooves as men galloped from the rear of the column.

"I must have nodded off. I didn't mean to."

Wilhelm shoved a finger at him. "Saddle that carbine, trooper. Keep it unloaded."

Gratz obeyed, swinging the carbine to his back.

"You need to exercise some trigger control. What if that hit one of us?"

"I'm sorry." Gratz lowered his brown eyes.

"Sorry don't bring back the dead."

Colonel Dahlgren emerged with an aide, Lieutenant Gordon. "Who discharged that weapon?" His eyes were fierce with rage.

Wolf and his men were quiet. "I will court-martial every single one of you if you don't answer the question."

Gratz's head dipped even lower.

Wilhelm responded without hesitation. "It was me, sir. No excuse. It was my fault."

The colonel's face twisted in surprise. "I'm to believe that you, Sergeant, are to blame for that negligent discharge? The man that is supposed to be leading these men in a place of honor?"

Gratz gaped at Wilhelm.

"It was my mistake. I take the blame."

"You men disgust me." Dahlgren lifted his kepi off his head and wiped his brow that glistened despite the cool temperatures. "Dismount your horse."

Wilhelm cocked his head. "With all due respect, sir, why?"

"You are to be punished for this grievous mistake. Get off your horse."

"Sir?"

Dahlgren's hand drifted toward his pistol. "Do I need to ask you again, Sergeant, or do I need to place you under arrest for insubordination?"

The two men eyed each other for a moment before Wilhelm complied. He dismounted, staring up at the tall colonel holding his reins.

"You, Corporal, take his horse."

Wolf steered close to Wilhelm, and the sergeant handed him the reins.

"You walk the rest of the way."

"Sir, we have at least six more miles," Wolf said.

"You want to join him?" Dahlgren pointed at Wolf then Roberts and Adams. "Huh? You all want to walk to Richmond?"

The men backed down, dipping their heads and grumbling beneath their breath.

"That's what I thought. We need discipline if we are going to succeed, and this man here will learn true discipline even if it costs him his life."

Dahlgren gestured at Wolf. "Onward. You, Corporal." He pointed at

Wolf. "You're in charge of these wretches until we reach Spotsylvania."

"Yes, sir."

"Your sergeant has delayed me long enough. Forward."

The men continued their march, leaving their sergeant behind. Wilhelm fell farther and farther back as the horses' long strides overtook him. He kept his back straight and his chest out as he marched, ignoring the scrutiny and disdain the men gave him as they passed.

CHAPTER 11

Early Morning, February 29th, 1864
Hampton's Winter Quarters outside of Fredericksburg, Virginia

Major General Wade Hampton gently closed the brown leather book. The front was adorned with an emblazoned eagle gripping a shield with its talons, and the rest was decorated in scrawling vines and leaves. He set the book down on a side table, thinking of his grandfather in the War for Independence. *Is this the second War of Independence? Will there be a third or fourth? How many times will we have to rip open the same wound and fight the same battles? How many wars will we fight before we're truly free?*

He sat for a moment watching the fire crackle and burn in the fieldstone-encased fireplace in his parlor. The flames danced to no tune, only able to consume every scrap of tinder and timber until there was nothing left to feed upon. Then it would die out, leaving only dusty ash in its wake. Just like war. An action that corrupted and tortured everything it fed upon, leaving no one safe and no one innocent from its effect.

The war had consumed the entire nation, yet even as it encroached upon its fourth year, there was no foreseeable conclusion in sight. It was threatening to stretch on indefinitely, and even as the manpower of the South dipped lower and lower, he knew his men would fight until the bitter end. It was in their blood. There was a fire inside them, burning much more brightly than the Northern invaders. The flames leapt and wavered in flags of orange and yellow.

Despite his time resting over the winter as combat lulled, he was still tired. Tired from the saddle and the death and the war. *Yet what choice do you have, Wade? You cast your die early and no better option would present itself with Lincoln's Republican Congress. If you lose, your fortune will disappear as if it never were. If you win, you'll be one of the richest men in the country again.* They were laborious thoughts to digest. If Lincoln had never been elected, he could have carried on with his successful business without having to fight for his very existence.

It wasn't the main reason he fought, but if it was between living his days in squalor or as a rich man with lavish food and wine, he'd pick that life. He'd opposed the war and secession early before flames ignited the nation. War was bad for business. Every day, the residual hammer blows of war chipped away at his wealth. But when his home state of South Carolina was the first to leave the Union, it forced his hand. Now he fought to be free from the Yankee hordes that came to yoke the Southern people and destroy their entire way of life.

He stood from his chair near the warmth of the parlor fireplace. Books lined the shelving on the wall, and the window to the outside was dim around the edges.

His hip had healed from Gettysburg although he noted with a certain amount of disgust it had taken much too long. *To be young again.* The wound it left was a puckered indent in his flesh that only began to feel normal after extensive stretching or walking. He supposed it could have been much worse. It could have shattered his hip bone, leaving him an invalid, or he could have become infected and died like so many boys did in field hospitals. His surgeon had done an excellent job despite cutting into him like a piece of meat while Hampton guzzled rum and bit down on a wooden stick to keep from screaming.

Rubbing the wound vigorously with his hand, his eyes scanned the book. He hoped to find an answer somewhere in its pages. This war had gone on for far too long. While the man on the page was clearly a military genius, Hampton hadn't found anything that he might use to bring about a swift conclusion to this godforsaken conflict.

Often now, late evenings turned into early mornings, and his mind tended to race with an infinite number of battle scenarios that haunted him. His mind would jump to future battles to come, and he would sip on whiskey until his mind calmed and his nerves dulled. The strategies and military movements would slowly depart with drums and bugle calls. It was only then that his brother Frank's ghost would leave him be. He stood and made his way to a circular table.

He tipped the decanter of rich whiskey back, pouring himself two fingers worth. With a practiced hand, he swirled the glass in a circle, letting the liquid spin around the edges. He ran a hand through his curled dark brown hair, scratching at the scar running along his scalp. A saber blow from a crazed Federal trooper near the outskirts of Gettysburg. The wound was compounded due to the fact he'd been leading a charge he didn't intend to lead. Subsequently, he failed to meet his objective of reaching the Union rear. The similarities to the entirety of the war effort were not lost on him.

The oaky liquid slipped down his throat, a sweet fire that warmed his belly. As it traveled to this stomach then spread to his limbs, he let out a sigh. The effects of the whiskey were starting the process of finding him sleep. He stared back at the brown leather book. "Until tomorrow, Daniel Morgan. Maybe you can shed some light on our predicament."

A crisp knock sounded at his door. The house had been generously acquiesced by a local widow who went to stay with her sister when the rebels shifted their lines farther south and ceded the land north of the Rapidan River to the Yankees.

His Negro body servant emerged from a small side room in the kitchen. His temples were waxen with gray and the top of his head still held some of its youthful darkness. He was younger than Wade but had started as his father's man before begging to go to war with Wade. Still in his nightclothes, he rubbed his eyes, wiping the sleep from them.

"Ransom, I got it. Go back to bed."

Ransom shook his head, hurrying for the door. "I'll git it, suh." He beat Wade to the door and opened it a crack.

A country voice spoke from the other side. "Is the general here?"

"Who're you?"

Wade stood back, listening. He assumed someone pounding on a door in the middle of the night would need something. The possibilities were many. Perhaps a drunken soldier or someone searching for a place to spend the wet night, not knowing a Confederate general now resided in the Wilcox family home.

"Dan Tanner."

Wade's ears perked up at the name. Tanner was a part of Hampton's loose network of irregular soldiers that acted as his eyes and ears throughout Virginia. He was a South Carolina boy who had earned Hampton's trust early in the war with a quick mind and a good eye for the land. Hampton had about twenty similar men in the field at any one time, and they had taken the name the Iron Scouts.

"Let him in."

"Mistuh Hampton, it's mighty late to be a callin'."

Wade gave Ransom a slight smile. "It's okay. I need to speak with him."

Ransom bowed his head low, exposing a bald spot spreading on the top of his pate. He opened the door all the way. Tanner stepped inside, took off his black overcoat, and handed it to Ransom. He was a handsome man. Save for the trimmed goatee and stubble on his face, one might even have said he had feminine features: delicate eyebrows, petite nose, prominent cheekbones. His skin appeared soft despite the man's ride and exposure to the wilderness.

He wore a thin brown jacket over a dark blue vest and maroon bowtie. He removed his John Bull style hat, shaking it out near the door. He exhaled as if he'd run from wherever he came.

"General, I came as quick as I could."

"What news do you bring?" He waved the scout over. "Come into the parlor. Do you drink, son?"

The man followed him. He stood back on his heels for a moment, marveling at all the books. "I do not, sir. Forgive me, but I must be brief."

Hampton stopped in front of the decanter and poured more alcohol into his glass. The first drink was dulling his wounds just enough to fetch him some sleep. "Go ahead, Tanner."

"Myself and Private Scott were headed north on a mission to scout a

Union depot for destruction." He gulped. "We caught wind of a large movement of Yankee cavalry heading south."

"How many?"

"Must of been at least four thousand."

Hampton kept his demeanor calm. *Four thousand?* "Go on."

"Scott and I abandoned our orders and started to follow them near Ely's Ford. They must of been riding hard cause they was sleeping in their saddles." He gave a mischievous smile showing white teeth. "We bushwhacked a few of 'em and took their horses, falling back in line with the rear command."

His Iron Scouts were a special breed of trooper. Smart, savvy, extremely competent in the field. It contained men from Cobb's Legion and Jeff Davis Legion as well as the South Carolina and North Carolina cavalries. It was difficult to gain entry into their close-knit unit, but the men that did fall into it were some of his best. Men that he trusted to know when to take the initiative and when to follow through with their original orders.

"We rode with them for miles, listening to the men talk and learning as much as we could. They're headed for Richmond, sir."

Hampton stopped drinking his whiskey, his brow creasing. "Richmond?" The liquid torched his throat, speeding toward his belly like a runaway train.

"Aye, they are going to attack the capital and burn it. They're on their way through Spotsylvania now."

Ransom stood near the wall, head down, showing no signs of listening although Hampton was sure he'd been. He was a very loyal man.

"Put some coffee on. It's going to be a long morning."

His servant nodded and went back into the kitchen.

"We hadn't expected them to strike at Richmond so soon." His men formed the far right of the rebel line. At his disposal were two severely diminished 1st and 2nd North Carolina Cavalries, not more than three hundred men capable of riding. Many had returned home to rest and refit mounts on furlough, leaving him with a skeleton force at best. Most of their time was spent running picket duties and watching the Yankees north. It was by no means a force that had any business tangling with four thousand Union troopers on a mission.

"Who's in command?"

"Judson Kilpatrick."

Hampton sighed. "Kilpatrick, he's a wee little leprechaun, but a feisty one. He's one of their bolder leaders. No coward there." He shook his head, thinking about his enemy. "He'll attack and attack until each and every man from his command is dead or wounded or the city is burned down."

Ransom brought the men coffee. Tanner sipped his for a moment as the men thought about the invasion. "This is good. Mighty cold out there, sir."

Hampton took a long bitter gulp and grimaced when it burnt his tongue. He put the cup close to his belly. "You did good, Tanner. You were right to track these invaders. Where's Scott?"

"He stayed near to keep an eye on them."

"Very good." Hampton moved over to a writing desk and sat in a short-backed chair. He tugged out a thin white sheet of paper and laid it flat. He took out a glass container of ink and removed the stopper. Dunking his wooden-handled pen with its metal nib in the ink, he jotted down a note, his letters forming in harsh lines. *Sizable Federal cavalry force led by Judson Kilpatrick heading to Richmond. Requesting your guidance and deployment of additional support to assist in turning back invaders before they reach capital. I do not believe the 1st and 2nd North Carolina regiments will be enough to turn the tide. Regards, Gen. Wade Hampton, III.* He pressed the letter into an envelope and sealed it shut.

"You are to take this directly to Stuart's command. In his hands only. No one else. We're going to need help if we're to turn these inglorious bastards around." He handed the letter over to Tanner. "I know you're tired, but you must ride all the way through." He faced Ransom. "Give Mr. Tanner ham, bread, and cheese and get Honey saddled for him."

"Yaas'suh." His servant disappeared.

"I'm giving you one of my horses so you can make better time. You understand the importance that this message get to Stuart right away?"

"I do, General."

Hampton nodded. "Then be off. We have no time to waste."

Ransom returned a few minutes later.

"Call for Captain Blair. I have wires I need sent." The servant disappeared. He peered out the window. The sun crept upon the horizon, preparing to beat back the night. He sipped his coffee as it gradually made its entrance. Another morning. Another desperate fight awaiting him.

CHAPTER 12

February 29th, 1864
Spotsylvania, Virginia

Spotsylvania was a tiny town with spacious muddy roads that could fit six wagons across without touching. It was a crucial intersection that contained the most direct route to Richmond. At that very crossing sat the Sanford Hotel.

Morning beams of light illuminated the immense red brick hotel's front porch that was propped up with four sturdy three-foot diameter white pillars and four chimneys, two on each side of the hotel. There were outbuildings, stables, smokehouses, and barns.

On the other side of the intersection stood another smaller structure that mimicked the larger one in style and design. It too had white pillars and walls made of fine red brick. It was the Spotsylvania Court House. Here Dahlgren drew the troopers to a halt.

He made a loud declaration only for his men. "I deem this town under Federal protection and request that all citizens help in the war effort."

Adams flashed a fiendish grin at Wolf. "He's telling us to acquire supplies."

Union men scrambled into chicken coops and smokehouses. Healthy horses were commandeered. Blue-coated soldiers marched to front doors, fists reverberating upon them.

Nelson dismounted and wrapped his reins around a split log fence. "Get me some breakfast." He marched along a walkway toward a house.

"Better stock up, Corporal, or you'll run out of food before Richmond," Adams said, hopping off his saddle.

Wolf sighed. The man was right. He didn't like taking from the people they were supposed to protect. Another couple of days of hard tack and they'd be out, and there was no telling what they might run into south of here or for how long. "You heard the colonel. Take what you can but don't rob them blind." His unit dismounted, tying their horses on the fence.

Roberts pointed at a clapboard house painted a faded yellow. "Let's check this one out."

"Shugart?"

The old abolitionist stood next to his gray mare, stroking her mane. "I will not partake in this despite the villainy of their ideology."

Wolf smiled at him beneath his beard. "I'll make sure to get you some extra meat."

"You be careful. Those men." He nodded at the other house. "They take too much joy in this conflict. You would do well to avoid them."

"Come on," Roberts shouted. He waved him toward the house.

"Pray for me, Uncle."

"I do every day. I pray for all of us and that this war may end."

Leaving his pious comrade with the horses, he half-jogged after Roberts. The short trooper pounded a hand on the door, the sound echoing.

"Open up now," Roberts said in a low voice. "Union Army." He turned and whispered. "You smell that?"

"Biscuits?" Wolf said. His mouth watered at the thought of warm homemade flaky golden brown biscuits. Those were the polar opposite to hardtack.

"I'm gonna eat all of them."

Wolf wrapped an arm around Roberts's neck. "No you ain't."

"We'll share. We'll share."

"That's better. I told Uncle we'd get him some too."

"No one said nothing about splitting our spoils three ways."

Wolf squeezed his neck a bit with the muscle of his arm.

They waited a moment before the door cracked open. A suspicious eye glared at them through the crack. "What you want?"

"Ma'am, we have come to collect supplies," Roberts said, sounding much more official than he normally spoke.

"We ain't got any."

She went to close the door and Wolf put his flat palm on it. "Say there, Mum, do I smell biscuits?"

"You most certainly do not," the woman hissed.

Wolf grinned like a wolf. "But something that smells divine is coming from your kitchen."

"All I smell is your dungy filth." She pressed her weight into the door.

"A hungry man can always smell a feast," Roberts added.

The woman tried to force the door closed again, but Wolf pushed it open instead. The two men stepped inside to the shrieks of the old matron.

"You no-good, dirty, thieving Yankees." She pointed a finger at them. "How dare you come into my home uninvited like a couple of Huns."

"We only want some food. Nothing else."

"We don't have any!"

Roberts's head lifted into the air, his nostrils working like a basset hound's. "This way." The two men walked through a dining room toward the back of the home. Two female slaves stood in the kitchen. Both wore rough-spun cotton dresses and aprons with handkerchiefs around the tops of their heads.

The matron followed the men. "Don't you dare touch anything!" she chastised as she shook a fist.

"Ohhh, smells yummy," Roberts said. He rubbed his hands together in glee. "Some home cooking."

"Where are they?" Wolf asked the slaves. "We know there's biscuits."

They kept their heads down. Wolf addressed the women over his shoulder. "Don't you know you're free? You don't have to serve her anymore. You can leave."

The slaves didn't say a word but kept their chins to their chests and their eyes downcast. One gripped her hands nervously together.

The gray-haired matron tramped across the room. "How dare you come in here and tell them they're free. I'd never survive without my two girls. Not with me man off fightin' the likes of you blue-devils."

"Then give us the biscuits and we'll be on our way."

The matron huffed. "Thieves every last one of ya. Bessie." She pointed at the cast iron stove. The older of the two slaves used rags to open a door on the side. Gripping a pan with a folded cloth, she took it out and stepped backward.

Wolf and Roberts shared a glance, deep grins spanning their cheeks. They walked to the stove and hovered over top of the pan. Twenty golden brown biscuits lay neatly across, waiting to be eaten. The men dug their greedy fingers into the fluffiness.

"Ow," Roberts said. He tossed the biscuit from hand to hand trying to keep from burning himself.

Wolf didn't care, he shoved the top half of a biscuit in his mouth. It burned his tongue and he smacked his lips, chewing with his mouth open to let the heat dissipate. "Whew!"

The young slave woman smiled at him.

He tongued the floury biscuit in utter glee as it melted in his mouth. "Best damn biscuit I ever had," he said, his mouth full. For a moment he stopped chewing enough for a big swallow. "My compliments to you saintly women."

The younger slave let a giggle escape her lips.

"You Northern heathen, using the Lord's name in vain. Godless is what you are, and you'll pay for this war of aggression."

Wolf stared right at her. "Goddamn, this is good."

The matron's mouth dropped open, her sensibilities offended by these ruffians.

"Good shit," Roberts said, pointing at the pan.

The slave girl giggled again, raising a hand to cover her mouth.

"You be quiet," the matron said. She shook her head at the slave girl. "I'll wipe that smile right off your face with a switch."

"She didn't mean nothing by it," Wolf said.

Her face flushed red in anger, and she pointed at the men. "Get out of my house!"

The slaves filled a cloth sack with all their biscuits and tossed in a cured ham and butter. The men walked outside, their bellies content with deliciousness and their spirits riding on high regardless of Wilhelm's banishment to walk.

"You think Wilhelm will catch up before we depart?" Roberts asked.

"Yes. He's a tough buzzard. He knows he must catch us here or be caught behind enemy lines," Wolf said.

"Long walk on foot. Territory crawling with rebs."

"I wouldn't doubt him. He'd steal a horse and ride back to the Old Snapping Turtle before he got captured."

They walked down the house path to their horses.

"And don't you come back!" the matron called at them from the doorway.

"God bless the troops!" Roberts shouted back.

"Thank you for your support!"

The door slammed behind them, and the two men laughed.

Wolf ripped off a chunk of ham and shoved it between two pieces of biscuit. He munched the delicious combination, letting the warmth of the soon-to-be midday sun soak into his skin.

Screams leaked from the house Adams and Nelson had ventured into. Roberts and Wolf turned to look. The house was a two-story red brick home with white doors. The door in front was ajar.

"What you think's going on?" Roberts asked. His throat jiggled as he swallowed.

"Dunno. Sounds like bloody murder."

The screams abruptly stopped, the sound being strangled out of existence. The two men shared a glance, and a moment later, Adams appeared with a white cloth sack. He took a green apple in his hand and took a big bite with a smile and a wave for his comrades.

"Everything all right?" Wolf shouted.

Adams sauntered down the front path toward the fence. Nelson emerged in the doorway. He ducked through, hefting another bag, and closed the door.

"Everything's fine." Adams crunched his apple happily. "Some people need a bit more convincing than others to part with their belongings."

"What'd you get?"

"Apples, chickens, silver cutlery, and candlesticks. Thought about a fine engraved bed warmer, but it wasn't made with gold or silver, so wouldn't fetch a good enough price."

"You robbed them of more than food?"

A snort came from Adams between bites. "Wolfie, this is war. To the victor the spoils. And that's us." He reached out and wrapped an arm around Wolf. "You need to take advantage. Someday this war will be over." He spread his other arm open. "And all these opportunities will cease."

"Those weren't the orders that were given."

"Wolfie, Wolfie." He patted Wolf's chest like he was an obedient dog. "They have no use for these fine things. What are they going to do with them?"

"I dunno what anyone does with 'em."

"They're going to use them to buy supplies, arms, ammunition, and food for the enemy. When I relieve them of these valuables, I damage the rebel war effort. You understand?"

The man's logic made sense. It seemed that every time they left a town in the South, its people always accepted the rebels back with open arms, giving them refuge and food. Even the towns they controlled never really liked the Federal forces. It was as if they were only smiling on the surface, waiting for you to turn away to they could spit on you and tell you it was rain.

"I guess you're right."

Adams smirked and he took another bite of apple. "Of course I'm right." He patted Wolf's chest. "You need to take care of yourself. Thirteen dollars a month ain't enough to take care of you a long time from now."

Wolf considered his words carefully. They rang more true than Adams could ever know. He didn't have a job to go back to. He would struggle as a farmer. He didn't have any land. Even if he saved his money, he wouldn't have enough to purchase very much land. Nobody would take him in a factory. He had to blackmail the recruiting sergeant to take him into a desperate army. His future had never been bright, and this might be his only way to secure something. "You're right. I do have to look out for myself."

Tossing his apple core, he chuckled. "You're smarter than you look,

Corporal. You have command written all over you." He pointed back at the clapboard house that held the delicious biscuits. "You sure there wasn't something in there to supplement your income?"

"Might of been." The drapes in the window shuddered as someone let them fall.

"She has to have something of value. She had two slaves," Roberts said.

"Slaves ain't cheap."

"No, they ain't."

The two troopers marched back down the walkway. Wolf put a fist to the door and hammered away on it. "Open up."

They waited a moment before the matron's voice carried forth. "Go away. You already robbed us once."

"Let us in. Don't make me kick in this door."

"You'll have to to set foot in here."

Wolf shook his head. He lowered a shoulder into the doorjamb. The wood creaked beneath his bodyweight. Gripping his hands tightly, he slammed into the door again. The frame splintered, and on his next try, the door burst open.

The woman screamed on the other side. She pointed a finger at him. "You get on out of here. You already robbed us. Probably come for us women like the true Northern heathens that you are."

Roberts slipped into the back room.

"We ain't gonna hurt you."

She nodded her head in disgust. "Standard talk before they do the dirty deed."

Wolf held up a hand. "Just stay here."

He followed Roberts through the house into a back room. A four-poster bed rested near the far wall, blankets neatly folded and tucked on top. A mirrored vanity lined the other wall. Roberts stuck his hands through a miniature wooden box. His hand quickly dipped into his pocket.

"Look at this," Roberts held up a gold ring.

"That'll fetch something."

Wolf went over to a dresser. He scanned the surface, and seeing nothing of value, pulled open a drawer. A man's white undergarments lay inside. He dug through them, feeling an odd sense of euphoria like he was getting away with something he wasn't supposed to, but Adams was right. He had to look out for himself, and these people were slave-owning Southerners who'd rather shoot him in the back than rejoin the Union. He felt something solid in the drawer. He dug his hand deeper through the man's clothes, pulling out a pocket watch with a gold chain.

He clicked the button on top and the cover flipped open. The minute hand ticked, and Roman numeral numbers lined the edges.

"You filthy thieving Huns!" the matron shrieked. She had armed herself with a broom. She struck Roberts on top of his head with enough force to drive him back a foot. "And you! That's my husband's! Put that back!" She pointed the broom like a gun at him and charged, ready to bayonet him with the stiff bristles. When she got close, he caught the swinging broom and ripped it from her hands.

"Your husband's watch is being appropriated for the war effort."

He slipped the watch into his pocket right before she swung a fist at him. He dodged her. Tossing the broom down, he caught her wrist and shoved her on the bed. "You'll stay there or else."

A filthy man appeared in the doorway. Mud drenched him from his feet to his waist. His back was straight and his gray mustache thick and curled. "What in the name of Christ are you two dolts doing?" Sergeant Berles said.

Roberts and Wolf stood at attention. "Appropriating supplies, sir," Wolf said.

Wilhelm's mustache quivered in anger. "Were you threatening this woman?"

"No, sir." Wolf studied the ground.

"Was he threatening you, ma'am?"

She blinked back tears. "Aye, the rascal was. He be like Attila the Hun that one."

The sergeant's boots thudded over the floor and he slapped Wolf hard across the cheek. His cheek burned, each finger a bee sting over the side of his face. But it stung deeper than being emasculated by the sergeant. It stung inside his chest because he knew he'd failed Wilhelm.

Planting a finger in the center of Wolf's chest, Wilhelm pressed it hard into his sternum. "No women and no children. I thought you knew better, but maybe that wasn't clear." He took Wolf's cheeks in his hand and squeezed, forcing them face to face. "You know why?"

Wolf was silent, meeting his eyes.

"'Cause some things got to stay pure." He squeezed tighter, sending pain into Wolf's face. "We walk a fine line between hero and devil. One small step the wrong way, and you'll become a savage that needs put down." Wilhelm's eyes were chips of ice, clear and sharp enough to kill a man. "You understand?"

"Aye, no women, no children."

"Good." Wilhelm released Wolf's face with a shove. He turned on Roberts. "You understand?"

"Yes, Sergeant."

"Now get the hell out of here."

CHAPTER 13

February 29th, 1864
Near Mt. Pleasant, Virginia

The column began the process of splitting near a lightless plantation manor atop a hill. The home was left unmolested by the troopers passing by.

Colonel Ulric Dahlgren waited for General Kilpatrick, who traveled with the main force, to speak with him before they parted ways.

The raid commander was easy to identify, an entourage of a dozen other officers and aides tailing the short general like a medieval lord and his retainers. Dahlgren saluted him, a gesture that was hurriedly returned by his superior.

A wide grin split Kilpatrick's face. "Five thousand dollars we take Richmond by the end of the week."

Dahlgren's horse stomped its hooves, the left and then the right. He stared at the advancing troopers. "The men look good. The rebels are unaware of our progress."

"Resistance is light. General Lee hasn't shifted any forces. How about it, Dahlgren? Any wager on our success?"

"I won't wager on something I'm so vested in happening, sir."

"Such a serious lad. Pleasonton took the bet. Ha!" The jingle of sabers, tack, and saddles softly played a marching army's song. "If he'd seen how unprepared the rebels are, he'd never have taken it."

"It's a sure bet, sir. We will succeed."

Kilpatrick eyed him, his horse moving beneath him. "Look for my rockets. That will be the sign to attack. We will be chaos amongst them, and in that upheaval, our success will be secured. I'll see you in Richmond, Colonel."

"I look forward to it," Dahlgren said with a nod of his head.

Kilpatrick gave him a short salute and walked his mount back to his column, taking a fork in the road, tailed by his officers. "Oh, and Colonel," he called over his shoulder. "Do not fail me. We are building such a glorious partnership; it'd be sad to see your star fall so soon after it took flight."

"I will not." Dahlgren clenched his smooth jaw. By God, he wouldn't fail. This mission was his destiny, and his destiny was to end the war by severing the head of the Confederate snake and watching its body wither and die.

He led his column in the diverging direction of his superior.

A cool drizzle started, pattering his hat and shoulders. It nagged at his men, irritating them and causing them to keep their heads down. But soon the rain turned into a storm. Dahlgren secured his heavy dark blue greatcoat tighter around himself. According to the regulations, officers were allowed to wear the enlisted version as to not unnecessarily draw sharpshooter fire, but he preferred the difference it created between himself and the men. The coat was quickly soaked through and weighting heavily across his shoulders.

The column trudged for miles in the rain, each step of his horse causing his leg to ache. The ache started as a distant thought. It was something that was there but tolerable if one concentrated against acknowledging the irritant. With each sway of his horse, the throbbing grew worse. It was as if time were ticking against him, a painful reminder that Death came closer with every second.

In order to ride sufficiently, he had to strap his right thigh to the side of the saddle. He rested upon his left leg and groin, leaving them bearing almost his entire body weight. It was a chaffing, uncomfortable experience, and it battered him physically as the march continued.

Black birds circled close to treetops in the distance and he studied them with interest. Scavengers most likely. Crows or ravens, searching for carrion. *Were they already gathering to feast upon our enemies?* He put that thought away. It was too soon to celebrate their victory. They'd only just begun their journey, but it felt right. They would win this war. The ebony birds disappeared into the trees in a brief moment.

His mind wandered. He questioned whether or not he was ready for such an excursion into the field, but he kept his face straight and his nerves steady. *You must show no sign of weakness or discomfort in front of the men. A leader is calm, collected, always knows the next move, and must be strict to maintain order over the lower ranks.*

A rider trotted his way, a trooper from the 2nd New York. "Sah, we got a cabin ahead. Bunch of horses out front."

Dahlgren waved a young lieutenant forward. "Merritt, lead the charge and capture those within." He turned to his second-in-command. "Major Cooke, you provide support."

The two men took off at a trot. Merritt rolled his platoon out of the column trailed by Cooke and a hundred men. Ten minutes later he had almost thirty rebels captured. It was easily done; the surprised rebels surrendered without a fight.

The prisoners were shoved into wagons and given to the rear guard with Captain Yates's men. In another few minutes, they were underway again, this time with thirty more prisoners.

Healthy rebel horses were commandeered, the defective and lame ones given to the prisoners to deter escape.

Merritt reappeared with a smile. "Sir, we interrupted a court-martial. The man on trial would like to speak with you."

"Send him along." Gentlemanly duties would fall on him as commander, a task he personally enjoyed as befit his social class and rank.

The rebel was allowed to ride a swaybacked mount next to Dahlgren, a horse that would never warrant any kind of escape.

The Confederate officer had a pugnacious round nose and a thick mustache hanging beneath. He had a healthy air to him, well-fed, and gaping kind eyes.

"I'm Lieutenant Colonel Hilary Jones."

"Pleased to make your acquaintance."

"And I yours, sir. You prevented a very uncomfortable hearing on my behalf. I must say I am indebted to you."

Dahlgren felt pride swelling in his chest. Denying the enemy a court-martial gave him a new ally, but the general disruption of the adversary's military activities gave him a small amount of glee. "We intend to free all oppressed by the rebel government. If I may be so frank, why were you being court-martialed?" He pulled a flask from his jacket and handed it to his prisoner.

Jones scratched at his mustache, staring at the flask. "Many thanks, a true gentleman." He tipped the silver container and passed it back to Dahlgren, wiping his mouth with the back of his hand. "It wasn't for lack on the battlefield. I was well-liked by the men and performed when asked."

"So what was it?"

"Love, sir."

"They were court-martialing you for love?" Dahlgren let out a short chuckle. "Sounds like a bit much."

Jones nodded vigorously. "Aye. I left command without orders to see my boy. They called it desertion."

Dahlgren narrowed his eyebrows. "Why was leave not given?"

"It's a long story, sir, but my commanding officer did not like me much, but sir, I implore you. My boy, he's almost one. I haven't even seen my boy. I'd give my left foot to see him. I would."

And I'd give my right leg for my nation. "You haven't seen your boy?"

"Not once. My baby boy has never laid eyes upon his father. If I should fall, he'll never know." He glanced away, overcome by his emotions. "The officers back there were going to court-martial me anyway as soon as we arrived to our prison. No doubt in my mind. There's no hope I'll see my boy no matter how this war goes." He collected himself, running a hand over his uniform. "I appreciate the sip of liquor and hearing me out. Better than most officers I know."

Dahlgren took a nip of whiskey and placed the flask back in his breast pocket. He was not a man to overindulge but only drank enough to keep the pain under control. "Lieutenant Colonel, I'm going to tell you right now. I don't like Southerners. You are a backward people. I don't like rebels. While it may seem logical that Americans would be rebels, it is antithetical to our constitution." He cleared his throat. "I don't like cowards or men derelict of their duties."

The prisoner's head dipped low, admonished, for he was all these things.

"But I will say, no boy shouldn't know the outline of his father's face. Swear to it right here and now that you will never take up arms against the Union again, and I'll let you see your boy. On my honor."

Jones's eyes lit up with hope. "Sir, are you playing me? It's a cruel jest if you are."

"All charges are dropped," Dahlgren said. "If you swear to the Union and live in peace."

Rubbing his mustache, tears filled Jones's eyes. "You don't understand what this means to me and my family. Bless your heart, good man."

"I am a liberator. I give you freedom from the yoke of your corrupt government. Go to your family. Live in peace."

Jones bowed his head deeply, removing his kepi with a flourish. "I owe you my life, sir."

The thought of being this man's redeemer, a benefactor that held his fate within his hands and granted him mercy, warmed Dahlgren. "You may go. When this war is done, and it will be done soon, I'd like to meet your boy."

Jones flopped his hat back on his head. "Of course, Colonel?"

"Colonel Ulric Dahlgren."

"Colonel Dahlgren. No man of more outstanding character on either side of the Mason-Dixon line."

"I am humbled by your words." *I am a benevolent leader. Wise and just. A modern Julius Caesar in American form.* He waved the man away with two fingers. "Now go see your son."

"Your generosity is unparalleled, Colonel. I'll never forget you." Jones grinned like an idiot.

"You won't. I assure you of that." Dahlgren gestured at his lieutenant. "Merritt, lead him away from the column so he is not interfered with."

"Yes, sir."

With a deep bow, Jones departed with Merritt.

The two men walked their horses away, and Dahlgren felt a sense of righteous pride. He'd forever turned an enemy combatant, had shown him mercy and gained loyalty. It was men like Jones that would be key to healing the nation when the war was done, men that understood the importance of laying down arms and focusing on their family. He turned in his saddle, eyeing his column.

The soldiers appeared tired and bedraggled by the rain and saddle time. They were moving too slow to meet their deadline for they had much farther to go than Kilpatrick's command and were bogged down by the prisoners they'd collected. He wondered if letting them all go was appropriate given their rushed circumstances.

He sighed and urged his horse forward. "Bring me that Negro," he called at Cooke.

It took the men almost ten minutes to bring forward the colored boy traveling with Captain Yates's command. The young black man sat in his saddle with his eyes downcast, fear emanating from his person.

"Well, I'm not going to hurt you. What's your name?"

"Martin, sir."

"Ah yes, that's it, Martin." He gestured out at the road ahead. "You know these roads?"

"Better than most, sir."

"Can you take us undetected through Goochland to the James River then to Richmond?"

The boy gulped but responded with a clear voice. "I can. I know it well enough."

"Good boy. My scouts do a sufficient job, but we'll need you before this is done." He glanced over at Hogan who ignored his quip. The man was an adequate scout but one of low status who fought wars not as gentlemen did; he was more of a rogue than a true soldier. He supposed the army needed rogues as well as warriors and tacticians, but his skills were more adept to frontier warfare against the Indians than battles between armies.

"I want to help."

"You stick with me and make sure we stay on track."

"Yes, sir."

They swayed with their horses. He would accomplish his mission. He would win this war.

***

Lieutenant Colonel Hilary Jones pushed his broken horse to the limits. It galloped along the soupy road as best as it could. But he was forced to slow it down to a walk when he felt the beast faltering beneath him.

He would see his boy as a proud man, reinstated with his honor restored. All he had to do was make it to Richmond and warn the people there. Surely, leniency would be given with his vital input.

He knew the Union raiders had few men in their command, maybe five hundred at the maximum. He knew their target was Richmond. He knew their commander's name: Ulric Dahlgren. He knew they were moving in a flanking maneuver around the city. All critical information for the defense of the rebel capital.

Rain pelted his body and wind whipped at his clothes as he drove his horse onward to warn the capital.

CHAPTER 14

February 29ᵗʰ, 1864
Near Frederick's Hall, Virginia

Everything was wet. At a certain point, even their greatcoats could do little to shield them from the weather. Cold wind drove the showers, so even with their hats and caps sitting low, the rain struck their faces. Their discomfort grew as darkness encroached, and the order trickled down the line that there would be no halting for rest.

The congregation of prisoners in the rear of the column had grown. Those riding lame horses were forced to the center of the column by Wolf's unit.

The spirits of the rebels didn't appear to be too dampened despite the weather. They rode with heads high and chests out like proud men that knew their abduction was temporary.

"Better get comfortable, boys. We got a long night in the saddle," Wilhelm said.

"Bastard colonel is trying to make us sick," Nelson grumbled. He wrapped a thick fur blanket around his shoulders.

Adams closed his eyes. "Always have to be prepared to sleep where you can."

Wolf tapped his shoulder. "We'll take turns. You go first."

"Good idea. I always do better with some sleep beneath me belt."

Taking out his pocket watch, Wolf flicked open the cover. The hour hand hovered near the VIII. He clipped it closed. "I'll give you two hours. Then we'll switch."

"No cheatin' me now."

"Would never."

The troopers settled in. The chatter became quieter and quieter along with the wind and rain. The pattering of water upon puddled ground and troopers alike soothed them into a trance-like state. Even the rebel prisoners became silent, and the column seemed more like a troop of long-forgotten apparitions from the Revolution.

The horses' gaits rocked the men like infants in cradles, and Wolf found himself fading fast. Every tree looked the same. The road appeared to stretch on forever like a march through purgatory. He took his watch out and wiped the face. One hour. He tucked the pilfered watch back into his pocket.

Soon he blinked furiously, struggling to stay awake. His eyelids drooped over his eyes, bit by bit closing out his surroundings. He gave a lazy glance at the prisoners still sitting atop their horses, heads rocking with each stride. The rebels were as exhausted as their captors. He didn't bother to count, but there appeared to be fewer than there was earlier. The fuzziness of fatigue numbed him of caring. The rain and wind lessened to a cold drizzle. He let his eyes close and his chin slump to his chest.

***

"Get him!" echoed in his ears. Wolf's eyes shot open in panic. Shadowed trees surrounded them. Gnarled limbs with spindly branches reached for the troopers, grabbing at them. His eyes fluttered, trying to grasp his surroundings. Men jolted upright in their saddles. Startled horses whinnied. Hands leapt for pistols and sabers. Union troopers surrounded him, but the missing rebels were doggedly apparent.

Prisoners simply walked their horses away from the column. They had duped their captors into a false sense of security. Instead of attempting a mad dash, they had quietly and simply steered their mounts away from the sleepy column.

"Oh fuck," Nelson groaned. He drove his heels into his mount's flanks, drawing a pistol.

Ripping his Colt Army revolver from his holster, Wolf's eyes tracked the two rebels then two others. The prisoners whipped their horses into a gallop.

"Go with him!" Wilhelm shouted, pointing at Wolf. "Shugart and Dan, after those two." He pointed his unit into positions of pursuit.

Wolf kicked his horse behind broad Nelson, chasing the two rebels. Billy's hooves thrashed the wet earth, tossing mud behind them airborne. He fumbled with his pistol as he held on to reins.

On their healthy mounts, they gained behind the rebels. Fleeing prisoners turned back and forth, seeing that they were quickly going to be overtaken.

"Stop!" Wolf tried to line a shot and a wet branch slapped his face, forcing him to retroactively duck.

Nelson took aim with his pistol and it banged out gun smoke and lead. His meaty thumb quickly cocked the gun again, aiming. *Bang!* He missed and thumbed the hammer again. *Bang!*

The rear rider slumped in his saddle and his horse slowed. The other rider tried to continue onward, but his horse was lame at best. Wolf caught them first.

"Surrender!" he shouted.

The rebel hefted a hand in the air while holding his other arm tightly across his body.

Nelson pushed closer to the wounded rebel. He aimed his weapon point-blank and pulled the trigger on him. The boom was dampened by the meat of the man's torso. Sparks flew from his jacket. The rebel spasmed in pain, toppling from his horse.

The other rider jumped from his saddle, stumbled and fell. Wet dirt sprayed the air as Nelson missed his shot.

"Kill the bastard, Wolf!"

"They're surrendering."

"No, they running. Orders were simple. You run; you get shot." Nelson fumbled with his cartridge box. It would be at least a minute before his weapon was functional again. "Go finish the bastard before he sounds the alarm."

Wolf heeled Billy. Tossing his head, rider and mount pursued the sprinting man.

The rebel weaved through the trees, his body staggering and lurching. Billy took logs and branches in stride while Wolf covered his face from the lashings of tree limbs.

The prisoner tripped and fell on the ground, groaning in pain. Wolf slowed his horse, reining him to a halt. He pointed his pistol, staring down the sight. The prisoner backed along the undergrowth, crumpling soggy leaves in desperate fingers.

The rebel held a hand out. "Can't blame a man for trying?"

Wolf steadied his aim. "You're my prisoner. Yield."

"I yield." The rebel stood gingerly, wiping his hands on his pants. Something blurred in the air and Wolf was forced to cover his face. A rocky mass crashed into his arm, sending pain emanating along his elbow and into his shoulder.

"Damn!" Wolf grasped his elbow.

Like a hare, the rebel fled, scampering over underbrush and fallen logs.

"Kill the bastard!" Nelson screamed at him. Reload complete, his horse whinnied as he kicked his heels. He jerked his reins, riding along the flanks to cut off the prisoner.

Straightening his arm, Wolf took aim. The rebel ran as fast as he could. The bead sight hovered right above the man's back. The rebel twisted, staring over his shoulder, a look of panic on his face. The trigger surrendered easily to his finger. The gun popped, fire momentarily illuminating the darkness. Just above the shoulder blade, the bullet struck. The rebel's jacket indented beneath the impact of the bullet. He fell forward on his hands.

Through the dead leaves, Wolf walked toward the fallen prisoner, Billy's hooves thumping. The prisoner lay still, facedown. Blood seeped from the hole in his back.

"Wolf," Nelson growl-shouted through the forest.

"Over here," he called back. He could hear Nelson driving his mount through the brush like a plow. The large trooper emerged from the darkness, revolver pointed in the air.

"He dead?"

"I shot him."

Nelson jumped down and holstered his pistol. An eight-inch knife emerged from his belt. He crouched down and grabbed the man by the hair, plunging the blade into his neck. Roughly, he forced the knife to the hilt then ripped it free. He wiped the blade on the rebel's coat and tossed him back to the ground like a dirty rag doll.

Wolf had seen men commit acts of violence against one another but not like this. The indifference in the way Nelson slit his throat reminded him of a butcher. The man was no more than a pig in Nelson's eyes, a piece of meat to be carved up. No, Wolf was sure it was done with less feeling than a butcher has for the pig.

The big trooper sheathed his knife.

Wolf suspected that when it came down to it man was no different than swine, easily butchered. Nelson patted down the rebel's pockets. They'd already been searched once for weapons and valuables.

"Sometimes they hide stuff." He unceremoniously rolled the body over. The face of Captain Young stared back. Nelson dug his hands in his pockets. Young's body shook under the inspection, but he didn't respond or protest, his throat a jagged mess of red gore.

"Fucker didn't have shit. Come on." He walked back to his mount.

The unfeeling brutality shocked Wolf. The escape and response had happened so quick he didn't have time to think. "They were unarmed and we killed them."

"So." Nelson checked his girth strap on his saddle.

"They'd already surrendered."

"They un-surrendered by running." Nelson's saddle groaned as he remounted.

They walked their horses back to the road.

Nelson spoke, "Not all men have what it takes to shoot a man in the back. You do. There's hope that you might survive this war."

"Is there?"

Nelson's mouth tightened. "Don't go crying to Papa Berles. You killed a man. You're a soldier. That's what we do, kill."

"There was no honor in that."

"Aye. There's no honor in it."

Horse hooves stamped the muddy ground.

"Who said there's honor in killing?"

"I've killed men before."

"Was there honor?"

"We stood toe-to-toe slashing, stabbing, and shooting. It was a fair contest."

"Surprised you've made it this far with that honorable notion. Let me tell you a secret about fighting."

Wolf knew enough. *What could this man teach me?*

"Don't fight fair. Never fight toe-to-toe. If you can kill a man while he sleeps, do it. It's easier. If ya can't do that, cheat, trick, deceive, and shoot 'em in the back if you can. Ain't no rules when it comes to a fight."

"It felt different. Shooting an unarmed man in the back." Wolf shook his head.

"But he died all the same."

"He did."

"Then what's the difference?"

Wolf wrapped his mind round and round shooting the rebel in the back. Branches scraped their greatcoats and took swipes at their caps. The trek back was much slower than the frenzied sprint into the forest.

"Dead's dead, boy. Does it matter how you get to be worm food?"

"I dunno."

"Don't think too much. War is simple."

"How so?"

"Kill them before they kill you. Ain't hard unless you start thinking. Thinking slows a man down. 'Member that one. A slow man is a dead man."

Gruff soldierly voices carried out from the road. Shapes of blue-clad men materialized as they neared the rear of the column. Loudly, Nelson said, "Wolverines coming up."

Guns were averted in a safe direction.

"What happened to the prisoners?" Wilhelm said.

"They died," Nelson responded.

Wilhelm watched Nelson for a moment then eyed Wolf. "Is this true?"

"Aye, they both died."

With wary eyes, Wilhelm stared at Wolf as if he knew the answer already and nodded all the same. "Corporal, go tell the colonel what's happened."

Wolf nodded, leading his horse down the side of the column. *This wasn't my fault*, he thought. But it had been. He'd fallen asleep, and when the rebels ran, he'd hunted them down and killed them for his negligence.

Angry with himself, he pushed Billy to a gallop. He passed sleeping soldiers and exhausted men. He met the slender colonel riding near the front and brought his horse alongside. The colonel leaned to his right as if he were trying to shift his weight to counterbalance to make up for his loss.

"Sir, I have a report from the rear."

"Carry on, Corporal."

"The prisoners escaped."

Dahlgren didn't turn his way or acknowledge their defect.

"All of them?"

"No, the ones in the wagons are still with us. We killed some on horseback, but others just disappeared in the night."

"You did well to hunt down those you could."

"Thank you, sir."

"They would only slow us down when it mattered the most. Our command isn't here to take prisoners." He turned, eyes scrutinizing Wolf. "Do you understand?"

Did he mean they'd be killing rebels instead of capturing them going forward? "Yes, I do, sir." They rode in silence for a moment, the orders settling in.

"We are done here, Corporal. You may return to your unit."

"Yes, sir."

Dahlgren stared forward again and Wolf promptly left his side, fearing the colonel would change his mind and make them all walk for their failures. Every time he blinked, he could see Captain Young's lifeless face, dead from a bullet in the back.

CHAPTER 15

Morning, March 1ˢᵗ, 1864
Goochland County, Virginia

The air smelled of fire.

A blanket of silver fog covered the rolling hills in the morning. Thick black smoke swirled together with the mist. The troopers' vision was obscured in the haze as the remains of flour mills, a factory, and small watercraft were eaten by the flames.

The rain had stopped, leaving Dahlgren's entire column wet, tired, and worn-out. Dahlgren had split off a company under Captain Mitchell, a well-liked officer in the 2ⁿᵈ New York. His hair hung almost to his shoulders, and he had a black beard. His stern eyes could discern your secrets, and he was easily distinguished by a saber scar that ran from the bottom of his cheekbone to his ear. He was known for bravery and calm under fire. His detachment went to burn and destroy anything that could aid the rebel war effort. The men disappeared into the mist.

The command traveled east beside the river road, guided by the former slave Martin who never left Dahlgren's side. They journeyed at a slow pace with low visibility until they came across the largest house that Wolf had ever seen.

The massiveness of the mansion dominated the area and he thought a mighty king must live there. The opulence was breathtaking, and the mist gave way before it as the morning sun ate at it from the sky.

"Would you look at that?" Wilhelm said.

"Bet they won't let us within ten feet of her," Adams said.

Roberts chimed in, "You think old Jeff Davis lives in there?"

The men continued to gawk at the extravagance. The mansion was all white with four monumental Corinthian-style columns in the front and behind that, a capacious porch. The building had been expanded at some point and more wings stuck out from the sides made up of newer, cleaner white-painted wood and brick.

"Some high-class ass in there," Nelson said.

"What man could possibly need such opulence?" Shugart added. "Devil's work."

"That a ballroom?" Roberts said, scratching behind an ear.

"Dunno." Wolf was stunned by the grandeur of the home. More wealth than he'd imagined was possible to have. He'd seen rich people and rich houses, but nothing like this. To him, it may as well have been Solomon's Temple or the Taj Mahal. "Whatya know?" He pointed to the far end of the mansion.

Slaves emerged from short stumpy cabins on the edge of the property cluttered in a village like setting. Rough homes that were not meant for more than sleeping with dirt floors and clay chimneys.

The slaves stared at the Federal soldiers. They wore dirty hats and raggedy tan and brown clothes. Most were barefoot despite the cold, raw weather. Some held hoes and shovels. They gaped with a mixed amount of suspicion and excitement. Until now, the Union army probably seemed like a myth to them, a faraway boogeyman melded with saviors, a vilified horde of ruffians and renegades that would be beaten back.

"You ever seen so many darkies?" Adams said.

"No, I haven't."

"I bet old Abe Lincoln would have a hard-on for so many in one place."

"Maybe."

The command stood on the edge of the property, gaping as if they'd come crashing into a whole new world and didn't know which way to proceed. The fear of the old world stayed their hand and kept them in place. With such grand wealth such as this came power and status.

In the distance, three great barns rested along with stables, a mill, a cookhouse, washhouse, smokehouses, and numerous sheds. They were the product of an almost self-sustaining agricultural unit.

Dahlgren pointed. Two companies of troopers continued down the road toward other towering mansions. Captain Yates's command stayed with the colonel.

Waving a hand, Dahlgren ordered, "Forward men." His horse lazily moved down the plantation lane.

The company followed suit, closing on the mansion. The lane stretched hundreds of yards from the river road magnifying the grandeur of the property. The slaves continued watching the troopers with wariness. No men from the house emerged to run them off. No overseer was present.

Captain Yates kept his men in ranks to the edges of a massive porch.

"There'll be some loot up in there," Adams said with a look at the house. "Some serious loot." He nudged Wolf. "Remember what we talked about. Take care of your future."

"I remember." He also remembered Wilhelm's rule of no women, no children. But Adams was right: if he didn't look out for himself who would.

A black-haired woman in a morning dress came outside without hurry. Her morning wrapper was exquisite. It was dark blue and patterned with red and orange flowers. Duel dark-blue buttons ran down the center with a blue weaved rope tying in the front. The collar revealed her pallid neck that made it obvious she'd never been inconvenienced by the sun.

She gave the men a welcoming smile beneath high cheekbones, inky eyes, and a slender face. Her skin reminded Wolf of a fresh snow, the opposite of what the men had been riding through.

"Gentle soldiers, I do say it is early to be calling."

"My lady, I apologize for our sudden appearance. We mean no harm."

She ran a hand down toward her hip. "Yes, you must forgive my attire. I'm only in my morning wrapper."

"You look most splendid, madam. May I take a rest? It's been a long ride."

"Why of course, Colonel?"

"Ulric Dahlgren, ma'am. At your service." He gave a tilt of his head.

The company of cavalry stood in formation, watching the Northern man and the Southern lady exchange pleasantries.

"You think he's gonna fuck her?" Adams asked under his breath.

"I'll do it if he won't," Nelson grumbled.

"Quiet, over there," Wilhelm hissed.

Dahlgren awkwardly climbed down from his saddle. For a man that looked so tall riding his mount, his dismount made the aristocratic-looking man appear frail and beaten. He removed a single crutch from his saddle and wedged it beneath his armpit.

"You poor man," she said. She went down the steps and wrapped an arm around his elbow, leading him toward the porch. "Did you say your name was Dahlgren?"

"It is, ma'am."

"My best friend in Philadelphia was married to a Dahlgren after we finished school. Mary Bunker."

A grin crossed his lips. "That's my mother. She still lives there."

She patted his elbow. "I remember her fondly. Always one for lemon cakes."

"She is fond of them."

She ushered him over to a rocker. "I'm sorry. I can't have you come in. You see, my daughter is deathly ill and I don't want you introduced to the sickness. Physicians say it's really bad." She nodded affirmatively. "The pox."

Roberts leaned over. "Older than she looks."

Wolf would have pegged her for her early thirties, but she must have been in her early if not late forties.

"I understand, my lady. Perhaps some wine to take the edge off the road?"

"Why, of course." She snapped her fingers and a slave disappeared back inside the house.

Gray smoke rose in the distance as the other troops went to work on the surrounding plantations. The wood fire smell hung in the air, stinging the nostrils, letting them know flames conducted their destructive work.

The matron eyed the blackening smoke in the distance. "I do say, Colonel, does your mother ever mention me?"

"I can't say I recall you coming up in our conversations, but I could say that for many folks."

"Of course, it has been a long time, but our friendship always felt like one that would stay forever."

"It does appear so. Such a splendid coincidence."

The slave returned with a platter of wine and tea. She set it down on a side table, splitting the colonel and the matron.

Dahlgren picked up a fine crystal glass and sipped his almost black wine in long gulps. "I will say this is some exceptional land you have here, madam."

"Some of the best in Goochland County."

He pointed out. "There, whose plantation is that?"

"That's Sabot Hill."

His tone darkened. "I didn't ask its name. I asked whose it was."

"I am sorry, Colonel." She quickly sipped her tea. "The Seddon family home."

"Seddon sounds familiar. Secretary of War for the Confederacy?"

"I cannot speak to his position. You know women don't trifle in such manly institutions. But he is a wealthy man."

"And there?" He pointed farther away at more pillars of smoke rising into the air.

"Eastwood, Colonel. Home of the Hobsons."

"Very well." He downed his wine and set the glass on the table. The slave woman was there quickly refilling it with blackish-red liquid. Dahlgren sighed. "This has been a refreshing stop. The saddle is a tiring place."

"I can only imagine, Colonel."

"But it will all be over soon."

She gulped and smiled reassuringly. "We can only hope."

Dahlgren drank more wine. "We can do more than hope, madam. We can ensure it." He took another sip of wine then used his fingers to wipe the corners of his mouth. He pointed at Yates and shouted. "Let's bring down the outbuildings!"

She set her tea down with a clank. "Gentle sir, please, this is our home. Our way of life."

"It doesn't please me to be the harbinger of defeat, but I am his messenger all the same." He gestured out at the grounds. "The sun is setting on the South."

"Please, it's all we have. You will drive us into destitution." She leaned closer to him, grasping at his arm.

"You do have your Southern hospitality. Excellent wine, by the way. Very superb. Virginia grapes?"

She shook her head. "Yes, but sir."

"No buts," he said to her. He gestured out. "Captain. Show the matron of this home some Northern hospitality."

Captain Yates turned in his saddle with a grin. "You heard the Colonel. Let's do our dastardly duty, you stinking Wolverines!"

The command went about their business with the efficiency of professional raiders.

"Come on, lads," Wilhelm said. He led his unit at a trot around the side of the plantation house. They rode past the slaves to one of the livestock barns.

"Empty it out."

Long sticks were found and torches were lit. The men put all the barns to flame. The fire spread quickly, engulfing everything in orange and yellow.

The stables were raided for fresh mounts. Adams brought a fine Kentucky stallion out.

"Good-looking horse there."

"For the Colonel."

The stables were put to the torch, and like tinderboxes, they ignited easily, the fire spreading almost as fast as the men could run clear of the inferno. Soon every structure on the property was alight with a fiery blaze except the mansion. Heat emanated from the fires, blackening the air like night despite the rising sun. The troopers reconvened back to the front.

Dahlgren still sat in his rocker drinking wine with the matron. She was disheveled now, and her eyes were reddened around the corners from pleading desperately.

The Union soldiers acquired more wagons from the property filled with flour from the mill, food, and supplies. A cask of bourbon had been found, and the men topped off canteens with the stuff. Swigs were taken by soot-covered horse soldiers feeling the burn of revenge down the backs of their throats.

Dahlgren stood unsteadily with his crutch. "Madam, this has been a most *pleasant* morning. Catching up with one of my mother's best friends is a small joy in the desolation of war." He bowed as deeply as he could on his crutch.

Her eyes narrowed. "How could you have done this? You've ruined my family."

"How many families have been ruined by this war? Be thankful I didn't hand your over to this lot."

Her mouth snapped closed. There were a few hoots and hollers from the troopers. Nelson laughed loud and Adams smiled. Wolf grinned too. To be feared was a powerful thing.

"It's places like this that have ensured the South stayed in the war. It is time that support evaporated." He waggled his fingers, imitating the dissipation of support. "Wait. That's not right. It's time the support went up in smoke." He turned away and crutched down the steps. Each step was the slow and calculated one of a man in pain. Yates jumped down and helped the colonel back into his saddle, ensuring he was strapped in.

"You men are monsters," the matron shouted.

"No, we're soldiers." Dahlgren turned to walk his horse down the path back to the river road.

She screamed behind them. "You're monsters. You'll burn for what you've done."

Dahlgren threw up a fist into the air drawing the men to a halt. Turning in a circle, he faced the woman. "No, this is the act of a monster." He waved Yates forward. "Burn the mansion."

"Sir? The sick girl."

"There's no sick girl. She was lying to give her husband time to escape."

"But, sir, we could have given chase."

"It would have been a wasted effort. No. The die is cast. We will sack Richmond. No effort they could scrounge together now will be worth a damn."

"Of course, Colonel."

Major Cooke trotted back toward them, joining them with his company.

"Any sign of Secretary Seddon?" Dahlgren asked.

"None, sir. Must be in Richmond," Cooke said.

"We'll bag the bastard that hung John Brown on the morrow. First, we must cross this river." He pointed out at the slaves. "You people are free, by the decree of President Lincoln. Head north."

The slaves stood silent. An old man with gray hair stepped forward, rubbing the bill of his hat. "But, suh, they'll catch us before we reach your lines. They'll hunt us with dogs. We seen it done."

"They will not. Go north, or east to Fort Monroe. I don't care which. You are no longer property of these people."

"Yes, suh." The slaves stood back from the horsemen, fear in their eyes. They were free in name only. They knew their fate if they were caught fleeing the countryside. They knew what it looked like. A burnt-down plantation and slaves on the run was a revolt regardless of how it happened. Revolts brought swift and brutal responses. Naked bodies swinging from trees, beaten and shot, mutilated and hung, sometimes set alight while they still were aware enough that the real torture had begun.

"Why are you still standing here?" Dahlgren shouted.

The slaves stepped back. Dahlgren pointed north. "Go!" He whipped his horse around back toward the road. He turned back to Yates and lifted his chin. "Burn the house."

Wolf found himself following a handful of men. Adams handed him a torch. Nelson marched up the steps and grabbed the woman by her hands. He picked her up like a sack of potatoes and threw her over his shoulder, carrying her down into the yard. She beat him with her tiny fists. He set her down with a smile. Her slave raced to her side, trying to comfort her.

Wolf and the others jogged over the steps. With his torch, Adams smashed a window and tossed it inside. A luxurious rectangle rosewood piano rested near a corner. It had carved curling legs and an ornate grilled music rack which depicted the "STIEFF" name in the woodwork. Plants on tile floors and exquisite rugs decorated the lavish room. The crash of more glass shattered the air and the flames roared inside the home.

"Hurry, Wolfie," Adams said with a smile. "You want to get caught in the flames?"

Wolf walked to a far window. He took out his pistol and smashed it into the glass. Shards clattered, sliding along the floor. The matron cried in the yard, moaning in desperation.

Taking his torch, he aimed for a stack of linen. Wolf tossed it on top. The linens caught fire quickly, flames running upward along the wall to the ceiling.

The men made for the safety of the front yard. Mounting their horses, they watched their handiwork go up in smoke.

"Good lad, ain't it grand?" Adams said.

Wolf couldn't help but marvel in the destructive beauty of the flames. Adams handed him a canteen. The bourbon was sweet on his tongue and burned like fire in his belly.

Yellowish-orange tongues of fire lapped the house, thirsty for more to consume. The fiery ballet continued for some time until the mansion was a charred outline of what it once was, and the cries of the matron had faded to whimpers. They kicked their horses, leaving her to her misery.

CHAPTER 16

Morning, March 1ˢᵗ, 1864
Goochland County, Virginia

Two miles down the river road from the plantations, the command was called to a halt. A troop of cavalrymen near the front of the column veered to the left and disappeared through the trees. Yates's company filed forward to take their place.

"Would you look at that?" Dahlgren said with a chuckle. Roughly twenty ramshackle horsemen stood in their path. Civilians by the looks of them. A random smattering of brown and gray coats, shotguns and muzzle-loaders, all manner of horses. One man even rode a tan pony.

"A good charge will send them running, sir," Captain Yates said.

"I'd rather wipe them clean from the earth. Major Cooke will hem them in, and we only need give him a moment to get into place."

"They have to know they are about to be routed," Dahlgren said in fascination.

"Mere farmers," Nelson grunted.

"Couldn't fight so they stayed home. Easy pickings," Adams said.

Wilhelm's mustache twitched. "Men with guns are dangerous."

Nelson's lips flattened. "Bah! Ya old yellow dog."

The sergeant ignored his grumblings.

"I'm with Nelson. It's been awhile since we had a proper fight," Wolf said. He felt much more in place dealing with an enemy in front of him instead of the secrecy of a raid.

"That a boy, Wolfie. Little blood lust in ya," Adams said.

Prompted by the support of his squad, Wolf urged Billy next to Yates.

"Captain," Wolf said.

The reddish-haired captain glanced at him. "Requesting to run the rebels into the ground." The impending fight butterflied his gut, but it wasn't like his first fight. It was more excitement than fear. Dread always lurked in the shadows, but the thrill of a deadly scrap outweighed it.

A smile crawled on Yates's face. "You boys are a bit ornery today, ain't ya?"

Wolf grinned. "Just want to show them resistance is futile. Too much raiding. We want a fight."

Yates barked a laugh. "Not sure these fellows will offer much." He faced the colonel. "Can my boys run them off?"

Dahlgren shooed them with a gloved hand. "Be my guest."

Yates waved his company forward. "All right, Wolf. Do your work."

Wilhelm brought the men in two tight lines of five troopers each. Wolf fell along the right flank of the squad. The more senior non-coms would flank the squad to keep the horses paced well and to keep order, and if there was a flanking attack, they could wheel the squad in response, keeping the more novice riders in a proper line.

The rebels saw them forming. A few of their horses turned around in circles. Fear oozed forth from them like a flock of sheep smelling a nearby wolf. The realization that they were about to be charged crashed around them. Heads swiveled, frantically peering for an escape route.

An entire unit of Federal cavalry was about to punch through them like piss through snow. Heads twisted, looking for a way to escape. One of their number discharged his musket in a puff of smoke, the bullet falling somewhere in the muddy road ahead of them. *Harmless.*

"Untrained dogs," Nelson said.

Wilhelm sat erect in his saddle. He was a professional soldier, disciplined and conducting his duty with precision. His voice called out beneath his mustache. "Men. Draw sabers."

Wolf reached for his saber and released it from its sheath. The sword freed with an audible *shashing*. The troopers around him did the same and metal scraped on scabbard.

"Carry - Sabers," Wilhelm called. "No point in burning out before it's time to do the devil's work."

Wolf rested his saber on the hollow of his right shoulder.

"Trot march!" Wilhelm shouted.

Their horses moved to a quick trot. Men bounced in the saddle, using their legs to absorb the animal's gait. The squad kept together like a tightly packed ball of flesh and pointed steel.

The rebels let off another hurried volley. Smoke shrouded them, but their rounds again fell short. A few whizzed high above the men before sailing harmlessly in the wilderness. As they reloaded, Wilhelm turned his men up another notch in an attempt to catch them before they could reload. "March gallop," he shouted.

The distance between the two forces closed even quicker. Wolf could see their faces now. Teenage boys, white beards, not a piece of professional gear on them. No soldiers, just what war left behind.

"Charge!" Wilhelm shouted.

"Ja!" Wolf called out. The men around him sounded off in a hearty cheer to steady themselves before the slaughter. Their formation was tight in order to maximize the shock of impact. He raised his saber high in the air and then brought it level with his shoulder. It was a three-foot violent steel extension of his arm. The rank behind him held their sabers higher in the air with the tips slightly to the rear. Hooves dug deep, throwing mud as they rushed the rebels.

The rebels had seen enough. They started to turn and ride, but their escape was disorganized and fear-driven, leading to a jumble of riders. Only a few men, either the stupid or brave to a fault, didn't pivot their horses until it was too late.

The unit cut them to pieces on the way by. The gray-bearded man across from Wolf closed his eyes just before impact. Arching his blade over Billy, Wolf penetrated his opponent's breast. The saber sunk deep into his chest, piercing jacket, shirt, and flesh like his chest was a giant pincushion. The old man let out a gasp and then a whimper.

Violently, Wolf shoved him from his horse, keeping a grip on his hilt. The man's body begrudgingly relinquished the blade. He felt alive, and the excitement of battle surged through him like he was a wild man pitted in the most primal of conflicts. He yanked the reins, turning Billy toward the retreating rebs.

A spattering of gunfire came from individual riders as they retreated. A young boy sat in his saddle less than thirty yards from Wolf, aiming his shotgun that was almost too big for him.

The gun boomed, but nothing happened. The shot could have gone anywhere. Into a nearby tree, the ground, overhead, but Wolf knew one thing, it hadn't come close to him. He drove his heels into Billy's sides.

The boy turned to flee, but his piebald mount was old and swaybacked and had no business being asked to perform. Wolf rode him down, gaining several feet with each stride. The freckle-cheeked lad looked back as Wolf slashed into his neck, cleaving a gaping wound into his underdeveloped muscle. The words that Hampton spoke to him outside of Gettysburg echoed in his mind. "This is war, boy. Men die. Boys die easier." And he knew Hampton was right.

Moments later, Cooke's troopers charged into the flanks of the retreating rabble, cutting the rest down. It was over quick and not a man escaped. The domestic warriors were slaughtered, and their mounts gathered for the command.

The young man struggled to breathe, trying to crawl away. His mount stood nearby, head low. The boy coughed blood as he stared, dilated eyes blaming Wolf for his early demise. Wolf stared back, observing the results of his handiwork.

"Mama," the boy whispered. He choked on his own blood as he fought to stay alive.

Wolf rested his saber on his shoulder, watching the young man pass to the next world. The whole thing didn't feel right. At the root, it felt wasteful. *Where were the real rebels? Where were the knights of the South? Stuart and his giant, Hampton? Where were they when the North ravaged their capital?* The ones that were unstoppable and formidable. The men they'd fought at Gettysburg. This wasn't war. This was outright slaughter. These men never stood a chance, yet they planted themselves right in the path of enemy cavalry with some godforsaken idea that they'd slow them down.

The boy expired with his mouth and eyes open, his teeth stained red with his own blood like he'd died with a mouthful of berries. Wolf guided Billy back to reform with the column. Men from Cooke's command and Wilhelm's unit trotted their horses back to the advancing command. He linked with Adams.

"Fine saber work, Wolfie," Adams said. He sheathed his sword. Nelson gave Wolf a mean grin, cleaning a knife off on a fallen rebel.

"Weren't much of fighters," Wolf said.

"They just die faster than fighters, but they still die," Nelson said.

"My large friend has a point. Boys and old men die like the rest."

"One was no more than a boy. Makes me pity them."

"Should have stayed home then," Nelson said.

"Working the land was their way of life. They should have stuck to that. Ours is war," Adams said.

Gripping his scabbard, Wolf sheathed his saber. "Aye, it is."

Wilhelm trotted joining them. "Reform on the colonel, boys." He glanced at Wolf. His eyes searched him for something. He blinked concern away.

They reformed in ranks of four troopers. Yates's command took their position as the lead company along with Dahlgren and their guide, Martin.

Dahlgren pointed ahead. "We've been north of the James for too long. Take us to a ford."

"Yes, Colonel," Martin said.

"Forward to victory!" Dahlgren shouted. They kicked their animals with their heels and trotted closer to Richmond.

CHAPTER 17

General Judson Kilpatrick's main body of cavalrymen penetrated the outer defenses of Richmond like water through lace. The intelligence was summing up nicely, playing out exactly as he had surmised. A weak line of pickets and skirmishers had been swept away like an irritating fly. The only disconcerting event so far was the silence from Major Hall's column, but long distances in enemy territory made communication difficult and his orders were clear. Arrive today, March 1ˢᵗ, and strike a feinting movement to spread their meager forces like a pinch of butter over rough bread.

He was precise in his timing of the assault, to the minute. He checked his pocket watch, eyeing the face and scrutinizing the road ahead. 9:36. He'd told his men they'd reach Richmond by 10 o'clock, and by God, he would do it. He scanned the trees surrounding the thoroughfare, wondering about Colonel Dahlgren and his column flanking the rebels to the south as planned.

Cannon fire barked from the front of the column, and he waved a portly captain to join him in his jaunt forward. The man accompanied him with little hesitation, and they passed rank after rank of almost a third of his three thousand troopers.

They emerged from the trees, and the earthen fortifications of Richmond sprawled before them over a mile away. It wasn't a continuous line of defense but was split to allow roadways, like arteries, to access the heart of the

Confederacy. A tiny blackened cannon in a cutout of the immense mound boomed.

"Spirited clerks and boys, aren't they?"

Cannonballs sailed through the air, harmlessly crashing into the earth hundreds of yards away.

Captain Gloskoski grinned beneath his mustache. "Bunch of quartermaster hunters." His grin faded with the realization that the term implied men in his current position at the rear of the line. "A few guns. Once we're close, they'll run off."

"We'll be the fox in the hen house for sure," Kilpatrick said. He smiled at the terror that must be building in Richmond at this very moment. The Confederate artillery continued to boom away. The head of the column had stalled on the road, having taken causalities. It's all part of the game.

"Major, send Captain Ransom's battery up to support."

He rubbed his long nose before he waved over a portly captain with a mustache nearby. "Captain Gloskoski, send up some rockets. I want Dahlgren to know we are almost ready to begin our coordinated assault."

"With pleasure, sir." The rotund captain retreated to his wagon to prepare the signal rockets. It was the only way for the commands to successfully communicate in a timely manner, otherwise they would be forced to send messengers far and wide throughout their adversary's territory.

Kilpatrick eyeballed a bleak gray sky then looked back at his signal officer, questioning all its effectiveness. He dismissed all worry. Regardless, the enemy capital would fall.

His subordinate general cantered his way. General Davies had a mustache that curled down the sides of his mouth. His far-set worried eyes appeared even more concerned because of a crease in his brow. He'd always been a loyal man and their careers had risen together. He gave Kilpatrick a quick salute.

"Sir, my men are taking heavy fire from the fortifications."

"I've seen."

"What are your orders?"

"Your orders are to wait."

"Of course, sir."

"We have to wait until Colonel Dahlgren is in place. Then we will launch a full-scale assault on the fortifications." He envisioned his men galloping over the field and then making quick work of the rebel forces as they retreated. The next telegraph to Meade would be a message of victory. The next communiqué after that would be to Pleasonton, ensuring he knew to pay his better's debt.

"Sir, I've dismounted ranks of skirmishers to drive off any rebels in the field. I've also sent a company to scout for any gaps in the defense. Perhaps we can take them even easier."

"Very fine work, General."

"Thank you, sir."

"Continue your scouting while we wait for our forces to consolidate."

Davies saluted and galloped away. Kilpatrick popped the top of his watch, eyes calculating. "10:22," he said aloud. "Everything is going according to plan."

***

An hour and thirty minutes passed before Gloskoski fired off his signal rockets. The man had taken extreme precaution in setting up his contraption.

A lengthy wooden frame, almost as tall as a man, along with six rockets spaced at intervals which he measured by hand. Each rocket stood atop the end of a long slender stick, a cylinder tube filled with gunpowder capping the ends.

"Captain, what is taking so long?"

Gloskoski was covered in mud and grime from crawling over the ground. He twisted a long fuse between the last two rockets, letting it sag almost to the wet ground. "My apologies, sir. There is a very precise prearranged sequence that I have worked out with Lieutenant Bartley of Dahlgren's command. If the rockets do not signal correctly, he will think the message is different or a ruse put on by wily Confederates."

Kilpatrick lifted his head sucking in air. "I am not worried about those things. Dahlgren must know that we have to strike today and now. We must maintain our initiative."

Standing back from his work, Gloskoski scrutinized his work. "All is well. It is ready, but I must say, the cloud cover has a very low ceiling. It may interfere with our signal."

Fire spit from Kilpatrick's mouth. "You listen here, you Polish imbecile. We've let the rebels take aim at us for over an hour while you set up your precious rockets. Now you're saying they might not work?"

"Well, sir, they don't work well in wooded areas or in bad weather. And all we've had is rain and snow of late." Gloskoski scratched at his temple beneath his kepi.

Kilpatrick steered his horse toward the man, walking it within feet of his subordinate. Gloskoski nervously sidestepped out of the beast's way. "You fire those damn rockets, or you can go find Dahlgren by yourself."

"Of course, sir. I understand the urgency of the situation." The signal officer gulped.

Leaning off his saddle, Kilpatrick jabbed a finger at the captain. "Do you?"

The man nodded, retreating toward his contraption. The rebel cannon continued to fire away but only enough to make a broad display. A seasoned ear knew that it wasn't enough to actually deter an assault of any magnitude.

In disgust, Kilpatrick glared as the man scratched match after match, trying to get a light. After a few tense minutes, one of his assistants returned with hands cupped around a burning ember. Gloskoski thanked him by snatching the glowing branch. He lit the rocket on the left end, each rocket attached to the others by cords. Holding the ember close, the fuse sparked to life with a crackling hiss.

The flame ate away at the fuse until it reached the underside of the first rocket's cylinder. With a loud swoosh, the projectile took flight. It traveled skyward, gaining altitude until it disappeared through the cloud cover. An audible pop could be heard, but the signal couldn't be seen.

Kilpatrick glared at Gloskoski.

"The others may have success. Lieutenant Bartley knows the sequence."

The next rocket took flight. Each man watched it ascend and disappear into the opaque sky. With every flight of a new rocket, anger built in Kilpatrick's chest. This imbecile was impeding his hard-fought glory.

The last rocket launched into the air, disappearing without even a whimpering pop. Kilpatrick raised an eyebrow at Gloskoski.

"Must have been a faulty one, sir."

"Must have been a *faulty one*? At this point, I have to pray that one of those sailed high enough in the air to perhaps hit the colonel so he knows that we are in fact in position."

Averting making eye contact with him, Gloskoski instead gaped at the frame. "I could set up more rockets."

Kilpatrick shook his head. "No, no. There'll be no need for that."

Gloskoski's shoulders slumped in defeat. Suddenly, his eyes lit up with an idea. "Perhaps he's heard the cannon and knows the time is now?"

Kilpatrick wavered his head back and forth. "Perhaps, but I need to be sure. You may go."

His signal officer sighed. "Frasier." He waved a private closer. "Sorry, boy, but the matter is urgent."

The man is dimmer than I thought. Kilpatrick shook his head. "Captain."

Gloskoski blinked at him.

"You will go, not him."

"Sir, I am of much greater service to you here and now rather than acting as a mere messenger."

"Are you?" He stepped his horse alongside the captain. "You are my lead signal officer. I am asking you to signal Colonel Dahlgren by way of mouth. Am I understood?"

"But, sir. Surely other men are better suited to the task."

Kilpatrick close-lipped smiled at the man. "Surely, there are not. Move swiftly, my good captain."

Gloskoski gulped. "Frasier, get my horse."

"They'll be south of the James River about four miles to the west." Kilpatrick pointed.

The captain struggled to find a hold in the stirrup for much too long. After a moment, he finished his ungraceful mounting, his horse tossing her head in complaint. Finally seated in the saddle, the signal officer stared worriedly at the trees. "Sir, where shall I cross?"

"We are depending on you." Kilpatrick ignored the mewing of the lamb. If the man wanted to be a signal officer then he bloody well would do it.

Gloskoski's eyes darted from side to side. "Of course, sir."

"Make haste. I want this city by the morning."

The captain spurred his horse, holding his hat atop his head, riding into enemy territory. Kilpatrick monitored the man's fading blue back as he galloped down the road, disappearing into the plain gray timber.

"He'll be lucky not to get shot," said Davies. He'd come along on the interaction unnoticed.

"He won't be shot. That man will be captured." He faced his general. "Report, sir, from the skirmishers."

Davies sucked in some air through his mouth. "My scouting company has found a gap in the fortifications. They've slipped through and await orders."

Sneaking through the earthworks was the last thing on Kilpatrick's mind. "I would prefer not to sneak into the city. Doesn't sound very thrilling, does it?"

"Yes, sir. About that." Davies pointed, his hand covering the land between where they stood and the ring of fortifications. "The ground between here and the defenses is a bog. Pure mud. I've got my dismounted men over it, but atop a horse, it will never work. Patton's men have been thrown back with heavy resistance."

"Heavy resistance? Tell Patton to try them again. And may God damn this weather. Everything kicked off to such a grand start, and now it seems that every idiot and every obstacle are showing their faces today. "He glowered, studying the field. "Not you, of course."

"Never thought you meant me in that sad mix, sir."

Kilpatrick eyed him. Ransom's battery unleashed on the fortifications.

"I suppose surprise is out the window on this one. Tell your men to stay in place. Our action still hinges on the young Colonel Dahlgren."

"Of course, sir. A wise move to keep them in place."

"I will have this city."

"Of course, sir."

"I will liberate our men."

"Of course, sir."

Kilpatrick became more comfortable knowing he had his men's support. The bells of Richmond tolled across the city, ringing with fierce determination.

CHAPTER 18

Afternoon, March 1st, 1864
Goochland County, Virginia

The constant barrage of rain over the past few days had swollen the James River like the carcass of a waterlogged cow almost bloated enough to explode over the lands with a flood. Dahlgren's command sat on the river's edge staring out at the other side.

The plan had been for Dahlgren to lead an attack against Richmond from the south. In order to do this, they needed to cross the James River, an action that should have already taken place.

The tired and irritated troopers were ready to finish their mission. Wolf felt it in his belly too, a sense of excited irritation like they were close to victory if only they could find it.

"This is not a ford," Dahlgren said.

Martin shook his head. "It's a ford."

Dahlgren walked his horse closer to the edge. What had once been dry land was now smaller trees jutting out of brown waters. His mount stepped carefully on the muddy banks. The current swirled and twisted, rushing to reach Chesapeake Bay as fast as possible. He gestured with a white-gloved hand. "That is not a ford we can cross." He was right. The water was much too deep and flowed much too quickly to cross on horseback. They would need multiple boats to reach the other side safely.

Having seen enough, Dahlgren tugged the reins back to the head of the column. "Martin, you said you knew this area."

The colored boy stammered. "I do, Colonel, but I never saw the James higher 'dan now." He turned, looking in one direction then the other, attempting to gather his bearing. "Tryin' to 'member."

"Boy's got us lost," Nelson said, spitting on the ground in disgust.

Adams sighed. "His days are numbered then. The good colonel won't put up with this for long."

"Quiet back there," Yates yelled at them. He kicked his mount forward within reach of the commander and guide.

"Martin, lad. There has to be another way," Yates said. "Another way across?"

"There is. There is." He licked his lips. "'Bout three miles further east. I'll stake my life on it."

Captain Yates smiled with a glance at Dahlgren. "See sir? The boy is sure of himself."

Dahlgren's steed nipped at the guide's mount. "This entire assault is resting on your shoulders, boy. You take us where we need to be, or I'll put you in the ground. Am I clear?"

"Yes, Colonel," Martin said hurriedly.

The command continued to walk east down the riverside road. They burned a sawmill and an ironworks factory along the large tributary. The high waters due to flooding thwarted their efforts at complete destruction, but after a satisfactory torching, only the stone foundation remained, blackened from the flames.

Thick clouds were heaped like piles of gray snow in the sky. Thunder carried through the air and eyes lifted upward in worry.

"Storm coming?" Roberts asked. He peered at the clouds like a rat who'd been drowned one too many times.

"Nonsense, boy, it don't thunderstorm in the winter," Shugart said.

The low rumble cracked in the distance, the sound of stones dropping on one another.

Roberts appeared miserable. "Sure as heck sounds like it."

"Ain't thunder," Nelson said, staring.

"That's cannon," Wilhelm said, straining to obtain a better view ahead.

They weren't the only ones to hear it. Dahlgren and Cooke exchanged a glance. Martin heard it too, and he slumped even lower in his saddle.

In anger, Dahlgren shook his head. "Kilpatrick is attacking. Goddamn it." He waved the guide forward from Yates's side.

"You hear that?"

Martin's shoulders hunched in further defeat as if he were trying to disappear. "I do, Colonel. Sounds fierce, sir."

"Fierce? That's the attack. Our attack." He pointed to the other side of the James River. "We're supposed to be over there. The fate of the Union rides on this. The fate of those imprisoned men rides on this. Does this mean nothing to you?" He grabbed Martin's shirt and the man cried out. Spit flew from his mouth as he yelled, "The fate of your people ride on this very mission."

Martin blinked as if every word were a slap to his face. Quiet words came from shaky lips. "Only another mile, sir."

Dahlgren snarled, releasing the boy. "All I need is my men to be tired before we begin the attack." He exhaled sharply. "Doesn't matter now. Forward at a trot, men."

The five companies of selected troopers trotted down the riverside road. The waters continued to gush in angry swells beside them, and the cannon fire grew louder, going from a low rumble to audible booms. Rockets screeched through the air with fiery tails only to disappear into the cloud cover.

"Those are Kilpatrick's signal rockets," Wolf said.

Roberts scratched at his head nervously. "Which means we're missing out."

The horses chewed the ground with greedy hooves until they reached a clearing. The command of halt filtered down the column.

A weathered signpost hung nailed to a tree, its rusty nails bleeding corrosion on the wood. In white faded letters it read Manakin Ferry, except there was no ferry and no way to cross. The waters here were the same as the ford, impassable.

"River be more swollen than a sow," Gratz said.

"It's all God's work," Shugart said.

"Send him a prayer and ask him to stop. Tired of being wet," Wolf said.

Adams chuckled. "And ask for some ham and cheese." He nudged Nelson. "What do you want big fella?"

"For everyone to shut the fuck up."

Adams's face contorted in a playful sneer. "Such a mean one."

The men quieted down and stood in formation awaiting orders. It was well into the afternoon, and weariness yoked them from the hard ride. The sun was only a brighter gray dot through the clouds. The manmade storm raged over the northern part of Richmond.

Dahlgren brought his horse along Martin's. "*This* is the ferry we're looking for?"

"Yes, Colonel." Martin's eyes danced, peering every which way to avoid Dahlgren's at all costs.

"How the hell am I supposed to transport my men across?" He pointed at Cooke. "See if someone can cross it."

"You. Try and ford the river."

A trooper from Yates's command walked his bay cautiously forward. He was one of the boys on loan from the 7th Michigan, a clean-shaven young man that went by the name Ollie from Kalamazoo.

He urged the bay into the water. The mare was skittish at first, stepping with reservation. Each hoof splashed down with hesitation. "Come on now," Ollie said, squeezing his mount with his legs. The horse ventured farther into the freezing water lapping around its legs. "Get moving. Come on," Ollie said gruffly.

The chocolaty waters surged to the horse's belly and with another step soaked the trooper's boots. He drove the animal farther in, and the water came dangerously up to the horse's neck. The horse could swim with the rider, but the fast-moving waters were dangerous.

"Come back, Ollie," Yates called over.

"Keep going, Private," Dahlgren threw back. "See if you can make it."

Yates gave the colonel an angry glare. "Sir, the water's too deep. He'll be swept away."

"He'll make it," Dahlgren said. A moment later Ollie's voice pierced the air. His mare, suddenly overwhelmed, dumped the rider into the frigid water. The trooper splashed, disappearing for an instant before emitting a short cry until he went under the water. His head bobbed back out, arms flailing. His greatcoat stuck to his skin, the wet wool weighing him down. "Help!"

Troopers dismounted with ropes. They ran to the edge of the river and tossed the rope in, but the man disappeared forced downstream by the rapid waters. Both man and horse sank below the brown surface.

"Christ!" Yates cursed. He scanned the river in apprehension, watching for the man to reappear somewhere.

Dahlgren rounded on Martin. "His death is on your head."

Martin stared at the ground in practiced subservience. "Yes, sir."

Hogan, still dressed in a gray coat like a rebel, maneuvered his horse back to the colonel. "Sir, perhaps we should abandon the idea of crossing? The river doesn't appear to be letting up. We may still reach Kilpatrick for support."

Dahlgren sighed, shaking his head. "You're right. We aren't any closer to fulfilling our part of the mission." He stared down the path, and without looking at the guide said, "Can you take us to Richmond?"

"Yes, Colonel." Martin's eyes lit up and he pointed down a split road running away from the riverbanks. "It's this way."

"Forward at a trot." The column rode for less than thirty minutes along plantation fields, passing brown dirt awaiting the end of the frost and the introduction of tobacco seeds into its bosom. Martin led them left at a fork in the road and the command followed.

The barren cleared lands of the plantation disappeared and were overtaken by thicker timber, birch, tulip poplar, and sycamore tall enough for a substantial undergrowth to finger upward from beneath their towering brethren. Dahlgren called them to a halt with a tight fist held high in the air near a gnarled ancient sycamore.

Limbs snaked from the tree. Its bark chipped and peeled from its trunk, revealing white. Even in age, every branch maintained its sturdy strength.

"You think this is a game?" Dahlgren shouted at Martin. "Men's lives are at stake, and you take us in the wrong direction." He shook his head with a nasty sneer, edging his horse closer to the terrified man. "Are you a spy for Jeff Davis?"

"No, sir. Please. I ain't no spy. I worked for Van Lew, a loyal Union woman."

"He's a worthless colored traitor," Major Cooke said. He massaged his drooping mustache repeatedly.

"He ain't no traitor. I never would have made it north without him," Yates said.

Cooke spun on him. "And how do we know you haven't gone soft on us either?"

"You calling me a *coward*?" Yates's chin lifted higher, and he licked his lips. "Nobody calls me a coward."

"Your boy here has led us astray time and time again, and we are no closer than when we moved out this morning. He's gone *foul*."

Yates's shook his head, spitting out words. "He ain't foul. He made a mistake."

Dahlgren eyed his men, watching the exchange and skillfully guided his mount alongside Yates. "You aren't in charge here, Captain." The two men eyed one another like dogs preparing to fight. "I want this man hanging from the end of a rope."

The men sat on their horses staring at one another. They'd been issued the command to execute a noncombatant. Wolf scratched at his beard nervously and glanced at Wilhelm trying to gauge his perception of the altercation.

The sergeant studied the officers just as intently, his face expressionless.

Dahlgren's eyes enlarged, his mouth forming a resolute snarl. "End of a rope, or you'll be shot for insubordination." His hand drifted to his holster and the tension between their leaders increased.

"No, Colonel. I didn't do you wrong. Please," Martin pled.

Without removing his eyes from Yates, Dahlgren said, "You had your chance to save your skin. Now you'll receive justice."

Yates shook his head no. "This is an honest man."

"Even if he is honest, he has done his country an incredible disservice. Major," Dahlgren's hand rested on his revolver.

Cooke gestured at the nearest troopers. "You heard the colonel. String this boy up."

"Do not follow that order," Yates said over his shoulder.

The tension built between the commanders and the enlisted men caught in the middle.

Cooke pushed closer to Yates. His mustache shook as he spoke. "How dare you delay my orders." He pointed at the troopers. "Hang the Negro."

Men ushered their horses toward Martin. "Stop!" With a sleight of hand, Yates drew his pistol. "Don't you lay a hand on him or you'll be shot." He twisted in his saddle, pointing his weapon at one man and then another.

Flames flared in Dahlgren's eyes. Cooke's mouth puckered like he'd eaten a hundred sour grapes. Most of the soldiers gawked as their captain, just a few feet from them, turned the cold metal barrel of his gun waiting to speak fire toward his superior.

"I want to kill Jeff Davis as much as the next man but murdering this Negro ain't going to get us any closer to Richmond. We turn this column around, and we can reach Kilpatrick by evening."

Hogan held both hands in the air. "I think the captain is right. Myself and Magee can find a way."

"Both of you shut up," Dahlgren said. He edged his horse near Yates, growling, "You'll put that gun away, you insubordinate prick. That's an order from your commanding officer."

Yates reached out and grabbed Dahlgren's greatcoat, scrunching it between his fingers. "Not while his life is at stake."

Guns scraped along leather as they were drawn from holsters.

Dahlgren resisted him, pulling himself upright in his saddle. "You take your hands off me or you'll hang next to him."

Begrudgingly releasing the colonel, the fiery captain turned to look. Some men merely held their weapons while others followed the colonel's orders. Wolf found himself holding his pistol loosely in his hand, unsure of what was about to happen. *Who would you defend if it came down to shots? Your commanding officer? Or the man that was right?*

Enough troopers followed Dahlgren's orders for Yates to know his defiance had come to an end. He flipped his pistol around and handed it to Cooke. The major snatched the weapon, and the captain placed his hands above his head.

"You are relieved of duty until we can give you a formal court-martial."

"Pleasure to be removed from this command," Yates said, hands in the air.

Cooke gestured at his troopers. "You men fall under my direct orders now. String that boy up or join your captain in chains." He leveled a finger at Wolf's men. "Do your duty."

Wolf blinked and gulped. He didn't want to be a part of this. Killing the man for making a mistake was harsh and a reality he didn't want to live with. What if that was him on the failing end? What if they threw him into a stinking disease-ridden prison like they were going to do to Yates?

Adams and Nelson kicked their horses out of rank.

"Come on, lads. Not all work is fun," Adams said, dismounting.

Wolf urged his mount after them.

"Please, no." Martin looked at them with wide-eyed fear.

Like a straw man, Nelson manhandled him from his saddle. The boy squirmed in his powerful arms.

"Easy, boy, and I'll make it quick."

Slowly Wolf dismounted Billy and hobbled toward the other two men. Adams took a spare halter from his saddlebag. It was horse headgear used to lead or tie up the animal and fit over its ears and around the muzzle. He placed it over Martin's head like he was a beast of burden.

A rope was procured, and Nelson handed Adams the end to be looped through the leather. After knotting the rope, Adams led Martin beneath the ancient sycamore and tossed the rope around a branch.

"Should do, huh, Colonel?" Adams asked. He tugged on the line, testing its strength.

Dahlgren shooed him away. "That's fine. You just get this traitor dangling."

"Be dead soon enough," Nelson chimed in. He nudged Martin with a large paw. The young man's body lurched as he tried to steady himself through panicked tears.

"You're making a mistake, Colonel," Yates said. His cheeks were red with anger, but his voice was calm and steady as if he were asking for drink of water, not a friend's life.

"You'll close your mouth unless you want to hang next to him."

"Court-martial me if you must, but let this boy go."

"Another word and you'll hang for treason. Try me, Captain, I dare you."

Yates dipped his head, his jaw clenching.

The Union horsemen drifted closer. Troopers pushed their way in around the tree for a better view. There was no love for their guide. His errant escort had gotten Ollie killed only hours before. The sight of the leather around his neck brought forth pent-up frustration and hate.

Wolf stood to the side, staring at the command that resembled more of a mob. The other two men worked. They needed no direction; they were experienced killers. Wolf oversaw them, an equally culpable party. Curses flew his way.

"Black devil!"

"Stupid boy!"

The troopers drew in tighter like an angry pack of dogs, jeering at the guide with loud voices. Martin had been the means of their failure. He'd been why they'd missed the deadline. Their voices rose into a death chant. How dare this Negro deceive them when they were bleeding and dying for his freedom? They spit toward Martin, and he cried beneath the weight of their hate.

Martin's eyes pled for someone to intervene, tears rolling down his cheeks in droves. Snot dribbled from his nose, running off the tip of his chin. "I didn't mean it, Colonel. Please. I didn't mean it."

Ensuring that the makeshift noose was tight around Martin's neck, Adams handed it off to Nelson. He drew the rope taut and faced Dahlgren for the order of execution. The troopers all watched their commander, awaiting his condemnation of the guide.

Dahlgren's eyes held a haughty fire. He was to be responsible for assassinating Jefferson Davis, president of the Confederacy. Woe to any man that stood in his way.

Martin wiped his eyes. "Please. I'm good. I'm loyal."

Tension, as heavy as a wet blanket, weighted the air around them. A bird called in the distance. A squirrel jumped in the timber. Dahlgren's chin lifted in the air. Every man held his breath. The colonel gave a curt nod, short and concise like a Roman emperor deciding the fate of a defeated gladiator.

Nothing more was needed. Heaving, Nelson threw all his weight upon the rope.

Martin's feet lifted off the ground. He dangled only a few inches away from solid earth. His feet kicked, toes searching for flat ground to stop his suffocation. He choked, his hands grasping the strap around his neck. Adams jumped up higher on the rope, yanking him farther away from the earth and sweet relief.

Wolf fell in along behind him, watching Martin's struggle for life. Gurgles escaped Martin's mouth, his fingers grasping at his neck. His nails dug into his flesh trying to stop the halter from cutting off his air supply.

The troopers cheered as he paid the ultimate sacrifice, releasing their pent-up frustration and rage. Yates watched his friend attempting to stay alive, unblinking, a frown on his lips.

"Corporal, I want him higher," Dahlgren said and he flicked his wrist at Wolf. "Now!"

The rough rope found its way into Wolf's hands. It felt wrong and callous, and his will to contribute to this man's death evaporated.

"Come on, Wolfie. Get him higher," Adams said over his shoulder with a smirk. "Let the traitor have it."

Wolf stared at the rope in his hands like a venomous snake. Nelson snarled, straining to hoist Martin even higher. Belligerent hands fell upon him.

A trooper shoved him to the ground and took his place in the execution line. "Yellow-bellied, coffee cooler," the black-and-gray-goateed soldier spat. Wolf lay there for a moment watching. Another trooper joined them, taking up any slack.

They hauled Martin higher and higher into the air as he grasped at the halter tightly constricting his neck. His feet kicked harder, scissoring as his time without air grew longer. Then he crossed a threshold, and his struggle became weaker until only his foot twitched, but the rest of him swung.

Dahlgren gazed at the body, a satisfied look passing over him as if he finally had relief for the first time in days.

"Good enough?" Nelson said.

"Fine work, Private."

Nelson grunted as he lowered the body then tied the rope around the tree. Martin's body hung stretched at the neck, inches longer than it should have been. Adams dug through the man's pockets, avoiding the piss that trickled down his leg.

"Nice to see this army still has some loyal men left in it. Faithful to their country. Despite this black treachery, we can still win this day," Dahlgren said. He walked his mount back the way they'd come without a second glance at the man he had condemned to death.

In a daze, Wolf mounted his horse with the other men. Questions plowed through his mind. Wilhelm watched him. "You didn't kill that man."

"It felt like it."

"You carried out an order from a commanding officer, however wrong." He reached for Wolf. "Men like Dahlgren have no sense of right from wrong. They sit in their positions subjecting others to harsh rule with no regard for human life." He squeezed Wolf's arm tight in an iron grip. "Wars are filled with these men, but you are not one of them."

"Nonsense," Adams interjected.

Wilhelm's hand loosened on his arm as he acknowledged his subordinate.

A smile settled on Adams's handsome dark-complected face as if he were the devil himself. "Wolfie gave us the orders. Didn't you, lad?"

Wolf shook free from Wilhelm. "I bear the same responsibility as these men." He wrestled with the actions they'd carried out.

"You bet you do. You're one of us," Adams said.

"I am," Wolf said softly, his eyes downcast.

Nelson scoffed at them. "Quit your whining. We killed a man. That's what we get paid to do. You want us shot for disobeying, Sergeant?"

"No, I don't. I want my men to come out of this in one piece."

"Then let us do what we do best. Kill men," Nelson said.

Wilhelm eyed the man with concern and steered his horse back into formation. "Fall back in, troopers."

The men formed into a column in ranks of four. Each trooper received a full view at the traitorous guide as they passed.

Martin's skin had a bluish tint as if he'd drown. His tongue hung from the corner of his mouth like he was making a jest. His eyes were open, staring lifelessly forward. The rope creaked in the wind gently, swinging his body like he was a babe in a cradle. His eyes followed Wolf as he passed, condemning him for his part to play in his untimely demise.

Most of the soldiers gazed on with an indifferent spitefulness. For how important was the life of a Negro? Especially one that couldn't take them where they needed to be. Southerners would have done much worse had they caught him helping their enemies. A level of justice settled in their minds. He'd failed his task and paid the price. Now, they had more significant business to attend to like winning the war.

The command walked their horses away from the gnarled sycamore, but Wolf could feel the shadow of Martin watching them leave the scene of the crime, his silent reprimand tailing the men like a curse.

CHAPTER 19

Midafternoon, March 1st, 1864
Goochland County, Virginia

A driver whipped a mule hauling a wagon as he bypassed the troopers. The column's short wagon train had grown as they'd rampaged through the South, and now they drove onward separating from the command. They took spare horses, rations, prisoners, wounded, and a dozen or so Federal horsemen.

The rest of Dahlgren's command sat around small campfires, resting their horses and eating whatever rations they still had. Troopers had a bad habit of eating all of their food supplies as soon as they were given or taken. Watching anything extra leave with the wagon train brought more than a concerned murmur from the soldiers.

"Where are they goin'?" Roberts asked between mouthfuls of hard biscuit. He gestured with his chin at the file of wagons struggling through the mud. "Plenty of food still in there."

"And bullets," Wilhelm said.

A young man with a light beard passed them by with his kepi sloped forward on his head. His nose was sharp like the point of a sword.

"That be Lieutenant Bartley, Dahlgren's signal officer," Wolf said. Crossed flags—one red, one white—decorated his sleeve. "Must be trying to signal Kilpatrick."

"Not much to signal now. Guns are dying down," Wilhelm said.

"I got to take a shit," Gratz said.

"Not too far now. Don't want to leave ya," Wilhelm said.

Gratz gave him a half-smile. "Sure, Sergeant."

The men sensed they'd missed an opportunity to link with Kilpatrick's command. That and the wounded at the mine brought feelings of uneasiness among them. Despite this they ate quickly, not knowing when they would be able to eat again.

"Never should have stopped at the coal pits," Van Horn said. His dour mouth tore into a piece of pork.

"Aye," Wilhelm added.

"It was an omen. God is angry with us," Shugart chimed in. The elder man's eyes drifted toward the heavens for a moment.

Adams rolled his eyes. "For what, old man? Hanging a colored boy?"

"For just that. Unjustly taking a life."

"The boy was working for them."

"The way those mines blew. Wasn't natural," Van Horn said. Over a dozen troopers were wounded when Dahlgren had ordered the destruction of the coal pits. They'd rolled a barrel of powder in a cart with a fuse on it. When it didn't immediately blow, men from the 5th New York went to investigate. As they approached the mine entrance, fire leapt forth like the gate to Hell itself was opening. Scalding rock and wood lanced the troopers, sending them to the dirt peppered with wounds, blood leaking from their ears.

"You believe God's will was at work here?" Adams said.

"Or the devil's." Van Horn spit on the ground.

"What about you, Wolfie?" Adams said with a sneer.

"I don't know, but the weather's been foul since we started this mission. Feels like a curse to me." Martin's hanging form plagued him and was always hiding in his thoughts. Swinging from the tree, his dark eyes blamed Wolf. Every time he closed his eyes, Martin was there.

Nelson waved a hand. "Bah, ghost stories and goblins."

"Ghosts be real. I seen one," Roberts said.

"Yer grandma been playing tricks on ya," Nelson said. The well-built trooper guzzled coffee as quick as he could, angrily eyeing the rainy sky as if he could change it.

Shugart's voice shook. "I'm telling you, men. You repent for your sins. God is angry with us." His eyes locked with Wolf. "He knows what you've done."

Wolf gulped, the old abolitionist's words chipping away at his conscience. His soul had an ache, but what could be done now? He'd been there. He'd let it happen. He'd held the rope in his hands.

Adams spoke, "We done no less than what these Virginians would do to the colored folk. We done no less than what Abe asks us to do."

"President Lincoln would never ask us to hang a colored boy," Shugart said.

"But he don't care neither as long as it wins his war. Old honest Abe was gonna let them keep their slaves." Adams's tone became mocking. "I have no purpose to interfere with the institution of slavery." He wavered, exasperated by his own words. "He don't even care. The Emancipation was a military policy to hurt the South, nothing more. Don't apply to the border states. Only the states still in the Confederacy. What Southerner in his right mind is going to abide by a proclamation passed by a government they are in rebellion against? Ha. Now tell me, is that right? If we were so benevolent, shouldn't all the colored folk be free by the power of existing everywhere?"

Wolf shook his head in disagreement. "We set them free."

"Then what? Told them to run north. Every Southern man between here and there is rounding them up. Beating them, sending them back to their owners. We did nothing but cause them trouble," Adams said.

Shugart's voice wavered. "Lincoln's proclamation made this a war of abolition regardless of how he felt when it started."

"Don't matter why we fight," Nelson said.

"It does," Shugart said.

"It don't. Cause there's always a war to be fought."

"My big friend is right. Where there's war, money, land, and power lurk nearby. Greedy men wring their hands together for the reaping." Adams shook his head. "You can sing your praises of abolition all day, but we know why men fight. And there will always be war as long as there's men."

Shugart's face reddened. "Then we should use those motivations for the betterment of mankind."

Wilhelm cut in. "Where's Gratz?" The men stood, scrutinizing the cold hard woods surrounding them. Their Austrian comrade was missing.

"Can't a man shit in peace?" Nelson growled.

The sergeant inspected their horses. "His horse is still here."

Wolf followed, hobbling over, carbine in hand.

"Woe to the man who does the devil's work," Shugart lamented.

Wilhelm spun on him. "We were following orders."

"But from whom?" Shugart's gray beard quivered.

The sergeant brushed past Shugart and pulled Wolf aside. "We ain't leaving any of our boys behind. Help me."

From the soggy ditch lining the road, they moved into the timber. Wolf limped through undergrowth. He made sure the percussion cap was in place and the carbine was cocked and ready to fire.

The saturated leaves squished beneath his boots. He searched for any sign of man or beast but only forest rolled before him, gray and dormant in the wet winter. The trees were indistinguishable from one another and every other woodland they'd ridden past. Patches of white lay intermittently among roots and limbs, snow that had failed to melt.

Out of the corner of his eye, he saw something move among the trees. With a snap, he lifted his carbine to his shoulder, aiming down its sights. A ruffling sounded to his right and he turned that way. Nothing stirred. He held his breath. The hair rose on his neck, sticking out straight. Through slate and charcoal trunks, he could see Wilhelm stalking with his carbine, the barrel dipped slightly toward the ground.

A rock struck the tree next to him. Wolf spun. The woods were motionless. His heart pounded in his chest. "Hello?" he called. Rain softly pattered around him, the only sound. He cautiously closed on the tree. A white growth from the brush caught his eye. At first, he thought it was a mushroom or some other kind of fungi.

He kicked at it with the toe of his boot. The leaves beneath stirred as if they were connected. He dug his foot into it again, revealing more pale white curled in the shape of a hand. He whirled in a circle, scanning for something or someone to point his gun at. Only knobby uneven tree trunks stared back, creaking with the wind. They were all different shades of gray, some with crumbling bark, others with furrowed lines running along them like bark ravines.

"Sergeant!" Wolf shouted. He set his carbine against the tree and dug at the brown and black decaying leaves disintegrating in his hands. He tossed moist clumps to the side. Slowly, a blue Union uniform emerged dark and wet beneath the loose cover.

Wilhelm huffed behind him. He glanced over Wolf's shoulder. "Don't tell me."

Wolf threw more compost away from the body until Gratz's handsome face surfaced. His eyes and mouth were open as if he'd tried to call out. Dirt and jagged leaves had found their way inside, blackening his throat. He brushed his pale cheeks. "Goddamn."

Wilhelm puffed air through this nose, sighing. He studied the forest for a moment. "We need to keep better track of our boys." He crouched next to Gratz, sticking a hand into his pockets.

"They took his boots and socks." Pale feet contrasted sharply against the brown shades of decomposing leaves and rich soil.

"Shoes wear out fast in war."

All his valuables and weapons were gone save for a letter for his next of kin, labeled Karl Gratz in Grand Rapids, Michigan. He handed the letter to Wolf.

"Keep this safe until we make it back to our lines," Wilhelm said.

"All right." He took the envelope and placed it in his pocket. "It's open."

"We'll sort it out later. Maybe send a few greenbacks for his folks."

Nodding, Wolf said, "Who did this?"

Wilhelm stared out at the offending forest. "This isn't friendly territory. Locals. Militia. Partisans. Don't really matter." He grasped Wolf's shoulder. "I failed him. Come."

They hoisted the body, taking him back to the bivouac.

Shugart shook his head as they approached. "You see." He wagged a finger. "He takes us one by one for our sins."

Adams licked his lips. "You'll be next if you don't shut your mouth."

"I don't take my orders from you, Private."

A knife flashed in Adams hands before Shugart finished the word private. The blade neared Shugart's face, threatening to slice him open. "Sure you don't." Swords and pistols were drawn and pointed at one another. Wolf aimed his carbine at Nelson.

The towering man scowled. "Careful where you point that."

"I'm not the one who needs to be careful."

Wilhelm growled low. "They're will be none of that under my watch. We got enough people out there that want us dead for us to be killing ourselves. Weapons away."

Adams lifted his knife from Shugart first. "Just trying to keep up morale in this godforsaken rain, Sergeant."

Weapons scraped leather and metal as they returned to their homes. Wilhelm lowered his head in thought. "He's right. Shugart. Let's tone down the revelations. Gratz's death is a deadly reminder. We are in enemy territory. They will harry us and kill us if they can. Everyone must stick together." He eyed his men. "Nobody does anything alone. We have to keep our heads on a swivel out there." He stared at Gratz's body for a moment.

The young man's throat had been slit, leaving a grinning knife wound across his neck. The wound exposed the pink insides of his throat.

"Now help me bury him."

They couldn't take the body with them. The wagons had departed, and the mounts were worn out from days of continuous marching. The unit dug as much as they could, and for a change, were thankful that the earth was wet.

"Mount up, men," Lieutenant Peters shouted. He trotted his horse alongside Yates's company. With the captain's arrest, they fell under the order of Major Cooke, and in turn, Peters was given command. The twenty-six-year-old lieutenant from Brattleboro, Vermont had a pointed brownish-blond goatee that stuck off his chin like a short bayonet.

"You men. What are you doing?" Peters stepped his umber gelding to the unit.

"They killed one of ours," Wolf said.

The lieutenant crinkled his nose. "Who?"

"Rebels. Didn't see them."

"They killed your man, but you didn't see them? No gunshots?"

"Slit his throat while he shit," Nelson said.

Peters blinked at his words, perhaps contemplating the intricacies or the vulnerability of a man shitting that he hadn't thought of before.

"Should we send out scouts?" Wilhelm asked.

"No. We are preparing to depart and that will only slow us down. Do him service, but hurry." He turned away, joining the formation of troopers.

The unit stood around the makeshift grave, heads dipped.

"May God take his soul. Another boy taken before his time. Another angel for his army," Shugart said softly.

"Amen," Wilhelm said. "Nobody alone. Always in pairs. Understood?"

A round of ayes went up from the men. They quickly tossed dirt on his fallen form and remounted their horses.

Major Cooke waved them on angrily. "You men, hurry! The colonel is adamant. We will enter this city this day! Flounderers will be left behind." He glanced at the fresh mound on the side of the road.

"What's that?"

"One of our men."

"What happened? Sick?"

Wilhelm ripped his shovel from the earth. "Someone killed him."

"Who?" The major's horse turned, resisting getting closer to the dead man.

"Don't know, sir."

"His death will not be in vain." Cooke eyeballed the sky. "By sundown it won't matter as we bask in the glow of a burning Richmond."

The men mounted their horses unhurried by the major. "Let's ride," Wilhelm said, weariness clouding his voice. The unit trotted to catch the rear of the column, but Wolf glared hard into the woods, thinking he saw something in the trees. He wiped his eyes with his free hand and looked again, but this time nothing was there.

CHAPTER 20

Evening, March 1ˢᵗ, 1864
Goochland County, Virginia

Dahlgren had sent a dozen scouts and messengers toward the cannon fire of Kilpatrick's guns and over the last eight miles heard nothing in return. No signal rockets soared through the air from Bartley or Kilpatrick. He kept his outward demeanor calm and respected as he rode at the head of his command, but inside his heart pounded his chest.

All was not lost regardless of the assault's commencement before Dahlgren was in position. Originally, the attack was to take place at dusk to give his men the cover of darkness to conduct their destruction of the city. *That damn guide. Goddamn guide. Traitorous bastard.* His solace was the coming victory.

"Sir?" Major Cooke sauntered along next to him, his slender supporter.

"What is it?"

"The cannon fire. It's gone."

Twisting his head to the side, Dahlgren listened. Hooves clopped in sloppy mud. Chilled rain tapped upon dead leaves and brims of hats. Rebellious sabers rattled in sheaths. Even a crow had the audacity to let out its violent song. *Caw-caw-caw.* But no distant rumble of artillery from the north of Richmond. They'd ridden miles after he let the men take their first break in over thirty-six hours. All the while they rode to the drums of cannon, and now it was simply gone. It was an odd silence as if the land and beasts in it missed the dueling fusillades.

His words had a hollow ring, his tongue not refusing to believe him. "A lull in the action is all."

"Did he not say the attack was to commence at dusk?" He glanced at Cooke for confirmation. He'd been in the same briefings.

"That was my understanding, Colonel, but it does not matter." At the end of his last word, he smoothed his mustache outlining his mouth. "Our assault was to be two-pronged. Three if Butler sends men from his command at Fort Monroe."

"And I haven't heard a lick of anything from anybody. Butler could be in the city by now."

"I doubt that, sir."

"It's of no matter. We will test their fortifications on the western part of the city. Boys and old men cannot stand before us."

"Of course, sir. Arguably, a southern approach would be a better maneuver for our smaller force. Less expected. Our reports say the fortifications are much weaker there, and if the defenders are stymieing Kilpatrick to the north, surely the southern part of the capital is drained of all resistance."

The major's words irritated the young colonel. He knew exactly what was supposed to be happening. He knew exactly what Kilpatrick had asked of him, and he strove to accomplish his task with impeccable care. But if Kilpatrick was getting cold feet now, it was of no consequence to him. His men knew the mission they'd undertaken and would not be deterred by weather, enemy, or tardiness of allies. Of that he was sure.

Dahlgren brushed aside the major's assessment with a wave of his hand. "Major, that way is shut. We will approach from the west and send them scurrying like the rats they are."

"I have no doubt, sir."

Of course you don't. Was Julius Caesar plagued by the incessant droning of lesser men? He wondered if he was surrounded by cowards and lackeys or if his commanders were men of honor and sound mind.

Not that Major Cooke wasn't of sound mind. He was an experienced tactician but seemingly couldn't grasp the reality that this mission would end the war. The man was always insisting on flankers and scouts. None of that would matter much in a few hours when he held Jefferson Davis's head on the point of his sword.

"Sir, if I may be frank?" Cooke's voice caused Dahlgren's leg to begin to throb again almost in sync with the tapping of rain on his hat. It was an ebbing of more pain followed by less, and it was incessant, making it hard for him to concentrate.

"Carry on."

"We had two men go missing from the rear guard at the last stop. That's almost twenty men today and yesterday."

"They are lost. They know to follow the gunfire or rally at Hungary Station. Bartley should be there now. Mitchell has been all over. There is ample opportunity to rejoin the command."

Cooke massaged his mustache. "I find this no mere coincidence. Yates's company found one of their boys dead in the woods. Throat slit when he went to relieve himself."

"Bushwhackers and brigands. They matter not. The war will be done by tomorrow morning."

"Sir, I think it's prudent to deploy scouts and flankers. Perhaps we can bring some of these brigands to justice."

"I've sent out almost a dozen men to link with Kilpatrick and heard nothing. If I send out more men and they do not come back, I won't have much of a command left." He shook his head. "No. Keep the men together, concentrated and ready to punch a hole through any force we meet. Just like that Home Guard on the road." He smiled at that. Ridden into the ground like the rabble they were.

"I believe it prudent, especially if Kilpatrick has called off his attack to the north. We want to know what we are walking into."

"Stand down, Major. These things are of little consequence on our crusade. Did Caesar stop because the mighty Rubicon stood in his way?"

"Sir?"

"No, he crossed the river and sealed his fate as emperor."

Cooke's brow furrowed. "Sir?"

Dahlgren brushed his subordinate's questions to the side with a flick of his wrist. "I wouldn't expect you to understand, but if you're so concerned, you may send a company of men ahead to ensure we are not set upon."

"Thank you, sir."

Cooke waved a lieutenant forward. "Yates's company to the front."

"Excellent choice. If those men are anything like their captain, perhaps some additional duties will make them more compliant."

"My thoughts exactly, sir."

Yates's mixed company from a cluster of different units cantered past them. The men had no flags. It had been part of their orders to keep them unidentifiable in the dark or daylight hours. No bugles sounded, another factor to increase their stealth although Dahlgren didn't care much about that now. The fire burned in his belly, but his body was cold and fatigued. He drew from the flames to fuel himself, knowing that all fires ended in smoke.

The enemy knew they were there, at least from an assault standpoint. What they didn't know was that he was about to attack with the ferociousness of a tiger, not to be discouraged until Jefferson Davis was dead.

Another mile was tread beneath their hooves. One of the prisoners had named the main road as Three Chopt Road, a sure way leading to Richmond. An excited shiver ballooned in his chest. Today would be the day. A sprinkling of gunfire peppered the air ahead of them. It was faint, almost as if the rain had taken on an angrier fall from the heavens.

He raised a fist. "Move with haste, men."

The column moved to a trot, and before long, the road gave way to earthen mounds. Horsemen trotted toward them and his command halted. A sergeant with a curled mustache and a trooper with a brace on his leg thrust prisoners before him.

"Colonel, sir. We have prisoners for you. There were only a few men guarding this point."

"Naturally, Sergeant. They are wholly unprepared for our attack. They have built a house on a rotting foundation. One little shove and the whole thing will collapse."

A young bearded corporal pushed a man in front of him, and he ignored the rebel, eyeing his man instead. "Corporal, what happened to your leg?"

The Union man clenched his jaw. "Before the war, sir."

"Ahh." Dahlgren slapped his thigh, sending pain cascading through his remaining limb. "Gettysburg."

"I was there as well, sir."

"What unit?"

"13th Michigan."

"Ahh, the Michigan Brigade earned some respect that day." He flashed a smile at the trooper and glanced at the Confederate for the first time. He was a dirty man with a brown coat and a wide-brimmed hat and a thick mustache. Nothing designated him as a rebel aside from the fact he fought Union men.

"And who are you?"

"Benjamin Wallace."

"Which unit?"

"City Battalion."

"He was armed with only this, sir," the sergeant said. He held out a sword by the blade, offering it to the colonel.

Dahlgren grinned, taking it by the hilt. It felt a bit off in his hand like at some point the sword had been reforged by a hasty blacksmith. Rust flecks dotted the almost straight blade.

"Looks like a reforged 1840 Model, wrist breaker, sir," Cooke said.

"It does." He examined the blade. "The rebel only had this?"

"Yes, sir. A few pickets had muskets, but they ran off before we got close."

"You stood your ground with but a sword?"

Benjamin glowered, eyes downcast. "Yes, sir. Was me pappy's."

Dahlgren belted a chuckle. "See, Cooke, they aren't prepared for this assault. They try to stop us with only swords. I at least expected an odd piece of artillery or a company of graybeards."

"Thousands of men gather now. We are unafraid. We will throw you back from whence you came."

Dahlgren stared the man in the eyes. "With a sword? No, you won't. I'd take this column against ten thousand of you vagabonds in a heartbeat." Then with a flick of his wrist. "Send him to the rear."

Light faded with the day. The time had come. With the outer fortifications easily taken, now an actual test presented itself: the inner earthen walls. Dahlgren pointed at Cooke. "Get your company out front. Tonight we take Richmond!"

CHAPTER 21

Evening, March 1ˢᵗ, 1864
Outskirts of Richmond, Virginia

Wolf's adopted company continued to scout for the main column under the direction of Lieutenant Peters. The first pickets had been easily run off and the horsemen captured.

An excited fervor took hold of the troopers over the chill of the rain. Richmond was close. Church bells tolled warning of the enemy's arrival. The rich stench of tobacco and the black stink of coal smoke infused the air.

They cantered down the dirt road in the low light. The land on either side of the roadway had been cleared into long rows of barren soil with almost no trees.

"For the tobacco crop," Shugart said.

"We'll be sure to get some before the city goes up in smoke," Adams said, but no one laughed. The men were tired and ready to see this mission through.

They rounded a bend in the road and a stone structure loomed. In the distance, earthen mounds that resembled ancient burial grounds for the native peoples of America stood defiantly.

Wilhelm pointed. "Those be breastworks on that wall."

"Wall?" Wolf stared harder, straining his eyes.

"Fortifications. Bet there's a ditch in front."

"That hill?"

"Ja, just hope there's no cannon on it."

Peters slowed the company with a raised fist. He jabbed a finger at the house, and six riders peeled off in its direction. The rest of the company sat in rank waiting. Their mounts shifted. Uneasy, they tugged at their reins.

"I don't like this," Nelson said. He spit.

"God must have blessed us with unimpeded entrance to the city," Adams jabbed at Shugart.

The old man ignored the swarthy private.

"Nelson's right. This is too easy," Wilhelm said. The sergeant's eyes scanned the earthen walls. He pointed. "Shugart, dismount and take three troopers with you. Move to a flanking position on that house."

"Bart and Dan, Van Horn, with me." The riders turned off to the side of the road, wheeling themselves to the rear of the house. Every other cavalryman was forced to battle the elements and anxious horses, waiting for the other men to make sure the way was safe.

Seconds ticked by. Wolf wanted to check his watch but held back. Without warning, gunfire ripped into the six riders like the roar of a lion.

Men twisted in their saddles and horses screamed as bullets tore through their flesh. In an instant, four of the six riders were unseated. The other two spurred their horses back to the company. Shugart dismounted and snuck his men around the other edge of the plantation manor. Carbines popped off as they engaged men on the other side.

In the road, one of the fallen troopers stood, trying to limp back toward safety. His leg failed to function, and he gripped the limb with white-knuckled hands, dragging it along. Each man silently cheered him on. He could make it.

"Hold," Peters said.

The wounded rider screamed as a bullet twisted him in a red mist before he fell to the ground.

Peters cursed at the top of his lungs. "Son of a bitch!"

"What are our orders?" Wilhelm yelled at the lieutenant.

"Stay in rank. Prepare to charge." He shook his head in anger.

Over a hundred rebels marched from behind the plantation house on foot.

They were armed with shotguns, rifles, and muskets. They wore a smattering of grays and browns, nothing uniform about them.

"They can hit us if we're close and packed together. Let's not give them the chance." Wilhelm pointed. "5ᵗʰ Michigan boys, dismount to skirmish. Keep them busy."

Peters mouth snapped closed and he blinked, registering that his sergeant's orders made sense. Cooler heads always prevailed while in command. He wasn't the only one.

"On the double, lads," the 5ᵗʰ Michigan sergeant shouted. The grizzly-bearded men practically jumped from their saddles with their carbines. They formed a skirmish line with a mixture of Spencer and Burnside rifles and carbines and stepped into the field. Their firepower would grossly counterbalance the rebels despite their advantage in numbers.

The rebels' line moved painstakingly forward in a disorganized mass. Shots smoked in the air and most ventured too high.

Peters blinked and visibly calmed himself. "Good call, Sergeant. Bring your men forward." He ushered them to the front, pointing at a detachment from the 6ᵗʰ Michigan. "Get me more men here." The other Michigan troopers filled in the gaps left by Shugart and his men.

Peters was in his element now as if he were in front of a class. "Stay in a rank of six. Once they start to scatter, we'll send you after 'em. Right to the wall with 'em."

"Yes, sir," Wilhelm said. "Keep it tight, lads. Draw sabers."

A soft *shiiiiiing* vibrated from sheaths as they drew their curved cavalry swords. The men kept close rank with knees almost touching one another.

The 5ᵗʰ Michigan skirmishers were experienced troopers. They fired with rapid efficiency, and the rebels struggled before them as gaps appeared where men once stood.

"Won't be long now, Wolfie," Adams said with a smirk. "Another few minutes and they'll scatter like leaves in the wind." He was correct. The enemy was close enough to see their panicked forms. Shugart and his men had crept to the side of the home, taking turns to fire into their flank from cover, and the rebels wavered.

Pounding hooves shook the ground beneath them. The colonel, with the rest of the men at his back, galloped on to the scene. He gestured wildly to the major behind him and more Union troopers dismounted, running to Shugart's men. The Federals went about forming a semicircle around the rebels, cinching off the route for escape and racking them with fire on the flanks.

Dahlgren nodded to Peters. "Nice work forcing them to commit. It is the only way we can ensure their destruction."

It was clear a single officer was holding the rebels together. He calmly walked his tan horse behind the ragtag company, his sharply pointed beard twisting as he scanned the field. Abruptly, he sat upright in his saddle then toppled from his steed, and his men scattered like sawdust in a breeze. Splintering, they ran for the safety of the fortifications. Peters waved at his men. "Finish them."

A routed man was an ugly thing to watch. Terror filled his eyes. He'd shove down his brother in fear after he'd pissed himself. The civilians had even less of a bond with the men around them. Wounded were abandoned. Weapons were tossed, and they sprinted every which way, but all were headed in the direction of the earthen wall.

The unit spurred their horses. Billy let out an irritated neigh, tossing his head. The Michigan men kept solid rank over the road and into the field as they gained on the militiamen. A cluster of rebels split from the others and raced for the walls. Wilhelm pointed his saber in their direction with a nod at Wolf.

Wolf called out. "My line, right half-wheel!" His men rotated their line in pursuit of the other rebels. He was on the outside, so he had to move Billy faster than the other trooper on the nearest end while the other troopers kept the same gait. Otherwise, they risked bunching out of formation.

Behind them a unit from the 2nd New York charged down the roadway for the city with hoots and hollers. Wolf's unit closed in on the slowest runners. He felt a sense of pity when he hacked his sword into a man's shoulder as he passed.

The rebel threw his hands up in defeat, collapsing on the ground. With a fierce battle cry, Nelson cleaved halfway through a gray-haired rebel's neck, sending a gush of scarlet bursting in the air. Adams slashed a man along the back, splitting his jacket and flesh underneath alike.

"Open pursuit!" The unit split into single troopers riding down individuals.

Adams grinned from ear to ear as a rebel cried for mercy and he jammed his sword into his belly. The man collapsed, whimpering in the soggy dirt. "You having fun yet, Wolfie?"

Wolf turned his horse, a sick feeling in his stomach. He carried on back to the man clutching his arm shattered by the saber blow.

The young man with angry eyes stared defiantly at him. "Just do it, you dirty Yank. But know this, you'll die out here."

The positions couldn't have been more reversed. He was atop his horse, sword pointed down at an injured unarmed man. "You're not a soldier, are you?"

"I'm a mechanic, but I would gladly die for Virginia."

"Any soldiers left in there?"

"There be five-thousand rebels led by Hampton himself that'll be here any minute."

Wolf lowered his sword. "Hampton?"

"What of it? And Custis Lee." The young man spit.

"General Wade Hampton?"

"Aye."

"Where is he?"

"Don't know, but he's gonna take your scalp."

Wolf lifted his saber level with the rebel's neck. "You want to live?"

The rebel glanced nervously around him. Confusion crossed his face. "Yes."

"Cry out and stay still."

Sounds of slaughter echoed from the earthen walls. A rebel held his guts inside his belly trying to shove them back in. He screamed, his slippery insides refusing to find their place.

Adams called over. "You need help with that one?"

"Just getting some intel." He turned back, grunting. "Fall over and scream, dammit. Or it's done."

161

The rebel shook his head. "Aah!" He threw himself on the ground. Wolf did a fancy display of whipping his saber. "Best of luck," he whispered. It didn't feel right slaying the civilian men as they ran. Or gutting a man as he called for mercy.

Adams rode closer. "Looks like the colonel was right. Clerks and mechanics, preachers and lawyers. Easy pickings for the likes of us."

A loud boom resounded off the fortifications. The Union troopers turned to stare at the men from the 2nd New York. A string of pops hurried off and riders crumpled in their saddles. Horsemen circled and another volley went out. More blue men fell. The cohesion of the company disintegrated. Sergeants yelled for order and to reform before the enemy.

"Wolverines to me!" Wilhelm shouted.

His unit reformed into a tight line of men and mounts in the plantation field.

"Might need our help," said a man from the 6th.

Sergeant Berles's eyes scanned the earthen walls.

"'Nother cannon," Roberts said, pointing.

The New Yorkers popped their pistols in surprise, not making a decision to drive forward or retreat.

"Not into that wasp nest."

The new artillery piece stopped rolling on the edge of the wall. Fire exploded from its mouth like a dragon. The sound was deafening as if the fabric of the heavens were tearing itself in half. Bits and pieces of metal sprayed into the blue-clad horsemen, easily shredding the flesh of man and horse alike. The New Yorkers broke like a brittle twig hightailing it back to the column.

"To the colonel," Wilhelm said. The unit galloped over dirt fields toward the plantation house, relinking with Shugart's men along the way.

Dahlgren rallied his horse, sweeping back and forth. "You see that boys! The walls of Richmond. Like the Greek heroes, here we are at the walls of Troy, and they are ready to fall before us."

The sky darkened further as night crept upon the Confederate capital. Light was failing the troopers, and the rain refused to relent. Soon they would be fighting a battle in darkness with only the calls of their sergeants to keep them in order and the orange bursts of fire to place their aim.

"Look, sir!" Cooke called out. Man-shaped forms moved in a line like infantry across the field where they'd run down the rebels. More forms collected between the gates. "Looks to be more than a regiment of the bastards. Cannon on the wall. We can't see a thing. It may be advisable to try and link again with Kilpatrick."

"Shut your mouth, Major. These are mere clerks and mechanics. They know nothing in the ways of war. They are gardeners in a war, and we are warriors in a garden."

The two guns on the fortifications boomed, sending balls screaming overhead and plowing into plantation fields.

Dahlgren breathed heavily. "Wipe them from the field."

"Sir, I would advise a withdrawal until we can better assess the situation." Cooke's horse danced as he spoke.

Jamming a finger at Cooke's chest, Dahlgren said, "You will charge, or you will be court-martialed here and now for insubordination." He blinked back his anger. "We are so close I can smell the stink of Davis's perfume. Through that wall lies our prize." He turned toward the men. "We have come too far to stop here. There are men at Libby who need our help. There are thousands on Belle Isle who need our help. Would you stand by while they suffer?"

A cheer went up from the Union cavalrymen, their spirits rising.

Cooke patted his horse in shame. He sat silent, not giving the order.

Dahlgren turned to the major. "I will not ask again."

"Yes, Colonel."

The major peered over his shoulder. "Captain Mitchell."

"Sir!" The scarred captain reported with a stern salute.

"Take your company and clear the road of rebels. Do not get close to the works."

"Yes, sir." Mitchell studied the darkness. His lips twitched in anger, but he trotted back to his command.

Wolf and his unit stood by as the company of blue formed. Sergeants yelled orders. Men kept their horses from bolting. They packed into a tight formation despite the rainy twilight conditions.

"Charge them!" Dahlgren cried.

The men galloped, a small dark blue thundercloud rolling over the field. The horsemen became a mass, a singular shadow with hundreds of heads and feet. The only sound was hooves tearing at the earth.

A line of fire lit the darkness, orange and yellow bursts of light like sudden blooms of nighttime flowers. Men screamed. The garden of night flowers bloomed again as another line of fire tore into their flank. More flowers blossomed from the berms in sporadic violent beauty. The blue cloud dissipated on and through the stalks of men, trampling those in the way.

"They're losing cohesion," Wolf said.

"Never good," Wilhelm said.

Screams of horses and cries of men filtered back to the Union troopers, but every man watching knew the outcome. And the outcome was death.

"Brave boys," Shugart lamented.

"Dead boys," Nelson added.

Horses bolted with no one atop them. Random riders galloped back to the column. Some in groups of twos and threes, but almost half the company didn't return.

The colonel's breathing came in audible hard breaths. "Did they break them? Did they break?" he stammered.

Cooke put a hand on his sleeve.

"Do not touch me." Dahlgren shrugged him off. "Did they scatter them?"

"Sir, our men are broke."

Dahlgren gestured at his men. "Send in another. One more go of it. Place flankers out. They'll think twice." He wiped his mouth staring at the field. "Yes, they will."

"Sir, we don't have enough men for this. A full brigade maybe, but one more charge like that and you won't have any men left."

Complete darkness held the land in a stranglehold. A cannon boomed, sending its shell over Union heads. A few men ducked. Dahlgren removed his hat, wiping rain from his forehead then coughing into his hand. An exhausted look spread over him like every ounce of energy he possessed had gotten him here, and now he needed to sleep for three days. It was as if his fire had been doused with the water of the enemy.

Wolf could commiserate with the colonel; he felt the same way. Hell, all the men did, and after watching their comrades charge headlong into a slaughter—it didn't matter if they were farmers with pitchforks—his soldiers were at the end of their tether. A regroup and modification of their attack plan was required.

"The best course of action," Dahlgren said as he smiled softly, the fight having gone out of him, "is to backtrack down the way we came and look for a way to link with Kilpatrick."

Wolf's unit stood in the road for a moment, staring at the earthen fortifications and the faint factories and warehouses, looming shadowy structures in the distance. They'd come to the edge of victory only to be turned away like beggars in the night.

Dahlgren placed his kepi back on his head. "Tomorrow we shall begin anew. Find me Hogan, Magee, and Woods. They will lead us to Hungary Station."

CHAPTER 22

Before Midnight, March 1st, 1864
Near Atlee Station, Virginia

Major General Wade Hampton wiped droplets of mud from his cheek. His uniform was splattered with the grime and he cursed the mucky roads and the worst weather he'd seen all winter. He hid a tinge of admiration for his enemy. They'd moved rapidly over terrible ground. *They are getting better at this, but they must have exhausted their animals and men.*

In the night, every roadway appeared the same. Shadowy timber flanked the lane. A pasture had been dug out of the land ahead. But if a man knew the land he was born in, each road became its very own map and each route upon it a path to success. Those were his men's advantages.

His Iron Scouts had shadowed the Federal troops and kept track of their every stop, the destruction of each piece of property, and each act of thievery. They'd come within an hour of catching General Robert E. Lee onboard a train near Frederick's Hall. It was almost as if it had been on purpose, and for a short time, Hampton thought perhaps there was a high-ranking spy inside the command structure. But the Federals moved too slow and Marse Robert evaded capture, and Hampton breathed a sigh of relief. His scouts would have died to protect the general, but in the end, they would have perished to the last man. Then Lee would be their prisoner and the war would swing drastically in the Union's favor.

A man emerged from the darkness. Hampton's company of North

Carolinians pointed pistols in his direction. Quickly, he lifted his floral engraved Manhattan Pocket Revolver into the air, a notch on the ivory grip for each Union man he'd put in the ground. Tonight that number would grow. He hovered it over the form.

"Deo," the shadow said.

"Vindice," he said in response. The simple Latin phrase was well-established within his scouting network as a means of identifying one another in covert positions. Weapons were lowered, and the shade stepped closer through the trees.

"George Tanner, sir."

"General Hampton."

The man removed a brown farmer's hat. He was the antithesis of his brother with a broad nose, plain face, and a beard covering it down to his chin. "It's a pleasure to meet you in person, G'neral." He paused collecting himself. "An honor."

"Thank you, George. How close are we?"

The scout squinted as he measured distance. "'Bout two miles. We've silenced the nearest pickets so we shouldn't have a problem. Follow me if it pleases."

The men dismounted their horses, walking them through a deer trail covered in brown undergrowth. Hampton walked next to George, his hip nagging him along the way like an old woman.

"Your brother has been of excellent use the past few days. I sent him to Stuart." He hadn't heard anything from Stuart in response to his pleas for orders and men, so he moved with haste toward the fight. What was a man to do with only 250 men at his disposal? Not much. Yet honor and obligation drove him into the field to serve anyway.

"You'd say then scouting is in our blood. But we be but simple folk. We know the land and its people, and they tolerate us well enough. A few pennies here and there to keep the louder mouths quiet about our back-and-forth."

Hampton's boots squished in mud; the sticky sludge tugged at his foot as he stepped again. "How large is the enemy force?"

"I'd say by the looks of the campfires and tents 'bout three thousand of the bastards. Look real serious about it as well."

Two hundred and fifty men versus three thousand. Not good odds, but he'd heard of worse. The Spartans and their allies at Thermopylae for one.

"That is a sizable force."

"Aye, general. But they didn't breach our beautiful city."

"For that, I am thankful. Perhaps we can make them rethink the entire endeavor," Hampton said softly. With such a depleted force of men at his disposal, he'd been forced into an irregular almost partisan-like status, which meant he would need to draw heavily upon his revolutionary forefathers' tactics to drag the enemy's attention away from their capital.

They continued their quiet stalk through the woods until Tanner waved him to a halt. Hampton's company slowed and crouched low behind trees in the murkiness of night. He followed his scout closer, stalking through a night that was dark as pitch in a barrel. The wet leaves underfoot masked their approach. Tanner gave him a quick tug on the sleeve, stopping the general.

He pointed out. Hampton's eyes weren't as sound as they once were, but the tiny glow of fires flickered through gray trunks. "This is only a portion of the command."

"Aye, I'd say about five companies. There's more down the road, but it'll take 'em awhile in the dark."

Hampton grinned beneath his bushy beard. Roughly five hundred men resting in the night versus his couple hundred drastically evened the odds, one might even say swung them in his favor. "You've done excellent work. You and your brother should get medals for this."

He could tell the young man grinned broadly next to him. "Thank you, sir."

Hampton gave Tanner a soft clap on the back and whiteness puffed from his shoulder. He studied the sky as white flakes floated for the earth.

"A winter snow to mask our approach."

***

The temperature dropped almost five degrees over the next thirty minutes. He felt it in his bones, especially his hip. His wound from Gettysburg always felt the changes in the weather.

Fog lifted from his mount's nose, and tiny flakes of white trickled from above. He sat with a company of roughly forty men on horseback while the rest of his companies were covertly surrounding the camp on foot.

Captain Blair would attack from the right flank, and Creek would come from the left. Hart's single piece of artillery would hit the center. They had strict orders to aim for the Union horses on the far side of the bivouac and to avoid hitting their own men. He'd brought two guns, but only one made it. The other was stuck somewhere in the frigid mud.

A horse smacked its lips in irritation from being forced to wait in the cold for so long. A night assault was the deadliest thing he could ask his men to do; the only thing perhaps more deadly would be asking them to charge a well-fortified and defended fort. But this was not well-defended.

In enemy territory, they should have had a host of sentries and layered them for better coverage. The encampment only had reserve pickets, meaning too few men, not far from the camp itself. It was as if they were afraid to venture outside the timid glows of the campfires. Exhausted heaps of sleeping Union troopers decorated the few buildings around the railroad station. He knew the rapid movements through Virginia were taking their toll on the men, something he would exploit with deadly efficiency in the next few minutes.

He drew his pistol from its holster and held it pointed upward. With his other hand, he made a sharp gesture at the camp, a lightning bolt snapping the heavens. He wavered it over a man he saw going from fire to fire, presiding over them like an officer. He sported a thick fur-trimmed hussar-style jacket. Hampton was curious about this man, and if he could, he would capture him if only to learn more about him.

Two of his Iron Scouts crept through the woods. He only knew they were there because Tanner had pointed the statue-like men out earlier in the night. Their movements were undetectable akin to stalking mountain lions, slow and precise.

A knife glinted in the firelight, and the two shadowed blue-uniformed pickets disappeared without a sound. His horse adjusted beneath him as if he could feel Hampton about to order the attack. Despite the silence imposed by his soldiers, quiet shifts and horse hooves scratched in the night air. His men breathed just a bit harder, knowing what was coming, but stayed steady.

A volley of gunfire shattered the night, flashes of orange spraying from indistinguishable barrels. Most of the lounging Union men didn't even move. They could only stare as bullets whistled by them, some into friends, others only sailing past before hitting the station and trees. Fragments of wood sprayed into the air as the bullets bit deep.

Creek's company unleashed a barrage from the other side. Federal soldiers still standing dropped to the ground. Hampton zeroed in on the man in the fur-lined jacket. He drew a pistol in one hand and called out, "To arms, men! To arms!"

Hart's battery let loose a booming shot. It crashed like lightning, striking twice and the earth trembled. The Union men crawled and scrambled over the ground, some crying out in fear. Scared eyes darted over the darkness surrounding them; they were kept in plain sight by their campfires. Horses screamed as shells struck over them, spooking them onto hind legs. Another salvo battered the bivouac. Bullets splintered wood and bodies alike. *They must think we are of equal number. My boys, yes, my boys, fighting like devils.*

The man in the fur-trimmed jacket rushed to organize their defense. He shoved a man toward Creek's flank, gesturing calmly. Union troopers hustled in that direction, those devastating Spencer carbines in their hands. He grabbed a grizzly-bearded sergeant and directed him toward Blair's company. *Smart fellow.*

Hampton didn't feel it until it was upon him. It rose like a volcano in his chest building fury before it burst from his throat. "Yeea! Yeea!" It was loud and guttural as if he screamed in a different language something unknown to man and only to beast. It was a mixture of every creature mankind feared that roamed the night with impunity. It was wolf. It was bear. It was ghost and devilry. It was why you didn't walk into the shadows. It was why men huddled around fires in the dreadful night. It embodied terror and the terror reigned supreme.

The battle cry was picked up by the men around him. Their blood boiled for revenge. The Yankee invaders came to take their land and their lives. Now they would pay with theirs. Shouts and screams echoed, bouncing among the trees. And the way the Union troopers cowered, they felt the yell deep in their bellies.

Hampton kicked his mount, screaming, "Yah!" The slap of hooves in mud loudly squelched, and his small contingent of North Carolina men galloped into the camp. He made straight for the man in the fur coat. Like most fights without effective leadership, these men would be doomed to the terror and chaos planned by their foes.

His horse flung clumps into the air, and Hampton zeroed in on the officer. They covered their ground quickly, even with the whistling of lead around them zipping like metal bees. The Union soldiers were still surprised by the unexpected charge of horsemen.

The enemy officer in the fur-trimmed jacket stared wide-eyed as the giant on horseback drew closer. Disbelief struck his face. He was handsome and well-proportioned with an educated demeanor surrounding him.

Perhaps he thought himself impervious to harm. None of that mattered. *Time to add another notch to his grip.*

His opponent slowly lifted his pistol, but Hampton was already aiming down the barrel of his. The bullet struck the officer in the side, spinning him into the freezing mud. The horsemen cut through the makeshift shelters. And Hampton bellowed with joy.

CHAPTER 23

Early Morning, March 2nd, 1864
Between Atlee Station and Mechanicsville, Virginia

Brigadier General Kilpatrick rubbed his hands together in front of a blazing flame, a quilted blanket cloaked around his shoulders. Warmth caressed him for the first time in days. He stood soaking in the heat, feeling it dry the weariness from his bones. His jacket and greatcoat hung nearby the stone fireplace, dripping away the chilly wetness.

"They'll break tomorrow, sir." Henderson said from behind him.

"Of course they will," he said. He didn't bother to acknowledge his subordinate. "That blasted Dahlgren."

Henderson's voice sounded out again. "He's a sound mind like his father. The roads are bad. I'm sure it's just a delay. He'll be there tomorrow."

"Have you spoken with the lad?"

The officer mumbled. "Well, no, sir. I just am optimistic."

"You're optimistic?"

"Yes, General."

Kilpatrick turned around. "Good. So am I."

The man visibly relaxed. His eyes were bright and blue with only joy held inside them.

"I didn't come all this way to return to Meade and Pleasonton empty-handed."

"None of the men did, sir. They are itching for a fight."

"As am I. These pesky rebels should have been driven back into the holes they came from. Not to worry. Tomorrow, we renew the assault."

"They will break, sir."

"Not in the same spot of course. We will feint a renewed attack where we were today. I'd say the boys from the 7th Michigan can handle that, and our main body will ride in from the east. If we are repulsed." The words tasted bitter on his tongue. "Then we can retreat easier to Butler's lines near Williamsburg and Yorktown."

His subordinate gave a mighty grin. "A plan guaranteed to succeed. If I may ask, we heard church bells today. I'd wonder if the city is being reinforced with men from Petersburg."

"Won't matter. Invalids and gray hairs to the last of them. Even if Dahlgren doesn't appear, we will smash through once they break. It will go quick."

"I share your optimism."

"As you should. It's a solid plan. Lincoln will thank us by the time this is over."

His man grinned beneath his mustache. "It will be a fine day indeed."

"Indeed." Kilpatrick stepped closer to the fire. He pulled a short cigar from his breast pocket. He'd been saving them for his staff when the battle was won, but the rich fragrance and the opportunity to take the edge off and keep the cold out superseded everything else. He smelled along the length of the cigar, giving his nose a delight.

"Henderson?"

"Yes, General?" A pleasing look spread on Henderson's face as if he were a loyal dog.

"Would you like to smoke a cigar with me?"

"It'd be an honor, sir."

I might as well pat his head for being a good boy. He sighed. "Come on over then."

The man approached him with a smile. Kilpatrick handed him one of his victory cigars. The man breathed in the tobacco.

"These are mighty fine, sir."

Kilpatrick side-eyed him. "Very fine." He bent at the waist and pulled a burning stick from the fireplace. Holding it near the tip of his cigar, he puffed until it smoked. He rotated the cylinder, getting an even burn all the way around the edges, and handed the ember to his fellow officer.

The man attempted to do the same but left an edge unlit causing it to burn uneven.

Kilpatrick ignored the officer's novice neglect of the quality cigar. "These were supposed to be for when we'd completed our mission."

"Very fine." The officer let out a short cough. "We are assured victory tomorrow."

"Nothing is assured. Never assume."

Henderson's smile flattened with the rebuke. "My apologies, sir."

"It's fine." He blew rich smoke from his mouth. "But when we're finished here, send Lieutenant Colonel Preston and Major Taylor to me. They will go with five-hundred troopers each to secure our entrance to the enemy's capital. We will wait here with the main body and cover their escape when the deed is done. Always be one step ahead. You can quote me on that, Henderson." He pushed smoke through his nostrils, feeling the smoky warmth.

"They are talented soldiers. Taylor's a veteran of the regular army?"

"He is. The 5th U.S. Cavalry spent plenty of time dueling the red skins on the frontier. He is well-suited for this kind of warfare." Taylor was a rough and tumble fellow. Short on words. Short on height. Broad shoulders. Like an enforcer for a gang. The man was always cool, never rebuked an order and his 1st Maine men were as likely to fight each other as the enemy. An unruly lot, more at home in a forest than anywhere else. The only regiment he'd bet over them in a fight was the 1st Michigan. Half of them should be in prison. "Regardless, if I have to send a cannonball through Jefferson Davis's bedroom window, I will."

His subordinate laughed too hard, but Kilpatrick accepted his enduring praise. Henderson was a lackey, but he was his lackey. All men on the rise had them, the clingers and men who held the coattails of those that were greater. Those that were more connected. He could have told the lieutenant colonel the sky was green and the rivers red and he would have nodded and told him how pleasant they were.

Henderson wasn't a poor commander. He lacked a bit of imagination and was maybe a touch hesitant in the thick of battle, but the man would follow orders like any dutiful soldier should.

Kilpatrick puffed, allowing the delicious smoke to run along the crevice of his mouth, gently letting it escape.

"Very fine tobacco, sir. Where did you come across it?"

Bluish-gray haze filled the room. "Imported from Cuba."

"Mighty fine."

Kilpatrick exhaled, finally feeling more relaxed than he had in days. He needn't worry. His plan would come through. If anything he was ambitious, and this plan was fit for a man like that, a man that wanted to improve his station. So he would succeed because he wouldn't have it any other way. He would sacrifice this man, and any number of men in his command, to complete his mission. It was a noble enough cause. They would go willingly to their deaths. Their brothers-in-arms counted on them. Their nation demanded it of them. They could cripple if not deaden the Confederacy in the water tomorrow. Then he would have something again.

Henderson grinned, staring at the flames. "Did I ever tell you about my family farm in Connecticut? Wonderful place. Right there upon a hill overlooking orchards and pasture. My father raised an excellent stock of horse flesh."

"You have."

"But did I tell you the time when my daughter found the winning apple at the county fair?"

Kilpatrick's lip twitched as he thought about his wife and infant son. His throat tightened like an invisible hand slowly squeezed. "No, you haven't."

Henderson continued with his chummy story, not even considering the fresh wounds that he may be ripping open for Kilpatrick. The man was oblivious, but his commander just let him jump happily along, talking about his child and wife as the general was too composed in his own thoughts to stop the man.

His sweet new wife, Alice. His precious baby. *Oh God, my child.* His chest ached like a bayonet pierced through the heart. He tapped the ash from his cigar in the fire. Just like that. They were gone too. Mere dust in the wind. Snuffed out before they began. The seed of his marriage clipped as a seedling while the leaves were fresh and green. Now they were a barren brown stalk, dead before they had a chance to produce any fruit. The cigar tasted more bitter now. He regarded the mocha cylinder in his hand, smoke tendrils lazily floating in the air.

"Won a ribbon and all, sir. Most fun we ever had."

"I bet," Kilpatrick uttered. He'd had a yellow streamer with Alice's name fastened atop his battle flag.

The man realized his fallacy now. Fear and worry cloaked his normally jolly features. "I meant no offense."

"No. No need."

"Sir, you have my deepest apologies."

Kilpatrick stared up at the man. "Do not apologize to me." He clenched his jaw in anger.

His subordinate shook his head, fear in his eyes that he offended Kilpatrick. "Sir."

"Drop it, Colonel. I said, there is no need to worry."

"But your family?"

Turning his head, Kilpatrick thrust a finger at the man. "I will cut you out of this command so fast you'll be on Halleck's staff by Monday. Do not apologize."

The thundering of hooves and shouts of men overcame the crackling of the fire.

"Sorry, sir."

"Dear God, would you have given me men with backbone this raid would be done by now." He turned away from Henderson. "We have an objective to focus on, so let's win this fight."

"Yes, sir."

More shouts infiltrated their small house. Kilpatrick went to the window, glaring outward. Men in blue scrambled over his camp. Others turned their horses nervously in the dark. "What on earth is going on out there?"

His subordinate joined him. "I have no idea, sir."

A fist pounding heavily reverberated off the door, shaking the walls. Kilpatrick beat Henderson there. He ripped open the door with a snarl. "What on—"

The officer before him had blood running from his temple. "Sir," he breathed.

"Better be good, soldier." Kilpatrick couldn't place the man. Whiskers lined his face. Unremarkable brown eyes.

"We come from the 7th Michigan at Atlee Station." The officer blinked.

"And?"

"We've been routed."

"You mean you've routed the enemy."

"I. We've been overrun. The men are retreating here now."

Kilpatrick shoved the officer out of the way, marching over soggy ground. Men galloped through his camp. Troopers ran from their shelters.

"You!" He jabbed a finger at a man sitting atop his mount. "What happened?"

"They came in the night. Must of been hundreds if not over a thousand. Snuck up on us. Cannon too. Shredded us near our fires."

"Impossible. Who's in command now?"

"They were led by a giant on horse."

Kilpatrick shook his head in disgust. "Who's leading your men?"

"No idea, sir. The giant brought down Litchfield himself with his first shot on horseback. Sawyer didn't show until it was too late."

"Giant?" Kilpatrick furrowed his brow. Sleet pelted the men and clouded his vision. "What do you mean?"

The officer joined them. "It was Hampton, sir. I'm almost positive."

The trooper turned his mare to stop it from following a platoon of horsemen out of camp.

The cracks of carbines sounded from the pickets his men had set in the forest near the edge of the bivouac. The sound made his skin prickle along with the chill of the night. The wet snow began to saturate his quilt, growing heavier with every droplet.

"Sir, what are your orders?"

The sleet continued down upon him.

He was joined by General Davies, who was hurriedly buttoning his coat. "What's going on here?"

"They've overrun our rear guard," Kilpatrick said.

"Impossible."

"Believe it, General."

"We had an entire brigade in that direction."

More wounded riders galloped into camp like a winter storm. Kilpatrick wiped the wetness from his face. A salvo of carbine fire reported from the nearby woods. Men called to one another in fear. More voices cried for help.

Pulling the quilt tighter around himself, Kilpatrick's body shuddered. His troopers stared his way silhouetted by campfires, clutching carbines in wet hands. He eyed General Davies; dark circles ringed his eyes, and water ran down his cheeks.

More riders charged into the camp, men without companies or order. Chaos and fear were beginning to rule.

A rider approached. "We're overrun, sir. They came out of the night like demons."

Kilpatrick held up a hand. The gunshots began to fade, and more riders entered the camp from the dark.

"I think we've repulsed them, sir," Davies said.

"Repulsed? We're in chaos, General." A fear took over his belly; it was something he hadn't felt in a long time. He didn't know if it was a fear of failure or the fear of being caught in the rout. Or if it was the rebels in the trees. Or if it was his failure to be there for his wife. Or was his career taking a dive having staked so much on this singular event, a raid he was sure he could master. The sleet beat his hat atop his head, a repeated mockery of his predicament. His cigar had gone out with a sizzle. A soggy mess of tobacco in his mouth, he spit it out.

"Get Major Taylor and Kidd to collect survivors and provide a screening action. Tell our men to follow the headquarters staff." He spat out loose clinging tobacco. He could feel the coldness running down his back, chilling him to the bone. "We retreat."

CHAPTER 24

Early Morning, March 2nd, 1864
Near Yellow Tavern, Virginia

The command stopped near a Baptist church painted white. The fleeing moon was hidden from the men below by the clouds. The plain structure had a single door and rose to an open steeple. Shutters were closed over the windows along the sides of the building as if it were abandoned.

A man hung from a towering oak tree nearby. He was hatless and wore a brown coat and trousers. His hands were bound behind his back, and his shoes were missing. Dahlgren waved a private forward to inspect the executed man. The private traveled close enough, quickly turning his horse around and coming back.

"Magee, sir."

Dahlgren lifted his chin. "This land is treacherous indeed. But no sign of Woods?"

"No, sir."

"Then he must have escaped. Good. Cut him down."

Troopers scrambled to obey the colonel's orders. They moved hurriedly with jittery movements, fear ebbing from them like a slow tolling bell. No one wanted to be left behind while the column moved ahead.

One man dismounted and held Magee's legs while another hacked at the rope with a short knife. The horsemen passed by at a walk. Their mounts were exhausted and wet. Wolf patted Billy's flank as they went by the man.

The process of death had already gripped the BMI agent. His face was bluer than a man's should be, lacking any of the vibrance of life. His tongue extended out of his mouth, a dull shade of gray. And his eyes bulged like those of a fly.

"Hanging our men like criminals near God's house. Blasphemous," Shugart said.

"The end of a rope or the end of a barrel. None of it matters unless you get caught," Hogan said. The willowy Irishman pushed his mount along Wolf's unit. He gave a glance back at one of his own. "Woods wouldn't have left him. He's either dead or captured."

"You don't think he escaped?"

Hogan's curls bounced as he shook his head. "Not a chance. Those two were inseparable."

"Means we still don't know where Kilpatrick is, and he doesn't know where we are."

"That be a fact," Hogan said.

The reality of the situation soaked into Wolf like the cold rain. The assault had failed. This was clear. Their five companies were exhausted, battered, and separated from the main army. Hampton was out there. The armed citizens picked them off one by one.

A new kind of fear settled in his belly. He wasn't afraid to die. Dying was easy. But struggling to survive when the land itself rose against you was a dire struggle indeed. He looked to the men around him. If not for himself, he must stay alert for them. Every man needed to do his part to come out of this alive.

Slender Cooke leaned in closely as he spoke to Dahlgren like they shared a secret. The gaunt colonel nodded, a weariness still about his long frame.

The major waved a platoon of horsemen from the 5th New York forward to scout ahead for any potential traps. The gray darkness embraced them and they disappeared.

Little time passed before a narrow byroad was discovered. The detachment from the 5th stood awaiting them in the dark, not knowing which way to go. They turned, facing the arriving column, their horses skittish.

A fusillade of gunshots destroyed the night. Wolf's heart leapt to his throat. His hand found his pistol as the blue-clad men galloped away down a track of road. He lined a shot but hesitated, unsure of friend or foe.

"By God, those traitorous scum were dressed in blue. Follow them!" Dahlgren shouted. "They'll hang for their treachery!"

"Sir, I beg you. It could be another ambush." Cooke sat high in his saddle trying to procure a better view in the darkness. "Won't that lead us closer to Richmond?"

"Major, you're treading on thin ice."

Roberts nudged Wolf. "Major's right, that route will send us toward the fortifications."

"These woods are hostile. The quicker we can find Kilpatrick the better," Wolf said.

"Unfamiliar ground is bad for a cavalryman," Wilhelm added.

Dahlgren wiped rain and sweat from his brow. "Track them."

The column turned down the small road and were forced into close quarter fours. Dahlgren pressed his steed to a trot and the men followed so as to not be separated from their leader. After a time, he brought his mount to a walk and his command breathed a weary sigh of relief.

They walked along, some men sleeping in their saddles. They'd traversed almost two hundred miles in roughly fifty hours over unknown terrain. Wolf didn't know as it happened, but the road narrowed further, forcing the riders into a double and then a single file. Long and strung out, they marched in the morning dimness.

Billy's sway knocked him in and out of sleep despite his heightened fear of being ambushed. Roberts gave a short shout awakening him. "Look!"

Lanterns glowed bright in the early morning, hanging off overhangs. Light flickered from the windows of a house. White-covered wagons rested near a train depot next to railroad tracks. A fieldstone square church stood across a muddy road from the depot. Even its windows were small squares that candlelight leaked from.

The exhausted troopers dismounted in the clearing between the buildings and tied their mounts to fence railings around the depot.

"Try to keep your horses dry," Wilhelm ordered. "Whatever feed you have left, give it to them."

Wolf gathered a handful of corn from a bag and hand-fed Billy. The hungry horse eagerly lapped up the kernels. He stroked the patch of white in the middle of the horse's forehead and muzzle. "We'll find you more soon." The gelding kept his head down.

The last of the men from the trail walked in and Wolf took quick stock. Hundreds of men were simply gone. "Sergeant," Wolf called over.

"What is it?"

"Where's the rest of the column?"

Wilhelm stepped closer, scanning. "Dammit."

They marched over to Dahlgren and Cooke who stood talking to Bartley near the church. They waited to be addressed.

Bartley swayed with uneasiness. A broken madness cloaked Bartley's eyes as if his mind had snapped like a frozen twig. A crooked smile stretched on his lips, and his eyes bounced from place to place, unable to settle on one thing. "Only wounded here, sir. Me and the wounded."

Wolf spied a glance into the church. Blue-uniformed men lay in pews and on the ground. They groaned and moaned in the quiet night while a civilian doctor made his rounds.

"Did you make contact with Kilpatrick?" Dahlgren asked.

"Shot all my rockets, yes, sir. No sign of him, but I can hear him."

"Get ahold of yourself man. What do you mean you can hear him?" Cooke asked.

Faint gunfire popped in the distance; it was almost the sound of rain in the early morning blackness. "He's out there. No doubt. But so are they." Bartley let out a nervous laugh and rubbed his pointy nose.

"He's right, sir. I can hear the gunfire," Cooke said.

Dahlgren eyed the night. "Me as well."

"He's left Richmond."

Dahlgren stared down for a moment, his mind speedily calculating the odds of overcoming their predicament. "He's called off the attack." Shaking his head, he cursed. "And I've been in the dark the whole damn time."

"Then we must make haste to Atlee Station, sir." Cooke leaned closer. "We don't want to get caught in enemy territory." He glanced at Wilhelm and Wolf for the first time straightening his uniform. "Sergeant, Corporal."

Wilhelm's back went straight. "Sir."

"Out with it, man. We don't have time for much."

Wilhelm peered at Wolf.

"Sir, you see. We're missing men."

The officers eyed the horses and men taking shelter from the rain. Cooke let out a tired sigh. "What do you mean?" There's men there."

Bartley squealed a short laugh. "So many men."

The two senior officers gave him a dirty look but ignored his outburst.

"No, sir, only about ninety or so. I'd say at least two companies are gone," Wolf said.

"They're gone. Gone. Gone. Gone," Bartley said, nervously rubbing his hands together.

"Be quiet, Lieutenant," Dahlgren growled.

Cooke held a finger out, counting each horse. "He's right, sir. Ain't enough."

"Nonsense. My orders were clear." He stepped back into the lights from the church. "They will catch up. Only a gap in the line. Where's Mitchell?"

"Not here, sir."

"He will emerge. He's a sound head on his shoulders."

"Of course, sir."

"Thirty minutes, we depart," Dahlgren ordered.

"The wounded, sir?" Cooke asked.

Determination settled on Dahlgren's face. "They must be left. Destroy the wagons, they mustn't fall into the enemy's hands." He pointed at the enlisted men. "You men hack the ambulances."

Wolf and Wilhelm eyed one another.

"And the prisoners?"

Captain Yates sat in a pew with four rebels.

"Release them, but I want that traitorous captain with me. I will be there when they court-martial him."

"Sure hope so, Colonel. So I can tell them how you botched this entire raid," Yates said.

Dahlgren crutched forward and slapped the man across the face. Yates took the strike in stride, blinked a few times, and said, "You think that's going to change my mind?"

"Watch your coward tongue before I remove it."

"If killing an innocent man makes me a coward, then take my tongue now."

Dahlgren turned away from the captain.

"Why are you two still here? Did I stutter? Those men will not make the journey, and I will not have Federal material falling into rebel hands. Chop it up."

"Yes, sir," Wilhelm said, echoed by Wolf.

They joined the rest of the unit. "Up and at 'em, boys. Colonel wants this material destroyed," Wilhelm said.

The troopers didn't have enough energy to complain but rose to tired feet and sore saddle bottoms. They took care to unhitch the mules used for pulling the wagons so as to not harm them.

Wolf trudged around to the rear of a wagon. A dark shape lay stretched along the bottom.

"Got to get out. We're breaking this apart."

The shape didn't move. The wagon rocked as Nelson took a giant swing into the front. "Hey, let me help you." Wolf placed a hand on the trooper's shoulder and shook. He was cool to the touch.

"He's dead," Wolf whispered to himself. They'd left him in the wagon to apparently die in the rain. The callousness made him balk, but nothing could be done now. "Hey, Dan."

The sturdy Polish trooper came his way. "Yes?"

"Dead." He pointed at the body.

Dan scowled. "Yes."

"Come on, help me." They dragged the man from the back and Dan hoisted him on his shoulder like a sack of wheat.

"Where?"

"I don't know. There I guess."

Dan lugged the body to the rail depot, setting him on the porch. Other troopers stared on with vacant eyes. Foggy breaths escaped barely living bodies.

In thirty minutes, the men were mounted back atop their tired horses. Every wagon and scrap of material that could be used by the enemy had been destroyed.

Troopers on makeshift crutches and bandaged arms and torsos cried out as the command clopped through the mud.

"Come back!"

"Don't leave us!"

"Please, sir."

Dahlgren waved them back. "The doctor will care for you, and we will be back."

His words had the opposing effect, exciting the men with fear.

A trooper hobbled alongside Wolf. He scratched him with grasping fingers. "Please, take me with you."

"I can't."

The trooper's hands held onto Wolf's boots. "Don't leave me. I'm light as a feather, I am."

"Get away, maggot," Nelson said. He drove his mount into the man, knocking him to the ground. The trooper splatted into the soupy grime. He slowly hauled himself upright in the stinking cesspool, bawling with his head in his hands.

They continued on the path to Atlee Station. By morning, every man left behind would be a prisoner of whichever local militia or Home Guard arrived first.

The rain began to lighten with the break of day, and a hearty mist clung to the trees and ground. The men cautiously made their way through the fog like apparitions marching home.

CHAPTER 25

Early Morning, March 2nd, 1864
Near Atlee Station, Virginia

They passed through Atlee Station, another train depot, in the early morning. All they found were bodies of the dead and wounded. The injured Federals and rebels were in the care of ashen-faced local women. Dahlgren gave the men a hasty salute, and his shrinking column of less than a hundred men carried on.

The command had yet to link with Captain Mitchell's missing troopers, but they knew they were on the right route after seeing the abandoned Union soldiers from Kilpatrick's command.

They trekked north and west, not in the direction of the Army of the Potomac. They would never make it that far with so few men, so they bolted for a closer destination of Gloucester Point, a fort that had been left in Union hands since 1862. In order to do so, they would need to cross the Pamunkey and Mattaponi rivers, both tributaries that melded together to form the York River.

Dahlgren's exhausted men reached the Pamunkey River with no issue. Any relief held by the men for reaching the river was swept away by the dangerously high brown waters. The river itself wasn't very wide, under two-hundred yards, but the only watercraft rested on the other side.

Two troopers from 6th Michigan, brothers from Manistee, braved the freezing waters to row the boat back to the banks holding the haggard force.

Rigging a tow rope, the men hauled themselves across. But they had no chance to rest, hurrying their horses through rebel territory.

Brown and gray timber surrounded the road, lifeless sentinels of the landscape. Dead leaves littered the ground like a wet blanket. Nothing appeared to be alive, including the beyond worn-out men around him. Yet they persisted toward the Mattaponi River.

Well after the sun had graced them with its muted presence, Wilhelm leaned toward Wolf.

"We're being followed."

Wolf coughed into his hand, grunting, "Where?"

"Our seven o'clock."

Twisting in the saddle, Wolf scanned the way behind them, searching for the culprits. A miserable Bart stared back.

"I don't see them," Wolf said softly.

"They're out there. Moving slowly so as to not catch our eye. Keep those pistols loose in their holsters, men."

Cautious eyes darted around the woods, but no attack came. Dahlgren's detachment moved with relative quickness in the daylight. It was amazing how much easier it was to navigate the land during the day. Traveling by night, everything was more complicated, especially in enemy territory.

Like its tributary brethren, the Mattaponi River was swollen from the rain and melting snow. It rushed before them, bleeding onto the land as if it wished to force life into its deadened state.

"Just across here, men. Then it's easy going before we fall under the protection of Union gunboats near Gloucester Point. No rebs dare go there."

A half-hearted cheer rose up from the troopers.

"Spread out and find a way across."

The men searched along the banks until a call went out. "We got an old scow here!" The horsemen drifted back to the clearing as the men dragged the boat along the shore.

"Look at that ancient craft. Must be from the Revolution," Roberts said. He may have been right. The flat-bottomed boat was used to transport goods and supplies down the river. It was perfect for rivers and harbors as it had a shallow flat hull to prevent it from running aground. It was less than half the size of the craft they'd commandeered earlier in the morning that could not transport horses. Rickety and patched, its buoyancy was debatable at best.

"You men get aboard. No more than six at a time," Cooke said. Soldiers took up oars, settling in the boat. "Horses will have to swim."

Troopers removed their mounts' saddles, loosely wrapping their reins to the craft. The horses splashed in the water, wading, and then paddling.

The remaining force watched in earnest as the tired soldiers struggled with their oars. The boat moved relatively speedily with six men rowing, but painstakingly slow as the single man rowed the three-hundred yards back across. Dahlgren observed the crossing with a dignified straight pose seemingly unconcerned by their situation.

Yates edged his horse closer to the colonel. "Sir, we should set skirmishers out."

Dahlgren turned on the captain. "You scoundrel." Anger creased his brow. "Your man was supposed to guide us. He's the reason we're in this mess. Now you presume to give me orders?"

"He deserved better than he got."

"He got exactly what he deserved."

Yates spit on the ground, lifting his bearded chin in the air. "He meant no harm, and please excuse me, sir, but you are one sorry excuse for a commander."

Dahlgren slapped the man hard across the face. Red stinging fingerprints lined the part of Yates's cheeks not covered in hair. His hand trembled as he spoke. "You will hang for this."

"I will not." Gradually, Yates's head drifted back upright.

A sneer formed on Dahlgren's lips. "I'll see to it myself."

"Sir, I agree with the captain. We should set skirmishers," Wilhelm said.

"I hear you, Sergeant."

A single man, struggling with two oars, rowed the rickety scow back over the river. He ran it aground and five more men hopped inside. Two others shoved them off, their horses resisting them the first few feet into the frigid waters.

The staredown between the colonel and the captain continued for a moment, the men waiting for the colonel to hit the captain again. Dahlgren pointed at Wilhelm. "Sergeant, you may set your men into a skirmish line."

Wilhelm wasted no time. "You heard the colonel. Wolf, take your men over there. The rest with me."

The 13th Michigan men dismounted, handing their reins to every fourth man. They divided and spread into the forest with their carbines.

Cautiously, they formed a line in the timber, knowing that even at this very moment, a rebel sharpshooter could have his sights on one of them.

Wolf crouched down next to a fungus-cloaked tree, its trunk turning a sickly shade of yellow. He placed his weight on his good leg, letting his braced knee rest. He scanned the woods for rebels. Roberts's small form kneeled nearby along with Van Horn as a bookend.

Despite the damp weather, Wolf's eyes were dry and bloodshot from exhaustion. He ran his eyes back over the forested land searching for movement, man, or both. He settled on a stumpy tree roughly fifty yards away. *Whiz!* A bullet whistled by his skull, and he dropped flat to the ground. He would never grow accustomed to the eerie noise of a ball sailing closely past. That ghostly sound made a man's heart race and his rear pucker.

Crack! Crack! He kept his hand atop his head as he lay for a moment. Wetness seeped through his greatcoat soaking through his jacket. One of his men returned fire. He crawled to the other side of his tree. He checked his carbine's percussion cap and ran his thumb along the hammer, moving it to full cock. Using his elbow to support, he quickly got to his knees and peered wide-eyed.

An empty forest sprawled before him. The only distinguishing mark left by a man was the gun smoke clouding the cold air. He located the gray shroud and searched for anything man shaped. There was something there. Staring at it from this distance, he would hesitate to call it a man. Steadying his arm on the tree, he took aim. *Bang!* He sent a bullet speeding in its direction. He had no idea if it hit the enemy or not but took cover behind the trunk, going through the process of reloading his Sharps carbine.

The rebels played this cat-and-mouse game with Union soldiers for about a half hour, neither side willing to expose themselves to the hidden men in the forest before them. After every shot, Wolf would crawl to another tree before scouring the dead terrain for another shadowy target.

"You there, men. It's time. Retreat to the boat," Dahlgren's voice came from behind, making Wolf jump.

Shocked, Wolf stared at the colonel on his crutch. The one-legged man had struggled through the woods to give them the order in person. With his tall frame propped up on his support, he made an easier target than a scarecrow. "Sir, take cover."

Roberts banged a shot from nearby, quickly crouching behind a log.

"Nonsense."

Thwack! A bullet thudded into Wolf's tree cover spraying splinters of wood.

"Sir, I believe that one was for you."

The colonel's eyes scrutinized the timber as if he didn't believe the enemy to be that close. He waved Wolf upright. "Move your men back to the river."

"Yes, sir."

Wolf rolled off the tree trunk, firing another bullet at something he thought was a man's hat. "Roberts, Van Horn, move to the boat!"

His men sprinted from their hiding places, bounding through the naked trunks, logs, and stumps to the shouts of rebels. Bart handed off the reins to their mounts. The troopers dragged their horses into the freezing water. Billy resisted in wide-eyed terror but let himself be tugged into the river. The blue-coated men hopped into the shallow boat. The leaky vessel rocked with the disruption.

"Hurry! We have to move," shouted the young trooper manning the oars.

Wolf grabbed Roberts's sleeve. "Where's the colonel?" Both men glanced back through the timber. Dahlgren crutched from the trees, pistol in hand.

"He's going with the last group. Pick up that oar," Van Horn said. He tied Billy's reins to the side of the scow and grabbed an oar. The rest of his men did the same.

Oars sliced through the murky water. Chilled droplets stung their hands. The horses huffed and puffed as they swam alongside, their eyes huge with panic. Faint gunfire continued in the background over the sound of men pushing themselves to exertion. The three-hundred yards rapidly disappeared.

They grounded the flat-bottomed boat and the troopers hopped out.

All the other troopers stared at the empty craft.

"I ain't going back," the young trooper said. He clambered out of the scow.

"What do you mean? They'll be captured."

The man shook his head no. "I ain't risking my neck no more. They'll find another way."

"Wolf!" Roberts pointed. "They're on the banks."

Blue-uniformed men stood on the river's edge. Pistols popped in their hands, barking fire toward the trees. One man stepped his horse close to the water as if he contemplated trying to swim it.

"Send me off," Wolf ordered.

Roberts and Bart lowered their shoulders into the hull. "Come on, Polska! Push!"

The ramshackle watercraft grated across the sandy bottom, convincing it to release its hold. Wolf settled into the center of the craft, an oar in each hand. He leaned into his rows, pulling like a mad man to increase speed, sending water splashing. He growled at himself as he heaved. "Come on, Wolf."

The scow plowed through the water riding lower than she should, gliding like a swimming rhino. The gunfire behind him increased in tempo. He chanced a glance over his shoulder. A blue-uniformed man lay in the dead grass on the banks.

Wolf hefted with all his might, and it wasn't long before the boat crashed onto the shore.

Adams hopped inside, keeping his head low. "Wolfie boy, knew you'd come back for us, the fact we're pals in all." He aimed his pistol jaunting his head to get a clearer shot and pulled the trigger. Wilhelm dumped Shugart's body into the bottom. The colonel stood defiantly on the river's embankment, staring out into the woods.

"Colonel!" Wilhelm said.

Dahlgren crutched hurriedly like a beggar chasing a meal, allowing himself to be rolled into the boat. Nelson capped duel pistols into the timber then holstered one, as he and Wilhelm took to shoving off the craft.

The overburdened scow ran shallow in the waters, grinding along the bottom as the two troopers pushed them further into the river.

Using his oar, Wolf propelled them off the riverbed, and Adams joined him until they were free-floating. The craft rocked as Nelson and then Wilhelm crawled aboard. Wilhelm scrambled over the other, lying next to Shugart for only a moment while he caught his breath. He snatched an oar and claimed a seat, helping the men row.

Straining, the group rowed across the river. Gray men emerged from the woods, standing on the shore. No more than seven men peered over the water.

The troopers had full view now as they rowed in reverse. Their enemy was dressed in varying shades of browns and grays, holding all manner of shotguns and muskets. They were militia on a good day. One took aim, discharging his firearm.

The Union men instinctually hunched near gunwales, nothing but the boat itself between them and bullets. The shot sailed harmlessly by, never even getting close to its designated target. A rebel swatted at the shooter that appeared more like a teenage boy than a man.

Between breaths, Wolf said, "Is Uncle all right?"

"He'll be fine." Wilhelm pushed air through his mustache. "A grazing round, more exhaustion than anything else."

"Just be thankful we don't have to hear his mewing for the next bit," Adams said with a smirk.

The men grunted and sucked wind as they quickly jabbed oars in the swirling waters. When they reached the other side, the rest of the command was already mounted and waiting. Jaded eyes watched them struggle ashore, relative indifference deep inside.

Wolf saved a glare for the man who wouldn't make the run. He rushed from the small boat. "You!"

The trooper gulped, looking for a way out. His horse mirrored his rider's emotions, stepping forward then backward.

"Johannes," Wilhelm said. "Not now."

Wolf stopped in his tracks, his eyes pummeling the man with anger.

"Help me," Wilhelm commanded.

They assisted the one-legged colonel from the boat. They wrapped arms around him and carried him to his horse. Together, they counted to three and hoisted him atop his steed.

The colonel regarded his men. "We are in need of a much overdue rest. If I remember what Kilpatrick said about the Stoneman raid, there should be a hamlet not far from here. We can dry out and recover." He pointed at Nelson and Bart. "You two break apart that scow." Looking down at Wolf. "You can strap my leg to the side here." He handed Wolf a belted piece of leather.

Wolf took the strap, running it from one edge of his saddle to the rear, resting it over the thin meat of the colonel's thigh. Dahlgren grunted as Wolf tightened it. "That's sufficient, trooper. Thank you." It would keep him from falling out of the saddle, especially if they had to ride hard. The colonel twisted, securing his crutch behind him.

Nelson and Bart went about smashing the scow to driftwood, a more natural state for the patched watercraft.

"Give me a hand," Wilhelm said.

Together they carried Shugart, propping him into a saddle. Wilhelm hopped up behind him. "We'll double until he's awake. No need to make a big deal of it. He'll be back to before we know it."

Wolf understood the sergeant's hidden message. Keep Shugart's injuries hush-hush or risk being ordered to leave him behind.

Dahlgren noticed the sergeant caring for his men. "Sergeant. You did well getting that wounded man to safety. If he isn't mobile, by the time we finish at the hamlet, then he will be left in the care of the locals. Is that understood?"

"Yes, sir," Wilhelm said.

"Very good. Forward march, men."

The exhausted troopers trekked down the country road until humble homes and a small mill emerged from the trees.

CHAPTER 26

Dusk, March 2ⁿᵈ, 1864
Garnett's Mill, Virginia

The hamlet had only four homes and a short mill that ran along a creek that fed into the Mattaponi. It was a modest mill, the exposed wheel not more than eight-feet high, not like the taller ones on the Grand River in Michigan with three- or four-story structures attached. Wolf supposed that the creek wouldn't support anything more. It ground flour during peacetime. Now it ground flour for the Confederate war effort.

The locals called it Garnett's Mill after the family that had owned it since the Revolution days, but everyone that lived there had a stake in the mill's operation. Local farmers would bring wheat to the mill for grinding into flour and pay for the service. In turn, the families of Garnett's Mill would ensure the operation and maintenance and in some cases storage.

The Union soldiers took refuge in barns and houses. A quick promise was given to spare their mill and the men filtered out into their respective regimental groupings.

A woman monitored the riders' approach from the porch of a humble two-story white brick home. Her arms were crossed over her waist. Wilhelm advanced near the home, stopping within a respectable distance.

"How can I help you, Sergeant?"

Wilhelm removed his hat. "Ma'am, we was wondering if we could take a rest in your barn over yonder?" He gestured at a small structure on the edge of her property.

Wolf guessed she was about thirty. Her face was slender, but her jaw was sharp. Her chestnut hair wasn't in a bun but hung loose around her shoulders, and her eyes crinkled along the edges like an aging parchment. She eyed the sergeant with mistrust. "You'll leave me out of this? Spare this land?"

Wilhelm gave a short nod. "I reckon we will. We have no ill-will toward the place."

"It's all I have left. I'll starve without it."

"Are you by yourself, ma'am?"

She visibly gulped and her slightly lighter brown eyes darted away from the men. "My husband is gone." Rushed she added. "And I have a gun."

"You have nothing to fear from us." He dipped his head for a moment. "May I ask your name? And where did your husband fall?"

"I didn't say he died."

"No, but your eyes did."

"I'm Mrs. Hemlick." She licked her lips. Her mouth tightened and her eyes drifted upward. "He fell at Gettysburg." Her lips shook. "I haven't even gotten his," she gulped, "things." She wiped her eyes, exhaling loudly. "Remains."

Adams's horse took a step closer to Wolf. "A widow, Wolfie. Has to be looking for another suitor."

"She suits me just fine," Nelson said from the other side.

"Best leave her be."

Mrs. Hemlick took a handkerchief from her sleeve and dabbed her eyes. "I'm sorry this godforsaken war is ruining our lives."

"I'll brighten her day," Nelson grunted.

Wilhelm glanced over his shoulder. "Quiet in the ranks." He faced the woman. "I am sorry for your loss. We will not disturb you."

"Thank you," she said, wiping her eyes harder. "I've got a few chickens and some bread. I'll bring it out."

"We would be much obliged to you, ma'am."

Her tone hardened. "But you spare my mill."

"I will do my best."

She tilted her head and nodded, accepting that an affirmation was the only thing she was going to receive from the sergeant. She disappeared inside her home.

The men were forced to one side of the barn as the other was used to keep four draft horses. The weather made both groups tolerant of each other. A campfire was made, and the chickens plucked and soon grease sizzled in the flames, skin charred. The unit ate their fill, the consumption of food after so long making them drowsy. Even their mounts lowered their heads in weariness. The horses were all left saddled with loose girths to prepare for a speedy departure if the need arose.

Wolf needed no help slipping into a deep slumber, the kind where you blacked out and no dreams came. When a hand shook his breast, he came to in a groggy stupor, unknowing where he was. "What? Where am I?"

"In the South," Roberts whispered.

Wolf brushed him away. "Why'd you wake me?"

Roberts scanned the outside of the barn. "You hear that?"

The soft crackle of the fire was the only sound.

A muffled scream trickled over the two men like mumbles of alarm. Roberts glanced back at the house. "You hear it this time?"

"I did." Wolf sat up eyeing the home. "It's coming from there." He pushed himself off the luxurious wooden ground that was infinitely better than the saddle and not exposed to the miserable weather. Every muscle in his body lamented as he stood. He rubbed his eyes and scratched his beard, tapping his hip for his pistol. Another call for help sounded out, light and feminine, a summer breeze in the harshness of winter. "The widow's house."

The two men half-jogged down a foot-beaten path to the humble two-story white brick home. Wolf fell behind his quick friend. Roberts reached the door first and twisted the knob, disappearing inside.

The entry was dark. Shadowed stairs led to the second story. A short doorway revealed a kitchen on their left and a room filled with an orange glow from its fireplace on the right.

"Where are they?" Roberts said.

Muffled screams traveled down the stairwell from the top floor. The two men exchanged a look. Roberts skipped up the steps and Wolf hobbled behind, using the walls to propel himself faster.

Roberts pounded on a bedroom door with his fist. "You all right?"

"Help!" a woman's voice called. The angered grunt of a man overcame her stifling cries.

"Open the door!" Wolf shouted.

Adams's voice came from the other side. "Go boil a shirt! Nothing to see here."

"You open this door right now, Private!"

Roberts tried the doorknob. It resisted him.

The woman cried out again.

"We go in." Wolf lowered his round shoulder into the door. *Bang. Bang.* Dust and dirt clouded the air. The wood creaked under the pressure. *Bang.* On the third thump, the door broke inward, and Wolf went with it, stumbling inside.

A pistol clicked next to Wolf's ear. "I told you to leave here, Corporal, while we finish our business."

"Let's put that gun away," Roberts said. He pointed his revolver at Adams. A coatless Nelson, his white shirt stained with yellow, held Mrs. Hemlick down on the bed by her wrists. Her shirt was torn, and the blankets were strewn about with white sheets.

"Meant no harm." Adams put his weapon toward the ceiling and smiled quick. "See?" He slowly slid the gun back into his holster.

The woman groaned, kicking her legs and ruffling her dress.

"Hold still," Nelson grunted at her.

"Let her go," Wolf said.

The broad, bearded man glanced over his shoulder. "You can have at her when I'm done, but I'm first."

Adams raised his eyebrows in a nonchalant way as if this arrangement was a well-known fact. The large man bent down and kissed her neck forcefully. The woman squirmed and kicked her feet, but the man was built like an ox and had the strength of one too.

"Nelson, stop." Wolf's hand went to his sidearm. "That's an order."

Deftly, he drew his pistol and cocked the hammer, glancing at the firing cone to make sure a percussion cap was there. He aimed at Nelson's back. *Big target.*

Nelson shoved the woman back on the bed, causing her to bounce. He exhaled like a bull and stood upright. Flexing his back with a series of cracks and pops, he turned on Wolf. "I said you could go next."

"I don't want to go next."

"Then don't. Get the fuck out." Nelson leaned back over her, and the woman turned away.

Wolf shook his head. "I ain't leaving."

Nelson flexed his meaty fists. "What you gonna do? Shoot me?" He took a step forward. "What you should do is shoot me." A guttural sound came from his throat as if he were a wolf threatening another to back off his kill. "'Cause if I get my paws on you, I'll rip you limb from limb."

Bringing his revolver more level, Wolf said, "No women. No children." His voice was rock steady with conviction. He'd seen enough of wars and raids and the depravity to make him sick, and just because it happened didn't mean he needed to perpetuate man's deepest darkest actions. He was rejecting these men and their outlook. He was drawing a line in the sand between them.

Adams spread his arms wide. "Wolfie boy, come on. We're only having fun. If the rebs catch us, they'll lock us up and throw away the key. Let the man have fun in peace."

"No. That's enough. This ain't right."

Lifting his chin, Adams said, "Who decides that? Who said she was innocent?"

"I'm higher in rank than you, and I say no women and no children."

"You're making the rules now?"

Nelson pointed at him. "Get out of here or you'll get hurt."

"Wolfie, we're friends. You're one of us. I know Nelson and I have always thought of you like a brother."

"I ain't like you."

Adams gave him a hurt look. "Sure you are. You robbed that old woman. You killed those boys when they ran, shot 'em in the back. You burned that mansion to the ground, and you laughed while you did it. You rode down those civilians that stood against us. You left the wounded. You hung that Negro. You're a murderin', thievin', burnin', and," he held a hand lightly in the air, "you're just like us. You were made for this war, just like me and Nelson here. Ain't that right."

"He's got a blacker soul than all of us."

"Maybe I'm not clean. Maybe I'll have to answer for the things I done, but no women and no children."

"You ran down those boys in the field," Adams said.

"They was armed and they came to fight." Wolf kept the gun on Nelson. "I let another one live. Told him to play dead until we left."

"Add cowardice to your list of sins."

"I ain't a coward."

"What's right? And what's wrong? Does the Bible tell you so? It's all perspective, Wolfie. You don't think if they was up north they wouldn't do the same thing to us? You don't think they would defile our women? Rob us, murder our boys, burn our homes?"

Wolf shook his head, pistol still trained on Nelson. "Hurting that lady isn't right. If a man wants to fight, then I will oblige him, but I ain't defiling a woman 'cause she grew up within the wrong boundaries of a war."

"You draw the line now? After all the fun we had? This is why we're here. This is why Old Abe let us back in after we were done, the hangman's noose around our necks. He needs us to do his dirty work. He needs us to win this war."

He couldn't step back from it now. "No women. I don't want to shoot you, but I will if you harm her."

"We're here to wreak so much havoc upon the enemy he gives up the fight and surrenders. What better reminder of what will happen than Nelson's babe popping out of her in nine months. We're here to take the wind out of 'em."

"No, we we're here to free our prisoners and kill." He stopped, realizing a rebel sympathizer was in their midst. "We failed."

A handsome grin formed on Adams's swarthy face. "Can you imagine if you was out fighting and you got a letter saying your woman's been defiled 'cause you weren't there to defend her impeccable honor?"

"I cannot."

"Exactly. 'Cause it's unthinkable. Soul crushing. Enough to make a man put down his blade. We have to be heartless. We have to show no mercy. Only then will they quit. They only respond to strength."

"You're not going to rape that woman."

Adams took a step near him. "She is but a casualty of this conflict. A war we didn't have to fight if her state wouldn't have joined the Confederacy."

"Stop, Adams. We ain't talking about that." Wolf shook his head in anger.

"You, Wolfie, don't understand what this war is and what it will take to stop it. They deserve every scrap of hatred in our blackened hearts."

Wolf's gun wavered in front of Nelson.

"It'll never be the same. We're firing a canister shot into their culture and you know what?"

"What's that?" Wolf said.

"It makes me glad."

"Why?"

"'Cause it ain't us."

"I don't love this war like you."

"There's still time." Adams stopped, his grin taking an evil turn. "Corporal." He snapped his fingers together. *Snap.* Like a shockwave, the sound rippled through the room, drawing everyone's eyes in his direction. All Wolf's attention shifted to Adams, a malicious grin still curved on his lips.

Nelson charged. His heavy footsteps pounded the floorboards. He growled like a rabid dog as he launched himself toward the barrel of Wolf's gun.

Wolf's split-second reaction was to pull the trigger. The shot went upward and to the left. Nelson flinched as the bullet entered his shoulder and exited out his back. The woman screamed.

With both hands, the giant trooper made contact like a bull ramming a calf who dared to test him. Wolf's legs flailed as he was lifted airborne, no small feat for he was a large man. His back slammed into the wall and pain shot through him. He grasped at the man's massive forearms as the brute hefted him even higher into the air.

The savage soldier's face twisted in madness. Foam collected on the edges of his mouth. Maniacal eyes stared as if he weren't there but a thousand miles away. Lightness filled Wolf's body as Nelson slammed him on the table as if he were a prized roast beef ready for a slow cook.

The table collapsed beneath his weight, and a fraction of a second later, Wolf's head rocked off the floor. Stars speckled his vision. He wrapped his hands around Nelson's. They squeezed around his neck, a vice of flesh.

Wolf gurgled, as the man continued the process of crushing his throat. His eardrums started to pound inside to the rhythm of his heart.

Fumbling at his waist, Wolf's single hand grasped for the only thing he could hope to free himself with. His fingers scratched and scraped at it. Nelson stuck his face near Wolf's.

The stench of stale whiskey emanated from his mouth. "You're going to die, and I'm gonna fuck your corpse when I'm done with her. Feed you to the wolves after that. Ain't that poetic. Wolf feeding wolf."

Wolf's numbing fingers found the bone hilt and he released the weapon. When he shoved the knife into Nelson's gut, it took the large trooper a few seconds before his eyes registered any pain. It was a difficult strike. Wolf's arm was almost trapped, and sticking a man with a knife was never easy. Muscle, bone, organs always got in the way. He ripped his hand free and stabbed him again.

Nelson growled and removed a hand from Wolf's neck, grasping for the blade. "I'll show you where to stick that."

Wolf grabbed the man by the back of the neck and hugged him tight, ramming the knife into Nelson's back.

The man lurched upright. Wolf's breath came in sputters and wheezes. He turned on his side, coughing.

Nelson stood, reaching for the knife hilt. The big man roared as he tried to remove the blade. Adams held Roberts at gunpoint on the floor.

Wilhelm and Van Horn barged through the door. After taking a half-second glance at Nelson, Wilhelm punched him square in the jaw, sending him to the floor. Bart and Dan followed behind them, their pistols drawn.

"What in the hell is going on? We're on the run for our lives, and you men are having an all-out brawl." Wilhelm eyed his troopers.

Adams holstered his pistol. "It's not what it looks like. We were just having some fun and it got out of control. You know women, Sergeant. Drive a sane man mad. A true siren she is."

Wilhelm eyed the widow, his eyes narrowing. "You all right, ma'am?"

Mrs. Hemlick stood, covering herself with a patchwork blanket. Her dress had been ripped and hung loosely over one shoulder. She kept her chin level as she visibly shook, nodding her head.

Wilhelm glared back at Wolf. His eyes knew exactly what had happened. "And how are we going to explain this trooper with a knife in his back?"

"Funniest thing, Sergeant. Nelson here fell on that knife. Nasty trick. Ain't that right, Wolfie?" Adams said.

"That's right."

Wilhelm shook his head. He already knew the answer but played ignorant anyway. "This man fell on that knife how many times?"

"Three, sir," Adams said.

"You going to live, trooper?" he spat at Nelson.

The large trooper spit. "It'll take more than a tiny prick to bring me down."

"When we get back north, we'll be having words with the general," Wilhelm said, eyes boring into Adams.

Adams blinked innocently. "Do I have a promotion coming my way?"

Wilhelm closed within an inch of his face. "You don't. You have a court-martial. You have no business conducting operations in my unit or this army. Ya been a blight on this unit, and I'll cut you away like a tumor if I have to."

Adams didn't back down. "I just have this feeling that somehow we'll find our way back."

"Not if I have anything to say about it."

"Of course, good sergeant." Adams placed a hand over his heart. "I can only stand by my honor."

Wilhelm growled at the small man. "Patch this ox up. The colonel wants us on the move in twenty, and I'm leaving no man behind despite how much I want too." His eyes settled on the woman. "My apologies, Mrs. Hemlick."

Her finger shook as she pointed. "Get the hell out of my house."

In silence, the men filtered down the stairs and to the outside. Nelson grunted, trying to reach the knife.

"I'll be needing my knife back."

Adams nodded. "Of course." He reached behind and ripped the blade from Nelson's back. The giant bellowed like a lion.

The swarthy trooper spun the knife in his hand for a moment. "Very nice. He flipped the blade in his fingers and stuck the hilt back to Wolf. "Very nice indeed, friend."

Wolf snatched the knife from him, sheathing it on his belt. "Thanks for holding it, Nelson."

The big man howled in anger. "Fuck you, Wolf."

"I guess we will have to finish this conversation another time," Adams said.

Wolf's eyes didn't leave Adams. "Yes, we will."

CHAPTER 27

Evening, March 2nd, 1864
Hampton's camp near Atlee Station, Virginia

"How can I help you, Lieutenant?"

The man was dressed in a farmer's coat and trousers with a gray kepi atop his head. A thick black belt held two pistols and a knife. His cheeks were gaunt, and a light black beard streaked his pale skin.

"Lieutenant James Pollard, H Company 9th Virginia Cavalry."

"I thought your unit was with Stuart?"

The man coughed into his hand, wiping the corner of his mouth. "They are. I'm on sick furlough."

"I can see that. I hope that you are recovering."

"I am, sir. Still a bit under the weather. Rain and cold don't help."

Hampton unconsciously moved his head away from the man. Chills, fevers, and poxes could all be the end of a man and one that was his age even faster. Even George Washington wasn't immune to such things, being taken much before his time. "Unfortunately, these Northerners have stirred us all from our well-deserved rest."

"That they have, but our wrath burns bright."

Hampton couldn't help but smile a fraction. Just like little Kilpatrick's camp. Tents and houses alight. Men screaming in terror. His lone cannon blasting their means for escape. He'd collected almost as many prisoners as he had men in a single hour. Their forms were outlined in the fires; they had been men silhouetted for slaughter. And slaughter they did.

"My men and I are looking for some assistance to string up a band of those blue-bellies running rampant across our land."

"I have no men to spare. We are harassing the rear guard and making the Yankees pay for every step they take on Confederate soil."

Pollard rubbed his brow. "There's another force. We ran into them this morning. Don't know where they're going. If you ask me, they seem lost."

"They will be rounded up in due time. My primary focus is the main body of the enemy."

"I understand, sir. Be as it may. These men don't know the roads, the swamps, the rivers, nothing."

Hampton regarded the sickly man with intrigue. "Carry on."

Pollard gave him a weak smile. "I do believe me and my boys can take the fight to them. Now most my boys aren't fighters. Hell, I got three preachers, four doctors, five lawyers, and seven young'uns. But we know the land."

"Continue." *Men that know the land are dangerous men.*

"Well, I know you ain't from Virginia, but I do believe that Stevensville and River Road be a place we can get 'em surrounded."

"Why is that, Lieutenant?"

"Well, there's a place along River Road where two creeks run north to south. They join together running into the Mattaponi River. The land on either side is real marshy. Never dry even when we haven't had rain in weeks. Murky place. Granddad always talked about a witch living near there. Nobody could ever grow crops." He waved a hand. "Neither here nor there. It's close to King and Queen Courthouse."

"I know the place."

"If we can hem them in, I don't see why we couldn't round up the lot of 'em without much a fuss."

Hampton knew enough of the area to know why the Federals would push that direction. Reinforcements lay that way. This command did not take the best route, but it was a way toward Butler's Union forces on the peninsula.

"You're sure these citizens are up to this task?"

Pollard's eyes studied the outside for a moment in hesitation. His lack of words spoke for itself.

"Lieutenant, I do not want these good people placed in needless danger. Fighting may not be their specialty, and perhaps we should leave it to others. In fact, I'm going to have to order you against it." Hampton went back to the fire and warmed his hands. The Virginia winters were much harsher than he was used to. He would have thought he'd have adjusted by now, but he never did. It made him yearn for South Carolina more and more with each passing day. "I appreciate your vigilance. You may continue to harass them but nothing pitched."

No affirmation came from the lieutenant. Only the fire popped in response. The general glanced over his shoulder. The pale man stood there apparently still contemplating his orders.

Pollard blinked rapidly. "General, sir, we can do this."

Hampton shook his head no, his bushy beard swaying. "The Federals are in a hasty retreat. I don't suspect they will make much of a fuss until spring."

"No, sir. This is principle. They came down here burning and pillaging, killed some of the local boys, scared some of the women and children. That ain't right. Those men should pay for what they done."

"Your enthusiasm is appreciated, Lieutenant Pollard, but with only a handful of men against veteran cavalry, however routed, you would be putting great minds and young minds in danger." He turned. Frank's ghost was there too. Silent and watching. Hampton hesitated a moment. *What hope have these men? You were a warrior and you didn't survive. Am I growing soft from your loss, brother?* Frank's eyes quietly followed him, but he emitted no sound. So Hampton carried on. "If it were just me and you, we'd try, but it's not. You are asking about taking preachers and doctors into battle. They are more precious to a community than a hundred prisoners to this war."

Pollard shook his head. "I respectfully disagree, sir. If those men out there had their way, we wouldn't have nothing left. They'd burn us out. Burn our fields. Torch our mills and our homes. One of the rail depots had twisted track. They made quick work of it too. Must a been no more than thirty minutes there. Left their own wounded behind. What kind of men do that?"

Hampton thought, emboldened by the younger man's words. *Desperate men. Aren't we all?* The retreat from Gettysburg came to mind. Many of the rebel wounded had been captured and now languished in Federal prisons in the North. It very easily could have been him. He thanked God. With severe wounds on his head and hip, surely he would have died in such captivity. That would have been a hell of a way to go. Richest man in the South dies a feverish death in a prison camp.

"What I can do is loan you a couple of my Iron Scouts. They should help you with the ambush. But that's all. Do not make me regret this decision, Lieutenant."

"I would not betray your trust." Pollard gave him a brisk salute followed by Hampton's slower one.

"You may carry on."

"Thank you, sir. I will report back in the morning."

Pollard turned to leave.

"Lieutenant."

"Yes, General."

"Make them pay."

A ghostly grin encompassed his bony face. "It'd be a pleasure, sir."

CHAPTER 28

Evening, March 2ⁿᵈ, 1864
Garnett's Mill, Virginia

The men stood in a loose formation, exhaustion still cloaking them despite their rest. The citizens of the tiny hamlet waited outside their homes, watching the Union troopers with unease. Murders of crows cawed from the nearby trees. Perched on lengthy limbs, they studied the men with avian suspicion. Ebony heads twittered back and forth, their black eyes jumping from man to man as if they were already pecking the soldiers' dead flesh.

Dahlgren lifted a hand in the air, drawing his men's attention. Dark circles encapsulated his eye sockets. "Burn the mill," he said from horseback.

"But, sir, we promised these people," Peters said.

"They are supporters of the rebellion and deserve to suffer. Burn it."

Wilhelm stepped his horse forward. "Sir, any nearby enemy will see the smoke."

Dahlgren turned on the sergeant. "Do you think for a second that the moment we leave here one of these bastards won't go galloping to the nearest militia and tell them our whereabouts?"

The sergeant closed his mouth.

"I said, do you?"

"No, sir."

"Good. Now burn that mill."

A gray-haired man stood nearby in civilian clothes. "Please, Colonel. We were promised to be spared."

"Your lives have been spared, but we mustn't let your treasonous industry carry on."

"You're gonna destitute us. We'd be better off dead."

Dahlgren coaxed his horse over to the man edging near him. "You'd rather be dead? You or you and your family?"

The man held out his hands. "No, please, sir." He bowed his head. "We want to live."

"Then be thankful for our mercy." He waved men forward. Adams willingly went, hopping down from his mount to light torches. Within minutes, the mill smoldered until the fire broke free from the doors. Thick black smoke snaked into the air.

"Shoot some rockets while we're at it," Wilhelm said.

The rest of the troopers observed the torching in silence. Sobs from the civilians and the sizzling flames were the only sounds. The thick stench of burning wood saturated the hamlet.

Adams kicked his horse back into line.

"All in a day's work, boys." Nelson grunted. He slumped in his saddle, holding some of his wounds. Bandages puffed from his coat in various places stemming the flow of blood. His face was much more pallid than normal.

"Lieutenant Peters, you may move them out."

The short column distanced themselves at a walk down a small lane leading away from the river. The colonel sat tall, ignoring the flames and the cries of the people until all his men had passed in rows of four. Then he galloped along his command back to the lead position.

***

Soon the inky darkness encroached. The troopers rode through the wooded region seemingly devoid of all human life aside from them.

Dahlgren, Cooke, Hogan and another scout positioned themselves at the front of the formation, followed by Wolf's unit and the other eighty or so men. Shugart had come too but wasn't exactly lucid. He stayed atop his mount out of survival but had a queer bearing to his eyes as if something plagued him deep inside. The dried blood on his head made him look like a robbery victim.

Winter darkness crept quickly upon the men as if Old Man Winter stalked them himself. A cool breeze tugged at the riders, nipping at their heels with frequent stinging gusts.

Captain Yates rode next to Wolf. He was under strict watch. Dahlgren had been explicit about court-martialing the man and didn't want him escaping. The reddish-haired captain turned, looking over into the looming trees. He shook his head. "We're walking into an ambush."

Wolf's eyes darted out at the dead gray and brown trunks of trees. Timber could be seen as far as the eye could go. Arching weather-beaten limbs tilted into the lane. Thick embankments lined the road as if the locals had carved it from the earth. The land gradually became a murky swamp with stunted trees on one side.

"Those berms keep the route from flooding out. I'd put a platoon behind it."

"I see it." He glanced over at Wilhelm. "You see this."

"Ja."

"Guns loose," Wilhelm said.

Wolf removed his pistol, resting it on his leg, so as to not give any indication that he was ready to fight. His sweaty palm gripped the handle.

The bog forest grew darker, a nothingness sucking them deeper inside. Dahlgren lifted a white-gloved fist in the air, drawing the troopers to a halt. Heads turned, nervously eyeing the growing shadows.

A dark man-made structure obstructed their path. Dahlgren waved at Hogan. He prodded his horse hesitantly forward. "Put silk on a goat and it's still a goat." The Irishman scanned the brush, expecting an ambush any second.

"Get those pistols cocked," Wilhelm said under his breath. Wolf thumbed the hammer. Soft clicks were audible as the men around him did the same. Bart held his carbine on his hip. Roberts laid his Army Colt revolver over his other forearm. Each man stared intently into the trees.

The horses could sense the riders' anxiety. Fog lifted from their noses as they breathed hard. A few stamped their hooves.

"Some kind of breastwork," Hogan half-shouted.

"They don't want us going forward," Dahlgren said. He glanced back at the dreary forest to their rear.

"They're just slowing us down enough so we're all bunched up for the ambush," Yates said softly to Wolf.

"Dismantle the barricade. Merely militia trying to impede our progress. We are closing on the Union lines, men. Our succor lies only a bit farther." He pointed back at Wolf's unit. "You men help the scouts."

Before they could assist, a shadow stepped into the road. He held up his hands as he approached. Every pistol within striking distance was aimed in his direction, and Wolf was sure more than one of them almost shot the man.

Dahlgren leveled his revolver. "Who are you?" He waved the scout forward. "Hogan."

The gray-coated BMI agent walked toward the man.

The newcomer wore a blue coat and had blond hair past his ears. "I'm Private Fleming."

"What unit?" Hogan asked, pointing a gun at him.

"10th New York."

"Who's your commander?"

"Cap'in Granger. Swear it on me life." His eyes darted from side to side. He reached a hand around his waist.

Dahlgren's voice cut the tense air. "Liar!" He sighted his pistol and pulled the trigger. The cap made a damp thud. Turning his revolver sideways, he stared at the malfunctioning weapon. "God—"

Gunfire trumpeted on both berms, a violent bugle call of battle. Each shot was an explosion in the night, coming from all sides. It sounded like the entire command had been thrown into a frying pan and they were the bacon crackling and popping.

Peters's horse reared, throwing him. Dahlgren fell from his saddle, the strap keeping him halfway on. His horse dragged him into the trees and chaos enveloped the command. Hogan dove off his mount, wrestling with the disguised rebel. Black barrels snuck through the barricade, blaring bullets at the column.

Wilhelm's voice carried through the madness. "Take cover!"

Wolf marshaled Billy off the road into the trees. He shot his revolver at a man stepping along the top of the berm. The rebel screamed and clutched his chest, rolling into the muddy lane. Yates followed him, ducking his head near his mount, trying not to take lead to the chest.

Voices bellowed as they fired in the darkness.

"Get me down!" Yates shouted.

Wolf pulled the trigger again. Fire bloomed from the barrel. Horses whinnied. Men cried. Another man screamed. Guns belched flames from the trees. Wild whoops came from the hidden rebels. Bullets riddled the timber, chipping sharp pieces into the air, some biting their way into the soldiers.

The Union men scattered in every direction in chaos. A layer of gun smoke masked the nothingness of night, obscuring everything in a smoky haze.

Wolf dismounted in haste. Yates practically laid flat on his horse's back, avoiding bullets. Wolf grabbed the reins. Gunfire cracked and a bullet buzzed like a bee past Wolf's ear. Billy bolted behind him. "Billy!" The horse disappeared into the timber.

Hooking Yates's elbow, he hauled the man down. Another bullet snapped between the men, pushing a cool wind in its wake. They sprinted into the dense timber.

The moonless night cloaked their rout, and he could only hear Yates sucking wind next to him. At a distance from the road, the men stopped. They crouched down, relieved to not have bullets sailing in the same vicinity as their heads.

Placing a hand on the rough tree trunk, Wolf peered from behind, trying to locate friends or foes. Gunshots worked back and forth, but who was who in the madness remained to be seen.

"Untie me, boy." The red-haired captain held up his wrists. "I told you, I ain't going back. Now untie me so I can die on my feet."

"No, orders."

"Fuck your orders. The colonel is fucking Swiss cheese. Untie me." Rage burned in the captain's eyes. "You know that him arresting me was bullshit. That boy didn't deserve to die."

"You're right, but we have orders."

Yates's face hardened. "Untie me. We need every man for this fight." Pleading eyes assailed Wolf. "This is a devil's apple barrel."

It was a fight for existence, and the only way to survive was for every man to take part. He removed his long knife and sawed through Yates's ropes. The captain was a desperate man, and they made dangerous fighters.

"Give me that carbine."

Wolf didn't hesitate. He unclipped his Sharps carbine from his sling and handed it over. Digging in his pouches, he gave him cartridges and percussion caps. Quickly Yates shoved everything into his empty pouches.

A shadow stalked through the woods. Yates brought the carbine to his shoulder. He aimed and fired, making the shadow collapse. Neither man went to see if it was friend or foe. Maybe they didn't want to know. Maybe they didn't care, but they had each other, and at this point in time, that's all that mattered.

The two men crept along, going from tree to tree for cover. Wolf fired at a shape and the man screamed, falling and writhing on the ground. Other forms turned and ran away, shadows retreating in the night.

A voice gurgled nearby. "Help me!" The man clawed himself across the forest floor. They sprinted to him and crouched down. His uniform was Union blue. The colonel's short-goateed face stared back. Without a crutch, the one-legged officer would never escape far.

"Grab an arm," Wolf said.

They dragged the colonel through the forest and propped the young man against a tree. His head lolled from side to side. His eyes widened as he recognized Yates. "You!" His head shook. "Who set you free?"

"Matters not now."

Dahlgren blinked and squeezed his eyes shut, letting out an exasperated breath. He raised a crimson covered glove from his belly. Blood leaked from him like a partially shut tap. He let his bloodied hand fall to his lap. He motioned at Wolf weakly. "You, come here."

He stepped closer, kneeling down on the ground. "Sir?"

The colonel opened his eyes and they darted around as if he saw imaginary fairies in the trees around them. "Listen now."

He waited while their commander overcame his pain.

Dahlgren gritted his teeth, "God damn." His breaths came faster now. He reached into the inside of his coat and gripped a white letter in his hands. It crinkled between his bloody fingers. "This," he growled, "this mustn't fall into the enemy's hands."

"Destroy it now then," Yates said.

"No." Dahlgren shook his head, audibly gulping. "No. You tear it up here, they'll find it. You must burn it. Until then. You must safeguard this with your life." He stuck it out, his arm wavering with exertion.

Wolf stared at the piece of paper in the young colonel's hand. "Sir, the captain should take it."

"By God, he will not. He is a treasonous fellow. You are not."

Yates shook his head. "I ain't getting captured again."

"Well, I ain't either."

"If you want to live, you will."

Dahlgren moaned, his head suddenly too heavy for his body. "Take the letter. The enemy must not know of our plot. It will threaten our moral authority. It will embolden attempts on Lincoln's life. That mustn't come to pass. Lincoln is the key to holding this Union together. Take it." He eyed the paper trembling in his hand. "Take it."

Wolf clasped the letter. The blood was warm on his cold fingers. He stuffed it inside the envelope in his jacket.

"We have to find Wilhelm and the men," Wolf said in a hushed tone. The sergeant would know what to do with the letter. They had to get to a place so they could burn it.

"Quiet now, boy."

A group of armed men slunk past their position as if they were hunting. Their guns pointed in all directions. Wolf raised his arm, silently aiming.

"No. Too many."

Gunfire rippled a couple hundred yards away. The hunters ran in that direction, disappearing through the trees. Wolf relaxed an inch, letting his gun lower.

Dahlgren glared at the two men, and for a moment, Wolf thought he'd expired. His words were laced with venom. "Surprised you didn't join your ilk, Captain."

Yates turned on the colonel. He knelt close to him. "You and me have some words to finish."

"Say your piece."

"That boy, Martin. He never harmed a soul. He's the only reason I made it back to Union lines. He made an innocent mistake, and you treated him with less respect than a dog."

"Our mission was of the greatest importance. I would have led every man to the scythes of slaughter to accomplish it."

"It looks like you have."

Dahlgren closed his eyes and pushed his head back into the tree trunk. "It was a noble cause, worthy of our deaths."

"At one time, you and me were in agreement, but not like this." He pointed the carbine at Dahlgren's head.

"Yates! What are you doing?"

"I call it justice."

"That is your commanding officer." Wolf put out a hand.

The colonel gestured Wolf away. "Corporal, do not worry. I am not long for this world. This man is just doing what is in his low nature. Treachery."

Yates placed his gun to his shoulder, taking easy aim. "An eye for an eye. You took his life. Now I take yours."

"Captain," Wolf said. "You'll draw them in."

"Won't be my problem. Then we don't need to play this cat-and-mouse game. They can come and find their death awaiting them."

Dahlgren spit toward Yates. "Do it, scum! Take your revenge. Won't make you less of a traitor."

"Nope. I'll still be a man who shot his commanding officer. And no one but Wolf will be any wiser. The only thing that matters is the story we tell."

"And the one we tell ourselves," Dahlgren said.

The carbine kicked in Yates's hands. The smoke stung Wolf's nostrils. Dahlgren slumped to the side. A bullet through the temple ended his life. Wolf stared at the colonel's body then at his captain. "You killed him."

"Aye. I ain't no hero. I ain't no savior. I just fixed what was wrong the best I could."

CHAPTER 29

Early Morning, March 3rd, 1864
A crossroads near Stevensville, Virginia

Captain Yates stripped off his blue cavalry jacket and shoved it into Wolf's hands. "Put that on."

"Why?" He held the officer's wet garment in his hands.

"They'll treat you better if they think you're an officer." Yates studied the forest from behind his tree.

"We have to find the other men."

Yates nodded, facing Wolf. "Well and good, boy, but don't mean much for me. I already told you. I ain't going back." He gestured with his hand, his eyes gleaming like blue sapphires. "Give me yours."

Wolf shouldered off his jacket, shoving his belongings into the captain's, and handing off his own. The man put it on. "You don't worry about me. I'm headed that way. You try to find your unit." He quickly offered Wolf his pale hand. The two men locked fingers around forearms in a warrior brothers embrace. "Good luck, Captain Wolf."

Wolf gave him a quick smile. "And to you, Corporal Yates."

The man jogged off in the direction of the last seen rebels. He slowed his gait, firing his carbine before taking cover. After a moment, he was on the move again, another shadow of death. He vanished into the gloom, and Wolf was left alone with the dead colonel and a letter that could threaten the entire war effort.

His commanding officer held the appearance of a pale boy in the dim light. Crimson leaked from the corners of his mouth, running down the short hairs of his goatee.

The step of boots over wet leaves swallowed Wolf's breathing. The air was scarcely able to fill his lungs. The sound grew closer, fumbling in an attempt to be quiet.

Slowly Wolf exposed himself around the tree. A man stepped cautiously through the looming timber with a pistol aimed in front.

Lowering himself to a crouch next to the colonel, Wolf held his breath. He tried to ignore the lifeless body, but being face-to-face with a dead man never sits right with one's nerves. He waited. His nose trumpeted a tiny whistle as he tried to mask his breath. His heart pounded his chest like a drum.

A single boot stepped out next to him. Then the other. The man stopped as if he too listened intently for enemies.

Using the tree to cover him, he rose like an apparition in the night. Inch by inch, he pointed his weapon at the man's head, the barrel grazing his sideburn hairs. His voice came out a harsh whisper. "Move and die."

The man froze like a statue in the winter.

"Make a sound and die."

"I yield. I yield."

Wolf grabbed the small man by the scruff of the neck and forced him against the tree. "You're going to show me the way out of here."

"Please, I don't know nothing!"

"You will or you'll die."

"I ain't from these parts. Please, mister."

He pressed the end of his pistol into the man's neck. "You're lying."

The man squinted. "Wolf? It's me. Roberts. You know, your old friend. Tent mate. Best pal?"

Wolf lowered his gun. "You sumbitch. I almost shot you."

"You made me piss myself."

Taking a step back, he said, "Jesus, take cover, man. Where are the others?"

"Wilhelm had us rallied in the swamp across the road. He's got us destroying our carbines and anything of value. Once we got moving, I lost 'em."

The letter in his pocket burned, a hot poker resting against his flesh. "I have to destroy a letter."

The snap of a twig brought them to a hurried silence. Wolf's heart sped like a galloping horse's hooves. Roberts's soft breath misted in the chilled air.

"Went this way, he did," came a deep voice with a southern drawl.

A higher pitched one sounded off with nervous energy. "No, he didn't."

"I won't have any of that tongue or you'll get a whooping."

"Yes, father."

"They went this way."

The men quietly stalked by the two Union troopers. After the two rebels traveled out of earshot, Wolf said, "Help me." He motioned to Roberts. Shouts carried from the road. There was a pause in the gunfire and some whoops of victory. He spied around the tree. Sparks flared as torches were lit that illuminated the forest in rippling yellow and orange.

What little light stretched their way, brought the colonel into focus. "By god, that's the colonel," Roberts said.

"Aye, it is. Take that coat off him."

Roberts brought the jacket to the side. "He's been shot in the head."

"And the belly." Wolf helped him strip the colonel.

"He's covered in himself! This don't feel right."

"Just do it."

Torches wavered and the light stretched shadows among the trees. "Take this." He handed him the captain's coat.

"Why on earth would I need this?"

"In case we get caught. They're going to treat us a lot better if they think we're important."

Wolf draped the colonel's fatigue coat over his shoulders. The material stretched tight; his back was much wider. After that, he stuck his arms through the colonel's dark blue greatcoat.

Roberts held Yates's yellow-trimmed short cavalry jacket. "Why do you get to be the colonel and me the lowly captain?"

"Look how long this jacket is. It'd be down to your boots. They'd never believe it."

Yates's jacket wasn't much better on the small-statured man, but believable enough.

"How many bullets you got left?"

"Two in me pistol."

"I have three."

"The colonel got any?"

The two men dug through his pockets finding a dozen more cartridges and corresponding caps. They split them evenly.

The sound of dogs barking roared in the distance.

"They got dogs."

"Run!"

***

Wolf knelt next to a tree, wishing he'd never dismounted Billy. His lungs burned with the frigid air yet cold sweat beaded on his forehead from the effort. He was painfully slow on foot, not to mention the pain half-running caused his ruined leg. The hounds had caught their scent almost a quarter mile back.

"Wolf, we got to keep going." Roberts breathed. "They're gaining on us." Torches and howls rippled through the trees like pebbles tossed in a pond.

"I ain't going to make it. Go on. I'll hold them off."

Roberts brow narrowed. "Now that's no way to talk to a friend. I been with ya from the beginning. We ain't separating now."

Wolf eyed the portable flames and shadows of men in the distance. Every moment they waited, their enemies closed on their location. "They're going to catch us."

"Then we put up a fight."

"I warrant we should. Being men and all."

The torches multiplied in number, and the two friends tracked them with their pistols.

"There's too many of 'em," Roberts whispered.

"I know." Wolf did a quick count at least a dozen men with torches and as many dogs. "We have to try." He trailed one of the leaders around a tree, letting his sight settle on him.

A voice came at them from the side. "How about we try laying down those pistols real slow like?"

Wolf started to turn in that direction.

"Don't you look at me without putting that pistol down." The two troopers let their weapons fall into the dead leaves below. They slowly got to their feet, hands in the air.

The man was surprisingly well dressed for war. His coat had a sheen to it with a matching vest and necktie. His white goatee was trimmed with neat edges. A silver pistol wavered in his hand.

"Anthony Cummings, esquire, at your service, gentleman." He peered over their shoulders. "Lieutenant Pollard, over here. You're going to want to see this." He licked his lips. "Bagged me a couple of officers."

The torchlight expanded, and soon the two were surrounded. Dogs barked violently, spittle flying from tooth-filled jaws. There were bloodhounds, bird dogs, mastiffs, and multi-colored mutts. Men jeered them with shouts and curses, some terms Wolf had never conceptualized before.

A man kicked the back of his knees, sending him crashing into the ground. Roberts followed him, tumbling into the leaves. A young boy kicked Roberts in the ass. "Take that, you Yank!" squealed the boy before his father could restrain him.

A pale, black-haired man with a gray kepi on his head stepped forward. He had a modest yet honest air about him, but he appeared gaunt like he suffered from an affliction. "You in command here?"

Roberts quickly blurted, "No!"

Wolf nudged him. "No, we're not in charge. That was Colonel Dahlgren. I am Colonel Wolf and this is Captain Roberts."

"Little young to be colonel, now, dontcha think?"

"Brevet promotions come easy these days."

Pollard let out a sorry laugh. "Ain't that the truth."

The dogs continued to bark. Pollard turned on the tracker. "Will, why don't you go back along the swamp trail? Look for guns and packs. They're stripping them off as they run. See if you can get me one of those Spencers I keep hearing about." Will left with his dogs followed by a pack of the men.

The sallow rebel leader turned back their way. "Thought you'd make it all the way to Gloucester Point, didn't you?"

"I did believe that was our goal." Wolf cursed himself as soon as he said it. His men still may be fleeing in that way, and now he had put them in danger.

Pollard peered in that direction, nodding slowly. "You boys had a lot of nerve coming down here like you did."

"I'll admit it was bold."

Pollard stared at the ground and back at the captives. "Bold? It was stupid."

"Richmond is weak."

"Strong enough to stand to the likes of you."

"We'll be back."

"And you'll bleed for every inch of ground."

Wolf gulped and stayed silent. He met the lieutenant's pale brown eyes. They stared one another down, neither blinking nor releasing the other from the contest.

"What's wrong with your leg?" He gestured at it.

"Gettysburg." He lied.

"That was a tough battle. Lost a lot of good men."

"As did we."

Pollard nodded his head, the men joined by their connection to the battle and the loss of comrades in the thick of things. "What unit are you with?"

"A detachment of the 13th Michigan."

"Hmm. Haven't picked up any from that lot. We'll sort this out later." He waved on his men. "Get 'em with the others."

***

Wolf and Roberts were taken to a cluster of captured Union soldiers. In the darkness, they sat with their heads down and spirits crushed. No one talked. Anytime any of them did, their guard, a pimply-faced teenager, would kick at them. A handful of other rebels stood nearby smoking with shotguns and muskets beneath their arms.

When the sky began to lighten, the soldiers were roused with another round of kicks from the teenager. Black facial hair sprouted from his acne-ridden face, and he had to constantly wipe his long hair out of his eyes.

"Get moving, lard ass," the teenage boy threatened Wolf. He planted a boot in Wolf's ass, sending him forward in the mud. Before standing, Wolf dug his hands into the sludge and wiped it over the bloodstains on Dahlgren's greatcoat. It would be difficult to notice now. Mud splattered everything he wore, making him various shades of brown.

"Enough, Vince. Treat the good colonel with respect."

Wolf gathered himself on his feet and with his most haughty voice said, "I will see to it that your commanding officer knows of this crude treatment."

The rebels laughed in response.

The guard called back, "Be my guest, Billy Yank. Can't save ya now."

The captives commenced the dead march of defeated men. The drudgery continued for almost two miles until they entered a hamlet shrouded in a light gray smoke. Along the small tributary was the burnt-down mill, charred and broken in the ashy aftermath.

"Wolf, we was here."

"I know. We didn't leave on good terms."

Soot-covered people stood silently, watching the captured troops. Their hands were blackened from attempting to salvage anything they could from the rubble. A dirty man hugged one of their guards and patted his back fiercely.

Mrs. Hemlick appeared like a ghost, white dust caking her clothes and face. She spit at them as they passed eventually retreating back to her home.

Near the middle of the hamlet's few remaining structures, the guards stopped them. "All right, you ugly goat fuckers. Take a seat."

The captured soldiers sat in a pile of mud marked by countless hoof tracks as the sun breached the horizon. The mill still smoldered, emitting black smoke into the sky. Guards casually kept an eye on them, knowing they wouldn't run. Where would they go? The swamps? The entire region was hostile to the blue-coated men. They wouldn't last with militia and rebel troops scrounging the countryside for any whiff of Union cavalry.

Later in the morning, Mrs. Hemlick emerged from her home. Her clothes were clean and her skin clear. She graciously walked forward, inspecting the Union men with a vengeful eye. She turned and spoke to a guard who shrugged his shoulders. Her footsteps squished in the mud as she stepped next to Roberts and Wolf. Hiking her skirts, she stooped down.

"I know you." She waited for Wolf and Roberts to explain themselves. Both men stared.

She reached for Wolf's jacket, tapping the greatcoat. "That's an officer's coat. And you." She tapped a finger on Roberts's captain's bars like a mother knowing her sons lied. "You boys aren't officers. Funny little trick you have going on here."

"You must have me mistaken, ma'am."

"Aye, me too," Roberts said.

Her mouth formed the fractions of a frown. "You burned my mill. I have nothing now. Your sergeant promised he would spare me and look." She gestured with her hand. "Look."

Wolf glanced over his shoulder at the smoking ruins of the structure, now only a blackened foundation. "We didn't."

"But your fellows did."

He had little to gain in his position, so he did the only thing he could do and nodded, telling the truth. "The colonel ordered it burned."

Her eyes were a shade lighter than her chestnut hair, and they measured the captives' character. Her voice spilled from her lips at a whisper. "You saved my life."

Wolf blinked, staring into her shiny brown eyes. "You must have us mistaken."

"You did," she repeated. "Part of me wants to see you lynched. Watch you dangle with the rope around your necks. If I tell those men over there, they will do it in a heartbeat." She eyed the guards then contemplated her mercy on the captives.

The two men gulped. She held their fate in vengeful hands.

"The other part of me wants to hug you." She weighed them and tears collected in her eyes but refused to fall. "And we've given so much for this damn war." She sucked her cheeks in, trying to contain her emotions. After a moment, she bit her lip. "And for what? Slavery? I don't even own a slave. Yet I pay like the rest of them."

"Sorry about your mill, ma'am."

She clenched her jaw. "That man who done it will pay. Is he here?"

"No, ma'am. He's dead."

She nodded and gulped. "Served him right."

Wolf stayed silent.

"But I owe my gratitude to you. Is there any way I can ease your captivity?"

"Set us free," Roberts said.

"I'm sorry, sweetheart. I can't do that."

Wolf exchanged a glance with Roberts. It was only a matter of time before they were subject to a thorough search. If not soon, for sure at the prison. An illiterate soldier may not know the significance of a letter, instead searching for money, but if they got the wrong guard, the letter would be discovered. "Can you send a letter for me? Mail it to my pa. Tell him I love him."

"You know we can't send mail to the North no more."

He gulped. "It could be all he ever gets to remember me."

His words struck her heart chords like a musician. She knew full well the heartbreak of losing someone you loved and the torment experienced from not having any of their effects. Items that could give closure in a person's life. Without them, it was as if they'd just disappeared one day and never existed.

"I know a man who can do such a thing." She nodded again. "I will see it done."

He hesitated, watching her eyes, judging if she played him false.

"It's in my jacket pocket. Along with a watch. Could be his only memory of his son."

The tears remained in her eyes as she watched him. "This war has gone on long enough." She removed the letter, holding it in her hand. "It's got blood on it?"

"Last night was rough, ma'am."

"It was," she said. Her eyes relived every moment of her terror. Then the desperation as her mill burned to the ground. Her torment and deliverance had been provided by men from the same unit. She stuffed the letter and watch under her gown and stood, smoothing her dress. "You men make me sick!"

The guards perked up, eyeing the exchange. She spit at the two troopers in disguise. "Sick!" She marched for her home. A man in a nice frock coat reached for her, but she shrugged him off along the way.

A civilian with a double-barrel shotgun strode toward the captives. "What'd you boys say to her?"

"Burned her mill."

The guard took his cigar from his mouth and eyed the wreckage. "Suppose she gave you what you deserve."

"Suppose she did."

The guard spit, plopping the cigar back in his mouth and sauntered back to the others. The sun rose like a yellow ball thrown into the sky, and the Southern woman disappeared into her home with a letter that could severely damage the Union war effort.

CHAPTER 30

March 3rd, 1864
Richmond, Virginia

Over one-hundred-and-eighty prisoners were collected into a horde of blue-coated men. Only about thirty came from Dahlgren's final command, but rumor had it the entire column of ninety men had been destroyed.

Wolf rode in the back of an overcrowded wagon pulled by a pair of mules with the sick and wounded. Roberts stumbled alongside covered head to toe in grime.

One of the men groaning on his back had pissed himself. The urine that hadn't soaked into the wood ran along the crevices of the planks. Wolf's legs dangled off the back of the wagon and he braced himself on the side of the bed trying to ignore the smell. His brace creaked as they wheels rocked the wounded men through the squishing of mud.

Confederates manned cannons built into large earthen mounds as they passed. They gave the Union soldiers waves with broad smiles and mock salutes.

"Chipper bastards, aren't they?" Roberts said.

Wolf scowled at the rebels with their gray beards. "Sent the raid to end the war packing." He kept scanning his fellow prisoners for signs of his unit. "Any sign of Wilhelm?"

"Nope. Not one of our boys." The two men locked eyes. "You think they escaped?"

"One can hope. Kilpatrick's still out there. Maybe they found him."

A man seated next to Wolf hacked. He was from the 1st Maine. His black beard was down to his chest. The pellets from a shotgun blast had taken out his eye, creating divots on the side of his head. A handkerchief covered the gaping wound. "Kilpatrick's gone. As quick as we came down from Washington, the quicker he rode out. Tail between his legs and everything."

"What about the prisoners we came to free?"

"Suppose that'll be an afterthought now."

A sense of fear gripped Wolf's gut. He was to be a prisoner. No war. No bullets. But death would follow nonetheless. Starvation. Illness. Abuse. At least on the field, one could fight back. Here they would be men not worth feeding. "We came to free them."

"And now you're one of them," the Maine man said.

Richmond loomed before him over sweeping hills. It was the third largest city in the Confederacy with five different railroads running through it. Early in the war, it had been the largest inland port for the rebels, but with the blockade, this had shrunk significantly. Over fifty tobacco makers resided in the city of 38,000 that had gained over 100,000 new residents with the war, but tobacco couldn't feed an army unless it could reach paying customers.

The war weighed heavily on those not on the front lines. Food shortages were common, and it was well known who was to blame. The people of Richmond turned out to berate the raiders that were causing terror in their city, a chance to take out their frustrations on a common enemy was welcomed by all.

The jeering started near the front of the disorganized column of prisoners. Wolf turned in the wagon for a better view. Throngs of Richmond's citizens lined the road. A chorus of boos came from the people. Men, women, and children raised angry fists at the captive soldiers. Then came the rotting food.

Stinking garbage sailed through the air at the men.

"How dare you!" screamed a woman in a bonnet.

"Should have put you all in the ground where you belong!" cried another woman.

An ancient man with a hunched back raised a fist at them. "Burn in Hell!"

"Colored lovers!"

The trash flew from angry hands. Rotting fruits and vegetables exploded on the filthy uniforms of the Union men.

Roberts dodged a browning apple core. "Have to be quick."

Wolf ducked down, avoiding something greenish-brown and smelling beyond ripe. Then he shook his fist at them. "Bugger off." But resistance was futile. The crowds were boisterous and cruel and cared little for any rebuttal the Northerners may have made. Soon all the prisoners could do was dodge and cover their heads. This carried on for city blocks. They passed houses and shops. The congregations were fewer, but people still came to gawk at the newest batch of captured soldiers.

A few streets away, the capitol building of the Confederacy stood upon a hill resembling a Roman temple. Tall white Ionic columns lined the front. There was no dome atop the building like Washington's partially built capitol building. It was the state capitol of Virginia before the war and the third in the state's existence behind Jamestown and Williamsburg and the second for the Confederacy. When the rebels first seceded, the Capitol building in Montgomery, Alabama, was used, the same place Jefferson Davis was sworn in as president of the seceding states.

The crowds grew larger as they marched closer to the river. Here men in aprons, clerks, mechanics, and machinists waited. This group was more violent. Some men were bandaged, and it quickly became apparent that some of these men had gone into the field against them a few days before.

A big man with a bald head punched a trooper from New York in the face. The trooper staggered and fell. Only the intervention from a guard saved him from being strung up on a post. The men continued their walk through the muddy streets chased by little boys and girls and the calls for violence from the citizens.

The road sloped downward. They passed a white-clapboard church with a sign that read St. John's church before they reached a street of warehouses on the edge of the James River, the same river that had stymied Dahlgren's men.

The smell of tobacco leaves clogged the air along with smog from the factories. A towering smokestack stood in the distance, a man-made blackness billowing from its top. Massive mills rose nearby and colored folk in flat-bottomed barges floated past, their tall oars propelling them along the canal.

The parade of prisoners slowed as a giant warehouse loomed before them, stretching the entirety of a city block. It was three-stories tall and gradually became four, increasing in size over the angle of the land toward the river. The top two stories were plain red brick and the bottom stories were painted white. Six chimneys stuck out from almost three buildings all linked into one. Black soot stained the window frames that were empty save for thick iron bars.

Nearby a vacant lot held a cluster of tents. Rebel soldiers sat lazily around cook fires, muskets stacked against one another. A couple glimpsed at the prisoners with relative disinterest. Another took aim at the building. *Bang!* His musket smoked. His comrades laughed. "Don't you be looking out here!" the shooter shouted. With little sense of urgency, he reloaded his gun.

The sergeant of the detail strolled to the door and laid a fist into it. A man answered, they spoke, and he disappeared back inside. The captives stood for a few minutes, waiting in demoralized discomfort.

Three men emerged from the warehouse. A diminutive man with a broad smile and spectacles followed by two men that looked strong enough to lift a bale of hay in each hand. Each man had a shaggy beard and held a cudgel two inches around in his hands. Mean grins rested on the faces of men who liked cruel work. The sergeant of the guards handed the short man a knife with a bone hilt.

"That's my knife," Wolf said under his breath. "That grayback's got my knife."

The studious-looking man regarded the blade for a moment with a smile of indifferent understanding. He passed it back to the larger of his two enforcers, who smiled a broad black-toothed grin. He shoved the knife through his belt.

The small man clapped his hands together. "Do me a favor now. All of you who are privileged to be an officer move over here." The men separated out according to rank. Wolf and Roberts joined the other officers.

"You men are excellent at following orders." He shared a glance with one of his enforcers. "This batch won't be any trouble, will they." He turned back to his eighteen prisoners. "Trainable and moldable." He nodded to the guards. "You may take the rest to Belle Isle for their internment."

"All right, you lazy good-for-nothing Yanks. Move on out." The enlisted men trudged down the James River in the direction of the infamous island. They would find no refuge there, only tattered and mildewed white tents to stave off the cold, and each other. Men holding one another in the night. They'd get quarter rations if they were lucky. The rebels could hardly feed the citizens of Richmond. Why would they waste food on the enemy? And most would muster out to the afterlife from rampant illness or freezing to death in a shallow ditch. The muddied bluecoats disappeared around warehouses and docks.

The spectacled lieutenant stepped forward. "Now that we've done away with the riffraff," he laughed as if he expected the Union officers to join in, "let's get you acquainted with your new home. This three-story warehouse used to house tobacco and rats. Now just rats." His grin deepened. When no one laughed, his smile faded. "Such a dour group. You should be happy. You're alive. No better time in history to be alive if I may say so myself." He shrugged his shoulders. "My opinion." He sighed as if his own internal debate had gone on for years. "I am Lieutenant Erasmus Ross, and despite our potential difference in rank, I am your superior."

Not knowing what to think of the Confederate lieutenant, Wolf and the men around him kept their mouths shut.

"Sure talks a lot, don't he?" Roberts whispered.

"He does." He knew not to trust a man who talked too much. A man that talked too much did little, at least that's what his father always said.

"Excuse me, fine gentleman," Ross said. He strolled down the line followed by his enforcers. "Did one of you have something to say?" He stopped in front of the man ahead of Wolf. "You, Lieutenant?"

"No, sir."

"Hmm." Ross took another step lining up with Wolf. "Or you, Colonel?"

"No, sir."

"Or was it captain?"

Roberts kept his head forward. "Roberts, sir."

"Ahhh, Roberts. Say, Mr. Roberts, would you care to step out of rank?"

"Happy where I am, sir."

Ross smiled, his cheeks lifting. "You are, are you?" He pointed with his head and a meaty hand shoved Wolf back. A burly enforcer grabbed Roberts by his jacket and hauled him out of line.

"Get your hands off me!" Roberts squirmed and fought the brute, but it was of no use.

"I think that officers in general have a misconception when they arrive here. A misconception that I like to curb quickly." The enforcer threw Roberts at his feet.

"Meant no disrespect," Roberts hollered.

"I am your commander now. You don't talk. You don't eat. You don't piss and you don't shit without my explicit permission. Is that clear?"

"Yes, sir. Meant no harm."

"I am familiar with your kind. They never mean no harm." He stood tall but couldn't have been over five feet. "Yet they harm the very order of this organization." He gave a swift nod to his enforcer. Stick in hand, he rapped it along Roberts's back.

"Ow!"

The man hit him again and continued with a merciless methodical beating. Blood spurted from Roberts's nose and lips as he tried to block the blows with his arms. Every time he gained his feet, the brutish guard clipped him again with his stick.

"No more!" Roberts moaned.

"Enough, Griff." Ross waved off his enforcer.

The hulking guard took a step back, with an evil grin on his lips. His eyes were almost entirely vacant, except for a cruel cunning lurking somewhere inside.

Ross lifted Roberts by his elbow, helping him upright. "Are you okay?"

Roberts cowered from him, spitting crimson. "Sir?"

"No more talking out of turn?"

"Yes, sir."

The small lieutenant slapped Roberts on the back, and he cringed in pain. "Back in line with you."

Wolf wrapped an arm around him, keeping him standing.

"You men may follow me."

The group of officers followed the short man toward the brick warehouse. "We had over a thousand rats until earlier this month. Happy to say that with this lot we might be over a thousand again." They neared the door and Griff pushed it open.

The men hesitantly stepped inside. Closed doors ran down a hallway. More guards smoked in a corner.

"Up the stairs," Griff grunted. The weary officers strode up the steps like men to their doom. About halfway to the second floor, the smell hit them. The putrid stench of unwashed bodies and piss. It grew ominous the closer they got to the top. It seemed to be leaking from the walls and floors itself. The guard shoved his way through the men and jingled a key before unlocking the door. The wood appeared to be new and freshly cut.

"Welcome," Griff said, pushing the door open. "Back, ya rats," he yelled inside the room.

Old feces and sickly men reeked from the room. It was a sour sewer of smells, making Wolf cover his nose.

Hundreds of sorry gaunt faces stared at the newcomers. Ragged beards covered sunken cheeks. Tattered uniforms and threadbare blankets draped around their bony shoulders. They were horrific shades of pallid white, starving and sick. Once proud and healthy, now they were defeated. If they were not broken, every day was another in a long siege of battles for their humanity. The number of faces staring at the new prisoners was staggering like they'd come to see a bearded woman at a carnival.

There were no beds and only a few patched together chairs and short tables. Only battered men as far as Wolf could see. Griff forced them inside to the murmurs of "fresh fish."

Ross followed behind them. "I hope you don't have any ideas of escaping. Anyone attempting to get away will be shot on sight. And well, the rest still here." He smiled. "I've personally seen to it that five-hundred barrels of gunpowder have been placed beneath the foundation of this place. We catch wind of another escape, and the entire place goes up in a conflagration of epic proportions." Joyfulness laced Ross's voice. "Welcome to your new home for the duration of the war. And I do mean duration. We haven't held a parole since '63." An evil smile embraced his lips. "Welcome to Libby Prison."

CHAPTER 31

March 3rd, 1864

Hampton's Winter Quarters outside of Fredericksburg, Virginia

Hampton sat at a small writing table, barely big enough for him to lean his large frame upon, in the corner of his parlor. The fire blazed in the fireplace. Ransom had stacked the logs high, but he hadn't been able to shake the chill from his bones. Between the rain and the snow, he was worried he'd caught something in his lungs.

He dipped a pen into its plain glass inkwell, letting any errant ink fall back inside. He scribbled pointed black characters on the white parchment. *Federal forces have been routed. They are on full withdrawal over the peninsula. There has been destruction of property and infrastructure, but the threat to Richmond has passed. Requesting two regiments of cavalry to be deployed to my position to deter future raids. However improbable, we must prepare. If they have attacked twice, why not a third? Until then, we are prepared to do our duty for this great nation.*

After signing his name, he leaned back. He flexed his fingers. His hip still ached, and his foray into the field with his nighttime raids did not help. But he didn't have a choice. This was his current position and he could not sit by while the enemy overran his capital. The cabinet had a backup plan. They would withdraw and reestablish in Danville, Virginia. Near the North Carolina border, it was a major supply depot. But the surrender of the capital would precipitate an end to hostilities. Hampton was sure of that. And for that reason alone, it must stand.

He glanced over at the leather-bound book that rested on a table by the fire. Daniel Morgan. The man was a leader far beyond the war he fought in.

Sealing his letter, he scribbled Maj. Gen. J. E. B. Stuart on the outside.

"Ransom."

Hampton's manservant stepped into the room. "Suh."

"Get me a rider and bring me a cup of coffee."

"Yaas'suh." The man disappeared.

Hampton stood, stretching his back and hip. It was always tight; he doubted they would ever go back to the way they were. He moved closer to the warmth of the fireplace. He bent over and snatched a log from the cradle, ignoring the complaints of his joints. He placed it atop the fire and was rewarded with snaps and pops from the fresh fuel. Taking a step back, he enjoyed the added warmth.

Ransom set his coffee at his side.

"Thank you."

"Pledjuh. An officer's yuh to see you."

"Bring him in."

Boots stomped the floor and he turned. A smile formed on his bearded lips.

"If I must say it is glorious to see you again," Captain Marshall Payne said. The handsome officer with unkempt curly brown hair removed his folded gray slouch hat and spread his arms open.

Hampton stood resolute for a moment. Payne's smile didn't quite touch his eyes. He gave a quick salute and Hampton returned it.

"My affection is not returned?" Payne asked.

With a curt shake of his head, he stepped forward and embraced the captain. "You look well, Marshall." Despite his ride, the captain had a hint of lavender perfume in his hair. "Is that perfume?"

"You like it?"

"Not particularly. It's fine I guess."

"My own mother gave it to me for the holidays."

Hampton waved at Ransom. "More coffee." The colored man nodded and disappeared into the kitchen. "How's your mother?"

"The arthritis keeps her pretty well sedentary, but she makes do."

"Good to hear. Sit?"

"I'd love to."

The two men situated themselves in their seats, the chairs creaking with the effort.

"How is Stuart?"

Payne smiled beneath his umber goatee. "Just a right old chap. Had a run-in with your friend, Custer, not a few days past. Ran him off. Nothing to worry about there."

Hampton nodded. "Welcome news. They've been active of late."

"You'd think those dandies would take a rest while we afforded them one."

"You'd think."

Ransom returned with a coffee for the captain. Payne took the cup and leaned closer. "I heard your attack on Kilpatrick's camp was a righteous affair. I am saddened that I missed all the fun." There was a glow in his eyes, or was it a yearning for battle?

Hampton eyed his subordinate. It was not a righteous assault as much as it was a desperate one. Speed, surprise, aggression. Throw in deception and he had success, but it was all they had. He couldn't have met the enemy in the field let alone the daylight.

"We turned them back."

"Sir, they sped for Yorktown the next day, tails between their legs! Two-hundred men versus brigades of seasoned troopers. I do say, there has not been a whooping like that in the entirety of this war."

This made Hampton smile beneath his beard. "It was a rout. I rode this fine tall fellow down. Put a bullet in him and took him prisoner. Gave one of the boys his exceptional fur coat. I believe it was astrakhan."

"Very exotic. I must say I prefer our native cotton, but who can deny the spoils of war?"

Hampton sipped his coffee with a grin. "Blood on it, but a fine specimen like that deserves to be worn."

They sat in silence for a cluster of moments sipping coffee.

Hampton set his cup down. "A few of my Iron Scouts performed excellent. The Tanner brothers in particular."

"I am happy to take them into my command as a reward."

"We can discuss that later. I regret that I did not call you here to tell war stories."

Cocking his head, Payne said, "Never would have crossed my mind. Duty first. Once we have lifted the tyranny from this land, we will have time for stories and celebration."

Hampton gave him a brief nod. "And celebration." He wasn't sure their acquaintance was one of that kind. He liked the man. His subordinate did outstanding work and was wellborn. But he was not sure that he would call him a friend.

They shared battle, war, and loss, but there was something off in Payne. Hampton saw it in his eyes sometimes. He tried to write it off as a part of war. It changed a man. Most men were never the same. Perhaps Payne had seen too much of the elephant.

He'd rationalized the things he'd seen long ago, but even he still masked the impact with a hard exterior. But a hard exterior never prevented the visits from his brother Frank's ghost. The men would sit in silence staring at one another. And every single time, Hampton would ask himself, why Frank? Why not me? I am older and have seen enough of this life and this war. You should have taken me. Not him. Yet Frank was the shade, and he was alive. His brittle bones and sore joints still forced to fight this war.

Payne was different though. There was a glint of joy in the misery itself. He supposed that was what made him adept at certain tasks. Tasks that might make other men uncomfortable.

"I need you to go to Richmond."

"If this is a staff position, I must wholeheartedly object."

Hampton poured back the rest of his coffee. Ransom was there in a flash filling his cup with more. "It is not."

Relief flashed in Payne's eyes. "Praise the Lord, General. You gave me quite a fright."

He smiled close-lipped. "Not my intention. Let me be clear. This is an information gathering mission."

"Information?"

"We need information from the prisoners. I want to know everything. There's been rumors among some of the men about a letter."

"Letter?"

"Yes, a letter signed by Lincoln."

"Surely there must be many signed by the tyrant."

"This one is specific. It has particular orders."

"Orders?"

"Orders to assassinate President Jefferson Davis."

Payne blinked as if he'd never heard of something so preposterous. "Those blue-bellies don't have it in 'em. It'd be like raising the black flag. No quarter. Open field day."

"I didn't believe it, but one of the prisoners said as much. I asked for proof and he didn't have any."

"Why would the poor bastard lie?"

"Don't know. But we must find the truth. And if there is a letter, we must acquire it at all costs."

Payne nodded. "I understand, sir."

"Everything is authorized in this. Your leash is off so to speak."

The left part of Payne's cheek lifted as he nodded again. The flames flared in his eyes.

There it is again. That queer look.

"It has been a while since I've been in Richmond. This promises to be a fruitful trip."

"I pray that it is, Captain. Make haste." Hampton stood, quickly followed by his subordinate.

"I will ride hard to Richmond. You will have the information you need."

"Carry on." Hampton dipped his head in thanks.

Payne saluted palm outward. "I look forward to getting into the field again soon with you."

"As do I."

The captain marched out of the house. Sounds of him urging his mount to speed and a thunder of hooves marked his departure.

He sat down again. Another man took the seat where Payne had sat. He was calm and his quiet face expressionless. Hampton ignored the newcomer. He gazed at the flames in their endless dance. Sipping his coffee, a vacant look grasped hold over his eyes. They grew unfocused as he stared into nothing.

"Frank," Hampton whispered. He was the spitting image of Wade but thinner and a few inches shorter. No wrinkles around the eyes. Only what was once a fresh and playful face combined with a youthful vigor that young men held. A man coming into himself. A man cut down by the scythe of war.

The pale man said nothing, but silently looked on.

"We'll win this war yet."

The ghost of his brother didn't say a word.

CHAPTER 32

Afternoon, March 4ᵗʰ, 1864
Libby Prison, Richmond, Virginia

A rough hand shoved Wolf onto the stairs. He gradually took each step down. Every foot exposed him to cleaner air and it felt wonderful in his nose.

Griffin growled behind him. "Go, colored lover."

The first floor of the prison was an administrative floor for their captors. A couple of guards lounged; one chewed noisily on a piece of hardtack. There was a kitchen in the center; the prisoners took turns using it depending upon which they were being held in. There was also a dingy two-bed hospital for the sick, a large guardroom, and multiple offices.

Wolf hobbled along a hallway. The tip of a stick in his back forced him forward. The kitchen reeked as he passed by and sunken-eyed Union officers stared back. When they reached a door at the end of the hall, Wolf halted.

"Which way?"

Griffin jabbed his cudgel into Wolf's back. "Here." He reached around him and turned the handle. "Go," he said, shoving the door open.

Lieutenant Ross sat in a chair behind a desk. He neatly signed some documents with intense focus. He glanced at the two men. "Ah, welcome, Colonel. You may go, Griff."

The brutish man left without a word. Wolf contemplated strangling the lieutenant with his bare hands. No weapon rested on Ross's hip. In fact, as he looked around the room, he saw no weapons at all. Only a window toward

20th Street leading perpendicular to the river. A wagon creaked by filled with wooden crates. The driver swung a short whip. "Get up now," he called to his draft horses.

Ross did not address him but continued to scribble on a sheet of paper. He dotted an i with fierce diligence. Without looking up he spoke, "Do you know why I let him go, knowing full well you could beat me within an inch of my life?"

"No?"

"Because where will you go? Twenty armed men inside this building. Over forty outside."

"Maybe it'll feel good to kill you."

"Then you haven't been here long enough. You haven't been taught enough."

Wolf eyed the door. If he could strangle the man and cover his mouth, no one would know, including the brute waiting on the other side of the door. He could arm himself. Kill Griff. Take his well-earned knife back. Then he could find a way to sneak out the back. Maybe make it to the river. It was a wishful thought, one that would easily lead to his death or his recapture.

"You don't want to kill me. Wait, that's not right." His eyes darted forward from the page. "No, you won't kill me because you can't as much as you want too."

Wolf continued to stand. "I'll choke you until your eyes pop."

Ross set down his dip pen. "You could. I doubt you would succeed in the venture." He shrugged his shoulders. "Men have tried. I'm not a warrior. Clearly you can see this. This is why you desire to overpower and kill me."

Wolf stood silent.

"I was a clerk's assistant. Granted rank in the absence of Turner. Deathly ill that one. They are obsessed with numbers and their bookkeeping. Count you boys twice a day. And here I am talking to a Yankee colonel that fantasizes about strangling the life out of me." He hefted his pen again, immersing its nib in a small inkwell jar, shaking his head at the thought. "They think numbers will win this war, but how can they if ours go down faster than yours?" He shook his writing utensil at Wolf. "Don't answer that. Perhaps later but not today."

"Then why am I here?"

"I have a friend who wants to talk to you. A true gentleman and patriot. Quite a charming fellow. Through that door there. The one you were thinking about making your escape through." He shooed him. "You can go."

Wolf laid a hesitant hand on the rusty doorknob. It slowly twisted in his fingers. The door creaked open. Griff gripped his arm in a clamp and led him down the corridor. Wolf gave a fleeting glance at Ross's office. They reached another closed door.

"Go in," Griff commanded, releasing him.

He opened the door gently, not knowing what awaited him.

A man in an impeccable gray uniform stood in the corner staring out the window at the murky James River. A boat with a large sail maneuvered along the waters.

The officer clasped his hands behind his back. Fine black leather boots went all the way to his knees. A silky maroon sash swathed around his hips along with a curved saber, and a gray slouch hat rested atop brown curly hair that hung down to his shoulders. The faint trace of perfume wafted in the air, making Wolf acutely aware that his smell was infinitely worse.

There was no way out of this room. A brick wall on one side indicated they were near the structure's foundation. The officer stood in front of the singular window. Only a table and chairs decorated the sparse room. Crisp air nipped at his skin despite a small fire in a fireplace.

"You may sit down," the Confederate officer said.

"I'd rather stand."

The officer turned around. A red shirt billowed from underneath his fine gray jacket. He was handsome. A grin spread on his face but barely touched his eyes. "I am sorry. We haven't met, have we? My name is Captain Marshall Payne of Hampton's irregular company. Colonel?"

Shock rocketed through Wolf like an electrical current. This man was the leader of the infamous Red Shirts, the same men his unit had tangled with at Gettysburg. The most ruthless of Hampton's units. He always had a full company because men strove to join their ranks. The most wellborn cutthroats of the war. The best of the best.

His words floundered like the first uncertain moos of a newborn calf. "Colonel Wolf."

"The Union must be in desperate shape to be promoting officers so young." Payne's grin widened at his opponent's weakness.

"It was more luck than anything else. We lost most of our officers at Gettysburg." A lie, but surely this man would buy it.

"Which regiment?"

"13th Michigan."

"Must be a relatively new regiment. Hordes of you blue-bellies up North, and all you boys tend to blend together after a while." Mirth transformed into fierceness, and his eyes judged Wolf's martial prowess. "Got some fight left in you, don't you, Colonel?" He squinted an eye. "I reckon you would be formidable enough for a try."

"Mustered in October of '62."

"Ahh, I see. Green as a willow tree. Would you care to take a seat? I do wish to have a cordial conversation. Nothing like that serious little Lieutenant Ross and his numbers. Ha." He waved a hand toward Ross's office.

"I don't like to sit, sir."

"Doesn't have chairs in his office, does he?" Payne smirked at him. "If you won't tell, I won't tell." He closed the door and latched it shut.

"How about it? Shall we have a pleasant little chat?"

Wolf took a seat across from the captain.

"Would you like some lemonade?"

He nodded, watching the rebel.

Payne took a pitcher and filled two glasses and leaned back in his chair. "It's out of season, but I can never turn down a glass of the stuff." He put an elbow on the table. "Keeps the scurvy away too. You're going to have to be careful of that here in Libby. She's a mean old hatchet wound liable to kill a man."

Wolf snatched the yellow lemonade and took a drink. The sweet, sugary, and tart liquid screamed its way down his parched throat. He waited a moment, tasting for any abnormalities. Finding none, he gulped the rest down.

"Very good. Here, have some more." Payne poured him another glass. Wolf drank that too. "Not too fast. You'll get a bellyache. Not like the dysentery and disease running rampant above us, but it still could be bad. I mean, think about the man spooning you at night." He shook his head in mock dismay. "He would be mighty disappointed waking up to that mess."

He set his glass on the table. "Would have been better if it was beer."

Payne grinned. "Beer would be a tough find here. Maybe a whiskey next time."

"I wouldn't object." He crossed his arms over his chest. "Why am I here?"

"Astute question, Colonel."

"You're one of the last I have to interview. You see, I'm looking for some information."

Wolf was silent. Information could cost lives in the field.

"You understand. There's this rumor going around. And the funny thing about a rumor is that most of the time it's true. At least part of it, and it's my job to figure out what's real and what's not real so we can dispel rumors and make sure there's only truth out there. Not like those damn newspapers. They're liable to write anything now a days." He raised his reddish-brown eyebrows. "Does that make sense?"

"Yes."

"You see why we have to be friends? So I can straighten this all out."

"I don't see what these rumors have to do with me."

"Well, maybe nothing. Maybe everything."

"What do you want to know?"

"You're a quick learner. Faster than most in here." He squinted with confusion. "It's like captivity dulls their senses. How fast they forget things." He sighed. "Who was your detachment commander?"

He probably already knows. It's a test. "Dahlgren."

"All right then. Exactly the fellow I want to know about. The last man in here, he said that Colonel Dahlgren and General Kill-Cavalry had a special plan. And that special plan involved an assassination of the most vile nature. Were you aware of this plan?"

Don't give him a reason to hang you. "No."

Payne cocked his head. "Well, this other officer said every man in his command knew about the order." He leaned back in his chair. "In fact, every man chose to go about this evil endeavor rather than turn around and scurry back to the holes whence they came. Is that true?"

"I don't know what he's talking about."

"So you're telling me that Lieutenant Peters fabricated a story that would sign the death sentence for all thirty-six captives of Dahlgren's raiding party? He must not have liked his fellow man."

"He must be mistaken."

"Then what of it? You're an officer. You know. They are going to hang all you men off his testimony. You want me to read what's already been written by the Richmond papers?" He unfolded a paper and snapped the edge to straighten it. In a politician's voice he recited with some theatrics, "He told them his true evil purpose, an order of diabolic intent. To a man they all cheered, electing to follow the one-legged colonel in their treachery, voiding their character as soldiers and embracing the basic cruel intentions of murderers, thieves, outlaws, and mercenaries. Yes, they followed Ulric the Hun and they paid the ultimate price for their devilish ways. But what of the rest of his men? Calling them men is a stretch by any means of the word. What do they deserve? Trial? Or swift justice?" He looked over the paper. "Pretty heavy indictment. But again. This is just one man's word." His head wavered from side to side. "Could be denied by others." He tossed the paper on the table. "Newspapers. Should take them with a grain of salt, huh?"

"He's a liar."

"Figured you'd say something like that." Payne stood, walking to Wolf's side of the table. "I always like to know my man before we start the next phase of conversation. See what kind of man he is on the inside."

"I'm not lying. He's the liar. We weren't sent to assassinate anyone."

"Peters isn't the only one to admit it." He raised his fingers as he listed the names. "Peters, Coleman, Welch, they all said the same thing. This was no regular raid. This was an attempt on the president's life."

Wolf shook his head, staring away from the captain. His mind raced. *They got Peters. I don't know the other two. Peters could sabotage my entire ruse. The lieutenant knew me as a corporal. What will they do if they find out I'm not an officer?* "I don't know what you're talking about."

"You have a hard exterior. Almost enough to make me think you're enlisted."

"They lie. I don't know why."

Payne exhaled. "They didn't lie. Why would a man tell a lie that would hang every single soldier in his command?"

"I'm not sure why, sir, but they do."

Joviality crinkled around Payne's eyes. "Can a man lie when his balls are in the hands of another?" He smiled. "Snip, snip and you're no longer a man." He made a scissoring motion with his fingers. "Now don't get me wrong. I'm no barbarian. No. No. I come from gentle stock, but it is just as easy as gelding a horse."

"There was no plan."

Payne leaned closer. "Wolf, I know there was a plan. What I want is proof."

"I don't have any."

"But there's proof somewhere."

"No."

"Perhaps there is a letter that your coconspirator showed to his men as they crossed into rebel territory?" A smirk settled on Payne's face as he weighed him with his eyes.

Wolf glowered over the captain's shoulder, trying to avoid his smoldering blue embers for eyes.

"There's a letter." Payne wagged his finger. "No need to deny it. Everyone's said there was a letter."

"I never saw it." He blinked past the officer, hoping he accepted the lie.

"We are on the right track then." Payne's eyes glanced over Wolf's shoulder. "Come on in."

A door opened. Wolf tried to look over his shoulder, but he couldn't make out the men.

"Go on, boys."

Thick hands wrapped around Wolf's neck, forcing him downward toward his belly. "Stop!"

Griff and Hank wrenched his arms behind his, securing him to the chair. As he stared at the floor, he noticed the stains for the first time. Dark brown stains all along the floorboards where the wood absorbed the blood. The two brutes gave him a shove and stepped away.

"Ross was kind enough to loan me a couple of his stalwart men for the afternoon."

"I never seen it."

"You sure? Do you know where the colonel is?" Payne tapped his cheek.

"No."

"Did he escape?"

"You tell me."

"*Tsk. Tsk.* Mr. Wolf. I will ask the questions."

The officer rounded the table. He grabbed Wolf's face with firm fingers, pinching skin between them. "You will tell me where the letter is."

"I don't know."

Forcefully, Payne released him and gave him a swift backhand to his cheek. Wolf's face was thrown to the side, and the coppery taste of blood filled his mouth. He spit on the floor.

"Are you aware that we have ways of coercing the Negroes here if they step out of line? Usually the threat of the whip or harm to a family member will do, but in certain select cases, more stern measures are applied. Do you know what I am talking about?"

"No."

"Suppose you wouldn't since you elect to live with our chattel. An unnatural arrangement you Northerners make." He smiled, showing teeth. "I must be clearer. I could rip out your tongue. Whip the skin from your back. Burn your flesh. Cut your balls off." He let the potential removal of Wolf's manhood sink in. "I hope it doesn't come to that. A man is never quite the same afterward." He looked at Wolf's leg. "Could maim your other leg I suppose?"

Payne's words had a certain puckering effect on Wolf, but he surrendered to the fact that he was going to suffer. "I don't know."

"But it must be somewhere." He nodded. "Griff, go on."

A clenched fist slammed into Wolf's cheek. Shooting stars rained in his vision. Griff pulled him back upright by his hair. Wolf blinked, staring at the captain, the stars continuing their celestial assault.

"I never saw it."

Payne smiled. "Wrong answer."

Griff ran a fist into his gut, flashing pain through his midsection. He struggled to catch his breath, sucking in air.

Payne raised his eyebrows. "Letter?"

Wolf closed his mouth and Payne shrugged. The brute punched his face again. This time he spat a tooth on the floor. The tiny white object rattled along the wood coming to a stop.

"I don't see why you are protecting Dahlgren."

"I'm not."

"Griff." The stocky man socked Wolf in the belly again. Then the face. Then his other cheek. The sound was like a slab of steak landing atop another. The skin swelled around his eyes and mouth. After thirty minutes of denial, Payne sat on the table next to him. "You are very adamant about the whole letter confusion. More adamant than some of your fellow officers. I must say you are a tougher nut to crack." He rested a metal object on the table in front of Wolf, eyeing it with a certain amount of respect.

"Now, boy, I admire your loyalty. I really do. And I want this to be easy. We can get you some extra rations. Clean blankets. Hell, I can even move your name up the list for parole, not that it will do much good. But I need that letter."

Wolf spit more blood. "Never seen it."

Payne appeared more than a little amused. "Untie him." The two brutes untied his hands, pulling him closer to the table. The device resembled a vice in his father's shop, but the press went downward instead of opening on the sides.

"Put his thumbs in there."

"No! No!" Wolf struggled, his voice rising, but he was overpowered by the larger men on each arm. He tried to keep his hands in tight fists, but the men wrenched his fingers, forcing his hands flat. They shoved his thumbs into the metal contraption like wooden logs into a sawmill.

"They say this came from the Spanish Inquisition. Such a petite little thing, but I first learned of it from the captain of a slave ship. He was a cheery fellow. Never had a problem." He twirled a nut on the top of the press, letting it spin upward, all the while smiling. "Simple and very effective at getting the truth. Aren't we all just animals without our thumbs?"

Payne twisted a nut, spinning it downward. Pressure built on Wolf's right thumb. The captain leaned over, his fingers were delicate as he wound the left nut as if he were an artist and Wolf his canvas. "She starts off gentle." He locked eyes with Wolf. "Finishes most rough." The slow click, click of the metal nuts turning forced the solid metal bar painfully into his fingers. The pressure made his breathing come heavy like he was in a fight.

"Okay. I seen the letter before."

A smile curled on Payne's lips. "That's all I asked for. A bit of cooperation."

"Dahlgren had it at Ely's Ford."

Click, click, click, the nuts went round and round, the pressure building with every fraction of a turn.

Wolf spoke faster, his breathing picking up pace. "I didn't read it. He read it."

"But what did he say it said?" Halfway around the nut went and Wolf could feel his nails splitting down the center. He wanted to get away, but he couldn't escape. His lungs were unable to inhale enough air despite the coolness of the room.

"He said something about freeing prisoners."

"And?"

"And burning Richmond."

Payne tightened the screws more and Wolf's fingers threatened to explode.

"Kill Jefferson Davis! It said something about killing Jefferson Davis!"

"That is what I was looking for." Payne unscrewed the nuts a fraction, releasing the pressure from his thumbs. Wolf leaned his head near the table catching his breath, forcing air in and out of his mouth.

"So where is the letter, Colonel Wolf?"

"No, I don't know. Dahlgren had it."

"Wrong answer." He wrenched one nut, forcing the screw downward, and Wolf could feel his thumbs pop like green grapes, breaking the bones inside. He screamed at the top of his lungs. He hadn't known that much pain was possible. Tears streamed down his face. And Payne drank it all in like it was a cheap wine. He unraveled the nut upward, releasing the metal press and Wolf regained possession of his wrecked thumbs. He held them close to his chest, sobbing in pain.

"The letter?"

Wolf controlled his breathing enduring the pain. "I don't have it."

"Who does?"

"Dahlgren."

"Wrong answer. We have Dahlgren's body. We found it next to a tree. Coatless. We knew right away 'cause he was missing a leg. No letter on his person. Which means someone else has it, and you're going to tell me who has the letter. Is that understood?"

"Please, I don't have it."

"Who does?"

"I don't know."

His torturer gestured to one of the brutes. Wolf tried to see over his shoulder what the man was doing. Hank grabbed a hot iron out of the fire and handed it to Payne.

"I'd like to say this is gonna hurt me more than it's going to hurt you, but then I'd be lying."

The enforcers stripped Wolf's coat off him, tearing the shirt from his back. His skin prickled from the cold. Payne ran a hand along his black sash. "Fine piece of cloth." He ripped it from his body and draped it over the thumbscrew.

"Now let's find the letter, shall we?" Payne reached closer and Wolf couldn't retreat any further. He screamed as the metal sizzled into his skin.

CHAPTER 33

Late Afternoon, March 4ᵗʰ, 1864
Madison Court House, Virginia

General George Custer was drenched in cold mud like the men around him. Every single man and horse under his command was splattered and soiled with the countryside grime. His legs and rear muscles were sore from riding hard through almost 150 miles of enemy territory. Sharpshooting from the windows and forests that sent bullets buzzing like hornets didn't make a man feel any better either.

He led his column to Madison Court House. They'd already crossed through the pickets from General Sedgwick's command, meaning that they could let their guard down. He wasn't looking forward to his conversation with the patriarchal commander of Union forces near this end of the Army of the Potomac's winter quarters.

The Sixth Corps headquarters flag was all blue with a white St. Andrew's cross in the middle. A blood-red number 6 centered the flag. Divisional flags drooped in front of a home with a long covered porch. All flags were variants of the corps flag minus the number 6 but had different combinations of St. Andrew's cross, red cross on white, white cross on blue, and blue cross on white.

Custer made for the porch and the outline of a heavyset man. A soft orange glow silhouetted his face as he smoked, observing the tired riders. "Major, carry on. Get the men settled. I will find you later."

"Yes, sir." The major continued on with the troopers. Despite their exhaustion, there was still a considerable amount of energy in his command. That was good. It meant morale hadn't been hampered by the excursion.

He steered his mount from the column to the home of the 6th Corps commander. His mind was still unsettled from the ride. The reality of his orders only provided him with three possible options to survive his part of the raid.

Strike boldly across Lee's rear and make for Kilpatrick's command. He'd imagined thousands of rebels chasing and hounding his men, chipping away until they were surrounded and captured. Charge southwest and try to reach Sherman, an equally dire proposal. Or feint toward Charlottesville and return the way he came before rebel troops could cut him off from Sedgwick.

The first two options were extremely risky. Death or capture was the most likely outcome for his entire command. If by chance he made it on the long dangerous ride, he would've been a half a world away from his dearest bride. The thought of her made his heart ache and excitement jump in his belly. If he'd gone to Sherman, it would have been months before he returned to Washington.

Truthfully, he didn't have much of a stomach for being away from Libbie that long. A wife changed a man, and he only ever wanted to be by her side. The army always called to him, but now he was a split man. Torn in two directions. He never doubted his calling to the military, but now, if he must pick, how could he not choose love?

He dismounted from Roanoke's back. The horse had recovered well from his wounds at Gettysburg, and a viable energy still embodied his mount despite the long ride.

His boots squished in the cold mud. Taking the reins, he wrapped them around a railing. After he spoke with his commanders, he would have his orderly take the animal for a rub down.

A gravelly voice carried over from the porch. "Our lost boys have returned home so quickly."

Absent in his own thoughts he'd forgotten the man on the porch but recognized his voice immediately. General John Sedgwick. He was an old-timer for sure. His men called him Uncle John. A veteran of the Seminole, Indian, Utah, and Mexican Wars and now the War Between the States. To say he had experience was an understatement. He had a jovial face, affable eyes, and a graying beard. A career soldier with plenty of war under his belt, he knew when to kid and understood the times to hunker down and do work. Either way, one listened to his words. Having neither wife nor child, the Army was his family, his junior officers his sons.

"General, sir. I didn't see you there." He tried to cover his surprise.

"You didn't see a pot-bellied, gray-bearded general braving the cold and having a smoke?"

Custer looked for a way out. "No, sir. I was distracted by my thoughts."

"Hopefully none of them are too disagreeable."

"They are not." Custer took a few steps forward, eyeing the general. "We rode over 150 miles and didn't lose a man."

"You exhausted almost 1500 mounts on your ride. What do you have to show for it?"

"We burnt mills and destroyed rail. Captured some fresh mounts."

"Did you burn the bridge at Rivanna?"

With a hand, he brushed errant hair behind his ear. "No, sir. We met stiff resistance. Four batteries, two infantry brigades, ran into Stuart himself near Stanardsville. Almost caught the bastard too."

"Capturing Stuart would have been a feat for the ages. The papers would have made you a legend."

Custer smiled. "It would have, sir." *I still have time to be a legend yet.*

Puffed on his cigar, Sedgwick clouded the air with gray haze. "Where are my manners? Why don't you come inside and have a glass with me?"

The men met on the porch and Sedgwick put a fatherly hand on his shoulder. "Whiskey warms the belly after a ride like that."

Custer remained silent and looked out at the quaint village. A faint snow fell from the slate sky. Cold whiteness layered the earth and buildings alike, wet and dirty at the same time. The combination of rain, sleet, and snow churned everything into a wintery wetland. Smoke escaped from stone chimneys. The two men watched the passing mud-splattered troopers. His mind drifted to Libbie, how she would stare up at him with her sparkling eyes and divine smile. He was that much closer to seeing her again, and that simple knowledge made him grin like a buffoon.

"It was a ride."

"You can finish your reports while we enjoy a fine bottle."

"That sounds like the end to a profitable sortie."

Sedgwick gave him a slight shake at the shoulder. "No men lost?"

"Not one."

"'Twas a success then."

CHAPTER 34

Late Afternoon, March 4ᵗʰ, 1864
Yorktown, Virginia

Brigadier General Hugh Judson Kilpatrick walked his column through the entrance to Yorktown, Virginia. The town had been under Union control since 1862 and was snuggly surrounded by earthen walls. The ugly mouths of six-pound guns bristled at even intervals, a constant threat to any rebel contemplating a daring attack.

Yorktown was on the other side of the York River from Gloucester Point. Roughly twenty-five miles farther south sat Fort Monroe run by fat General Butler, who'd failed to move a single soldier past New Kent to assist in the raid.

New Kent was directly east of Richmond and provided a chokehold on access to the peninsula that mostly fell under Union control, including Fort Monroe on the southernmost point. *The obese cross-eyed bastard must be salty about his failed raid and now has condemned us to failure.*

Once inside, they could see the walls had been reinforced with logs and wood, hardening the fort to assault.

"They really are quite trainable. Let me tell you. One can see how that is entirely suitable for their race's current disposition, but I must say they make very capable soldiers. You might even say robust," said Colonel Livingston.

"Is that so, Colonel? I am surprised," Henderson said.

"I understand your reservation. I was plum surprised myself."

Kilpatrick's men had run into the Butler's relief column on the road near New Kent. Only a single brigade of infantry had moved to support. They may as well have sent them to Timbuktu for all the service it did Kilpatrick's command. His men had prepared for another cold fight until it was clear that General Duncan's brigade was friendly. Duncan rode with his column while the nearest infantry colonel, Livingston, had taken to talking Kilpatrick's ear off like he was a part of a knitting circle. The man was infuriatingly insistent about the martial prowess of colored soldiers, something that Kilpatrick did not care about and Henderson felt obliged to comment on.

"Have you seen a colored regiment in battle?" Livingston asked.

"No," Kilpatrick said. He glowered on ahead, trying to ignore Livingston's analysis.

"Fierce boys. Some argue even fiercer than the white race."

"I doubt that," Henderson said. "Captivity for so long, how could they comprehend the fight for freedom?"

Livingston nodded. "Sure, there are many doubters. But could you not say that they would fight even harder to gain their freedom?"

Henderson wavered his peanut-like head. The debate was only philosophical in his mind. "Interesting. I'd never thought of it that way. My feeling is that men knowing what they could lose, would fight harder than a man who knew little of what he could gain."

The Negro regiments cheered Kilpatrick's men as they grew closer, and when they'd stopped to rest, the colored soldiers had given over all their rations to his exhausted troopers in goodwill.

"What say you, General?" Henderson asked.

"I'm sure they would fight and die like any other man," Kilpatrick snarled.

"Sir, surely you are not saying they are equal? Let me put it this way," Henderson said. "You take a dog, and as a pup, you lock him in a cage. You beat him when he's bad. You feed him your scraps. You train him to sit and stay and hunt. Now you take him out of his cage, and you say, 'You're free, boy. Hunt. Fight. Live.' And you send him out into the wilds. He meets a stray dog. Been free his whole life. Had to hunt, fight, and lived outside captivity his entire life."

"Make your point, Colonel Henderson."

"Well you see, my point is, who would you pick? A beaten dog whose been caged his whole life and doesn't know to piss without command? Or would you bet on the wild dog? One that's roamed the earth doing as he pleases, fighting for every piece of meat he eats."

Genuine fascination marked Livingston's face by Henderson's interpretation. "Interesting analogy, but you forget something important."

"What's that?"

"They aren't dogs. They're men, and men have an uncanny desire to rise above their station. And those men. They can fight." He faced Kilpatrick. "General, what say you?"

"I'm saying I don't know. I've never seen them in battle. I am sure they will serve adequately with proper training."

Livingston pointed out. "Of course, of course. Perhaps we can put on a drill for you to show you their discipline."

"I am very intrigued by such a demonstration," Henderson chirped.

"If there's time." Kilpatrick didn't want to debate the prowess of colored troops. He lamented about the failure of his raid and how he would have to pay up to Pleasonton.

He glanced over his shoulder at his column. *Dahlgren is still out there.* The last he knew, he was somewhere near King and Queen Court House. The firebrand was probably holding strong, refusing to give up the mission. The boy had guts, he'd give him that, just lacked experience.

Yorktown was a dismal sight for his eyes. The gray sky and dreary weather didn't help his mood. The whole raid had soured. All the fervor to end the war. Every bit was gone from his men, and it left his soul even more empty. *Where do I go from here?* This was the heroic raid to end the war. A historic thrust to liberate the prisoners and burn the city. A move that would laud him with the laurels of victory and propel him into congress and someday the presidency. All of that faded now like a distant memory. With this blemish, where would he go? No use in thinking like that. He would find another way. It was all about the narrative. *Who was to blame here? Butler didn't show. The intelligence was faulty. Enemy resistance was much stronger than anticipated.*

Custer? That pompous dandy. I wonder if he even carried out his operations.

Freed slaves watched the troopers from hovels and makeshift housing, all newly built since the Federals had liberated Yorktown. Livingston gestured out. "More come all the time, ever since Butler started labeling the coloreds as contraband. Only men that is. They all come anyway. Liberated rebel property. Free. You should hear the townsfolk squeal in misery about it." He chuckled at the thought.

"We brought our fair share of them with us," Henderson glanced over his shoulder. A long line of colored folk followed the troopers as fast as they could with the hopes of being deemed "contraband" and free.

Union gunships steamed along the waterfront patrolling the York River. They also protected the unfortified harbor from any rebel activity, of which really only amounted to smuggling, something Butler had been rumored to be making a fortune on.

"Can you take me to a telegraph? I need to make my report."

Livingston smiled beneath a wispy mustache. "It would be an honor, sir."

"I will stop by your quarters later, sir," Henderson said.

Kilpatrick waved him off. *I'm sure you will.*

The two officers peeled from the column toward a single-room building near the edge of the town. Sagging wires ran from the roof overhangs to a tall pole. In turn, more wires stretched from that pole to another and so went the cables linking the technology that allowed almost real-time reporting to command from the field to Washington. It had spread like wildfire across the continent, and thousands of miles of wire had been erected for the war alone.

He dismounted, adjusting his saber and hat. It was all about the narrative he put forth. It was all about how you worded it. His legs were sore and bowed from all the saddle work. He kicked off mud from his boots as he crossed a wood-planked sidewalk.

Livingston opened a short green door, ushering him inside. A single civilian with a brown frock coat and a blue bowtie sat behind a desk with a telegraph. He tapped his finger rapidly on a metal piece atop a rectangle wooden block. A wire came from the device, running along the wall and to the outside.

Every time the civilian pressed the flat-headed metal, it would click. Click. Click-click. He concentrated, tapping away at the machine. After a moment, he glanced through spectacles, beneath a straw boater-style hat, noticing them for the first time. "Sir," he said, lifting a finger to wait. "Sorry, concentrating on the message."

Livingston smiled. "Abel Tawney. This is General Kilpatrick."

The telegraph service was a civilian component of the Quartermaster Department, meaning they didn't fall under military authority. This caused friction between the officers and the operators as they refused to conform to military standards, and since they were outside the military's jurisdiction for the most part, they were generally distrusted.

The operator adjusted his spectacles on his nose. "I know of the general, sir."

"I assume it's all pleasant?" Kilpatrick said with some venom.

"I've heard stories of your boldness in the field."

This softened Kilpatrick's bite. To be bold was a strong characteristic of determined leaders. "Very good. I need you to relay a telegraph to Pleasonton."

"It would be a pleasure, sir." He sat back in his seat, setting himself to transmit the message, finger poised on the telegraph machine. "I am ready."

"To Major General Pleasonton."

The operator tapped furiously.

"I am happy to report. Confederate infrastructure, communications, and property south of Rapidan severely damaged. Period."

Taps filled the room. At the end of his line, Tawney glanced upward.

Kilpatrick took a deep breath before he started. "Grand objective not reached. Period. Rebel forces much greater than expected. Period. Lacked support from Butler. Period. Colonel Dahlgren continuing to raid countryside. Period."

The operator tapped rapidly, keeping his head down. "One-hundred-and-fifty casualties sustained. Period. Awaiting further orders. Period." Pleasonton should be pleased with that report. Much was done despite the failure to breach Richmond's walls. He could spin this as a moderate success. He had too. His mind went calculating onward.

"Operator. Another message."

"Yes, sir."

"Request update on General Custer's movement. Period."

He imagined the golden-haired dandy face down in a ditch, a bullet through his chest. To be free of such an upstart would be a blessing, provided he wasn't cursed with a glorious death. Then all he'd hear in papers for the duration of the war was about Custer. Nation's young hero slain in battle. Legendary last stand. Statues would be erected in his honor. Maybe Kilpatrick would attend the unveiling. Place a comforting arm around Libbie's shoulder, whisper a sweet word. Perhaps she wanted more than a little comfort. The entire fantasy lifted his spirits a fraction.

Clicks from the telegraph filled the room, and the civilian began jotting down notes. The clicking stopped and the operator held up his note.

"Well, come on, man. What does it say?"

"Custer's raid success. Property destroyed. Stuart diverted. No casualties."

"God damn that man," Kilpatrick said. He pounded a fist into the table and shook his head in disgust.

Tawney blinked behind his spectacles and he ignored him.

Will I never be freed from him? He'd sent him on a suicide mission or at least away from any opportunity to make real impact, yet the man sat pretty. Full command. No losses. The thrill of tangling with Stuart. Damn him.

"General, isn't that a good thing?" Livingston said.

"Of course, it's a good thing, you imbecile. It's a bloody well great thing for him."

The lieutenant colonel gave him a cautious smile. "I'm not sure I understand."

"Not sure you would, Colonel."

Kilpatrick swung open the door with some force, stepping out onto the planked sidewalk. His column of troopers walked their horses into the fort. The first glimmers of happiness were sprouting on their grime-covered faces. Every man was saturated with mud, some with blood. Wagons carried the severely wounded.

Major Taylor gave him a salute on the way by. His eyes held a mean glare.

Kilpatrick observed his men as they passed. The lead of the next command of riders peeled his mount from the column, walking it in his direction. Captain John Mitchell from Dahlgren's command came to a halt, looking down at Kilpatrick.

The horse jerked at his reins, shuffling its hooves in the soft ground. The captain's face was stern, his black beard puffy. He would have been handsome save for the saber scar running along the bottom of his cheekbone all the way to his ear. Kilpatrick waited for the man to salute him as was customary military protocol.

"Captain," he started to say, but was cut off by Mitchell's open-palmed salute.

Kilpatrick's lip twitched, but he quickly returned it. "Yes, Captain?"

"Sir, he couldn't have had more than ninety men when we were separated. That is not enough of a force to conduct any kind of operation in enemy territory. I am requesting to go back and search for the colonel."

"You conducted operations on your own, Captain."

"Within range of the main body of troops. If Dahlgren is indeed still in the field and not lying in a ditch somewhere, we should move to his aid."

"I will not waste more men on this errand. The colonel is capable. He will continue harassing the enemy or rally here as was discussed. The men and horses need adequate rest behind a stout wall."

Mitchell removed his hat. "On that we agree. Isn't there a unit here ready to ride?"

Livingston joined them. "My apologies, Captain. We have explicit orders not to traverse past New Kent."

"That is not near far enough," Mitchell said.

"Watch yourself, Captain," Kilpatrick said.

"That is not sufficient support. Sir."

Kilpatrick pointed at him. "I know that. For Christ's sake, even that blubbering ox, Butler, knows that."

"Sir, there's been a rumor."

"What's that?"

"They were ambushed."

"Nonsense." He stood scratching his head. *But then, where is he?* "You know how men talk."

"If there is any truth to it, they will need aid now. I respectfully request to lead three companies from the 2nd New York back into the field to provide support to Dahlgren's men."

Kilpatrick stared at the man. "Denied."

"But, sir."

"I will not waste more men without due cause. We will rest for three days. If he is not heard of by then, you can conduct a relief expedition."

Mitchell nodded his head and gave a snappy salute. He rejoined his command without a second glance.

Livingston gawked at the gritty captain as he walked his horse away. "Eager fellow, isn't he."

His men passed their commander and Kilpatrick gritted his teeth. "He is." Fear laced his belly, the kind of dread a poor man feels when another reaches to steal his last piece of bread. If the letter was discovered, it would be political suicide for at least him. He wasn't a religious man, but he said a prayer that Dahlgren was alive and the letter not found. That the young colonel was in fact still on his way to Yorktown. His men passed and the fear grew because deep down he knew he'd failed, and his star was falling faster than it had risen.

CHAPTER 35

March 5ᵗʰ, 1864
Libby Prison, Richmond, Virginia

Wolf's broken and battered body was taken to the second floor of Libby Prison. They threw him on the ground like yesterday's chamber pot. His whole body shook, and his shirt had been torn from his back. Griff tossed his colonel's coat back on top of him. Hank let out a bass chuckle and the two enforcers left.

Ghostly prisoners crowded around, whispering to one another until Roberts appeared. He went to his knees. "Give him some space." He eyed Wolf, worry creasing his brow. "Worked you over pretty good, huh?"

Wolf squinted through only one of his eyes; the other was swollen shut. "Not too bad." He didn't know what hurt worse, but his thumbs throbbed like they were going to burst. From where they melted the skin on his back, raw pain emanated outward shooting over his body. Payne had used the orange glowing iron with glee, reheating it when it had deadened to a light smolder. The stench of his own burning skin had permeated his nose like a roast pig on a spit and would never leave. He'd wished he'd had worse in his life, but he knew he hadn't. He knew it could never get worse. If he wasn't going to die, he knew he was close.

An older gentleman pushed his way through the crowd. He had a white beard and disheveled hair. "Out of my way." He bent down next to Wolf. "Help me get him to the corner."

In a daze, the prisoners hefted Wolf into their arms, and they lugged him to the corner, setting him down gently. There was no furniture, so he lay atop his jacket shivering.

The white-bearded officer went about cleaning Wolf's wounds with dirty rags. "Sorry, son, this is all we have." He studied his thumbs for a moment. "This is bad. Very bad. You." He gestured at Roberts. "Find Major Olmsted. Hurry."

The elder officer rolled Wolf over, inspecting his back. Concern spread over his eyes. "Surely no secret was worth all this, young colonel."

"Who are you?"

The old man grimaced. "Captain Harold Reynolds, Assistant Surgeon of the 5th Iowa Volunteer Regiment."

Wolf coughed violently, sending pain throughout his body. "They didn't get it." He hacked again. "Didn't get it."

"I'm sure they didn't, son."

Roberts returned with a thick-bearded major. "Olmsted, I need your needle and penknife." The major willingly handed them over without a question. "And hold him down."

"No. Nobody holds me down." Frenzy and panic built in Wolf's chest. "Don't take 'em, doc."

Reynolds hesitated. "I'm not going to take them." He turned and waved more prisoners over. "I have to drill your thumbs to release the pressure."

More gaunt men wrapped firm hands around him. Wolf fought them, but every movement was weak. The men overwhelmed him, holding him panting on the floor. The doctor spindled the needle in minuscule circles, each movement sending pain firing through his fingers and running along his arms like rivers until a tiny pop was heard and blood sprayed from the hole. It shot into the air almost five feet, but the relief was unbelievable. His eyes faded to black to the voices of the prisoners.

***

When he awoke, it was to the clamor of excited voices. His crusted-over, swollen eyes cracked open. His vision was severely impaired. His night had been plagued by fevered dreams of Payne and the comfort of Roberts and Reynolds.

Light shone through a glassless window, and he discovered he wasn't packed tightly with other men like a can of sardines. The room was cool with the open air from the outside. There were two stoves for heat. Men fought for a place by them at night. It was one of Libby Prison's six rooms that held countless prisoners.

A blanket had been draped over him, and he tossed it to the side. A black rat scurried away.

"Get 'em Dick!" a man squealed. The man scampered after the creature, slapping at it with his boot. Another officer followed, his arms spread wide in an attempt to hem the rodent in. But those men weren't the ones who woke him. It was the congregation of prisoners by the door.

Hank yelled at the Union men. "Make way for Crazy Bet!" He jabbed his beating stick at a man, creating space.

Wolf crawled on his elbows. The floor was cold to the touch. His whole body felt like everything was out of place and everything had been broken. He stared at his thumbs. Sticks splinted the purple robust fingers. Black cloth was wrapped around them. He reached around, finding his colonel's jacket and delicately draped it over his shoulders.

Men crowded around a woman dressed in an almost all black velvet dress for the cold weather. White lace engulfed her neck. It was plain but well-crafted, symbolizing at the least a modest form of wealth. She handed out baskets of food and packages to the soldiers. The men cried thank you to the woman, singing her praise.

She waved off Hank with a whip of her hand. "They will not harm me, you fool. Not the hand that feeds them."

Hank laughed like a booming bass drum. "You're on your own then, good lady." He twirled his stick and disappeared through a doorway.

The woman walked through the prisoners, engaging in pleasantries with them. Grinning faces met her, and the captives reached for her hands. She knelt by a man and wiped his brow. He lifted a hand for her and she took it, holding it dearly.

Roberts crouched down next to Wolf. "Glad your awake. You scared us there." He handed him a cup of yellowing water.

Wolf sniffed it first before drinking. "Who's that?"

"You'd think she's the Blessed Mother Mary with the way all the men are carrying on."

The woman drifted closer. Reynolds appeared to be her escort, pointing out sick men. "I need more supplies. Every day more and more men are ill. Without treatment, they will die."

"I will do what I can," she said. She reached out a hand to him and squeezed his, and he mouthed his thanks.

"He's this way."

Roberts gave Wolf a short grin, holding out a golden wolf head. "It's all we could save. The rest were used as bandages."

He took the emblazoned wolf head in his fingers. Dark brown stains caked the snarling wolf. Carefully, he placed it in his pocket.

The congregation of prisoners led by the woman stopped near Wolf's space on the floor.

"This is him."

She smiled at him with a sad mouth. Her jaw was square, her nose aristocratic, and her black hair with a smattering of gray was parted down the center and drawn around the back. Her presence was that of a matriarch or even a queen if America had such things.

"My good colonel, I hear you have a story to tell." She eyed him, her eyes becoming stern. "They took to eliciting information from you most harshly." Her hand reached out, and she touched his battered face. "Get these men back. I must speak to him in private."

Major Olmsted pushed on the other men. "All right, lads, give them some privacy."

The prisoners shuffled away, a spirited version of "Yankee Doodle" lifted up from worn mouths.

"My name is Elizabeth Van Lew, but most call me Betty. What's your name?"

"Wolf, ma'am."

"I heard you were with Dahlgren's band when they were defeated."

"I was, ma'am." Wolf glanced at Reynolds. He smiled back. His beard made his cheeks appear rounder than a prisoner's should. "She is our patron saint."

"I read this in the papers today." She handed him a Richmond Sentinel newspaper and tapped, pointing to a spot.

The newspaper read: *A letter was discovered on the person of Colonel Ulric Dahlgren stating the raids intent to assassinate the President of the Confederacy, Jefferson Davis. The wretched North has resorted to debauched and sullied tactics to win the war at any cost. All true Southern men must now know that any and all measures must be taken to ensure our survival and win this war. Just as a true lover of freedom pierced the breast of the tyrant Julius Caesar thousands of years ago, a retributive strike at the tyrant Abraham Lincoln himself by such a man is desirable if we could be so lucky.*

"No." Wolf shook his head. "It can't be."

Van Lew studied him with a keen eye. "You know this to be untrue?"

"I was there when he died." He gulped, eyeing Reynolds for a moment. "You trust her?"

"With my life, son, and you should too."

His words could send him to the end of a noose, feet dangling like Martin. "He gave me the letter."

Her sad smile grew urgent. "Then you gave the letter to Ross or some other Southerner?"

"No, ma'am."

"You have the letter?"

"No, ma'am."

She shared a glance with Reynolds. "I suppose I should be thankful of that. Where's the letter?"

"I gave it to a widow with a comrade's final letter. She was going to see it home."

Blinking, she digested his information. "Do you think she turned it over to the Confederate government?"

"She had no reason to."

"Why wouldn't she?"

"I'd saved her from some bad types. She thought she was doing me a favor and didn't know what it was."

Van Lew took the newspaper again. "So this alleged letter is a forgery?"

"Yes, ma'am."

"No papers were on Dahlgren."

"No."

"And you're sure?"

"Of course. He placed them in my hand."

She stood abruptly, smoothing her dress along the sides. A pleasant smile curved on her lips. "Then, Colonel Wolf, I will see to it that you are free of this place."

The swish of Van Lew's black skirts whisked over the men as she walked like a sovereign ruler over her prison domain. Men bowed and scraped almost as if they asked for her blessing. Wolf watched her leave. *Who was this woman? Why did she want to help him?*

He knew none of the reasons mattered. He knew that she held the key to his escape. He'd volunteered for Dahlgren's northern hunt. They'd raided and pillaged, burned and killed, and now, the only men that remained were prisoners of a hostile people in a dank rat-infested hell. He leaned his unburnt shoulder on the wall. He may pay with northern blood, but they would win this war.

Historical and Personal Note

When I was researching the history of the Michigan Brigade, I came across the Kilpatrick-Dahlgren raid that took place in early 1864. I hadn't heard of this raid before and thought it displayed the perfect backdrop for Wolf's external struggle for survival complemented by his internal conflict over what kind of soldier he was going to become. *Northern Hunt* was born in this crucible.

Colonel Ulric Dahlgren was an extremely interesting historical character in the Civil War, although controversial. He was completely fictionalized for this novel, but the real-life person was no less interesting. His father, Admiral John A. Dahlgren, was a powerful man who had the ear of Lincoln throughout the war.

Ulric was one of the youngest men to be made colonel in the Civil War. He lost his leg during the Gettysburg campaign and was chosen by Kilpatrick to lead a portion of Kilpatrick's command on the fateful raid, and as a result, was killed during its failure.

There were a host of stories that sprang up surrounding the raid, including the hanging of Martin Robinson. That may not have been his real name, but it is clear Dahlgren did order the hanging of a black guide. Another story was Dahlgren taking tea/wine with Sarah Bruce "Sallie" Seddon (changed for the novel). A similar story arose around the Tuckahoe Plantation and Virginia Allen meeting Dahlgren on her porch with two pistols strapped to her. Both stories are most likely false and used to promote a legendary post-war image of Southern women. The last story was the letter with orders to kill Jefferson

Davis. I say stories because the validity of these events is widely debated. Some may have been enhanced in their retelling, others may be true. Personally, I love a good myth or legend, but then again, I write fiction. Today, we can only speculate with the sources at hand.

Probably the most controversial story surrounding the raid was the letter Dahlgren supposedly carried in his prosthetic leg with orders to kill Jefferson Davis, president of the Confederacy. While this letter was written about in Southern newspapers at the time, it was lost as were countless reproductions at the end of the war. A reproduction from Lee to Meade still remains today.

The Northern government made many declarations that those were not actual orders given. Many facts are in open debate. Who knew about it? Who ordered it? Evidence chains for the Rebel command? Ulric's name was misspelled and abbreviated in a fashion that he never employed in any other writings. Many people came forward after the war, including Hogan (BMI agent) and stated that they were never given such orders. However, most historians claim the letter was authentic. It was in this realm that I created this novel. Ironically, the Northern president, Abraham Lincoln, was the one to be assassinated soon after Lee's surrender at Appomattox, some claiming the green light having been given because of this raid.

Much of this novel was based on true events however fictionalized. If you have interest in this whole affair, I would highly recommend, *Like a Meteor Blazing Brightly* by Eric J. Wittenberg. He does an incredible job bringing this relatively unknown raid to light with a focus on Ulric Dahlgren. If you'd like to learn more about the raid in its entirety, check out *KILL JEFF DAVIS: The Union Raid on Richmond, 1864* by Bruce M. Venter. Both paint an excellent picture of the forgotten raid. If you are interested in Hampton's Iron Scouts, check out *Wade Hampton's Iron Scouts* by D. Michael Thomas.

While I attempted to stay within the guidelines of the history, I did fictionalize this event. Times, locations, and troop movements may not be completely accurate. In particular, Custer's arrival at Madison Court House was actually sometime on March 1st. Sometimes historical timelines don't adhere to our stories. Garnett's Mill and the widow, Mrs. Hemlick, were not real. I fictionalized point-of-view characters like Custer, Dahlgren, Kilpatrick, and Hampton, but their struggles were very real. This is not meant to be a non-fiction rendition. The authors above have done a more than admirable job relaying that message.

This novel is a continuation of Wolf's story as he becomes a soldier and warrior, embracing the struggles surrounding war, combat, captivity, and life in general. Like all books in this series, it is meant to entertain while showing the clash between the North and the South primarily through Northern eyes. It is also meant to shine a light on the common soldier's life but also to get into the minds of the leaders of those men. This has been my favorite story in Wolf's saga to write, and I hope you enjoyed reading it as much as I enjoyed writing it. The next book in the series is coming soon!

Best,

Daniel Greene
November 19th, 2019

Thanks for reading! I hope you enjoyed the second novel of the Northern Wolf series. As you may have gathered, there are more books in the series coming your way. Pick up **Northern Blood Book 3 in the Northern Wolf Series!**

The Greene Army Newsletter: Want exclusive updates on new work, contests, patches, artwork, and events where you can meet up with Daniel? An elite few will get a chance to join **Greene's Recon Team**: a crack unit of talented readers ready and able to review advance copies of his books anytime, anywhere with killer precision. Sign up for spam-free Greene Army Newsletter today here: http://www.danielgreenebooks.com/?page_id=7741

Reviews: If you have the time, please consider writing a review. Reviews are important tools that I use to hone my craft. If you do take the time to write a review, I would like to thank you personally for your feedback and support. Don't be afraid to reach out. I love meeting new readers!

You can find me anywhere below.

Facebook Fan Club: *The Greene Army - Daniel Greene Fan Club*
Facebook Page: *Daniel Greene Books*
Instagram: *Daniel Greene Instagram*
Website: *DanielGreeneBooks.com*
Email: *DanielGreeneBooks@gmail.com*

A special thanks to all those who've contributed to the creation of this novel. A novel is a huge feat and would remain as a file on my desktop without the contributions of so many wonderfully supportive people. This includes my dedicated Alpha Readers, Greene's Recon Team, Greene Army, my editor, Lisa, my cover artist, Tim, and Polgarus formatters and especially my readers. Without readers, this is an unheard/unread tale. I can't wait to share more stories with you in the future.

About the Author

Daniel Greene is the award-winning author of the growing apocalyptic thriller series The End Time Saga and the historical fiction Northern Wolf series. He is an avid traveler and physical fitness enthusiast with a deep passion for history. He is inspired by the works of George R.R. Martin, Steven Pressfield, Bernard Cornwell, and George Romero. Although a Midwesterner for life, he's lived long enough in Virginia to call it home.

Books by Daniel Greene

The End Time Saga
End Time
The Breaking
The Rising
The Departing
The Holding
The Standing (Coming Soon)

The Gun (Origin Short Story)

Northern Wolf Series
Northern Wolf
Northern Hunt
Northern Blood